Until the End of the World

of the

World

SARAH LYONS FLEMING

For Sadie and Silas.
I love you, my nerdlings, until the end of the world and after.

CHAPTER 1

Today is the kind of spring day that used to make me feel like anything was possible. That it would all work out in the end. I used to love days like this. Of course, that was before I started avoiding spring altogether.

It isn't easy to avoid an entire season, especially one this glorious. But for the past three years I've managed it. I close the blinds, stay out of the sunshine and keep to myself, so as not to dredge up memories of that first terrible spring.

But this year feels different. I can't help but enjoy the breeze that promises summer is coming. It's the kind of day that puts a spring in your step, where you believe hope does spring eternal.

I dreamt about Adrian last night. But it wasn't the usual dream, the one that wakes me up in tears with that empty feeling in the pit of my stomach. We were sitting on the porch steps of my parents' cabin. Our legs were stretched out, feet resting on the ground. I was wiggling my toes. There was nothing else. Sure, the bees buzzed among the flowers and the trees whispered in the wind, but that was it. There was just quiet. And peace, the kind of peace that didn't seem to follow Adrian as much as it was a product of him. When I woke up that feeling stayed with me, and I started thinking that maybe it could be mine again.

My friend Penny's dark ponytail swings as we pass the brownstones and apartment buildings of our Brooklyn neighborhood on our way to work. I haven't told her about this feeling, even though I tell her almost everything. I'm like a squirrel with a nut, wanting to hide it away for safekeeping, to turn it over and over and examine it.

Penny glances at my feet. "You wore your new shoes."

I nod. It's still too cool, but I wore the delicate straw sandals anyway. I thought they might make me feel feminine and strong. That maybe they would help me to embrace and welcome spring again. Relying on shoes to do all that is pretty dumb, but I need all the help I can get.

Penny raises her face to the sun and sighs with pleasure. She moved here from Puerto Rico when she was ten, after her father died. Even after all these years she still takes winter as a personal affront.

"My mom was called in last night, something to do with the LX virus," Penny says, and pushes her vintage glasses back up where they belong. "She says there are a lot of cases in New York now."

Bornavirus LX has spread across the world in the past few days. So far it's only been found in the Midwest and West. I haven't been paying much attention because in the spring I never do.

"Did she say how many?"

"No. But she's pretty certain the quarantine of St. Louis means it's going to get bad."

"They quarantined St. Louis?" I'm shocked that it's come to that.

"Yeah, late last night. Chicago, too. And air traffic is suspended from the West." We stop at the front door of the Sunset Park Community Center, where we both work. "How do you not know all this? You're usually the one telling me these things."

"I've been distracted. I didn't listen to the news this morning."

I want to tell her more, but I'm not sure what there is to tell. It's just a mental shift or something, and if it comes to nothing I don't want to advertise the fact that I've failed. Penny glances around and twists her lips.

"James kissed me last night," she says to the concrete.

"James what?" I yell. She shushes me and I lower my voice. "We just walked all the way to work and you tell me now? At—" I look at the time on my phone, "crap. There's a meeting. I have to go."

Penny smiles. She did this on purpose so I wouldn't bother her about it the whole way to work.

"I knew it!" I say, and narrow my eyes even though I'm grinning. "We're twenty-eight years old and you still won't tell me when you like someone! Nelly and I have been waiting for this. You're gonna tell me later, you know."

"Gotta go," she sings out, as I head upstairs.

CHAPTER 2

I'm at my desk, considering beating my uncooperative computer with my stapler, when I hear a voice.

"Psst, Cassie." Nelly's head appears over our shared cubicle wall. "Drinks later."

I open my mouth, about to refuse, but he shakes his head and flashes me his white-toothed smile. "Don't even say no," he drawls, before he sinks down.

I sigh and slip on my sandals to go argue my case. I'm sure this is one time Nelly will be glad I'm backing out of plans. I sit down opposite Nelly's desk and swing my foot.

"New shoes?" he asks.

The magical properties I imbued them with this morning have not materialized. So far the only thing they've done is create a suspicious pre-blister itch in several places. My toes are freezing. I notice my toenail polish is chipped, as usual.

"You like?"

"Yeah, yeah, they're great. Have I ever given a rat's ass about shoes?" He runs a hand through his messy blond hair and tries to look despondent but fails. "No, you've come to tell me you aren't drinking with me."

Nelly's tall, broad and exceedingly healthy. It's obvious he grew up in a place where they ate beef and drank whole milk and were out in the fresh air and sunshine. Without the ever-present smile, his face can look stony. He perfected it playing high school football in Texas, where a good game face is essential, especially when you're gay.

I sigh. "Believe me, I'd rather go out. But I'm going to try to break up with Peter tonight."

He whoops, Texas-style. Now that I've told Nelly I can't chicken out of the breakup at the last minute without getting tons of grief. I already regret it.

"You are not going to *try*, you wuss!" He bangs a pen on his desk and points it at me. "You're going to do it this time. But, first, we'll have a drink for fortification."

I laugh because of course he's going to get his way.

His blue eyes are serious. "You'd better make a clean break. Or I'll do it for you. I swear I will this time."

I give in. I'm going to need that drink. I could use it right now, actually. "Okay."

He looks doubtful.

"I will. I promise." I lay my head on his desk and moan. "I hate this. Why do I have to break it off?"

He pats my head. "Because, darlin', you date the wrong people."

I stick my tongue out at him just as James, our part-time IT guy, pokes his head into the cubicle. There's a flush of excitement on his angular cheeks.

"Guys, come see," he says. "The virus is in New York."

We follow him down the hall to the conference room. I refrain from asking him about Penny because she would kill me, although I'm dying to.

Our coworkers are perched on chairs and the long table, eyes trained on the newscaster.

"Bornavirus LX has been found in all five boroughs since yesterday. The virus first appeared in Long Xuyen, Vietnam last week, and has since spread throughout the world. As of last night, cities in the middle and western U.S., including Denver, Chicago and St. Louis, are quarantined, and state governors have instituted mandatory curfews. The fast-moving virus causes brain damage, which triggers the infected to aggressively attack and spread the disease through their bodily fluids.

"Authorities state that the virus is under control. People with a high fever and joint pain should be seen immediately by a doctor or emergency room. Please do not try to care for your sick loved one yourself. The CDC and Health Department are not releasing estimates of the number infected so far. We will be following up with more information as it becomes available."

James cocks an eyebrow at me, lets out a *harrumph* and heads to his work space. His hands fly over his computer keyboard. I don't ask what he's up to because I know he'll find me when he's done.

Nelly and I amble back down the hall. Usually, I would comb the internet for news about the virus, but it's gone in one ear and almost out the other by the time we reach our desks. My thoughts are consumed with the tactic I'll use to break up with Peter. There's the let's-be-friends and the it's-not-you-it's-me and there's the fact that I'm an idiot for dating Peter in the first place and then dragging it out this long.

"Hey," I say to Nelly, "how about this: 'Peter, I'm an idiot. And I can't be with you anymore because I'm an idiot?'"

"You suck at this." He puts his arm around my shoulders to stop my shivering. I don't handle this kind of anticipation very well. "I'll coach you over drinks. By the time you get to Peter you'll only have to recite your lines. Okay?"

I give a somber nod. "Nelly, why can't I just marry you?"

"Darlin', we both know who you should marry, and that door is probably still open."

He's talking about Adrian. We were engaged until I ruined it.

"That ship has sailed, Nelly." I can't say Adrian's name out loud because I'll start crying, I know I will. "It's been two years."

"He's in the northeast, Cass. I could find out where. If you wanted me to."

My face is hot. I haven't done many things I'm ashamed of, things where I've been hurtful, but what I did to Adrian is the biggie.

Nelly's bringing it up today of all days must be a sign. What if I said, *Sure, go ahead and find him*? I can't imagine that Adrian would be happy to hear from me. But that feeling from my dream still lingers, and I want it for real. I want it so badly that maybe I'm finally willing to take the chance and find out. I open my mouth, trying to find the words, right as my phone rings. Nelly raises his eyebrows like he'll be waiting for an answer and leaves. I pick up the phone.

"Hey, Cassandra," Peter yells over loud rumblings.

"Where the heck are you? It sounds like you're standing on a runway or something."

"I am. We're at the private airport here in D.C. waiting for our jet to New York. It's been delayed. They're saying we have 'low priority.' There are ten senators and their families ahead of us."

"Philip Morris must be giving out vacations if you vote yes on a pro-youth smoking bill," I joke.

"Yeah." He doesn't even chuckle. Sometimes Peter is lacking in the humor department. "Anyway, I don't know about tonight. I'll be in late, but maybe I'll come to your apartment so I can see you first thing in the morning. I miss you."

"Sure. Good. Just let yourself in whenever," I squeak, painfully aware that I don't miss him back. "I'll see you in the morning."

"See you then." The phone clicks off.

I can see him standing at the airport. He'll slip his phone into his designer-name-I've-never-heard-of coat pocket and rake a hand through his dark hair. Then he'll stride off to find the most important-looking person at the airport and convince them his flight has priority over Air Force One.

My stomach stops roiling now that I get to put off the breakup. When I get home tonight I'll pretend I'm really tired or drunk or something. I know I'm being spineless, but I don't like to hurt people's feelings, even if I don't like them very much. Or, in Peter's case, when they pretend they don't have any. But, mainly, I'm chicken.

I've spent the past year convincing myself that Peter isn't as superficial as he seems, but now I'm not so sure. Honestly, at first I kind of liked how easy it was to date him. He didn't push me to talk about my feelings. He couldn't compare me to the person I'd been two years before. When I met him I was coming out of a two-year fog. But as the fog has cleared and I've become more like the old me, he's never given me more than a glimpse of something real.

In true passive-aggressive fashion I've been waiting for him to break it off. I've gotten more and more distant and even blatantly annoyed with him. This approach obviously hasn't worked. I need to imagine the after, not the part where I do it. I just need to do it fast.

Nelly's voice floats over the wall. "You've got to rip him off you like a band-aid."

"How do you read my mind, Nelly? It's so freaking creepy!"

"Sounds like you got a reprieve. More time to drink. *Practice*, I mean."

James enters holding an unlit cigarette and his iPad. He reminds me of a praying mantis: all long, skinny legs and arms. He spends all his time folded over a computer or tablet, smoking madly. I imagine him making the moves on Penny and smile.

"Hey," I say.

He plops down and hands me his iPad, which is open to a blog page. "Look at this, Cass. It's about Bornavirus LX. It's more serious than they say."

My family's dinner table was a place where Roswell and Peak Oil and the New World Order were debated with enthusiasm. I've found a kindred spirit in James. He loves that kind of stuff.

I read aloud. "As the LX virus has spread it appears to have mutated. The last reports received suggest it may be only a matter of hours from infection to the final stage."

"In the final stage the person goes crazy," James says. He tucks his light brown, jaw-length hair behind his ear. "Then they attack, which is how a lot of people are getting infected. It's in the saliva and blood. One site says they've been showing the same footage of Chicago for twenty-four hours because Chicago's a wasteland. I know a couple of bloggers out there and their sites have been down for the past day."

A graph estimates that fifty thousand people in New York City will be infected as of noon today.

"That's crazy," I say. "Fifty thousand? There's no way they could hide that many sick here. And they're still telling us it's not serious?"

He fiddles with his cigarette. "I know. They wouldn't quarantine major cities if it wasn't serious. The hospitals are filling up faster than they can handle."

I think of Penny's mom, Maria, who's a nurse. She'd know what's going on.

"Yeah, well, I definitely wouldn't put it past the government not to tell us anything until we're fucked." I sigh. "I have to finish this newsletter. My computer is being a pain."

Any mention of a computer problem lights a fire under James. He nudges me out of the way and pokes around on my computer.

He shakes his head. "Dude, look at your desktop. Sure you don't want another shortcut on it?"

I don't mention that I recently cleared it and thought it was neat.

I pull up a piece of his hair and peer under it, choosing to ignore his defamation of my character. "Are you coming out tonight?"

"Ah, yes, tonight." His smile lights up his face. "The priming for the great break-up."

"Nelly, you have a gigantic mouth." I know he's listening. "No, I got out of that. Tonight is just good, old-fashioned fun."

Nelly's voice comes over the wall. "And coming up with Cassie's breakup tactic, James. Maybe you can help. Cass's gotten herself mixed up with the wrong guy, as we all know."

"Will 'You never get off that computer and I can't stand it' work? That's the one that I know best," James asks with a grin.

"How about 'You care more about that Hot Pocket than me!' " Nelly calls.

James laughs as he finishes whatever magic he's worked on my computer. "Girls are more trouble than they're worth. I'd like a Hot Pocket, though. It's been years."

"Penny's coming tonight," I say innocently. He ducks under his hair. "And you, Nelson," I point my finger at the cubicle wall, "are not one to talk about wrong guys. How many boyfriends have you had since I've known you?"

There's no reply. I smile in triumph. James is already engrossed in his iPad.

"Wow, I have to see this," he mutters, and wanders out.

CHAPTER 3

A little while later I whisper over the wall Nelly and I share. "I have gossip you don't know. Ha ha."

"Get your ass over here right now," he commands.

"No. I'm busy."

"You are no such thing. You barely even work. You just design newsletters and organize artsy crap for the community."

I smile. "Well, all you do is act all charming and get people to give us money. And—"

"And that's how you get paid. So get your ass over here or I'll purposely pull in less this year so you lose your job."

I laugh and head into his cubicle, where he sits with a smug smile. "So, James and Penny kissed last night."

He rubs his hands with glee and I grin back. "When a bunch of us went out last week they talked all night," he says. "I thought I saw a spark. I forgot all about it because we'd given up on them ever getting together."

"Well, we've got our work cut out for us there. James says he doesn't want a girlfriend, but—"

"But what?" asks James, who leans against the cubicle entry and smirks.

"But there are certain people I don't think you'd kiss if you weren't interested in them, like girlfriend-interested," I say, and tug on the sleeve of his t-shirt. James doesn't exactly dress up for work.

"That sentence made almost no sense," he says, in an attempt to deflect the accusation, but his face is scarlet.

I bounce up and down like a three year-old but don't want to scare him off, so I change the subject. "Hey, any more news on Bornavirus?"

Nelly gives an exaggerated shake of his head. "Y'all and your conspiracy theories. Now what, this is a government plot to overthrow society as we know it and implement a new world order?"

James rolls his eyes. "Dude, no. It may be some sort of disease or weapon gone awry. But, whatever it is, it's everywhere in the world. They're saying to get to a hospital if you're sick, but they won't say if they can actually cure it. And no one can find anyone who *was* sick and got better. Some cities in China are already under martial law. They're shooting people on sight."

"Really?" I ask.

"They're always shooting people on sight in China, my friends," Nelly says. "Oppressive government, remember?"

Nelly is the foil to our belief that someone, somewhere, is up to something that they're covering up. James and I would have packed up for the apocalypse ten times by now, had Nelly not brought us back down to reality.

"True," James admits. "But here's footage of a city in Germany, taken hours ago."

James hands us his iPad. Soldiers hold back bystanders while they fire on a group of advancing figures. They drop to the ground as the onlookers scream, but it's shadowy and hard to see, so Nelly is unimpressed.

"Let's see what they're saying on the news," Nelly suggests with a sigh. He steers us to the conference room. "The only way I'm going to get any work done today is if I can stop you two before Cassie has us living in her bunker until this blows over."

"Hey," I say, "don't make fun of my bunker!"

"You have a bunker?" James asks. "How do I not know you have a bunker?"

"It's just my parents' house upstate. It's still full of food and stuff. Like a year's worth."

James whistles. He knows that my parents were weekend homesteaders and had lots of food, but I guess I never mentioned all the stuff is still there.

I miss the log cabin after my dream last night. It's secluded; my parents always half-kidded that it would be the perfect place to ride out the apocalypse. It was a place where I would read for hours in the hammock under the trees, make a salad from the garden five minutes before dinner and spend all summer playing with my little brother, Eric, and our closest neighbors.

It's also the place where Adrian and I sat and waited for my parents to arrive, one Friday night in April three years ago. They never came. They never knew Adrian had proposed the night before. They would have been ecstatic. They loved Adrian almost as much as I did.

***

Adrian and I had sat in the warmth of the wood stove. He leaned back on the couch and leafed through one of my dad's solar power catalogs. My feet were still freezing from falling into a creek on our hike and I plopped them in his lap.

"Hey, handsome," I said, and wiggled them for a foot massage.

His dimple showed. I loved the way it made him look like a little boy, even with the dark stubble that was back by evening.

"I don't know," Adrian said, picking up our previous thread about the wedding. "I kind of like the whole obeying part of the vows."

I rolled my eyes, not even rising to the bait.

"I already obey you." He smiled and held up my foot to prove his point. "It's about time you started doing the same. Or at least take it into consideration when I tell you not to leap from one rock to the next because it's slippery. I'm just trying to keep you dry."

He was referring to earlier, when I had eschewed his outstretched hand while crossing the creek. I could jump to the next rock just fine, I said, right before I slid off it.

"Do you know Laura Ingalls told Almanzo Wilder she wouldn't have the word obey in their vows? She said she wouldn't be able to obey anyone against her better judgment." When I first read that as a little girl I'd been so impressed.

"Your hero. But you *mis*judged those rocks. And your, um, athletic ability."

His mouth curved up. He was one of the only people in the world who found my clumsiness endearing.

"I am the very picture of grace." I wiggled my feet. "Back to work!"

He picked up my foot and kissed it before giving a little bow and obeying.

When headlights finally shone through the front window I jumped up. My parents might have been cell phone-hating hippies at heart, but they always called. I was uneasy enough to have a mini lecture prepared.

I stepped out on the porch and was surprised to see Sam, the sheriff. His hands shook as he took off his hat. The beam from the motion-activated light left his face in shadow. It's never good news when the sheriff comes to your house and removes his hat. I hadn't had personal experience with it before then, but I was pretty sure of that. I backed into the doorjamb as if I could escape what he was going to say.

"Cassie? Cassie, your mom and dad were in an accident on the other side of town."

Sam walked toward me, his hands out in a supplicating gesture. His face was haggard when he stepped into the rectangle of light the open door threw on the ground. Like gravity was working overtime on his jowls and the corners of his eyes. I gripped the door. Adrian put a hand on my shoulder.

"Are they okay, Sam?" he asked. "Where are they?"

Sam shook his head and blinked. "I'm so sorry. Cassie, I'm so sorry." He gripped the hat in his hands so tightly that his knuckles were white. "They both died at the scene. It looks like they slid on a patch of mud. They hit a tree."

"Okay," I said, and walked back in the house on shaky legs.

I sat down on the couch. Adrian sat next to me and took my hand. He was crying, I noticed, as he tried to hug me. I sat there, wooden, wondering what I was supposed to do or say next. It was like I had forgotten how to be human. I couldn't remember what people did in these situations.

"Okay," I repeated helplessly. "Sam, what should I do?"

I wondered if Sam thought I was cold because I wasn't crying. He and my parents were friends. They would talk gardens and hunting while relaxing with a home-brewed beer on the porch.

There was nothing but pity in his eyes, though, when I looked up. He'd been the bearer of this kind of news before, and it occurred to me that if I was the only recipient who was numb and dry-eyed then maybe he wouldn't look so sympathetic. Then I wondered why I was thinking these ridiculous thoughts instead of feeling anything.

"You'll need to come down to the hospital, Cassie. I'm sorry. You can take your time."

I got up immediately because I couldn't think of anything else to do, and walked out the door with Adrian's arm around me. I've gone back there once, to scatter my parents' ashes on the land they loved and planned to live out their lives. I haven't seen it since.

***

The news blares in the conference room.

"...not to panic. They say that there is much false information on the internet and to visit the CDC's website for information concerning Bornavirus LX. There are a suspected few thousand cases in New York City right now, the CDC states.

"If you have a high fever or joint pain or have come in contact with someone you think may be infected, please go to the nearest hospital for treatment. Doctors say that antiviral medication must be administered immediately for optimal effectiveness."

I raise an eyebrow at James.

"First I'm hearing of it," he says.

"Stay tuned to New York One for updates on Bornavirus LX. There will be a live statement by the Board of Health in one hour."

Nelly turns to us. "See? A few thousand cases, not so bad. We'll just steer clear of crazy people and get some drinks."

"Maybe we shouldn't go out." I feel a pang of foreboding. "Even if it's nowhere near as bad as those sites are saying, I'm sure it's worse than 'authorities' are saying. Maybe we should hang out at my house."

"No!" Nelly grimaces. "We are not ruining Friday evening!"

I punch him. "Thanks. I didn't realize my house was second only to hell."

"You know what I mean. How about we go to Paddy's, and we can always walk the four blocks to your house if we think we should. Which we won't."

"That's fine with me," James says. "I don't imagine it will be so bad that we can't go out. And the only thing that would keep Nel from going out on a Friday night would be a nuclear bomb detonation."

Nelly nods emphatically.

"Fine, you win," I say. "Maybe I'm being a dork."

There's just too much of a disparity between what we're hearing unofficially and officially. The difference between fifty thousand and a few thousand is huge. Someone is wrong, or they're lying.

CHAPTER 4

I catch Penny in the upstairs kitchen on her break from the preschool, where she's lead teacher.

"So, you're really going to break up with Peter this time?" she asks, her joy at the news unmistakable.

I groan. Nelly must send out emails or texts or something.

"I'm going to kill Nelly. I would have told you in the next three seconds anyway. I decided this morning. At this rate I won't even have to do it, he'll hear the news before I see him." *I wish.* "Yeah, I'm going to, but not tonight. He's stuck in D.C."

Penny squeezes my hand; she knows how much I'm dreading the breakup. "Who else is coming for drinks tonight?" she asks, suddenly intent on the refrigerator's contents.

"Well, James is coming. I just saw him. He said you're a great kisser."

A blush spreads under her honey-colored skin. "No, you didn't say anything." Then she freezes and her brown eyes widen. "Did you?"

"Of course not!" She pretends to throw her water bottle at me and I duck. "I'm just bothering you because you didn't tell me right away. Jerk." I sit and pat the chair next to me. "So? Tell."

The pink creeps up her neck again. "Okay, okay. I don't know. Last night he asked if I wanted to hang out and we had coffee and then we kissed. I guess I kind of already liked him a little. It's weird, because we've been friends for so long."

"He likes you too-oo," I sing, and rub her shoulder.

She leans forward eagerly. "Really?"

"Totally. He blushed when I—"

Penny shakes her head, and I shut my trap as James walks in and heads to the refrigerator. She looks down at my feet and changes the subject.

"Can you even walk in those gigantic, one-inch heels?" she asks with a laugh, because she knows I can't.

"It's been a challenge." I wiggle my toes. "I think I'm getting blisters. April may be too early to be out with sandals on. My feet are icicles."

"Nice polish." I poke her in retaliation.

James peeks at Penny from under his hair and smiles. "Hey."

"Hi," Penny says.

"You're coming tonight?" he asks, as he leans into the fridge.

"Yeah."

He straightens up and pops open a soda.

"What, no Hot Pocket?" I ask. He laughs. Penny watches us with a look of confusion.

"I decided to go with the other thing," he says, and looks from me to Penny.

They smile shyly at each other. I kick my shoes off and stand up holding them. I think they might want to finish this stimulating conversation in private.

"I'm going to go wait for that news conference," I say. When I get to the door I look back and smile when I see he's already in my seat.

***

A blond reporter stands in front of a hospital.

"Many hospitals have a backlog of cases. Police are busing the sick to other hospitals throughout the city. Nurses and doctors are being asked to come back in for emergency shifts."

Penny takes out her phone and furrows her brow. Her mom might be on her way back into the thick of things.

"The New York City Health Department's statement is about to begin."

A man with a bit of gray hair and a sizeable belly stands at a microphone. He looks tired. He rubs his hand on his chin and begins.

"I'm Michael D'Angelo, of the New York City Health Department. As you are all aware by now, we have an outbreak of Bornavirus LX in New York City. While it is a serious virus, we don't want anyone panicking due to incorrect information.

"The CDC is providing treatment for those who have contracted the virus. We have set up emergency treatment areas throughout the city. It is very important that you receive treatment if you suspect you've been exposed. Do not try to care for an infected person yourself. The risk of transmission is great due to the nature of the virus."

"What do you mean by the nature of the virus?" a reporter shouts.

D'Angelo holds up a hand. "Bornavirus LX causes aggression in the final stages. This leads to a transmission of the virus through bodily contact, as patients will bite and scratch their caregivers.

"Transportation is set up at local hospitals to take people to the new treatment locations. Time is of the essence. As of now we estimate there are twenty thousand people infected in New York City."

The reporters and all of us in the room gasp. He nods.

"I realize that sounds like a lot. But it is the same number of people that Madison Square Garden holds, to put it into perspective. We can keep it at that number if New Yorkers follow our guidelines. We recommend that people go out in the next few days only if necessary. We can use the weekend to treat those affected and eliminate any new cases.

"Please visit our local CDC website for information on the treatment centers. Your local news stations will post the locations. We all know New Yorkers do their best under pressure, and we will have Bornavirus knocked out by Monday. We need help from all of you so that we can do our jobs to the best of our abilities. Thank you."

He mops his brow with a handkerchief and steps down, ignoring the reporters' shouted questions.

Everybody talks at once. Julio, our boss, uses his deep voice to catch our attention. "Listen up, everyone. We're going to finish up early today. I don't want you guys out in this any later than necessary. I'll call preschool parents to see if they'll pick up the kids early. The afterschool program will have to go on as scheduled, but I want the rest of you home."

People applaud and Julio smiles under his thin mustache. He raises his hands for silence. "All right. That means home, not *out*."

He looks at Nelly, who pretends to look behind him as everyone laughs. "Really, let's all take care. I'll see you on Monday."

There's a holiday atmosphere in the room as people leave to get their stuff. Penny hangs up her phone, her eyebrows straight lines with concern. "I left a message for my mom. I have to get back downstairs to the kids. I guess I'll meet you later?"

"I'm sure she's fine," I say. "I'll wait for you. You're not walking home by yourself. As soon as the kids are gone, we'll leave."

"Yeah," Nelly says. "And then we'll get that drink."

I face him with my hands on my hips. "Seriously? Did you not hear Julio?"

He shrugs as we stare at him.

"Dude," James says. "Pretend it's the nuclear bomb of viruses. Let's just go to Cassie's."

"Fine, fine," he says with a sigh. "But we won't leave without you, Pen. Just come up when you're done."

CHAPTER 5

James reads me and Nelly choice snippets of virus information as we wait for Penny in my cubicle. My cell phone buzzes. I can hear my brother talking before the phone even reaches my ear.

"Cass? Are you there?" He sounds worried.

"Hey, Eric!"

"You're okay?"

"I'm fine. Fine. Why?"

"Well, it took me eight tries to get through. They're reporting that New York's crawling with infected people. Something like one hundred thousand sick."

"They're telling us it's twenty thousand and they're busing them to treatment centers. Where'd you hear that number?"

I think about that estimate from earlier: Fifty thousand by noon. It's almost three o'clock.

"About five minutes ago. On CNN. They did their own estimate based on what they're seeing by helicopter. And right after they said it, the screen went black."

"Really? Are you sure they shut down CNN?"

Nelly and James look up at that.

"That's what it seemed like. Cass, you guys should go to the apartment. You've got Dad's supplies, in case you can't leave for a while."

"We're heading there after work. Julio let us out early, but we're waiting for Penny."

There's camping gear and food in the basement below the apartment we grew up in. Our landlady insisted I move in after my parents died.

"Eric, how about you? What's it like in Pennsylvania?" Eric's always so sure of himself that I forget to worry about him sometimes.

"They're reporting that there are some people infected. But, you know, it's pretty rural here. Rachel and I are going to sit tight all weekend. I've got a couple of extra cans of food," he jokes.

I laugh. He's always planning for an emergency just like Dad was.

"Cass, Rachel's brother called and said he can't leave his place in Philly."

"What do you mean, *can't*?"

"Too many infected in the streets. He can't go outside at all. People are getting attacked, and the police aren't doing shit. Maybe you should head for the cabin if it gets worse. That's what I'll do, too. We'll meet there if we can't get in touch again. Promise me, Cassie."

Eric knows I won't break a promise.

"Eric," I say cautiously, "I can't promise that. We'll be fine in the apartment, I'm sure. How would I even get there? The F train?" I try to lighten the mood by reminding him I don't have a car. None of us does.

"I'm fucking serious!" he says.

He sounds scared. Eric doesn't get scared. It's that edge in his voice that makes me listen as he goes on.

"You know what to do. You're resourceful. Don't let your brain get in the way. Cass, I have a really bad feeling."

I'm silent. I *am* thinking too much. My dad used to say that nothing will get you killed faster than ignoring your instincts. One hundred thousand people. That's five Madison Square Gardens. Five Madison Square Gardens' worth of people wandering around, basically rabid.

"I promise, E. I'll leave if it gets worse."

He lets out a breath I didn't know he was holding. "OK. I love you, Cass. Until the end of the world."

"And after. Love you. We'll talk later, okay?"

I tell Nelly and James what Eric said, and we head for the TV. But where CNN should be, there's a Time Warner Cable technical difficulties screen. James flips to NY1 News. It's still on, at least. They say the situation in the west is resolving itself. The virus is expected to be gone by Monday in all of the United States.

"Bullshit," James says.

"What's bullshit?" Penny says as she walks in with her bag.

"That this will be over by Monday. They've shut down CNN," James replies.

"Really?" Penny frowns and points at the TV. "But they didn't shut down everything."

"Just the stations telling the truth, maybe," I say, which earns me an eyebrow raise from Nelly. "I spoke to Eric. He says there are more infected here than they're saying. He made me promise I would go upstate if it came to that."

Penny's eyes go round as she nods. Then she looks at her phone and remembers something.

"I left another message for my mom, telling her we're going to your apartment, but I have to go home first. Ana left a voicemail. The phone didn't even ring. She said she was coming home after work but she forgot her keys. I can't get her to tell her to come to your house instead."

Ana is her little sister. She's always forgetting her keys, even though she's twenty-five years old. And she expects someone to be there to open the door, just like she expects people to do anything else she wants. Penny wouldn't normally rush home for her, but today is different.

"So we'll go to your house and head to mine later," I say, like it's no big deal. But I picture a street in Philly where you can't even go outside, and I shiver.

CHAPTER 6

I take deep breaths of the soft air as we head up the avenues. I grew up in this neighborhood, in a mixture of Irish and Puerto Rican families, and I've always loved it.

The old ladies, their lined faces ranging from a pale ivory to a dark brown, are in their aluminum-legged chairs getting up to speed on winter gossip. Salsa music pours out of windows. Barbeques are lit and kids race around. I'm always glad I decided to move back when I walk home from work.

Nelly watches the outdoor festivities and pouts. "See? Everyone else gets to have fun. But, no, we have to go hide inside."

"Stop being a crybaby," I say.

He laughs. But I know what he means. It doesn't seem like things could be bad, the way the neighborhood is out enjoying the day. No one seems to care.

"I don't know why no one is listening to what's going on," James says, and shakes his head.

"What's going on is that everything is fine, according to the news," Penny reminds us. "Not everyone is dissecting everything they say and spending hours on the internet. Don't get me wrong, I'd rather be safe than sorry, but no one else thinks this is a big deal."

Every step in these shoes has become torture. That's what I get for going for form over function. I can't even wear platforms without wobbling like an eight year-old playing dress-up. I should've stuck to my boots. I consider taking them off, but the sidewalk is covered with a layer of what resembles congealed fat.

We wait for cars to pass on the corner. I nudge Nelly and point to James and Penny's intertwined hands. He winks at me as I catch a glimpse of someone coming out from behind a dumpster. He's probably been taking a leak and I don't want to embarrass either of us, so I avert my eyes.

A rasping exhalation makes me turn again. An older man with dark, matted hair shuffles forward with a dirty hand out. At first I think he must be asking for change, but his skin is gray and his mouth gapes. Almost half of his neck is gone, like a bite was taken out of it. He must be infected. The wound is edged with black and filled with clotted blood and bits hanging that I really don't want to identify. The stench of something rotten wafts past.

"Let's go!" James yells, and yanks Penny's hand.

My ankle twists as I turn, and I gasp at the jolt of pain. I have to get out of these stupid shoes. Nelly steadies my elbow as I kick them off and we race across the street. Half-Neck follows. By the time we reach her building he's halfway there. Penny scrambles to get her key in the lock of the outer door. Maybe we should just keep running.

"C'mon, c'mon," Penny begs.

Her hand shakes but her key slides in. We fall into the small vestibule as Penny works on the next lock. Half-Neck appears and spreads his hands on the door. Brown flakes smear off his filthy fingers onto the glass. His eyes are filmy. He sniffs the air with a guttural moan and paws at the door.

"C'mon, before he breaks the glass," Penny says.

We rush through the second door. Once inside the second floor apartment, the door locked behind us, I collapse on the couch. James runs to the window.

"Oh my God," Penny says. Her hand's at her throat, like she's trying to hold in a scream. "What the fuck was that?"

We're all silent, our chests heaving and eyes wide. That's not what I thought an infected person looked like. He didn't look sick; he looked like a monster from a horror movie. And he chased us. My skin crawls when I realize he might be chasing other people right now.

"I'm calling 911." My voice sounds far away as I dial with a shaky hand. "We can't let him walk around."

After twenty rings I hang up and try the landline. An automated voice tells me they're too busy to answer. "They're not answering." This is not good. This is New York fucking City. "They're too busy."

Nelly watches out the window. "Still there. Penny, when's Ana coming home?"

Penny jumps for the phone and presses redial over and over. "Ana!" she yells, when she gets through. "Where are you? Okay, listen. There's a guy out front trying to attack people. Go to the service door. I'll stay on the phone with you. James and Nelly will open it so you can run right in. Do not come in the front!" A shrill voice sounds on the other end. "Ana, please. Just do what I'm telling you to do!" She turns to Nelly and James. "She's five minutes away. Will you go make sure it's safe? One of you run back up if it's not." They nod and leave.

"They're on their way down," she says into the phone. A couple of minutes pass in tense silence. "Is the door open? Go. I'll see you upstairs."

Penny grabs Ana in a hug as soon as she enters. Ana gives her a cursory pat then pulls away and smoothes her long hair. It's lighter than Penny's, with hints of gold. She wears brown suede knee-high boots and a long sweater with leggings. The sweater must cost as much as my yearly clothing budget, including my sandals back on the corner. Ana looks a lot like Penny, with her dark eyes and small nose, but she doesn't have Penny's curvy softness.

"So, what's with the crazy guy downstairs?" Ana strides over to the window. He sits slumped against the glass of the door. He's not moving. I hope he's dead.

"He tried to attack us on our way here," James tells Ana. "That's what the infected people are doing. You get the virus through bodily fluids."

Ana turns from the window and shrugs. "So, this is that swine flu or whatever? I can't believe people are going so crazy over it! The bar we were going to go to closed early. Now I get to spend Friday night here."

Now that she's safe, I want to put her out there again. "Ana," I say, in my best stop-being-a-little-shit voice. "Sorry your Friday night is ruined. But did you hear James? The man tried to attack us. Your mother is stuck at the hospital with these people. There may be a hundred thousand infected in New York. And it isn't swine flu."

Ana sticks out her bottom lip. "Fine, whatever."

She picks up her bag and saunters off to her room. I love Ana the way you love a little sister that you also don't like sometimes. That sweet little girl she'd been must still be in there. One summer at my parents' cabin she had found an injured rabbit and nursed it back to health. She didn't trust anyone else to do it. When she and my dad let the healed bunny go, she sobbed and spent the rest of the week looking for more animals to save.

"Whatever, indeed. At least she's safe," Penny says, and she raises her eyes to heaven.

Nelly pops the tops off four beers. James puts the TV on a local channel. CNN is still off air. I listen as I dial 911 over and over.

"Buses are filled to capacity with the sick. Family members are being asked to pin a note with the infected person's information onto their clothing and leave the area, with promises that they will be informed of the patient's progress. Police say this is to protect family members from being infected. We're going live to the scene at Lutheran Medical Center in Brooklyn."

I set the phone down and move closer to the TV. A reporter stands outside of the hospital where Maria works. Penny leans forward like she's trying to catch a glimpse of her mom. The number of people out there is staggering. They're lying down, standing up, sitting. They shuffle forward onto a waiting string of buses. As each bus fills up and pulls away, it's replaced by a new one. City buses, school buses, Greyhound coaches—it looks like anything with more than four seats has been pressed into service.

"They've been funneling people onto buses for several hours, but more arrive to take their place. We were just informed we are being moved to an area a few blocks away for our own safety. We will continue to monitor the situation down here. Back to you."

Nelly lowers the volume as the news anchor lists the treatment centers again.

Penny sighs. "Well, I don't imagine my mom's going to be home soon. There must have been five hundred people waiting out there. I just hope they're giving the nurses the anti-viral medication."

Penny grabs her phone and walks to the window, trying her mom again. Her beer hits the wood floor in a foamy crash that makes us jump. One hand covers her mouth and the other points to the street.

CHAPTER 7

There are four of them in front of an apartment building down the block, bent over on the shady side of the street. One is Half-Neck, astonishingly still alive, his head canted to the left. There's an old lady wearing a flowered housedress and wispy gray bun, a hipster with off-kilter aviator sunglasses and a Hispanic man wearing a half-tucked shirt and jeans.

The housedress lady stumbles away to reveal something meaty and glistening and pink. Only the hands and feet give any indication that it was once a person. The four of them are coated in fresh blood. It's smeared around their mouths and drips from their hands. It runs down the concrete into the street. My stomach heaves, and I lean on the windowsill. I want to scream at them to stop, but that would alert them to us, and the person is obviously dead. I run and dial 911. Fast busy. I try again and again as the others stare out the window.

"Nine-one-one, what's your emergency?" a voice asks.

"I'm watching four of the infected on the street. They're ripping someone apart! I'm on—"

The voice cuts me off. "Ma'am, is the person they're attacking dead? Can you tell?"

What kind of question is that? "Yes, I think the person's dead, but—"

"Ma'am, we can't send any police out now. If you give me your address, they'll take the infected into custody as soon as possible."

I give her the address. "Do you know when they're coming? I'm afraid they'll hurt someone else."

"No, ma'am, I don't." She has that officially harried voice every civil servant in New York City adopts. "And please stay in your home. The police will be there soon, and they are equipped to handle the situation."

"Yes, of course. Thanks." I hang up, adding, "For nothing."

I move back to the window. "They're not even coming."

"Well," James says, without tearing his eyes away, "at least they answered this time."

I can't stop watching either. It's so horrifying that the minute I stop looking I think there's no way it can be real, so I look back.

"They aren't just attacking, they're eating," Nelly says, and shakes his head in disbelief.

He heads into the kitchen and sits at the table. I follow him to get paper towels to clean up the spill. He's as pale as I've ever seen him, but his mouth is set in a firm line. "I know you promised Eric you'd leave if it was bad." I nod. "I thought that was a little over the top. But now I don't know. What do you think?"

What we just saw wasn't simply someone a little ill and violent. I don't want to sound like a maniac, but I'm scared. And I promised Eric. "I want to go upstate," I say.

James comes to the doorway with his arm around Penny's shoulders. "They don't have this under control," he says. "I mean, there are people eating someone on the corner and it's not even a fucking priority. They're not telling us the truth. People still think it's safe."

It's true; I can hear music and the sounds of happy shouting blocks away.

"Okay," Nelly says, his hands fisted on the table. His expression is incredulous, but his nod is firm. "Then we should leave. I can't believe this, this is insane."

I've always thought it would be great to have Nelly's total belief, just once, in my and James' crazy imaginings. But I find that this is one time I really, truly want to be wrong.

CHAPTER 8

A yell from the street snaps us out of our silence. Five young guys grip baseball bats and pieces of rebar and move in on the infected, who are so busy with their meal they don't notice.

A length of rebar connects with Aviator Glasses' head, while the owner of the rebar yells with the effort. It splits his head open with a crack that carries down the block and through the window glass. There's surprisingly little blood, although my stomach lurches at the sight. Another bludgeons the older man. Half Neck and the old lady turn toward the three men left.

"Now!" yells the biggest guy.

Half Neck and Old Lady don't stand a chance. They're down in seconds and bashed repeatedly until their heads are just a memory. The big guy straightens up and wipes his forehead with a bandanna from his back pocket. Before I can stop myself I throw the kitchen window wide open.

"Hey, thanks!" I call.

They look up and around until they see me and move to stand under us. Penny leans out of the living room window and waves.

"Oh, hey. You Maria Diaz's girl, right?" the leader asks. Penny nods. "Listen, you need to stay inside. They're everywhere." He gives us a stern big brother look.

"Are they all like this? So violent?" I ask. "They said they were attacking people, but it looked like they were eating—"

"Oh, they're eating." He grimaces. "Make no mistake. And you have to get their heads or they don't go down easy. Cut their necks or something. Crazy shit. You know, like zombies."

A younger kid wearing a baseball hat chimes in with lit up eyes. "It is, man. They *are* zombies. It's just like that game. You know, the one where you—"

"Christ, Carlos," the leader says. "This is no game. You see that body? That could be you or your moms or your sister." He looks up at us as Carlos surveys the remains and quiets.

"Sorry. We got to go. I'm picking up my little sister from a friend's house. Stay inside. Be safe. Tell your moms Guillermo said hi."

Penny says she will. We watch as they walk down the rest of the block and pause before every doorway.

"Zombies," James mutters. "Jesus."

It's silent. Penny finally speaks. "I'm willing to entertain the idea that this virus is out of control. I'll leave New York as soon as my mom comes home. She'll know how bad it is. But, zombies? C'mon."

She crosses her arms, her face tight. Penny is practical and even-tempered like her mother, but I can see the doubt in her eyes even as she insists it can't be true. They were eating that person, as hard as it is to believe.

"You just saw them, Pen." James gestures toward the window, then squeezes her shoulder gently. "I can't rule anything out, can you?"

Penny shakes her head, arms still crossed. He knocks a cigarette out of his pack. I haven't smoked since I quit again a year ago, but I think I can break the rule this once. James is smoking out the window, as no one in their right mind would send him outside, so I drag a chair over. He knows what I'm after and hands me his, lighting another for himself.

"Thanks," I say, and take a deep drag. The nicotine tingles down to the tips of my fingers and toes. "I can smoke if it's the zombie apocalypse, at least. What's my life expectancy anyway? One week, maybe two?"

James chokes on his smoke as I grin at him. "You're sick."

"Humor is the last refuge of the damned. That's what my mom used to say." I take another drag. "I don't know what else to do."

James closes his eyes. I stare down to where Half Neck and Old Lady are sprawled on the concrete. The windows of the building across the street are filled with people. A little girl with a ponytail waves at me, and I wave back. I can't imagine what her parents are telling her about all this.

James's eyes open suddenly. "Does it really matter?" he asks us. "I mean, I'm sure they're not really zombies, but they're acting like them. If this is spreading fast we need to get out of here before the rest of New York figures out the same thing. We can't afford to sit around waiting."

He's right. The trick is to leave before everyone else does.

Ana wanders into the living room. "Zombies?"

I stub out my cigarette and answer. "Yeah, it seems the virus is creating something close to zombies."

"Ew." Ana makes a face, not about zombies, but about the cigarette. She waves her hand at the smoke that's nowhere near her. "So, what are we supposed to do?"

"Leave the city," Nelly says. He sits next to Penny, who's chewing on a fingernail, and pats the couch on his other side.

"And go where?" she asks.

"My parents' house upstate," I say. "If we can get there."

Ana purses her lips. "Seriously?"

"We'll talk to Mama first, Ana, and bring her too. Don't worry." Penny reaches across Nelly and squeezes her hand.

"I'll try her," Ana says, and grabs her phone. "Oh, Mama texted. It looks like she texted us both, hours ago, but I'm only getting it now."

I wonder why no one is panicking when even making a simple phone call is a challenge. But I guess it was the same during 9/11 and the blackout. Maybe we're used to it now.

Penny checks her phone and shakes her head. "I don't have it. What's it say?"

"Virus very bad. Meet you at Cassie's after work. Bring clothes. We leave city tonight. Explain later. Love you, Mama."

Penny's eyes are huge behind her glasses. Ana shakes her head. "No way. Mama's as bad as the rest of you!"

I'm relieved. Not that it's turning out to be as bad as James and I thought. But that we've gotten permission to follow our instincts. That maybe we're not so crazy after all.

CHAPTER 9

Penny and Ana pack bags for themselves and their mother while we wait. Nelly smiles at me, but the smile doesn't touch his eyes.

I plop down next to him on the couch. "What's wrong? That's a stupid question. I mean, specifically, what's wrong?"

He looks down at his hands clasped between his knees. It's been years since he's worked on a ranch, but they still look like he does. He raises his eyes. "All those people out front of the hospital. If they're all like those four, then how are they going to control them?"

"I know. It's still early. Maybe there's some way…" I change the subject. "Have you spoken to your parents again?"

"My mom emailed before we left work. They're fine. Just a few sick there. They're together, so I'm not too worried."

Nelly's mom and dad and five siblings live near each other. They have cattle and a lot of guns. On my first visit Nelly had let them swagger around and show the City Girl how to hold a gun. Then I picked up a twenty gauge and blasted a can on a stump. Their mouths hung open until Nelly laughed and explained that my dad had taught me how to shoot when I was a kid.

"Yeah," I agree. "They'll be okay." I rest my head on his shoulder and wish I had parents to call.

My dad was always ready for an emergency. When I was young it had been fun: target practice, pioneer skills, food storage, conspiracy theories. As I got older I'd thought he was wacky in a loveable sort of way. And as life went on with no great emergencies lasting over a three-day snowstorm, I ceased believing that something could go monumentally wrong. It was unimaginable that anything worse than both my parents dying in one moment could happen. There'd been no way to prepare for that.

"So," James's voice breaks into my thoughts, "I'm seeing over two hundred thousand estimated infected here. The government has to be stretched pretty thin at this point. Especially since the rest of the country is fighting the same thing."

My dad always said it was better to be over-prepared than under-prepared. That he wouldn't feel like a fool if nothing ever happened, and that only in recent decades did people think planning for a lean future was a waste of time.

James taps a finger on his tablet. "The cities that were hit first are at forty percent infection. So that means if infection rates hold true, we could be looking at those numbers in days. Of course, this is all dependent on if they've quarantined most of the sick by now."

That's almost half of the city. I can't even fathom what that would be like. Maybe these websites are wrong and the Department of Health is right.

"Maybe they can stop it," I say. "You would think that they would've seen what should have been done in the Midwest and started doing it here."

James gives a sardonic laugh, and I admit he's probably right.

I miss my dad. It always seemed like nothing bad could happen if he was there to protect me. I remember standing down in the basement of their apartment as Dad showed me all the organized bins.

He had handed me a heavy backpack. "This is for you."

"What's in it, an anvil?"

"Funny. It's your BOB. Your Bug Out Bag. It has what you need if you have to leave the city quickly."

I hugged him and laughed. "Okay, nutso."

He hugged me back, smiling but serious. "Keep it in your closet. I hope you never need it. But when I got to thinking about how you didn't have one with you, now that you're out of the house, I couldn't sleep."

I patted his bushy hair. He tried to keep it tamed, but it grew in cowlicks and puffs with a life of its own.

"Of course you couldn't. How could anyone sleep soundly without a backpack full of escape gear?"

He smiled but then shook his head at my levity. "All this," he motioned at the bins, the cans of food, "is for you and Eric. I hope you never need it. My greatest fear is that I wouldn't be able to take care of you guys. It's a nightmare. You'll understand one day."

I gave him a kiss. "Well, thank you, Daddy. I do appreciate it. Truly. I'll keep this handy."

I knew it gave him a modicum of feeling in control, and it was harmless, really. He wasn't one of those people who sat around hoping the world would end; he just felt more secure when he was prepared for anything. That bag is in the basement right now, still packed with what he thought would keep me safe. I'll go through that first.

"So, y'all, it's great we're leaving town and all. But just what are we leaving town *in*?" Nelly asks.

"I was thinking we could take one of the vans from work," I say.

There are a couple of ten-passenger vans in the lot behind the building. Nelly and I both have driven them in the past.

"I was thinking the same thing," James says with a nod.

A rumbling echoes down the hall. Ana enters rolling a suitcase and wearing ballet flats.

"Huh," Nelly says, completely straight-faced.

"I'm thinking someone hasn't grasped the gravity of the situation," James mutters to Nelly.

I attempt to keep my voice light. "Ana, do you have a backpack?"

"I still have one from school. Why?"

"Maybe you should pack in that." I look down at my bare feet. "And shoes you can run in would probably be good."

Her upper lip curls. "Fine. Do you want to help me pack?"

"Why not?" I wink at James and Nelly, who are still snickering, and follow her down the hall.

Ana must have thought we were heading to the Caribbean, since I removed gauzy tank tops, a makeup bag and a pair of heeled sandals from her bag. Now she's outfitted in a pair of decent shoes, jeans and a sweater. Penny's in a similar outfit.

"I'm scared, you guys," she says.

Her lower lip trembles and I give her a hug. "Whatever! So there are thousands of people who want to eat us alive. I don't see what the big deal is."

The face I know almost as well as my own breaks into a smile. We can always make each other laugh, no matter how bad it is. We always have, ever since that sad girl whose papa had just died walked into my fifth grade class.

"Love you," she whispers and grabs my hand.

"Love you back." I squeeze. "It'll be all right."

James opens his arms and she steps into his gangly embrace. I nod at Ana's look and she grins. She's always dying for Penny to meet someone, so I know she's pleased, even if she thinks he's a geek.

Nelly stands up and claps his hands. "Shall we?"

"We shall," I say, as I link my arm into his.

CHAPTER 10

The streets are empty of infected, except for the bodies. The bodegas on the avenue are open, and people lug full bags as they hurry home. Some hang out, completely ignoring the pleas to stay indoors.

By the time we reach my garden apartment my neck hurts from looking over my shoulder constantly. We troop down the hall into the living room. Someone's in the kitchen, and for a moment I think it's Eric, but that would be impossible. It's Peter.

He's making himself something to eat and has his sleeves rolled up and his tie off. It's the most untogether that Peter ever appears. He always looks so out of place in my apartment amidst the clutter of papers, books and art supplies. Not that I've used art supplies much in recent years, but I can't bring myself to admit defeat and pack them up. I'm sure I look the same in his apartment with its big windows and clean lines. The minute I get there, it looks like I've exploded all over, even when I try to be neat.

"Hey, babe. I was worried." Peter wraps his arms around me so hard my air cuts off. I hug him back in surprise. I didn't think Peter got worried. "We got a ride on another plane to LaGuardia, so I came straight here. And when you didn't answer your phone…"

I feel a pang of guilt at the concerned look in his eyes. All I've felt is relief that I won't have to see him. I'm a horrible person, and I'm probably all he has. He lost his little sister and parents in a car crash when he was twelve. We have that in common; it may be the only thing we have in common. His rich, aloof grandma raised him until she died. He's alone. At least I have Eric.

My voice catches. "I'm sorry. I'm glad you made it back."

When I met Peter at a bar in the city I'd dismissed him. Smooth, charming rich guys from the Upper East Side aren't my type. He insisted on buying me a drink, though, and I chatted with him while I counted down the minutes I had to be polite before I could escape. But when he asked if my parents still lived in New York, and I mentioned the accident, he didn't make that uncomfortable face everyone makes just before they apologize.

His eyes were dark and liquid when they met mine. "It's like living in a house where the roof's been torn off, isn't it?" he asked, and I could tell he'd been waiting years to find someone to say that to. Someone who might understand.

I nodded, shocked, because the feeling that there was no protection, nothing left to shield me from whatever fucked-up thing the world was going to throw at me next, was exactly how it felt. And I'd thought that maybe I'd unfairly judged the book by its cover. But that guy, the one in the bar with the kind eyes and startling insight, hasn't shown his face in months, until now.

It's a brief appearance. Peter lets go abruptly and surveys all of us with a dark eyebrow raised. He goes from warm to cold so fast it can make my head spin.

"So, what's the deal with everyone here?" he asks.

"We're waiting for Maria, Penny and Ana's mom," I say. "She said we should get out of the city, so we're going to my parents' house upstate."

He gives a dismissive laugh. "Seriously? I think you might be overreacting a bit."

Ana nods in agreement with him. Traitor.

I feel my usual annoyance at him swell. "Well, if wanting to leave a place where people are eating other people is overreacting, then sign me up. Were you chased by a man with half his neck missing? Did you watch four infected people eating someone?"

"Cassandra, it's a small outbreak. They have it under control. I spoke to friends in Manhattan and they say police are everywhere and the streets are empty."

He looks like a petulant little boy. I saw pictures of him once in an old album on his bookcase. They were from the years when his parents were alive. Peter had been a cute kid, with freckles that matched his dark hair and a wide, easy grin. He hadn't looked bratty like he does now. When he'd gotten out of the shower and saw me looking at the album, he had smiled but put it away. The next time I was there it was gone.

Ana flips her hair and smiles at Peter. It's the smile she reserves for people who aren't us. "See? It seems like they're taking care of the situation in Manhattan. I'm sure we won't have to leave."

Ana has a huge crush on Peter. She thinks it's one of life's great mysteries that Peter and I are together. I'm alternately irritated and amused by her consternation. Sometimes I name a place we've gone and watch her burn with jealousy, just to mess with her.

James smirks. "I think I'll go by what Maria's saying. Cassie, I've got to charge my iPad. Can I use your computer?"

"Of course." I look at Nelly. "Want to see what's in the basement?"

CHAPTER 11

The plastic bins are stacked against the far wall of the basement. I've passed them a thousand times on my way to grab a can of tomatoes or something but never notice them anymore.

"So, where to begin?" Nelly asks.

"I guess we'll start with the BOBs. That's Bug Out Bag to you normal people. Filled with all the stuff you need to make a quick getaway."

We find four large backpacks on the top of the stack. Mine must weigh thirty pounds. The contents are neatly packaged in Ziploc bags and stuff sacks.

"Why don't you start emptying the others?" I ask. "Let's pile it up next to each bag and see what we've got."

"You got it, Boss," he says.

I sift through my bag. There are energy bars and dehydrated food, water bottles, water filter, first aid stuff, toiletries, and the dorkiest sweatshirt ever, among other things.

"Hey, Nels. What do you think?" I hold up the sweatshirt with a kitten painted on the front.

"Nice," he says. "You should totally wear that."

I laugh. "It had to be my dad. My mom would've known I wouldn't be caught dead in it. He must've bought it so there'd be some warm clothes in here. At least the jeans look normal."

I'm still smiling. My dad was convinced I loved kittens even though I had grown out of that sometime, oh, around when I was ten. He always put something in my Christmas stocking that made me laugh until I cried: a fluffy kitten calendar, a notepad with cats wearing Victorian hats, those types of things. Now that I think about it, maybe he did know and liked to see my reaction. Suddenly the sweatshirt is the best gift I've gotten in a long time. I pull it over my head and wrap my arms around myself. It's like a hug from my dad.

"It's from my dad," I say. Nelly nods and smiles; he doesn't need expounding. "Some of the clothes in the other bags might fit you and James."

The last thing out of every bag is a travel pouch with a wad of cash and papers. I unfold a map and see different routes highlighted, all leading up to the cabin. I count the cash, seven hundred-fifty dollars in smaller bills.

"Wow," I say. "Guess I don't have to hit an ATM."

"Same amount over here," Nelly says. "That'll make three thousand if the other two have the same." He looks quickly and nods. "Yeah."

The bags just need some unexpired food. My dad put a lot of thought into the contents; I don't think there's anything missing. Except weapons.

"Are the guns still here?" Nelly asks. He's talking about the small cache of weapons my dad kept in the city.

"I think so. Eric put them in a bin marked 'sewing stuff.' "

The bin is under others, one of which bears my name in Eric's scrawl. My curiosity gets the better of me, and I leave Nelly to unearth the guns while I investigate. My college diploma is on top. An old cigar box that I remember throwing out is in there, too. It smells faintly of dried flowers that Adrian brought me. I find the silver ring with a tiny star on it that Adrian gave me because he knew I loved stars. It feels warm in the cool air of the basement. I put it in my jeans and run a finger around the circle it makes in the pocket. Old concert tickets are in there, too. I think of something I haven't thought of in a while and start to giggle.

"Nelly, remember when we went to see The New Pornographers and Adrian smoked too much weed?"

Nelly puts down a bin and guffaws. "When he thought he'd walked into cobwebs and they were on his face and wanted us to help get them off?"

Adrian had been swiping at his face and looking frantic. He was always so composed that it made it a hundred times funnier, and the rest of us had crumpled to the ground, we were laughing so hard.

Footsteps sound down the stairs, and I can hear Penny laughing before she appears at the bottom.

"There's no way the candy bars that girl gave us were only chocolate," she says, and shakes her head. "No way."

"I never let him live that down," I say. "It still makes me laugh out loud, every single time. The look of panic..."

My stomach hurts from laughing, but when the laughter stops it continues to hurt in a different way. I never bring up Adrian. I stare into the bin as though I'm fascinated with its contents, but there's no fooling your best friends. Penny's arm snakes around my waist. I try to stop the tears. I hate crying in front of people. I cry over stray cats, old people eating dinner alone and lonely looking little kids. I'm a huge crybaby, but I like to cry by myself.

"I miss him, you guys," I whisper.

"Don't you think we know?" Nelly asks, like he can't believe I think it's a secret. I wipe away the tears, but the more I think about it the faster they come.

"You know, I could have chosen a better day to decide I've made a huge mistake. Only *I* would choose the day of the zombie apocalypse," I say, which makes them laugh. I smile through my tears, and the lump in my throat eases. "There's no way to contact him, even just to make sure he's okay."

"If anyone's fine, it's Adrian," Nelly says with certainty. "He's on a farm in northern Vermont. I can't remember the name. I had an email he sent, but it was my old account."

"I didn't know you guys still spoke." I'm jealous and have to remind myself I have no right to be.

"We've emailed now and then. The last time was about a year ago. I wrote him twice to tell him my new email address but never heard back."

He shrugs, but I know he cares. Adrian was his friend, too. When I broke up with him it must have been hard to straddle two friendships.

I touch Nelly's arm. "I'm sorry I made you guys lose touch." I mentally add another item to the list of things Cassie has messed up in recent years. It's growing by the minute. I'm dying to know what he and Adrian talked about. "Did he...? I mean, what did..."

"He wanted to know how you were, said he missed you. The last time he wrote he asked if I thought you would talk to him. I tried to bring it up, but you were so opposed to talking about Adrian that you shut me down. I told him he could try, but I didn't know how it would go over."

I finger the concert tickets and imagine how different my life would be if I hadn't been too stubborn and ashamed to admit that I fucked up, even to myself.

"I wish you would have made me listen," I say, even though I'm sure he tried.

Nelly raises an eyebrow. "Do you have any idea what you're like when you don't want to talk about something? I know you do. You are the most stubborn human being in the world. *Please.*"

His face is stern. I might be able to lie to myself, but Nelly won't stand for me lying to him.

"I know, I'm sorry. It's my own fault. I didn't listen. But you're the second most stubborn." I make a silly face at him.

"Hey, I can admit when I'm wrong. I just never am," he says. Penny groans and rolls her eyes. "Plus, I'm bossy. There's a big difference."

I raise my hands in surrender.

"Okay, enough memory lane, people," Penny says. "There's a ton of crap to go through before my mom gets here. James is on the computer, and Ana is mooning over Peter, so I figured I'd come down here and help." She reads the bin labels. "Sleeping bags, mats, lamps, cookware. Jeez, did you get rid of anything?"

"Nope. Eric organized it all. That's who put all this stuff I threw out in this bin."

I'm grateful he rescued the wooden box and promise myself I'll tell him when I see him. I wonder what Adrian's doing right now. If that farm in Vermont is his. The night I met him he already knew that was exactly what he wanted.

***

I was sitting on a couch at a frat house party at my upstate New York college and wondering what I was doing there. My roommate of a week was across the room. I watched as she draped herself over any guy with a pulse.

"Not your kind of scene? Mine either." The voice came from a guy who sat on the other end of the couch. His sandy hair was messy and his lips formed a wry smile as he saw me take in his shirt with Greek letters on it.

I looked at the letters and then back up at him. "Yeah?"

"I have no choice," he drawled, his accent more apparent. "I'm a legacy. If I don't embrace the life of a frat boy my daddy will disown me." He held out a big hand. "Name's Nel. I'm from Texas originally."

I shook it. "Cassie. Nice to meet you."

"So, Cassie, who are you and what are you doing here? You don't look like the usual clientele."

I shrugged and pointed at my roommate. "She begged me to come with her. I figured I'd give it a whirl. I'm from Brooklyn. Sociology major." I shrugged. "Boring."

"Brooklyn? That's not boring. I'm moving to the city once I graduate. *This* is boring." He took in the room. "The funneling and male chest-beating. The drunk girls and their screaming fights. A lot of the guys are okay if you don't take it too seriously, but the parties are terrible."

I knew he wasn't your average frat boy; his eyes twinkled as he made fun of it all.

"My roommate is auditioning for the role of Drunken Girl." I pointed to where she sat on someone's lap giggling.

"It's times like this I'm glad I don't like girls."

While I couldn't have cared less, fraternities aren't known as a hotbed of equal rights. "And everyone here is cool with that?"

"Yeah. Especially since they know they're not my type. They all think they're God's gift to women and were surprised to find it didn't extend to men, too." I laughed as he grinned. "I came out senior year of high school and took some shit for it. I refuse to hide anymore."

"Absolutely," I agreed. "But, Texas? That must have been rough."

"Well, it didn't hurt that I can beat the crap out of most guys who might have a problem with me." He made a mean face and then replaced it with a sunny smile. "I was a football player and my closest friends on the team knew. They stood up for me, too."

I tease Nelly that he told me he was gay right away so I didn't fall in love with him. Girls are always falling in love with Nelly. But there wasn't time for me to fall in love with him, because at that moment he spotted someone across the room and waved.

The guy made his way toward us. He was tall and lean, with dark hair and pretty green eyes. They really were pretty, and with his light olive skin and high cheekbones he might have been pretty, too. But his strong jaw and his nose, which was just slightly imperfect, were enough to make him interesting. He was wearing a t-shirt with some indie band's name on it and jeans. When he smiled one deep dimple appeared.

"Adrian, this is Cassie. Cassie, Adrian." Nelly said, just as someone called his name. "Ah, I'll be right back. They always want the gay guy for the things that involve food. You'd think I know how to cook."

Adrian sat down on the couch. I'm not very good at making conversation in general, and most definitely not with good-looking men. I smiled nervously and consoled myself with the thought that he was Nelly's date, even though he was my type, too. There was no reason to act like a tongue-tied second grader.

Adrian turned those eyes on me with interest. "Hi, Cassie. What year are you? I don't think we've ever met."

"Junior. I just transferred this year. How about you?"

"Junior, too. It's a decent school, people are pretty nice."

I nodded and tried to think of something to say, but my mind was a complete blank. It occurred to me that I shouldn't be allowed to participate in social interactions without a set of note cards. Adrian saved me.

"So, what do you want to be when you grow up?" he asked. His smile was disarming. And although it's the second question everyone asks when they make small talk in college, he gave the impression he really wanted to know.

"Well, if you mean what am I majoring in? I started out thinking of art. But that's not going to line up a decent job, so I switched to sociology with an art minor."

The corner of his mouth twitched. I knew what he wasn't saying and conceded to his unmade point. "Yes, I know sociology's not much better." I smiled. "But I'm not planning to work on Wall Street. I have to study something I love or what's the point? I'm thinking I'll work in a non-profit somewhere."

He nodded. "What kind of art do you make?"

"Mostly I paint." I felt too shy to talk about it and changed the subject. "So, how about you? What's your major?"

"Engineering."

"Now that's a grown-up degree," I teased. He was so friendly I could feel myself relaxing. "So what do you plan on doing with it? Building bridges and making tons of money?"

He grinned. When he shook his head his hair fell into his eyes, and he pushed it out of the way. "Not exactly, I'm majoring in environmental engineering. I want to create things that might be used for food production and soil conservation."

I shook my head. "Ah, a do-gooder!"

"Hey, don't worry. I won't start lecturing you on what you're doing to ruin our planet or anything." He held his hands up and the dimple showed.

"I'm just kidding. So you want to be off grid? Zero waste?" I asked.

"Exactly." He looked at me like I had caught his attention and my face grew hot under his scrutiny. "I spent this summer volunteering on a project and learned enough to put in a solar hot water system for my mom. Next I'd like to completely solarize her house."

I nodded and drank some beer so he wouldn't notice how pink my cheeks were.

"I'd like to create a farm that generates its own food, power, maybe biodiesel—" He stopped abruptly. "Sorry, sometimes I start to talk about this stuff and can't stop." He waved his hand in front of my eyes. "Are they glazed over yet?"

"No, it's like talking to my dad." I lowered my cup. My face had finally cooled down. "My parents are putting in solar at their house upstate. Their plan is to be entirely off the grid by retirement and raise most of their food themselves. I like to talk about it with my dad, until it gets too technical and I can hear the gears in my brain grinding."

I made a whirring noise that didn't sound at all like gears, but he laughed. "I wish I could pick your dad's brain sometime. I'd like to see what he's done."

"You could, you know. If you're serious. He's desperate to talk about it. My mom and I just nod and smile and wander off when he gets going. Now that my brother's away at school, he's slowly dying inside from lack of interest in his plans."

Adrian nodded like it was something he would consider. I had to say this for the lovers of solar electrical systems: they sure were a committed bunch. I recognized the dreamy-eyed look on Adrian's face.

"So how do you know Nel?" I asked. I wondered if they were serious or not.

"We were in a class together last spring and just hit it off. He's a great guy."

"He seems like it."

Right then Nelly appeared with a plate of burgers. "So, what'd I miss? I think you may have missed your roommate puking in the bushes and heading home, Cassie."

I stood up. "Maybe I should go after her." I didn't want to. Holding her hair back in the communal bathroom was not high on my list of things to do.

Nelly waved a hand. "Some other girl was with her. Bethany? Tiffany? Someone, anyway. She's fine!" He sat on the floor and patted my spot on the couch. "Sit. Eat."

So I did. My eyes wandered over to Adrian constantly. A few times I caught him looking at me and whenever our eyes met my stomach jolted. I told myself to get a grip. That maybe he was cute and nice, but he wasn't interested in me. He wasn't even interested in girls.

I always felt like the girl whose name people forgot. Usually the guys who ended up interested in me were the ones I'd known for a while. The ones I could talk to without being self-conscious. I was fine with it by that point; I didn't mind being a person who inspired love and loyalty over time. But it usually meant that I was overlooked, at least at first. And with Adrian I knew I would have minded that.

"Well, I have to work in the morning, library work-study," I said, after we'd talked for hours. It was the kind of conversation where you have so much to say that you despair of ever getting it all out, even if you're awake until dawn. I didn't want to break the spell and go home, but it was late. The rest of the party was passed out or making out at that point. "I might be able to drag myself out of bed if I go to sleep now."

"No walking home alone, darlin'," Nelly said. "Let me walk you."

I didn't want to make him walk me home along the safe, tree-lined streets. "Thanks, but I'm fine. I grew up in Brooklyn, remember?"

"Let's walk together," Adrian offered. "Our dorms are right near each other."

"Okay, thanks," I said. "Nelly—" I realized I'd called him Nelly, the beer having loosened my tongue, and blushed. I'd already concocted a nickname for him but hadn't meant to use it.

"I like Nelly!" Nelly exclaimed. "Like Nellie Oleson on *Little House on the Prairie.*"

"I used to pretend I was Laura!" I said. "When I practiced my pioneer skills." Adrian smiled at me. "Anyway, *Nelly*, it was really nice to meet you. Maybe I'll see you around?"

Nelly grinned and swallowed me in a hug. "Oh, you won't get away from me, Half-pint. Let's all meet for lunch tomorrow."

"I'd like that," I said, and beamed at him.

I moved away to give them a moment of privacy, and with a last wave at Nelly we set off. We walked to campus while Adrian told me about his mother, who'd raised him and his sister with lots of love but hardly any money. He was smart, funny, liked his mom and was environmentally conscious. I sighed.

Adrian poked my arm. "Why the long sigh?"

"Oh, nothing," I replied, watching my feet.

He pulled my arm through his. "C'mon. Tell me."

I made my lips a line and shook my head. Then I decided that if I told him it might be funny and also stop my crush in its tracks.

I sighed dramatically and elbowed him. "It's just depressing. No guys are ever interested in the same stuff I am. Even my dad would love you." Adrian stopped walking and looked stupefied.

"You know," I stammered, "because you're gay." Now I really felt like an ass. If only I'd kept my mouth shut.

"I'm not gay."

I thought I saw a tiny smile on his face but couldn't keep eye contact long enough to be sure.

"What?" I'd heard but needed a moment to think.

"Am I giving off a vibe or something? I was trying to give off a vibe that I wanted to go on a date with you."

I hardly listened to what he was saying because I was wondering if I could turn and run. The chance that I could avoid him on campus for the next two years was slim, however. Plus, I could only run a block before I got a stitch in my side and he still had my arm. I'd told him that I liked him and that my *dad* would like him.

The beer and food were mutinying in my stomach. "I just thought, because of Nelly, and you said you two hit it off..."

"I don't care about that. I do care about the date thing, though."

I stared at him blankly. He looked so relaxed, while everything inside me was buzzing and jumping.

"You know, the thing about wanting to go out with you?"

"Oh." I was pretty sure he knew the answer to that question, so I made a joke. "Okay. But maybe we could save meeting my dad for the second date."

His grin was huge, and I smiled back, relieved that maybe I hadn't made a complete fool of myself. I was still mortified, but underneath was a warm flicker of excitement. It hadn't been my imagination; there was something there. Somehow we got to my dorm without my dying of embarrassment.

"Here's my stop," I said, as he released my arm. "Thanks for walking me."

I bit my lip and glanced at him, hoping he'd say something about seeing me again.

"My pleasure. So, I'll see you tomorrow at lunch and we'll make plans?"

"Okay."

We smiled shyly at each other until I realized I should probably go inside. I started up the steps to the door and tripped. I hoped he was gone, but when I turned around he was still there. It looked like he was suppressing a smile. I tried to act flippant, but I wondered how many gaffes I could pull off in one night. This was going to be a record.

"Go ahead, laugh. I trip about ten times a day. Or knock something over. Or clobber someone by accident," I said.

He shook his head, amused. "Goodnight, Cassie," he said in a soft voice.

The way he looked at me, like I was something special, something worth staring at, made my legs wobbly. I waved and managed to walk in the door, not *into* the door, and headed to my room.

***

Nelly lifts the bin lid and takes a deep whiff. "Ah, I love the smell of gun oil." He probably does, too.

"So what's in there, you good ol' boy?" asks Penny. "Not that it will mean anything to me."

Nelly sets the long bin on the ping pong table. He opens the cases and pulls out two revolvers, one nine millimeter and a shotgun. They're clean and shiny. They look like my dad might have packed them up yesterday. Boxes of ammunition come next. Nelly stacks them according to size.

"There's nothing worse than an unloaded gun," he says.

He deftly loads the proper ammunition into its respective gun. I help him. The revolver feels heavy and weird in my hands. I haven't held one in over three years.

Penny backs away. "Jeepers." My dad taught her to shoot a rifle, but she's afraid of pistols. "Didn't your dad know it's illegal to have guns in the city?"

"Sure," I say with a grin. "That's why most of them are still up at the house."

Penny shakes her head and Nelly laughs.

CHAPTER 12

We finish up downstairs, for now. The cabin is only a four-hour drive, but if my dad were here he'd say not to count on that. We need to have enough supplies with us in case it takes days. In case we have to walk. I'm not a light packer, and left to my own devices I'd bring everything. James might be good at helping with it; he has an ordered way of thinking. So does Peter.

Peter. He's here, and it seems he's coming with us. I can't keep this up much longer. Every minute I spend still officially dating him feels like a lie. I head upstairs. James is intent on my computer. A giggle comes from the kitchen.

"Yeah, no one goes there anymore. And—" Ana stops talking and looks up.

I smile brightly. Peter smiles back. Ana looks at my cat sweatshirt with something akin to horror. I'm planning to put it back in my BOB to keep it safe but didn't want to take it off yet.

"So, we've had a look in the basement, and we have backpacks for everyone. Peter, you have clothes here." He nods. "You're going to have to pack things that you can walk in, just in case. Like jeans." I give Ana a pointed look.

Peter looks at me like I'm a silly little girl. It's maddening. "So, we're really leaving?"

"Well, Maria said we should. Ana, it's *your* mother. She's not one to blow something out of proportion." I stop short of telling him he's welcome to stay in New York if it's too much of a hassle.

Ana clearly doesn't want to agree, but she does. "It's true. My mom is the most practical person you've ever met. We should probably listen to her."

The unstated implication is that Cassie is not. She's spot on with that one; I'm not going to argue. Peter smiles and holds out his hands. I take one, even though I don't want to.

"No, Cassie's not the most practical, but she is the prettiest," he says.

Ana smiles at him, but after he turns to me she rolls her eyes. His skin, even in my terrible kitchen light, is gorgeous. But all that aristocratic perfection is boring when there's nothing behind it.

"Thanks," I reply, although it's not true. Ana could beat me in a beauty contest any day. Personality is another story. "Time to pack."

I pull on his hand. It's smooth but strong. He does things like faux mountain climbing and running, but only in climate-controlled environments. The one time I cajoled him into walking around Prospect Park with me, he bitched about the mosquitoes the whole time.

I've thrown some of my stuff on his shelf in my closet. Peter *tsks* at me as he pulls his clothes out from under mine and places them on the bed. Then he closes my door and turns to me with a smile. I bury my head in the closet and mumble something about boots to keep him at bay, but he comes up behind me and kisses my neck. I stiffen just a little, although what I really want to do is swat his hands away.

I bonk my head on the closet rod as I turn. "Peter, we have a lot to do."

He smiles and gently pats my temple. "And no time for a kiss? Come on, I haven't seen you in a few days."

I give him a kiss that's more than a peck but definitely not a real kiss. I smile and hope it isn't as fake looking as it feels. "Okay, now, there's a lot to do."

I can't decipher the look he gives me, but it's not a happy one. "Fine."

I let my breath out, relieved, and find clothes for myself.

CHAPTER 13

Peter helps to organize the basement, even though you can tell by the set of his face he thinks it's ludicrous. We have food and water and water filters. Compasses, duct tape, knives, flashlights, a radio, a tiny stove with fuel, two light tents, and other things for backpacking. Peter's made a list and checks things off once they're packed. Whether or not he thinks we're being ridiculous, he's being diligent. He's like a toddler; you have to give him a job or else he'll pout and annoy you.

"We'll have to get the van soon," I say. "Get it loaded and ready to go."

"I don't know," Penny says, as she zips up her pack. "I'd feel like we were stealing. Maybe we should cab it to the airport and rent a car."

"Julio said I could use the van. Like if I went to Ikea or something," I assure her. "We'll be back with it when work starts. Given the circumstances, he'll be happy we used it."

"Julio won't mind at all, Pen," Nelly says.

With urgency James calls to us from upstairs, where he's mapping out routes on my computer. "I guess you guys can't hear down there. Come here."

The noises grow louder as we climb the stairs. James has opened the street-facing windows in my bedroom. We peer past the decorative wrought iron that covers the glass, but my street is empty. It's coming from up the block.

"Let the looting begin," Penny says, over the sound of breaking glass. "Let's go up on the roof and walk to the avenue."

We pick our way along the attached brownstones to the end of my block and stand at the ledge.

Broken glass from the storefront windows glitters in the streetlights. Dozens of people cheer as they hand things out to their partners in crime. One guy dances along with his radio as he fills every inch of his car with plunder.

More figures head this way. At first I think they're more looters, but they don't show any interest in the stores. They begin to scuffle with the looters a few blocks down. It must be a group of infected.

"Holy shit," James says, coming to the same realization.

They make their way toward the looters below, who don't hear the screams that we can barely make out over the din. Finally, a teenager notices the infected, and his face slackens as they arrive. The sounds of rioting fade under the shrieks of fear. He grabs a friend by the back of his shirt and points.

Some manage to run. Those who don't notice, or don't know what the infected are like, or who think they have time to grab one or two last things, find themselves surrounded. The infected fall on them with their hands and teeth. Hoarse screams rise up and are abruptly cut off.

"Jesus. Get their heads," James mutters next to me.

It's a massacre. Blood splatters to the street as bodies are ripped open. A few escape after being bitten. I hope they don't go home to their families and infect them, but I'm sure that's where they'll go. That's where everyone goes when they're hurt.

Peter leans heavily on the ledge, looking pale. Maybe now he understands.

It doesn't take long until bodies litter the street. Some of the infected wander around like they've lost track of what they were doing, while others eat. Some sway in an invisible wind. The only sounds are the awful noises that rise from deep in their throats. I'm certain I can smell the tang of blood all the way up here. I put my cold hand to my forehead and close my eyes.

"All the noise attracted them," James says. "They heard the yelling. Look at them." We scan the group below. I don't know what I'm supposed to see besides all those bodies and all that blood. He gestures to the street. "Look at what they're wearing."

Over half of them wear hospital gowns, the kind they give you when you check in. But they don't let you leave wearing them, at least not while they're able to stop you. Penny lets out a gasp.

"Oh, shit," I say. My heart sinks as low as the street beneath us.

CHAPTER 14

Penny paces the hall with her phone. We sit in the living room, the news and James's clicking on my keyboard the only sounds. When my home phone rings, I jump for it.

"Thank God, Cassie," Maria says. "I've been trying you for an hour."

"Maria!" I say. Penny rushes in. "We got your text. Are you still at the hospital?" There are shouts and heavy things being dragged around in the background.

"Yes. Cassie, do you have a speaker on this phone?"

I find the button and tell her to go ahead.

"Thanks. Penny? Ana?" Maria's softly accented voice echoes around the room.

Penny bends over the speaker. "Mama! When are you coming?"

Maria takes an audible breath. "Penny, you have to leave the city right now. There's a man here from FEMA. I'm on his emergency phone. He's told us they plan to destroy all access out of New York sometime tonight or tomorrow. They can't control the spread of Bornavirus, so they're going straight to quarantine."

"What do you mean, *destroy*?" James asks.

Maria's laugh is short. "They're calling it quarantine, but they're leaving the infection to run its course. Bart, the FEMA guy, says they're planning to bomb or block off the bridges and tunnels. They don't want millions of infected spilling out of New York. He was supposed to leave the city tonight."

I never would have thought they'd trap us here like that. At least not while there were so many people still healthy. They're guaranteeing our deaths.

"So they'll leave us here to die?" Penny asks incredulously.

Maria sighs, and when she speaks again her voice wavers. "Yes, they will, *mija*. They are. There's more. There's no treatment. They're killing the sick. We were euthanizing them with a mix of drugs to the brain stem. But it was too little, too late. The hospital's been overwhelmed and patients are pouring out the doors. We're all hiding in the basement here."

"We saw them. I was so worried about you. They're eating people, Mama," Penny says. A sob escapes, and she covers her mouth. "They're all just lying dead in the street."

"Oh, *mija*. They may not be dead, as long as there's enough of them left. All of the infected are dead, or as near to dead as they can be, but still move around."

James meets my eyes. There's no surprise in them but a kind of awe. Like how people must have felt when man first walked on the moon or made a test tube baby. Except test tube babies didn't want to eat them.

"The virus is working in tandem with a parasite. The brain is its host. Somehow it stimulates all those processes that are primal: moving, fight impulses, hunger. I don't know every detail. The CDC's been studying it for the past month."

A month and they still couldn't stop it. We hear another loud noise on her end and jump. They must be piling up whatever they can find to keep them out.

"I'm here, I'm here. I have to go. Other people need the phone. We've got the morgue and cafeteria. We've got a generator. We're safe here. But you all need to leave the city now and go upstate." Maria knows all about the stash in my basement and up at the house.

"You mean we," Penny corrects her.

"Penny, there's no way for me to leave until the infected have wandered away or died or found something to—we're okay here. I need to know that you're safe."

"So we're supposed to leave you here? No!" Penny says with a screech. Her mouth is frozen in an O.

"You can't wait. Bart wanted those of us with family here to get them out. In forty-eight hours New York will be infected beyond belief."

"That doesn't make me feel better, Mama!"

"I know, but you need to know how dangerous it is. One little bite, sometimes even a scratch, can infect you. I know how to take care of myself. As soon as it's safe I'll head to Cassie's apartment. If there's a way out of New York, I'll head upstate. Cassie?"

Penny looks at me like she's wandered into a bad dream and I might be able to wake her up. But it's not just her nightmare.

"I'm here, Maria," I answer. "I'll put the key under the mat. We'll leave a map to the house."

I think of Maria here alone, with a few million ravenous dead people outside. Maria was always like a mother to me, even before my parents died. After they died, when Eric and I were frozen in grief, she handled the funeral arrangements. She made our first Christmas alone bearable. She's been here any time I've needed her. I can't leave her here when she needs us. "We're going to get a van from work. We'll come by and get you—"

"No! No," she says again, gently. "It's too dangerous. I'm sorry, but I have to get off the phone. I love you, *mijas*. Please, promise me you'll do what I ask."

"Okay, we promise. Please take care of yourself, Mama. I love you," Penny cries.

"I promise I will. I love you, Penny. I love you, Ana. More than anything in the world."

Penny's cheeks are wet with tears as she whispers back.

Ana clutches the table, her knuckles white. "I love you, Mama. It's Ana. I love you, too."

"I love you, baby. Take care of each other, all three of my girls, okay? I know you will." Her voice breaks under the strain and then she's gone.

CHAPTER 15

We stand around the phone base in silence. They really are dead people. They've lost all semblance of order. They're going to blow up the bridges. Maria isn't coming with us.

We're all thinking it, but James is the one to finally say, "Holy fucking shit."

Peter sinks into a chair and stares into space. Penny and Ana hover over the phone like it might start talking again.

I blink back tears and touch Penny's shaking shoulder. I don't know what to say. It might have been the last time she'll ever speak to her mom. Maria didn't mention how long it will be until the infection's run its course. There's enough food here to feed one person for a long siege, but she has to make it here. I have a feeling that'll be easier said than done.

Penny motions to herself and Ana. "We're not going." Her eyes are wild and red, daring any of us to object.

Nelly shakes his head slowly. "What?"

"It's our mother. How can we leave her here? I know I promised, but when she gets here we'll leave with her."

I tread carefully. I know I wouldn't want to leave my mother here either. But I also know Maria would die if her girls stayed in harm's way because of her.

"Pen, I promise you we'll come back for her as soon as we can," I say.

She and Ana exchange a glance. Penny gives me an apologetic look and shakes her head.

James clears his throat. "Well, then, I'll stay with you guys. Strength in numbers. We'll find a way out when your mom gets here." He shrugs, but his face belies his words.

We should leave. There's nothing I want more than to be in a van heading north. But I can't leave the few people left in the world that I care about. It might not be the smart decision, but it feels like the right one.

"I'm staying too, then, if you really won't go," I say, as Nelly nods. "We'll spend tonight and tomorrow getting any extra supplies we can. We should still get the van, so it's close by when we need it. Bring over all the food from your house. We're not leaving without you."

Peter shakes his head and turns away.

Penny looks from James to Nelly to me. "I can't have you all risk being trapped here. You must be crazy. No matter how much I want you to stay, I have to make sure you're safe—" The last remnants of rebellion leave her face. "I sound just like my mom, don't I?"

"Yeah," I agree. "Now times that by a thousand and you know how badly she wants you to leave. The rest of us have to stay because when she gets here and sees you she'll kill you herself."

She gives me the ghost of a smile and runs a hand along the earpiece of her glasses. "We have to go, Banana." She uses her pet name for Ana. "I don't want to leave, but Mama will kill us if we stay. We promised. When she gets here she'll be good until we can come back for her."

"This is ridiculous," Ana argues. "I think we should wait a few days and see how it goes." Penny tries to speak but Ana cuts her off with a glare. "I know what Mama said, Penny. But that FEMO or whatever guy could be wrong, you know. What are the chances that they're actually going to blow up bridges in New York City? That sounds like something Cassie would say."

It's heartening to see how she rolls her eyes at my name. Makes me know the real Ana is in there somewhere, dying to get out and disparage someone.

Penny's tears dry up. "Ana, stop! We're going, like we promised. Tonight. Let's get our bags ready."

Her no-nonsense manner shuts Ana up. She sounded just like her mama.

CHAPTER 16

Nelly and James elect themselves to get the van. I volunteer, but what seems suspiciously like misguided chivalry makes them refuse. I decide not to make a fuss even though, after Nelly, I'm the best shot with a gun. They each have a baseball bat from my dad's coaching stuff and a pistol.

"Remember," I remind them, "don't use those guns unless you have to. It seems like they like noise, the..." I trail off. I can't say the word.

"Zombies?" James says. He has that look of nervous anticipation guys get when they're doing something dangerous and probably stupid, but instead of being scared they're excited.

"Listen." I wag a finger at them and pretend it's not shaking. "Don't be heroes. Get the van. Pick the one with the most gas. Come back. The end."

Nelly salutes me. "Yes, ma'am!"

I hug them and lock the gate. It's hard to ignore the lump in my throat. They'll come back. I busy myself bringing the backpacks upstairs. Between the bags and larger equipment that we'll put in the van and leave behind if necessary, it looks like we're mounting an expedition to Everest. I hope that the van will take us as least as far as the city limits.

I put my hand to my jeans pocket and run my finger along the circle Adrian's ring makes. It's become my talisman; as long as I hold onto it, this will end well. Peter comes into the basement.

"Want to help me bring up the rest of the stuff?" I ask.

He ignores my question. "What were you thinking? Are you out of your mind?"

"What?"

His arms are crossed and he has on his superior, disdainful look. I've seen it before, but it's never been directed at me.

His face twists. "Saying you wouldn't go without Penny? I can't believe you would jeopardize our safety like that, for a person who most likely will end up dead!"

I take a couple of deep, trembling breaths. They don't help at all. Two hours ago he thought we were blowing this out of proportion, and now he's accusing me of jeopardizing *our* safety. All he cares about is himself, and maybe me, because I'm his ticket out of here. I'm somewhere to go. I don't know why it comes as shock to me, really. I suppose I think that people can be selfish, but when push comes to shove they'll do the right thing, the human thing. But not Peter. Rage boils up, but I tamp it back down, and what comes out is cold and deadly.

"You know, Peter, sometimes you do something that might jeopardize your own safety because you love someone. You love them so much you're willing to stick by them, even if it means doing things the hard way. Even if it means putting yourself at risk. Not that I expect *you* to understand that. And as for jeopardizing us, don't worry about that. As of now there is no longer any *us*."

His mouth hangs open. I'm cruelly happy to see the sneer replaced by shock.

"I don't want you to stay here where it's not safe, and you're welcome to come with us. Or go your own way, since you think we're all crazy. But don't you dare let Penny or Ana hear you. You, of all people, should understand that they want to make sure their mother's safe."

It's a bit of a low blow, and he looks properly chastened. "Fine, fine, sorry," he says, and reaches out for me.

His face rearranges back to its normal state. He's trying to charm me. He thinks Silly Cassie isn't serious. I cross my arms. I have never wanted to kick someone so badly in my life.

He exhales noisily. "Cassandra, stop being ridiculous. I'm sorry. I didn't mean it how it sounded."

But I know he did. My whole body shakes, but I also feel a palpable sense of relief.

"No, we're done. It's been a long time coming. Now's not really the time to discuss it. I'm sorry I did it this way."

I push past him and run up the stairs.

CHAPTER 17

Standing in my bedroom, hands in fists, I hear the sounds of Penny and Ana moving our stuff to the front door. I change into my broken-in leather boots and throw my slippers into the closet with more force than necessary. Being scared and sweaty has done nothing to tame the frizz in my hair, so I make two long, brown braids. I don't want to see Peter, but I can't lock myself in here. I head into the living room and stand in front of the TV, ignoring Peter's glares from the couch.

The virus is under control, the news anchor says. Now that I know they're lying, I understand why everyone is still at home, waiting for it to blow over. Unless you're looking for it, there's nothing but good news.

They're implementing curfews, ostensibly to stop the looting. That means roads should be clear, and if we aren't stopped we might make it out. They flash the locations of more treatment centers. I imagine mass graves. My feet tap the floor. We don't know what time they're taking out the bridges, and tomorrow officially starts at midnight. A car door slams out front. It's Nelly and James with the blue van.

I run to the door. "Well? How was it?"

"Not too bad," Nelly replies. "We turned a corner, right into one of them. He scared the shit out of us, just before James and I both knocked him with our bats." He mimes swinging a bat and blanches.

"Ugh," I say, as I remember the crack of the metal on Aviator Glasses' head.

"Yeah," James says. He no longer looks thrilled to be having a testosterone-fueled experience. "It was pretty gross. As we were driving back we think we saw a huge group of them. Going through Queens may be impossible. We need to leave now, while the streets here are clear."

The only other plan is the Verrazano into Staten Island and then crossing into Jersey. They didn't see many cars. People are still in their houses, doing what they've been told. That must be why they're bombing the bridges tonight. The panic will start tomorrow for sure, and by then it will be too late.

CHAPTER 18

I look around my apartment one last time. I think I can feel my dad and mom here. I hope I'm doing what I'm supposed to, what they would have done.

"Until the end of the world," I whisper down the empty hall.

"And after," Penny whispers from behind me.

I turn and smile. When I was a little girl I would argue with my parents about who loved who more. As big as the universe, we'd say. Forever and a day. Infinity plus one. Until the end of the world and after. Right now it seems fitting.

My block is still quiet, so we load the van quickly. Nelly's behind the wheel as we head for Queens. Shadowy figures fill the blocks far ahead. Nelly drives to the next avenue, but it's the same: a terrifying parade, headed our way.

"Yeah," I say, "Jersey it is."

There are a few infected people on every block. Some almost look normal, but their stiff bodies and staring eyes give them away. Others look dead and decomposing. I wonder how I didn't realize Half-Neck was dead; in retrospect it seems so obvious. You can't be alive when your carotid artery has a bite taken out of it.

I'm relieved when we're off the streets and on the expressway. The infected haven't made it here yet, and the bridge is only minutes away. I'm beginning to relax when the interior of the van flashes with police lights. A layer of sweat forms under my clothes, and my legs tremble. We've barely made it anywhere.

"Shit," Nelly says, and pulls to a stop on the shoulder.

Four police cars race up. I hope they'll let us go home instead of arresting us, but they whiz past without a glance. I drop my head back with relief and hear the exhales of my friends as we pull onto the road and cross the bridge.

The Verrazano has always been my favorite of all the bridges. It's tall and graceful and painted a light silvery blue, the exact color of the river and sky at dusk. It looks as if it's grown there organically, water turned to metal.

I imagine it tomorrow, a twisted hulk, with cables and chunks of concrete hanging down to the water beneath.

This seems too easy by far. I spin in my seat, but the road is empty except for a few cars far behind us. I face forward as we pull into the tolls. A police officer stands in the one open booth. He looks like the kind of guy who becomes a cop so he can legally fuck with people.

"Whatchoo all doing out here?" he asks. He has a name tag that says Spinelli, and he looks at us with absolutely no expression.

"Hi, officer," Nelly says. "Hoping to get to Jersey, we've got some family there."

He stares at Nelly without blinking. "What, you didn't hear about the curfew?"

"Well, yeah, we did. But you know New York City traffic. I figured this was the only time in my life I was going to get to speed on the Turnpike."

Officer Spinelli's veneer cracks a little bit. He's doesn't smile, but some sort of tough guy thing passes between them and he relents.

"All right. Listen, I'm not taking you guys in. We're supposed to, but after this shift I'm going home, and I'm not staying in the station filling out paperwork if I don't got to. I'm the only one here now, anyway, so I don't know what they expect me to do. Anyone asks, you got on the highway in Staten Island."

James leans toward the window from the passenger seat. "Thanks, officer. Are you planning on staying home or going somewhere?"

"Staying home. Like you should be doing. Why?" he demands.

"We have it on good authority that they're closing off New York tomorrow. Blowing up almost every access point and leaving the infection to die out on its own."

Officer Spinelli looks like he might be reconsidering not taking us in. It's obvious he thinks we're off our rockers. I know James is trying to help him, but it might make things worse.

"This is straight from a FEMA guy high up. You might want to leave tonight," James says.

Spinelli's eyes don't change expression. "I'll take that under advisement. Godspeed." He lifts the arm on the lane and waves us through.

"I thought for sure he'd listen to me," James says, disappointed.

I turn back and see the arm hasn't come back down. A few cars have pulled into the lane and he waves them through. Then he rushes out of his booth to a police cruiser parked on the side of the highway.

"He is," I say. "Look." I hope he gets his family out in time.

CHAPTER 19

Nelly was right: I don't think I've ever gone this fast on the Staten Island Expressway. I cross my fingers as we turn onto the road that leads to the Goethals Bridge.

"We've got a roadblock," Nelly says.

Two cop cars block the road, surrounded by police barriers. A cop rises up from behind them and limps toward us, dragging his right leg. Nelly takes his foot off the brake, but the figure raises its arms and waves. The leg of his uniform is shredded. He leans against Nelly's door and pants.

"We were attacked by some guys," he gasps. "One bit me, but I shot him right in the head. I radioed for backup, but it hasn't come yet. My partner's dead and I can't drive with my leg." He points back at the cars.

"National Guard was here, but they were called away to some disturbance. You can't go through." He has a mustache that bobs up and down as he talks. "Curfew. Plus, I need medical help. You gotta take me to the hospital."

They must be telling the cops the same thing they're telling everyone. He doesn't know his bite is a death sentence.

"We can't," Nelly says. "We have to go to Jersey. We'll take you that way."

"You can't go that way. I just told you that. Stay here, I've got to get my stuff." He limps back to his cruiser.

James turns to Nelly. "Just go, dude."

I pull the revolver out of my bag and hold it on my lap. Maybe I could use it on someone who isn't already dead, if I know he'll be dead soon. Dead, and trying to eat me.

"Hang on," Nelly says.

He knocks the traffic cones out of the way and an orange striped barrier hits the van with a clunk and flies off into the grass. The cop waves his arms and yells. He gets smaller and smaller as we race across the bridge. I feel sorry for him; he has no idea why we abandoned him.

James turns to me, on the bench seat behind him. "He didn't even know there's no cure. What. The. Fuck?"

Peter's been silent the whole trip, but now he speaks up from behind me. "If they told you that you were fighting a losing battle and that they were about to lock you and your family on an island of infection, how many cops do you think would stay on the job?"

"True." James leans back in his seat. "Do you think that's it? Just that roadblock?"

"That'd be pretty hard to believe," Peter replies. "But who knows? Everyone in the know may have left already. I wouldn't have flown back to New York, had *I* known. I would have hopped on one of those choppers with a senator and be cooling my heels somewhere in Montana right now, perfectly safe."

I can feel his eyes boring into the back of my neck. That makes two of us that wish he was in Montana. He's taking the breakup well.

"Well, since they can't spare the manpower to stop the infected eating people on the street, I'm betting they don't have the time to stop people who are driving along minding their own business," Nelly says. "That cop said the Guard was called away. It must have been pretty important for them to leave a major roadblock."

My shoulders come down a centimeter on the other side of the Goethals, and I loosen my grip on the pistol. I've been waiting for an explosion to rip up the roadbed underneath us. There are few cars on the Turnpike, but that wouldn't be surprising this late on a normal night. A convoy of Army trucks passes us southbound. Maybe they're heading for the bridge. Maybe they're setting up the explosives.

"We've got about twenty miles until the Palisades Parkway," James says.

The only sounds are Penny and Ana's sniffles. There's nothing I can say to make it better. Maria's all they've got left besides each other, and I know exactly how that feels.

The van slows as we come up on the George Washington Bridge. The highway beyond our exit is blocked. When we make our way down the ramp, we're stopped at the intersection.

What looks like a kid in an Army uniform shines a light into the car. "Sir, the bridge to New York is closed. Where are you headed?"

"We know, we're heading to the Palisades," Nelly replies.

"Sir, that road is closed. All civilians need to go home and stay there. A curfew is in effect in New Jersey."

"Well, seeing as how we're from New York, we need to go somewhere else. We don't have anywhere to go in the area. We're heading upstate to our house."

The soldier nods. "Sir, we have temporary quarters for anyone traveling through. Make a left, head up that road about a mile, and you'll see big tents and an office building. All persons without valid local identification are required to go there until morning."

Swell, I think. They're forcing us into a government corral. Now I sound just like my dad and his friend John, our closest neighbor up at the house.

"C'mon," Nelly argues. "We do have a place to go. We're trying to get there right now. I'm sure y'all could use the room to house someone who doesn't have somewhere to go."

"Sir, those are my orders." He motions to an older man who's been talking on the radio. "These folks say they're heading upstate. They don't want to head to the temporary quarters."

The man, who's not much more than a kid, says, "You have to go while the curfew's in effect. Besides, roads are only for official vehicles right now. You won't get far." He runs his hand over his crew cut and smiles apologetically. "Sorry I can't help you out. We're getting a lot of sick around here. They're not taking any chances. Turn left and head down. Can't miss it."

Nelly sighs and puts the van into drive.

CHAPTER 20

Afew tents surround a two-story, suburban office building. The road beyond is blockaded with Road Closed signs. An older soldier with a beard flags us into a parking lot and then gruffly demands the keys to the van. We all gape at him.

"Our keys?" James asks. "Are you nuts?"

"I give you a tag, I give your van a tag, and you give me the keys. You get the keys back when you leave," he says, like we've somehow missed the point.

"You're basically taking our vehicle away," James argues. "You can't just demand our property."

The big man sighs, like he's heard this from every driver of every car in the lot. "Listen, the keys are hanging in that tent right there." He points to a tent at the lot entrance. "We need them in case we have to move things around. Think of it as the U.S. Army running a valet service."

Nelly reluctantly hands over the keys. The soldier nods his thanks and points us in the direction of the building. Four soldiers stand at the entrance. Thankfully, they don't demand to search our bags.

"Do you know when we'll be able to leave?" Peter asks one. He's got on his Important Voice, but the soldier only shrugs and motions for us to follow him inside.

The lobby narrows to a carpeted hallway lined with doors. We're led through one, into a large unfinished space. A dozen people sleep under army-issue blankets in cots against one wall. Chairs are grouped in the front of the room.

I swing off my pack and sit down. People eat at the folding tables that fill the back. A woman at one holds a little curly-haired boy on her lap. Next to her a kindergarten-aged girl swings her legs and chatters away while she eats a plate of cookies. For her, at least so far, this is an adventure that involves unlimited cookies, and that's all she needs to know. The woman smiles fondly at her. Above the table she seems calm, but on the floor her feet are restless. Underneath the glare of the fluorescents I can see her cheeks wobble with the effort of keeping that smile on, of not giving into the panic.

Against the far wall stand a few more tables loaded down with food. My stomach growls loudly enough to turn Nelly's head in the chair next to me.

The soldier who brought us here motions at the tables. "There's plenty of food. Someone will fill you in soon."

CHAPTER 21

"Do you have another cigarette?" I ask James. "I'm sorry I'm grubbing. It's not like you can just run to the store or something."

We stand outside the building, having just feasted on bagels and cold cut platters. There were fruit baskets, which was pretty surreal, like we were at some corporate symposium on our lunch break.

"I grabbed what was left of my carton at the office," he replies, and hands me one with his lighter. "I've got plenty."

I light it and sigh. I could get used to this again.

"I'll take one, too," Nelly says. He looks like the Marlboro Man with the butt hanging out of the corner of his mouth.

"How long has it been?" James asks.

"Five years," Nelly says. He sinks back against the building as he exhales and closes his eyes. "How can they still be this good after so long?"

"Isn't it evil?" I ask, as the smoke hits my lungs.

"And awesome," James responds, clearly having none of the guilt Nelly and I have.

My laugh is cut short by Peter, who comes out of the front door of the building and makes a beeline for us. "Can I talk to you for a minute?" he asks me, with a look of distaste at the cigarette.

I'm thankful I have it. If it doesn't keep me calm while talking to Peter, I can always put it out in his eye.

We walk away a bit, and when he stops I stop and wait for him to speak.

He shakes his head. "I can't believe you're smoking."

"Is that what you wanted to say? Because, yes, I think I can have a cigarette right now without feeling too guilty about it."

"Whatever, Cassie. That's not what I wanted to say." His dark eyes flash and his lips thin. "I think I'll go my own way now. Thanks for helping me leave the city, but I'll figure it out from here."

I know it has to be hard being here with my friends, but it's just like him to pick on me about smoking because he's annoyed. Maybe he wants me to beg him to stay. Not happening.

"Fine," I say. "Good luck."

He looks at me coldly and shrugs. "You, too."

He turns on his heel. Now I feel guilty. Someone has to be the mature one here; we're both acting like babies.

"Peter." He turns around, but his face gives nothing away. I take a deep drag and crush out what's left of my cigarette on the side of the building. "Come on, this is silly. You can't go off by yourself. Just because we…well, we can still be friends, no?"

He shrugs. I am *not* going to beg him.

"So, we'll all stick together for now?" I ask.

"We'll see how it goes, but I don't think so. I'm sure I'll be safe here until I can get back to the city."

He holds his head high and waves his hand back at the building. He might just as easily be telling me he'll be staying at the Plaza until the decorator's finished with his apartment. I watch him walk away, amazed at how easily he believes this new reality conforms to any of the old rules. Nelly and James look at me curiously as I make my way back to them and carefully relight my crushed-out cigarette.

"What was that about?" asks Nelly.

"I broke up with Peter at the house, before we left."

"Really?" Nelly asks. They're both trying not to smile. "Great timing, as usual."

"Oh, be quiet. I just couldn't take him anymore. He's saying he's going to go his own way from here. And now I feel guilty about that, so I asked him to stay with us, and he said that he'd have to check his calendar."

A soldier with a friendly snub-nosed face strolls up. "Everything okay over here?" We nod. "I'm Sergeant Grafton."

We introduce ourselves.

"When do you think we'll be able to head upstate?" Nelly asks.

Grafton contemplates the question. His round face and pink cheeks remind me of a grownup version of the little boy on his mama's lap inside.

"Probably in the morning. We're not hearing anything but bad news, so I can't make any promises. In fact, there's an armory over in Teaneck where the two majors went for a briefing. We've lost contact. We sent out a team to find them." He looks like he thinks he's said too much and puts his hands out in a calming gesture. "Now, we can hold the building if we have to. Until help comes."

If help comes is left unsaid. But I know we all thought it.

He gazes into the distance. "We don't know if they were overrun by Lexers, but lack of radio communication is troubling."

"Lexers?" asks James.

"Yeah, you know, like the LX in Bornavirus LX? The Army is unofficially calling them Lexers."

"Can you tell us how many they think are infected?" I ask. "They aren't releasing new numbers."

The Sergeant snorts and anger passes over his features. "That's been a bone of contention around here. They were trying to keep us from contacting family, so we couldn't spread the word. That lasted ten minutes." He blows air from his nose. "They think that ten to fifteen percent of New York City will be infected by dawn. The major cities in the Midwest are at sixty percent. The rest are hiding out in their homes.

"I shouldn't be telling you this, but right now they're focusing on the smaller places, the ones that don't have a lot of infected. Hoping they can build up Safe Zones and leave the cities until they can clear them of Lexers. I don't see any point in keeping the information from civilians."

He shrugs, but the look on his face says he knows more than he's telling us. He's warning us that this isn't under control, without saying as much. He has no idea we already know.

"It's the best plan they've got so far. Now, look around here." He points to the building. "Not much in terms of defense, but we do have the Palisades right at our back, so there are no worries about defending in four directions. Fences are going up as we speak."

"Palisades. You mean the Parkway is right behind us?" I ask. It's useful information.

Grafton hooks a thumb at the trees behind the tent. "Yeah, head back, maybe a thousand feet, eight foot fence, you'll be at the Parkway."

James nods quickly and tries to look disinterested.

Grafton's radio squawks. "I gotta go."

CHAPTER 22

We're back in the waiting room. Peter sits in a separate grouping of chairs, but Ana's followed him and they talk quietly. I'm too tired and tense to do anything but sit here. Nelly sifts through the supplies in his pack. He finds a deck of cards in a side pocket and holds them up to me. Dad believed that boredom could kill you, too.

"Eh?" he asks.

I could use something to take my mind off of things.

"Sure," I say. "Spit?" Nelly and I have an ongoing battle in that game.

He pulls the cards out of the box just as Grafton enters the room and raises his voice. "We have word that there may be infected heading this way. Please stay where you are and keep your belongings nearby in case we have to evacuate."

The woman with the kids chooses the cot farthest from the windows and door. She covers them with a blanket and cradles them to her.

We grab our packs and sling them onto our shoulders. In the frenzy no one notices when we leave the room and head to the lobby. Humvees and jeeps are parked around the perimeter of the parking area out front, just inside the newly-erected fence. They're circling the wagons.

Bright lights, the kind you see on nighttime construction sites, are set facing out. About thirty soldiers take up positions outside. A soldier in the lobby tries to herd us back down the hall. I'm not too keen on heading to where I can't see what's going on. Neither is Nelly, and we follow as he ducks into the first door in the hallway.

The soldier leans in. "We need you to head to the back," he orders.

Nelly turns around after nodding approvingly that the windows face the parking lot. "Grafton said it was okay. Go ask." He's betting he won't do it.

The soldier backs down. "Okay."

Five soldiers file in and take position at the windows. We're in the waiting room of a mortgage company. There are stuffed chairs upholstered in that ugly pattern favored for its ability to mask any stain. One of the soldiers switches off the lamps on the scattered tables.

The lights outside provide more than enough to see by. We huddle at the back of the room. I sit on the floor, backpack in front of me, hands under my thighs.

Nelly sits next to me. "Take your gun out, just in case."

I pull it out. It gives my hand something to do. The others sit behind us on chairs. Penny murmurs to James.

James leans forward. "Penny doesn't think she can use her gun. Should I give it to Peter?"

Nelly twists his head back. "Pete," he calls softly. I'm surprised he followed us down here, but I'm glad too.

Peter tears his gaze away from the windows. "Yeah?"

"Can you shoot a gun?" Nelly mimes shooting a pistol.

"Um, I never have. How hard can it be?"

"Well, shooting is easy. Aiming's the hard part," Nelly says with a grim smile.

Peter's eyes narrow, but Nelly wasn't making fun of him and he knows it. "I wouldn't mind having it. Any pointers?"

Nelly kneels and gives him an informal two-minute introduction to handguns. Once Peter can sight and hold the gun properly, the lesson is over. The only other thing that would help would be target practice, and we hope for none of that.

Grafton pokes his head in the door. "Ready?" he asks the soldiers. "We have word they're about a half klick away, headed this way, most likely. Lights are going off, just in case that draws them."

"Ready, Sarge," replies a young Latino soldier. The others nod.

"Remember, head shots," Grafton says.

The soldier who spoke looks at his compatriots. "If I get bitten, man, take me out. No waiting, even if I'm still alive."

A dark-skinned soldier gives him a playful palm to the back of the head. "Rodriguez, I've been waiting for the chance to shoot you. I volunteer."

All the guys laugh, and Rodriguez cuffs his buddy with a smile. "I'll be sure to get you too, Park."

They all grin. It's the last thing I see before the lights outside shut off and plunge the room into darkness. A small light comes on by the window. Grafton's features are dark as he nears us. His jaw is tight, but he smiles and glances into the shadows, where we've lowered our guns. Nelly's shotgun is parked under the chair behind him.

"You have weapons?" he asks. Nelly nods reluctantly. "Well, we're supposed to confiscate them, but I'm not doing that."

I relax. I have my doubts we're getting the van back, but this gun isn't going anywhere.

"You might need them. We've seen the footage, and Lexers aren't easily fought. They just don't stop," he says with something like wonder then looks out the window.

"There's a good chance we can hold them off. If it looks like we can't beat them the best thing to do is run, if you can find a clear exit. Or head upstairs to the men on the roof. I've been told they're able to crawl up staircases eventually, but they can't open doors unless they can break them down. The door frames here are metal. It would take a lot to get through them. That one group in Chicago held them off for a week. We could do that, no problem."

His voice is a mumble; I think he might be talking to himself now.

"Maybe the Middle East would've been better. At least that enemy is human."

And I guess he knows the truth about the infection, or has figured it out.

"Okay, I've got to get back out with my men." He nods once before leaving.

CHAPTER 23

My mouth is stuck closed, and the water I sip does nothing. I strain my eyes and imagine things moving in the dark: a mass of infected like the ones who attacked the looters. Except I'm not safe on my roof right now, with months of food to eat and access to stored water below me. All we've got is what's on our backs. We have two places to go: the Palisades and the upper floor of this building. The Lexers may not be able to make it up, but if there's no water, all those people will be dead in a week, if not days, trapped up there.

After what seems like forever, one of the radios carries a warning. "We have approximately one hundred Lexers heading our way. ETA of two minutes. Be ready, boys."

The soldiers stand at attention. A figure advances out of the gloom and nears the fence. It's followed by another and another. The outside lights blaze to life, and I gasp at the sight.

The main road is full of infected, of Lexers. They stumble their way over the grass and into the lot. The guns and soldiers make no impression on them, except to draw them closer.

Shots ring out. A man with no lower jaw falls after the top of his head is blown off. A woman wearing a bright purple wrap dress drops to the ground with a well-placed shot. A little boy, who can't be more than nine, limps to the fence. His mouth hangs open and his baseball cap has slid down over one eye, giving him a rakish look. His parents must be so worried about him. His parents might have been the ones who did this to him, I realize, and my mouth goes even drier.

My legs grow weak. These people are dead. They're dead, and they're not. If I think about it too much I might go crazy, so I push the thought to the back of my mind. I watch the little boy stagger from a head shot, and it's only when he drops to the ground, face-first, that I see his shirt wasn't always brown. Before all the blood, it had been white.

There's an older woman who looks like an office worker, a doctor still wearing his white coat, a couple of men wearing orange road worker vests. They all fall, but the tide continues as they veer off the road.

There are so many of them. They make it to the fence, where they push and pull and yank. I can hear them through the window, even over the gunshots. It's a cacophony of low, rasping cries and drawn-out moans. It sounds like hunger, and we're the food. I fight the urge to cover my ears with my hands and use them to clench my pistol. The gate swings alarmingly, but it holds.

A flash of light out by the main road illuminates the room. The explosion makes us jump. For a few minutes they're killed as fast as they come. But then Rodriguez points out the window and shouts. I visibly follow his finger, and the sight forces the air out of my lungs. I tighten my sweaty hold on my gun.

A gigantic throng of infected follows the first. They trip and swarm over the road barricades they've knocked to the ground. All the noise must have attracted them. Rodriguez, Park and the others have a loud conversation over the gunfire.

Rodriguez turns to us as they run out. "We've got to get out there," he yells. "We're gonna kill those motherLexers!"

The Lexers at the fence push. Their fingers stretch through the wire, beckoning us. The fence buckles at the joints where the panels meet; the sheer force of hundreds of bodies is not something it's made to withstand. I back up, right into a wide-eyed Penny.

It sounds like the finale at the Fourth of July fireworks. My heart booms and my stomach pounds like a bass drum. *Please, please*, I chant along with it. *Please*. But, when the second group meets the first at the fence, it bends from the top and the bottom scrapes along the pavement. The seam between two panels of fence cracks. A Lexer on the ground slithers through. He's missing an arm, and his shirt hangs open to reveal shredded skin and coagulated blood.

"No!" Penny whispers.

When she grabs my arm it stops my trembling. I can't freak out now. She isn't armed. And if the Army can't protect us then we're going to have to protect ourselves.

The Lexer under the fence grasps a soldier's foot and drags himself toward his ankle with his one good arm. His teeth sink into boot. The soldier cracks his head with the butt of his rifle and fires on the infected who follow.

The bright lights turn their skin a garish white, which contrasts with the dark blood most wear. Some look like they're hissing, but it isn't with any real venom. It's instinct alone. Their eyes are blank, soulless.

The soldiers retreat into the building. Boots clatter and bang as some head to the roof and the shots resume in earnest. The gate bends lower and gives way with the sound of shearing metal. The Lexers pour through and squeeze between the vehicles. Now that the worst has happened, I'm calmer than I thought I could be. There's only one thing to do.

"We have to go," Nelly says. "Grab your bags."

I throw my straps over my shoulders. The others hurl their heavy packs on and look to Nelly.

"Out the back, to the Palisades?" he asks James and me. We nod.

The soldiers in the lobby pile desks and chairs in front of the glass, while others herd the civilians up the stairs. The mother has the boy in her arms, and a soldier carries the screaming little girl.

Grafton intercepts us. "Where are you going?" he yells.

"The Palisades," James answers.

Grafton nods. "I can't say when we're going to get any backup, but I can't leave them."

He gestures at the shell-shocked people. The glass of the front door shatters. A pale arm covered in dark brown hair pushes through the furniture. The jagged edges slice the skin, but it doesn't stop.

"Go now!" Grafton shouts. "We'll keep them back as long as we can. Take the exit doors at the end of the hall. It's clear behind us."

My pack's waist strap is unbuckled, and it slams into me and throws me forward with every step. A piercing siren wails as the door flies open. Everyone is through except Peter. He hesitates.

"Peter, come on!" I yell.

His eyes are huge and he jumps at a crash from inside. "I said I'd—"

I can't believe he's considering staying. We have to go now; there's no time to argue.

Ana leans in and pulls his sleeve. "Peter!"

His pack throws him off balance, but he rights himself and staggers through the door. I push it closed before following them onto the grass.

James raises his gun and shouts over the alarm. "Over there!"

Three infected have rounded the corner of the building. Nelly and I aim, but before we can fire they land in three thumps on the ground. I look up in confusion.

"We got you covered to the trees. Go!" shouts a dark form on the roof. I can't be sure, but it sounds like Rodriguez. I'm glad he's still alive.

CHAPTER 24

We stumble over tree roots in the dark until we hit the chain-link fence. Penny's hastily-produced flashlight throws a beam on the southbound lanes of the Palisades. No cars. No infected, either.

Nelly locks his hands together to give me a boost. I straddle the fence and hit the other side with a thud. Penny and Ana drop down. Dead grass crunches under our feet as we move back so the guys can follow. James hushes us, but there are no sounds of pursuit. I think we would hear them; Lexers don't have the sense to be stealthy.

We race across the grassy median to where the northbound lanes glow in the moonlight. Shots continue to ring out, but they're slowing. I don't know whether that's good or bad. The only other sounds are our breathing and footfalls. My breath is short and my muscles are tight, but I think I could keep walking along this asphalt road and never, ever stop. I'm not sure how long we walk before we see flashing lights ahead.

James reads the map by a light Penny shelters in her cupped hands. "Looks like an entrance ramp. We can make it down to the Hudson Drive here. What do you guys think?"

"Maybe we should," I say. "The farther away we are, the better."

We walk single file in the shadows of the trees. There's nobody in or around the police cars. Maybe they were called away. Maybe they're dead. Or maybe they're dead but alive, which still seems impossible. Penny spots a path in the woods, and we follow it until we hit a board with a map a few yards in.

We're on a trail called The Long Path. It runs along the top of the Palisades all the way to Rockland County. No one says anything. Every decision we make seems monumental, and I don't want to be the one to steer us wrong. At the thought of the distance ahead of us, of all the things that could go wrong, the energy drains out of me, like my feet have two rubber stoppers that have been left open. The lights flash through the trees. They turn everyone's faces red, blue, white, red, blue, white. It makes me dizzy.

"We have to get away from the entrance. Why don't we stay on the trail?" James suggests. He points to the map. "Here, here and here are trails that head down to the river. Let's just walk."

It's hard to believe we're surrounded by city as we trudge through the woods. Another mile and I want nothing more than to curl up and sleep. Ana stumbles every third step, and the only thing that keeps her upright is Peter holding her elbow.

The path opens up to an overlook with a view of the George Washington Bridge and Manhattan. It's darker than usual. I can make out the spire shapes of the Empire State and Chrysler Buildings, but the buildings themselves are dark.

"Looks like brownouts, maybe," Nelly says.

"Or power plants shutting down," adds James.

Penny shudders. "I'm so glad we're not there." Then she shudders again. Maybe she's thinking of Maria, or maybe it's because the breeze off the river is cold, especially now that the adrenaline is long gone.

"Let's stop here," Ana pleads. Her hair's come out of its ponytail and sticks to her face.

I drop my pack to the ground and rub the knots in my shoulder. This tiny park's not a bad place to stop. The lampposts will allow us to see if anything's coming, and we can stay out of sight, if we sleep just inside the trees. Everyone sets down their packs in exhaustion and agreement. There are only four sleeping bags; Peter and I were supposed to share one. Before things can get awkward, I unfasten mine and roll it to Peter.

"Here, I'll share with Nelly."

Peter thanks me, but lurking beneath his voice is an emotion that's definitely not pleasure.

Nelly points a finger at me. "No wiggling, woman. And no funny business."

The world could be ending, the world may be doing just that, and Nelly wouldn't be able to pass up the opportunity to make a joke. It may be the number one reason I love him.

"I don't know if I'll be able to restrain myself," I say, thankful he's saved the moment. "But I'll have to try, seeing as how we have first watch." He groans and yawns. "Only forty-five minutes. We all need some sleep."

Penny and James agree to share next watch. Nelly and I lean against a tree with an emergency blanket under us and the sleeping bag unzipped over top. I snuggle against him. Nelly always smells like the outdoors, like clothes that have dried in the sunshine. Maybe it soaked into him when he was a kid. We stare into the dark long enough for my heart to resume its regular rate.

"You know how we talked about what we would do if the world ended?" he asks.

"Of course."

It's fun to discuss over a beer in a warm bar, to imagine that it would be an adventure. And now here we are. I'm exhausted. I'm scared out of my mind. I already feel filthy and despairing.

"I'm glad we were all together. I knew working with you would pay off one day, even if you never let me get anything done." He pinches me, and I can make out his smile in the pre-dawn light before his face turns grim. "I feel like we've been thrust into a horror movie midway, you know? But we didn't do so badly."

"Well, it's certainly not as much fun as it's cracked up to be. But at least we're out of there."

I watch Manhattan's dark skyline and think about all of those people waiting for help. People who don't deserve what they're going to get. People, like Maria, who we love.

The time goes fast. James and Penny practically leap out of their sleeping bag with fright when I touch them. We zip ourselves into their warm nest, and I fall asleep wrapped in Nelly's arms.

CHAPTER 25

I awaken to the sound of thunder in the distance, but my face is warm with sunshine. I crack an eye. It's tired and grainy and begs me to let it rest, but I force it open and see blue sky overhead. I sit up quickly, having forgotten that I'm in a sleeping bag with another human being, and get thrown back down. Nelly grunts but doesn't wake as I ease myself out. Ana and Peter are fast asleep against the tree. Not that I can really blame them, it's been a rough night.

Plumes of smoke rise into the air over Manhattan. I move to the edge of the lookout in awe. It looks like a war zone. A louder roll of what I now know isn't thunder booms. Another plume joins the others to linger like smog over the city. There are exclamations as everyone wakes and joins me. Ana and Peter share a guilty look that they've literally fallen asleep on the job.

James leans on the rock wall that lines the cliff and peers into the distance. "The bridges. They're really doing it, aren't they?"

As if in answer to his question, a helicopter zooms from the New Jersey side to the middle of the George Washington Bridge, then swoops away and hovers at a distance. The middle of the bridge becomes a blur from the explosion. It thuds in my chest and up through my feet.

We all cry out. Nine million people are about to find out they've been left to the wolves. Terror seizes my insides, along with a breathless relief. We're safe. Safer than them, at least. The suspension cables of the bridge are still there when the smoke clears. They've only blown up the roadway. The helicopter retreats back into Jersey.

"Maybe they're thinking they might need to fix the bridge at some point," Nelly says icily. "Maybe some poor bastards will be able to walk across what's left."

I know what he's feeling. That could be us in there. That *is* us in there, people just like us. Peter's mouth hangs open. He doesn't think things like this can happen. I touch his hand. I'm so used to touching him that it doesn't feel strange until he moves his hand away. I want to say it'll be okay, but I don't think it will be. I think that's what's shocking him most of all.

James roots around in his pack for his iPad. He hasn't been able to get onto his internet all night, and our phones are useless. I try to send Eric a psychic message. *We're okay. I'm heading to the house.* He must be going crazy.

"Got it!" James yells. He sits on one of the benches as we huddle around him. On a news site the headline reads:

Major U.S. Cities Being Abandoned
President, from Undisclosed Location, Calls for Residents to Prepare for Long Siege
Medical Experts Report Infected May Already Be Dead

James reads aloud, "The president announced today that most major cities in the United States were 'unable to be cleared of infection.' Every major city in the country reports numbers of sick that are overwhelming and untreatable. Hospitals stand empty. The sick now wander the streets spreading Bornavirus LX.

"The virus, spread through bodily fluids, has torn through the world. All contact with China and much of Europe was lost yesterday. Both were hit with Bornavirus LX only days before the United States.

"Police departments and National Guard units are stretched thin. Many have abandoned their posts to care for their own families, leaving no one to answer calls for help.

"Projections showed that the cities on the East Coast, where the infection was least prevalent, would be fifteen percent infected by this morning, even with curfews in effect. A decision was made to abandon cities and focus efforts on less populated areas.

" 'This was not an easy decision,' the president said this morning. 'We have not forgotten you. I am sure you all understand the need to keep this infection in check. We ask that you leave your homes only if absolutely necessary. It will only be a matter of days until we can muster our forces to fight the virus. God bless you all.'

"The main arteries out of cities have been barricaded or destroyed. This leaves the president's detractors to ask how exactly the military plans to come back in after their forces are 'mustered.'

" 'They're not coming back,' said a highly-placed government source. 'Those cities have been written off until the infection dies out on its own.' When asked how long those infected with Bornavirus live, he replied, 'That's the thing. We just don't know. They aren't even alive.'

"The rumor that the infected persons may not be alive, even though they appear to be, has been floating around since yesterday. This startling statement was denied by the CDC, but backed up by medical professionals who have been treating patients with the virus. The CDC released a statement last night that read, in part:

There is no known cure for Bornavirus LX.
The transmission rate is one hundred percent if you are exposed to the virus and the mortality rate is also one hundred percent. We ask that all citizens take the precautions of staying indoors and not attempting to care for infected loved ones.

"We contacted the CDC to ask how long the infected survive. 'We have no idea,' said Marcia Dreyer, a researcher, and the only person who could be reached for comment. 'Tests have shown that they are not decomposing at the normal rate. Only an injury to the brain, or fire, have killed our test subjects so far.' Ms. Dreyer was then ordered to relinquish the phone to a superior, who had no comment.

"Whatever the case may be, it has become clear that Bornavirus LX is rampant and untreatable. The only course of action now is to find somewhere safe and wait out the virus."

James swigs water from his bottle and clicks on a live audio link. I recognize the voice of the morning anchorman on NY1 news. He has a grin that makes him look like a little kid. Other times, like when he's reading a particularly ridiculous newspaper headline, he wears an amused smirk that says, *Can you believe this shit? What these people are up to?*

His normally upbeat voice now sounds exhausted. I imagine the bags that must be under his eyes, how he must finally look his age. The terror he's trying to keep at bay. I imagine him, possibly at gunpoint, being forced to deliver these lines, to keep people calm.

"...and all access points into New York City have been blocked to make them impassable to infected persons. We are asked to stay indoors until the infection has run its course. FEMA plans food drops for those who need supplies. We will broadcast the drop locations as soon as they are available. All utilities will remain on in the coming days. The president has assured us that help is on the way. Please keep yourselves safe by following these instructions."

I hear the skeptical tone in his voice and can picture his smile, resigned and bitter, that asks, *Can you believe this shit? These lies?* And, no. No, I can't.

CHAPTER 26

We strap on our packs and walk. I wear my mom's shoulder holster. I don't imagine I'm going to get in trouble for carrying a gun in the city right now. When it's stuck in my waistband I become obsessed with the idea it's going to shoot me in the butt, however unlikely that may be. I chew an old energy bar until it feels like my jaw is going to give up and die. It's hard to swallow over the lump in my throat, and I sluice it down with gulps of water.

Every so often the woods open up, and we're treated to a gorgeous view of the Hudson River moving along under the imposing rocky cliffs. It seems like it should have reversed direction or stopped moving entirely on a day like today. I'm surprised that the sun can shine down from such a beautiful blue sky on all this madness.

The city now sports countless columns of twisting black smoke. It looks as if all of New York is on fire.

My chest tightens as I think of the best parts of the city: The gruff, gold-hearted Brooklyn guys who won't hesitate to help someone out. The way New Yorkers pull together when they need to. The museums I grew up in, where I stared for hours at the mummies or fossils or shrunken heads. Prospect Park. The library. The train cars and neighborhoods full of not only every shade of skin imaginable, but also every country, every language, every dress, every food.

Then there are the worst parts: The cashiers who completely ignore your outstretched hand and throw your change on the counter. The people who think lines are merely suggestions. The hipsters. The grime. The F train. The DMV.

My city, the city I love, the city I sometimes hate, which has both energized and exhausted me since I was born, is going up in smoke. I stop and stare one last time, because it was my home, a place to go back to if I wanted or needed it. But I'm pretty sure it's gone now, the good and the bad wiped out in one fell swoop. I cry for every last bit of it.

CHAPTER 27

We find a map at another signpost. The wind shakes the empty branches of the trees. It blows the smoke from the city this way, but it's high enough that it doesn't touch us. Only the smell of burning makes its way down to where we stand. Booms and sirens and loud noises carry from far off. Some of them I can place: a fire engine, gun shots. Others are guesses: A grenade? Gas line explosion? Godzilla?

There's a Park Headquarters with a police station several miles ahead. We walk slowly, our packs and fatigue weighing us down. Penny's face is pale, with dark smudges under her eyes. I match my steps to hers. She watches her feet as we walk, then looks up at me with bloodshot eyes.

"My mom," she says. She wipes her nose with the back of her hand.

"She's got the best chance of anyone there," I say, searching for something that will make her feel better.

"I know." But we both also know even that better chance is slim.

It's afternoon when we reach Park Headquarters, a stone building with leaded glass windows and imposing chimneys. We walk around it until we find the well-lighted police station entrance. There's a tall counter inside, but it's vacant.

Nelly opens the door and calls, "Hello? Anybody here?"

Silence. James sets his pack down and creeps behind the desk to check the hallway. He comes back shaking his head. A computer monitor sits on the counter, and I walk around to check it out. A cup of coffee and half a sandwich sit in front of the monitor. I feel the side of the mug.

"Well, the mug's cold," I say. "Whoever was here has been gone a while."

"What else, Sherlock?" Nelly asks.

"Well, I can deduce by the various keys hanging under here that we may also have a ride, smart-ass. If we want to steal a police car, that is." I wave a set of keys at him.

"Which we do, of course," Penny says. I guess she's gotten over her whole not-wanting-to-steal-a-car thing.

I nod. "Of course."

We settle on an SUV with Parkway Police written on the side. If someone sits in the way back behind the cage it might almost be comfortable.

We buy food from the snack machines. I guess we could steal that, too, but we feed money into the machine.

"We can use it in our defense if we're arrested for stealing the car," James jokes. "We may need more food if we get waylaid again."

"Not that you can really call this food," I say. Our found duffel bag crinkles with chips, cookies and fruit snacks.

He grins through the smudged dirt and tired creases under his eyes. "Hey, speak for yourself. I live on this stuff."

We take off onto the Palisades with Nelly driving and me in the way back. Unsurprisingly, no one fought me for the honor.

Tracts of suburban houses appear through the trees, and a few cars join us on the road. We're sticking to the main highways because the smaller roads travel through the main streets of towns along the way, and those may be impassable.

The Palisades turns into the New York State Thruway, and within minutes it's a sea of brake lights. There's a toll booth for commercial vehicles ahead but nothing that would block the passage of cars. It must be stopped for miles.

"Well, kids," Nelly says, "I guess it's back the other way, once we get to the next exit."

"I don't imagine it's going to get better," James agrees. "People are getting out, just like us."

He points to a blue sedan in front of us, with beat-up boxes and bags attached to the roof with double-knotted twine, just as it bumps into the SUV ahead of it. It's barely a nudge, but the door of the SUV flies open and a man with a graying crew cut jumps out. His chinos and t-shirt stick to him with sweat. He leans into the car and comes out holding a metal flashlight.

"What the fuck!" he screams.

Spit flies from his mouth as he storms the sedan. A small, dark-skinned man hops out. He raises his hands and gestures toward Chinos' car. Nelly rolls down the window so we can hear.

"Sorry. Hey, I'm sorry," the guy says in a calm voice, and takes a step back.

Chinos advances, his face well on its way to purple. His hand is white-knuckled as he lifts the flashlight menacingly.

"Look, man, nothing happened to your car. Take a look!" the smaller man says. He points to the SUV.

"*You* should be looking. Looking at the goddamned road!" Chinos yells. "You should be taking care, goddamn it!"

He lifts the flashlight higher. There's a dark spot on the underside of his arm. A purple wound with red streaks. Round like a bite mark.

"Did you see that?" I ask. Everyone nods and stares at the scene.

The smaller guy shuts his door and backs around the car as he talks to Chinos. He uses a quiet voice, the voice you would use to soothe a wild animal. He doesn't realize this guy has nothing to lose. He stops and Chinos moves quickly, the flashlight in the air.

"Oh, fuck," Nelly says.

He grabs the shotgun he's placed in the holster of the police truck and steps out. He cocks the gun and points it at Chinos, who freezes at the sound.

"Officer," he says. He smiles like he's been waiting for him to show up, instead of planning to beat the other party to death. "We just had a little accident. Nothing to worry about."

James gets out of the car and stands behind the open door. Suddenly it seems like a really bad idea for someone to be trapped back here. Nelly walks closer to Chinos.

"Drop the light," he orders. Chinos does and lifts his hands into the air. "Where did you get your wound?"

Chinos looks from side to side and his tongue darts out to wet his lips. He lowers his arms a bit in an effort to hide it.

"Doing some work in the garage. Screwdriver slipped." He gives a high-pitched laugh. "Not a good time to go to the hospital, as you know, so I figured it'd be fine. Putting lots of ointment on it. Nothing to worry about." He licks his lips again and takes a step back.

"Sir." Nelly sounds so official and calm. "You need to be seen by someone. Let's go to the toll booths right there, and we'll find you some help."

"You're right." Chinos nods wildly, eyes darting. "You're exactly right. I should have someone look at this. I—" He jumps the median and gallops across the oncoming lanes. Nelly lowers the shotgun and looks at the wiry man.

"You okay?" he asks. The guy nods mutely and watches Chinos disappear into the trees.

Finally, he speaks. "He was infected?" Nelly nods, and his eyes widen. "Thanks for stepping in."

He pumps Nelly's hand and looks him up and down. "Officer?"

Nelly smiles. "No, not quite. We need to get this guy's car out of the way. Maybe over to the tolls there. We can use the siren."

"I'll get it. My wife'll follow us."

James switches on the siren. Cars inch and scoot out of the way until we make it to the shoulder. We head to the right of the tolls, into a lot for highway trucks.

The man comes up to our window once he's parked Chinos' car. He looks to be in his late thirties, with close-cropped hair and the hands and face of a man accustomed to working long, hard hours. But the weariness disappears when he smiles and thanks Nelly again.

He holds out his hand, and Nelly and he shake. "Name's Henry. Henry Washington."

"Nel Everett. No problem, man. Where are you going?"

"North. Doing some long-term camping at a spot we know." Henry hooks his thumb in the general direction.

"We're heading back over to the Palisades. Northeast. If you want to follow, you can have a police escort," Nelly offers, his mouth half lifted.

"I'd appreciate that. I'm just trying to get my kids somewhere safe. Hearing anything on the police band?"

"We didn't even get a chance to turn it on," James says, and turns the knob.

A woman's voice repeats that she needs officers in the vicinity of somewhere. Other voices ask for help. "Shots fired." "Officer down." One man screams something I can't make out, but I understand the rawness in his voice. He sounds like someone who thinks he's going to die, and it makes my stomach clench. James switches it off, but the screams reverberate even after it's gone.

Penny points. "Oh, God. They're here."

A few dozen Lexers come out of the tree line and disperse between the cars down the road. They have different wounds, different clothes, different faces, yet they all look the same with their slack-jawed hunger and shuffling gait. Two of them pound on the windows of a gold hatchback, and the mouths of the couple inside open with screams I can see but not hear.

The occasional honk becomes a chorus of blaring horns and screams. But there's nowhere to go. One man leans out of his truck and yells at the traffic to move. He rolls up his window when the only response is for the infected to move his way. A heavyset woman throws her car door open and leaps over the median to the other side of the highway. And in that instant an entire lane becomes useless. A car bumps over the shoulder and heads for where we sit. The truck behind it follows. This lot is going to be as jammed up as the road in a minute.

"I know a back way to Bear Mountain," Henry says. "Follow me?"

Nelly nods, and Henry jumps into his car. He straddles the curb to fit past the posts that block cars from entering from the street. We follow him onto a street of suburban homes.

A Lexer, his bloody abdomen scooped out like a bowl, stands on one of the neat lawns and watches us pass. The houses all look the same; I don't know how Henry knows where to go in this maze. But he must, because we hit a main road and make another left.

A few Lexers move down one block, and a tense group of men armed with pipes and bats rushes to meet them. I watch out the back, but a turn throws me off balance, and then they're out of sight. I pick myself up and hang on to the hatch. I hope this guy knows where he's going.

CHAPTER 28

We follow Henry to two adjacent campsites in the back of the empty campground. There's a picnic table and metal fire pit at each site. Penny releases me from the cargo area, and I walk on the packed dirt to work the cramps out of my legs. A woman and two kids jump out of the sedan and follow Henry to where we stand.

"This is my wife, Dorothy. Dottie."

Dottie is petite, and her eyes are a striking light brown against her dark skin. Her smile is warm. When she speaks I hear the soft lilt of the Caribbean in her voice.

"I can't thank you enough for helping us. I was sure—" She stops and looks at the children.

"This is Corinne, she's twelve," Henry continues. He places his hand on the shoulder of a slight, pretty girl who resembles her mother, down to the eyes. She gives us a small smile. "And this is Henry Junior, we call him Hank. He's nine."

If there's ever been a child who looks less like a Hank, I haven't met him. He's small, like the rest of his family, but he lacks the compact strength of his father and the vitality of his mother and sister. His hair is short, which makes his glasses and the eyes they magnify look even larger. At first glance he looks frail, but when he says hello he looks me in the eye. I get the feeling he doesn't miss much.

"Thank you for leading us here," I say. "We wouldn't have made it without you."

"No problem," Henry says. "A couple of times there I thought I was lost, but I helped run the electric in those houses, so I gave it a shot."

He's so relieved that he beams at me, and I can't help but smile back. After the last twelve hours of jaw clenching, it almost hurts. We decide to stay the night and figure out a route in the morning. Our two tiny tents set up quickly. I'm not sure how all six of us are going to fit into them. I head to the water spigot a few campsites over, but it's too early in the season for the water to be on.

"Dry?" Henry asks from behind me. I nod. "There's a stream over on the other side of the campground. We should go before it's too dark to see."

"I've got a hiking filter," I say.

We grab every bottle and his two collapsible containers. It's a small creek, but he heads right for a spot where it widens into a swimming hole. I sit down on a rock beside it and dangle the filter in the water.

"I take it you've been here before?" I ask.

"We camp here every summer. Swim in this very creek. It's strange to be here this time of year."

It's still a winter landscape, minus the snow. It's getting cold, too. The creek water is freezing.

"Why did you decide to leave today?" I ask him.

He crouches next to me and wipes a hand across his forehead. "I went in to work. I didn't know how bad it had gotten. I figured I'd be just as safe in that building as at home. The curfew was only in effect until dawn, and I left just before the sun came up. I didn't get the paper. Dottie called me at work—it's a big job and the electric guys are getting double time for weekends—and said we had to leave. She told me about the bridges and that some of the neighbors were infected. That there were people who looked like they were out of their heads.

"If Dot says it's serious, then it's serious. So I left right away. We live in an apartment complex, the kind with lawns and parking?"

I nod. My hand pumps the filter faster, and I realize I'm getting nervous for him.

"I pulled into our spot, when out of nowhere people started rushing me. I could tell they were far gone, all bloody, so I backed up. I hit one behind me. That *thunk*, oh, man." He closes his eyes briefly.

"But I couldn't get out of the car. I knew I'd get bit if I did. I pulled back, hoping she was okay. Her foot was crushed, completely crushed, but she got up with her leg dragging behind her. Didn't stop her at all, didn't even act like it hurt.

"I called Dot and told her to be ready at the back windows and drove on the grass. I wasn't taking any chances by having the kids walk. She already had everything packed; she'd called me and then got ready.

"They were coming around the building, making these terrible noises. Have you heard them? I don't know how to describe it."

When he looks up his eyes are red and frightened. I know exactly what he means. It's unearthly, hungry; there are many words to describe the sound, but none does it justice. A crying baby awakens an instinct to comfort it; its cry has been carefully calibrated by nature to force nurture. These sounds do the opposite. Some primal part awakens, scratching to get out and take over, like a little rabbit running for its life from a hawk. I shiver as I nod at him.

"Thank God the streets were clear for the most part. We didn't have a plan, until we drove past our self-storage place. We used the code to get in, and for a few minutes I thought about staying there. It's got a fence and the units have metal doors, but then I realized we might end up surrounded. So we got out our camping stuff to head upstate."

I'm absurdly glad for a second that my life's gone the way it has these past few years. Adrian and I might have had a baby to protect against this. That little boy at the office building was Hank's age. I bite the inside of my cheek before my eyes can fill.

"Do you know where you're headed?" I ask.

"I spent a lot of summers at YMCA camps. We're heading to one that's pretty out of the way. You?"

I tell him about my parents' house.

"Sounds like the place to go." He takes over the pumping of the filter and speaks again. "Hank has some pretty interesting ideas about what's going on. You wouldn't believe it if I told you."

"I bet I would."

He gives me a look that says there's no way. "He says they're dead. Like zombies. Not Caribbean zombies, but horror movie zombies. I mean, they look like it, but it's impossible."

"He's right."

Henry looks up sharply. "But how can that be?"

"I don't know. Penny and Ana's mother is a nurse. She made us leave New York last night. She knew about the bridges."

I tell him everything she told us and how the CDC still denies it. His face is grim when I finish.

Back at camp, our table is cluttered with ramen noodles, freeze-dried hiking food and junk from the vending machine. The latter items are being eyed by Hank and Corrine, who jump to inspect the packages when Penny invites them over. She's started the backpacking stove and put on a pot of water.

Dorothy cooks dinner on a two burner camp stove. We decline her offer of fresh food. We have plenty, even if it's mostly vitamin-free. She watches the kids take one treat each and nods approvingly when they thank us. Dottie's quiet and has a soft smile, but underneath that is a woman who isn't going to let things just happen to her family. I like her.

The solar radio reminds us to stay calm and remain home. It repeats the addresses of treatment centers in an endless loop but doesn't say anything about the infected being dead or how long this will last. James curses and spins the tuning knob for some real news. We catch the tail end of an announcement that all government offices are closed until Tuesday before it turns to static.

"Chicken a la king or ramen noodles?" I ask.

Ramen noodles win. Nelly puts out the little tin plates he's been carrying in his pack. I spoon noodles onto the plates, and then the only sounds are slurping. It's warm and filling. Even Peter, who's a food snob, seems to be enjoying his.

"I'll clean up," he offers, when everyone's finished.

"I'll help you," I say.

I follow him to one of Henry's water containers. He scrapes and rinses plates and pretends I'm not here.

"Listen, Peter," I blurt out. "I'd like to be friends."

I know it's lame, but there's no other way to say it. The beam from the flashlight leaves his face in darkness, but I can hear the scowl in his voice.

"I don't really want to be *friends*, Cassandra." I wince. "Is it really so hard to understand that?"

I don't see much of an option at this point. Unless his plan is to hate me instead.

"Well, I'd rather be friends than fight. I'm sorry about back at the house."

I can't think of anything else to say. Usually when you break up with someone you get to leave and lick your wounds, not live with them in a tiny tent. He doesn't answer, and we finish in silence.

Henry insists on taking first watch shift, since we've barely slept. Nelly, Peter and I squeeze into our tent. When I accidentally brush against Peter, he recoils like I've stung him. I make myself as small as possible and curl into Nelly. What I wouldn't give for that third tent in the van.

CHAPTER 29

I want nothing more than to snuggle with Nelly when he crawls in after his shift and wakes me for mine. It can't be much more than forty degrees out here. I wish I could build a big, toasty fire, but it might attract attention. I duck back into the tent for extra socks and Nelly's fleece. When I come out Penny's zipping up her tent and yawning. She wears a hat and Eric's old jacket over her own. I put on water for tea as we face out into the darkness and shiver. It's not like we can see anything, so calling it a watch seems silly. It's more like a listen, and, thankfully, the woods are silent. So quiet that when Penny speaks I startle.

"I'm so tired, I feel like I could sleep forever."

"Why don't you go back to sleep?" I say. "I can sit out here by myself."

She shakes her head. "No, no." I'm relieved. I would've sat out here alone, but I would've been scared. "I'm not leaving you out here by yourself. Besides, it'll be nice. We needed some post-apocalyptic girl time."

I laugh and lean against her. "You okay?"

"No. Yeah. What choice do I have? And Ana, it's too much for her, with leaving my mom behind."

Ana's off the hook for watch because she's acting like she can't handle the responsibility. I think Ana could do watch, if she wanted to, but I keep that thought to myself. Penny gives everyone the benefit of the doubt, including me.

She stomps her feet quietly on the ground to warm up. I use the flashlight to pour us both a cup of tea. The powdered creamer and sugar don't exactly make it delicious, but it's warm, and that's what counts. The emergency blanket crackles, and we shush each other and giggle as we spread it over us.

The mood has lightened, so I ask the question I've been dying to ask. "So, you and James?"

"Yeah, me and James. Cass, I really, really like him."

"Well, Nelly and I already knew that. We thought you'd be perfect for each other, since you're both nerds." She elbows me. "Okay, you're both smart and funny and well-behaved."

She snorts. It's true, though. She's naturally good, she can't help it. We balance each other out.

"So what base have you gotten to?" I ask. Now I'm just bothering her.

"*Base?* What are you, in eighth grade?" But she's used to this question. I've been asking her it since, well, eighth grade.

I try not to laugh. "You know I am. So?"

"And what base do you think? Let's see, there was the night we kissed, and then the night we ran from hordes of dead people. And then tonight, in a tent with my sister. It's been pretty romantic so far. Why am I even answering you?" She laughs.

"Okay, okay! But, seriously, what base?" I whisper, and grin as she ignores me.

An easy silence falls and we watch the sky grow lighter. I turn the radio on very low. It's an actual broadcast.

"...has broken out in New York City. The bodies of those who have tried to swim to safety are washing up on shore. There is mass rioting and looting in major cities from Florida to Massachusetts, and traffic is at a standstill out of every major metropolitan area. Abandoned cars make it impossible for police to clear the roads. The president declared that the National Guard has the authority to stop illegal activities in whatever way they see fit.

"The president asked Americans to remain calm while Bornavirus is eradicated. He maintains that only a week is needed, but the quarantining of major cities has caused people to flee for less populated areas. There are reports of roads being blocked by infected persons. Authorities maintain that staying in the safety of your home is still the best way to remain healthy. Please stay tuned for updates."

I turn it down again.

Nelly steps out of our tent. "Well, that was depressing."

"Sorry, we were trying not to wake anyone," I say.

"Nah, I was awake."

He refuses when I offer his jacket back. He's got one of my dad's flannel shirts on, and I can't believe that he's warm enough, but I keep it on gratefully.

He sits and puts his arm around Penny. "So, how are you doing?"

Penny shrugs and the line between her eyebrows deepens. "I just hope my mom's okay."

The worried expression makes her look so young, like we could be sixteen the morning after a sleepover, and for a moment I wish it were so, even though usually I'd rather stick a pen in my eye than go back to high school. At least the world was relatively safe.

"I hope so too, darlin'." He squeezes her close and thanks me for the truly awful instant coffee I hand him. "And how about your new beau?"

She pushes her glasses up, flustered. "It's good."

"I was wondering, has James slid into second base yet?" he asks, and tries not to smile. She huffs and glares at us as we crack up.

The Washingtons give us a wave as they head to the toilet. I wonder if they have a plan and resolve to ask after breakfast. We need to figure out our next step.

CHAPTER 30

Hank and Corrine look at our breakfast spread of cookies and packaged danishes jealously while they pick at their eggs and toast. You don't appreciate real food when you're nine and twelve.

"I'd like to hear what you're planning next," I say, after everyone has finished.

James opens our map and runs his finger along the distance from the park to the house. Peter glances at the map as if it's rudely interrupted his staring into the forest and then resumes staring. Ana still hasn't woken.

"We're about a hundred miles away, more if we take a lot of back roads," James explains.

"Well, what does everyone think about getting on the road?" I ask. "Sooner or later?"

"Dot and I were thinking of waiting a few days," Henry says. "It's a gamble. There'll be more infected, but I'm hoping people will have gotten where they're going. I'm also hoping the situation will have improved."

He rubs a hand over his eyebrows. When he lowers it, there's doubt in his eyes.

Nelly nods. "I don't want to get stuck at another one of those treatment areas or a roadblock. We were lucky to get out."

"I have a feeling things are only getting worse," James says. "But waiting a few days might be a good idea either way. Henry, do you know somewhere we might be able to buy camping supplies?"

Henry's face creases as he thinks. "There are a few stores, mom and pop-type of places. We need some gear, too."

"What would you say to a team effort?" Nelly asks.

"I was hoping you'd ask that." The lines in his brow smooth out a tad. "And we're glad to have company for a couple of days."

We might have a couple of days before people arrive. It's pretty isolated here, and that's bound to draw others once they get unsnarled from traffic. We plan to head out in a few hours to a store Henry thinks is our best bet.

It's warming up. I take off Nelly's jacket and wish for a hot shower. My jeans are filthy, and after a few swipes I give up. I re-braid my hair. At least my teeth are brushed and we have deodorant. Feeling marginally cleaner, I sit at the table and listen to the radio repeat the same things.

"I hate talk radio!" Corrine complains.

She sticks headphones in her ears and plops down at the table. Hank sighs, scoots over so she isn't so close, and continues reading. Nelly, James and Henry have gone to get more water, and Penny's in the tent with Ana. Peter's fascination with the surrounding forest has not yet waned. I think about trying to talk to him but don't want to get shot down again.

"Hank," I say. "What're you reading?"

He looks up. "Oh, just a graphic novel."

"What's it about?"

"Well," he glances around and moves next to me, "it's about zombies. I know everyone thinks they're fake, but I brought it just in case."

I nod. "Your dad told me what you were saying about the infected."

His eyes are wary behind his glasses. "He told me I was right last night."

"You are right."

He grins but then tries to wipe it off because it really isn't anything to smile about.

"I didn't think it could really be true." He gloats for a minute, but then his face grows solemn. "But it means we're in big trouble. This is serious, Cassie."

The way he says my name is so grown-up that it's hard not to treat him like one.

"Yeah, Hank, it is."

CHAPTER 31

Dottie interrupts Hank's effusive showing and telling of every detail he's ever read about zombies to take him and Corrine to wash up. I don't know how much of it is accurate, but it can't hurt to know, I guess. Besides, I like Hank.

I straighten up the campsite and am about to drag out a book when everyone gets back from the stream. I call softly to Penny and tell her we're leaving.

"Where's Peter?" Nelly asks.

"Tent. Resting." Not that he had to do watch last night. Nelly gives me a questioning look, and I raise my hands in the air.

Henry's held on to the pistol we gave him to use during watch, and he checks it now. We make sure the rest of the guns are loaded and ready to go. I hand Penny one of the revolvers, and she takes it reluctantly.

Hank makes me smile when he mimes a whack at a head with a stick. I try to hide it, but he looks so funny with his determined little kid face that I fail. I probably shouldn't encourage him, but I think he's got a handle on the situation. He isn't about to head off to whatever make-believe land Ana and Peter are currently inhabiting.

"Wait," James says, as we pull out. He looks torn. "I'm staying. Penny and Dottie are here with the kids. I'd feel better if they weren't alone."

"I thought your friend Peter was here," Henry says.

"Yeah. Me too," James says, before he jumps out.

I think about staying too, but I want to go. I hate being left behind to wait for the bad news I'm always afraid is coming.

The park road twists and turns and finally deposits us on a two-lane road bordered by fields and a few scattered houses. After a few miles the houses get more frequent, although there's no one outside.

"About a quarter mile now, on the left," Henry says.

The sign says Sam's Surplus, and it looks like Sam lives in the back of the peeling blue house. Our feet creak up the wooden porch steps, and we peek in the dark window. There's a dusty glass counter filled with knives and other items. Bags and clothes hang from hooks on the ceiling and walls.

Nelly knocks on the door. "Hello? Anyone here?"

A figure makes its way through the gloom. Nelly and Henry back away from the front door as it opens. A pudgy man in his forties, wearing jeans and a Smith and Wesson T-shirt, looks at us suspiciously. His brown hair is streaked with gray, and what looks like a week's stubble coats the lower half of his face and neck.

"Yeah? You're not cops." He tells us more than asks us this as he glares at the Parkway Police-emblazoned truck.

"No, we're not," Nelly says. "We were hoping to buy some supplies. We're camping up the way."

"Ain't camping season."

"Yeah, well, we left the city and are trying to get further north. But we need a few things."

"Where?" We all look at him blankly. He tries again, with a sigh, like he has to deal with people as dumb as us all the time. "What city did you leave?"

"Oh. New York. Brooklyn," Nelly replies.

The man runs his eyes over us and swings the door open. "C'mon. Cash only."

The inside smells of dust and old clothes. Boxes are stacked on the shelves. We're going to need his help to find anything in here.

"What d'ya need?"

Obviously, with this guy, the less said the better, so I read off the top few items on our list. "Sleeping bag, stove fuel, siphons, a lantern."

He walks behind the counter and pulls out bottles of fuel and a lantern. After a couple of gruff questions, he chooses a sleeping bag for us and backpacks for Henry. Another minute passes before Nelly broaches the subject of weapons.

"Do you have any machetes?" he asks.

The man ignores him and leans under the counter again. Nelly looks at me and shrugs. The door to the back of the house is ajar, and I think I hear something familiar on the kitchen radio. I walk to where he's rummaging around under the counter. I hope I'm right.

"Is that Preparedness Radio?" I ask.

He raises himself up and looks at all of us in turn but finally decides that the voice must have come out of me. "Yeah. You know about Prepper Radio?" he asks doubtfully.

"Of course. My dad was a prepper." He raises an eyebrow. "That's where we're heading. His house."

"How'd you get out of New York?"

"Well, we had some information about the bombing and knew it was time to bug out."

He nods. I can tell he likes that I used the term bug out. "What's the house like?"

I keep it short and sweet. "It's a log cabin on twenty acres with an acre of fenced garden. A year's worth of food for four adults. Outbuildings, gravity-fed water, some solar. On a dirt road. We're the only house."

"How's the food stored?" He's testing me. But I know the answer.

"Oxygen absorbers and gamma lids. At least besides the home-canned food," I say, like there's no other way.

He looks impressed. "Nice set-up." He's not quite friendly, but he's no longer looking at us like we're aliens.

"It really is."

The rush of longing I feel to be there, to be safe, to smell the familiar smell of the house and touch all of the familiar objects, almost makes me swoon.

"Sounds like your dad knows what he's doing."

"He did. He died a few years ago." I still hate saying it.

"Sorry," he offers. I nod. He really does look sorry that another prepper has left the earth. He spreads his hands on the counter and leans forward conspiratorially. "So, what else you folks need?"

And we're in.

***

Ten minutes later there are machetes on the counter, and the man, who we now know is named Greg, not Sam, tells us about the area.

"They're setting up some sort of roadblock, I think. There's a meeting tonight." He waves a photocopied flyer in the air. "Says something about allocating resources. Which is doublespeak for they're going to take everything in my store. I'm bugging out tonight while the meeting's going. Got a place in the hills stocked up. Not as nice as yours, but it'll do."

He shrugs his sloped shoulders. "I can't take a lot of this stuff, so I'm glad to sell it to you. These folks been making fun of me for years for being a prepper. I even got a guy who'll be stupid enough to accept cash for a few things on my way out. You don't have gold, do you?"

I shake my head. "Any gold's at the house."

There isn't any gold. My dad was more interested in things that produced energy and food than money. I have a feeling that gold's going to be as worthless as rocks pretty soon. There's no such thing as gold stew.

"Well, like I said, I got a guy who'll still think cash is good."

"What we really need is more food," Nelly says. "We don't know how long it'll be until we get there. Any idea where we can get some?"

Greg looks up at the ceiling and then at me. "Move your car to the back. Don't need people seeing you're here."

Nelly obliges and is back quickly. Greg locks the front door and heads for his living area.

"Well, c'mon," he says. I get the feeling Greg doesn't have much social interaction. He shuts the door behind us and opens a door in the kitchen. "Basement."

The stairs are dusty, but the basement is shockingly tidy. Boxes and five-gallon buckets are stacked against the walls. A ham radio sits at a desk in one corner.

"So, food. I think I've got some down here. You got a problem with MREs? I've got a few."

He removes a box from the stacks and drops it on the floor. I realize all those boxes are full of MREs and laugh. There must be hundreds here.

"MRE's?" Henry asks.

"Meals Ready to Eat," I answer. "They feed them to soldiers in the armed forces. They even have heating packets included with them."

"Your dad did right by you," Greg says. He idly scratches the part of his stomach that peeks out between his jeans and shirt and looks me over. I smile at him. "So, I got eggs, sloppy joes, beef stroganoff, tortellini, chicken. I can let go of six cases total. Should get you where you're going. The rest I think I can haul out. I'm not leaving a crumb for those vultures in town."

His face darkens. I know that Greg's probably more than a little crazy, but I can commiserate. The people who for years have thought he was overboard are probably seeing him as their own personal store right about now. But, on the other hand, there's something to be said for pulling together. We put our chosen meals into the boxes he's set aside. Every time I say something offhand, he nods like I've just announced the meaning of life. He even throws in a bunch of freeze-dried food.

"On the house," he says. "Let's settle up upstairs."

Nelly and Henry each grab two boxes, and I go to do the same. Greg shakes his head and takes them from me. "Lady shouldn't have to carry a box when there's someone around to do it for her."

Greg heads up the stairs with a grunt. Nelly follows, but only after turning and giving me a glance that asks if I'm interested, to which I give him a look that shoots daggers. In the kitchen Greg names a fair price and we hand over the cash. We load the truck until there's just enough room left for me to squeeze into the back seat.

"Thanks a lot, Greg," I say. "We truly appreciate it. You've saved our lives."

He blushes. "Well, it'll help you out. I've written down a back way for you to get out of the woods without hitting town here."

He's written it on the back of the flyer for the town meeting. Nelly and Henry pump his hand and thank him. Nelly waits by the driver's side for me. Greg hands me the flyer along with another slip of paper.

"I wrote down where I'll be. In case it doesn't work out with them." He cuts his eyes over to the car.

"Oh. Thanks." I try to smile. It's always the strange ones.

"I don't have enough to take in anyone else. But I could stretch it for two. If you need me, you'll know where to find me." He smiles. It looks out of place on his face, and I see how lonely he must be. He's been real nice to us, so I try not to hurt his feelings.

"Thanks, Greg. I really appreciate it. I'll hold onto this, right here." I put the paper in my pocket with the ring and pat it. "It'll be there if I need it." I hold out my hand to shake, and he clasps it with both of his.

"Really nice meeting you, Cassie." He doesn't let go.

I disentangle my hand and try hard not to look like I'm escaping. "You too, Greg."

"Get his number?" Nelly teases, when we're back on the road.

"Got his address," I answer. "I think he may have asked me to move in with him." Nelly cracks up.

Henry shakes his head. "That guy was a nut job."

"A bit," I agree. "But then, who's prepared for this right now and who's not?"

"Yeah, but he was still off his rocker," Nelly says.

"I thought he looked lonely," I say.

I'm not sure why I'm defending Greg, since I'm relieved to be traveling away from him in a fast-moving vehicle. Maybe because he did us a favor by helping us and repaying it with jokes seems mean. He was harmless, even with all his bluster.

"Cassie Forrest, friend to loners and crazies everywhere," Nelly says. "He was very generous, though. Good call, Henry."

"Thanks, he did hook us up. One-stop shopping," Henry says. He drums his fingers on the door and looks back at me. "And we wouldn't have gotten all this without you, Cassie. How did you know all that stuff?"

"My parents were preppers. You know, people who store food and stuff for emergencies? Not the crazy militia kind, the homesteading kind. Although my dad was also a bit of a nut. I picked it up over the years."

"Yeah," Nelly says. "You did pick up being a nut."

I pull his hair from the backseat.

"Well, it sounds like your dad was pretty smart, too," Henry says.

"He was."

I watch forest flash by and wish with all my heart he were here.

CHAPTER 32

The tables from our two sites have been moved together. I guess this means we're a group, and I like it. Penny and James help unload. Ana and Peter don't.

"Wow," Penny says. "Nice haul."

"How'd it go?" James asks.

"Well, Cassie was asked for her hand in marriage and we got lots of food," Nelly says. "So, all in all, it was pretty good."

Penny and James look at me, but I just shrug and unload while I listen to Nelly tell them the story. He's playing it up, too. Pretty soon he'll have Greg down on one knee. It's afternoon, and camp is quiet after dividing our stuff. I look through my pack, tired of listening to the radio, and pull out my book.

"Of course you brought a book," Nelly says.

I hold up my old copy of *A Walk in the Woods*. "Actually, I brought two. This seemed like it might be fitting. And I could use a laugh."

I throw Nelly the other book and he reads the title aloud. "*Tom Brown's Field Guide to Wilderness Survival*."

"Seemed fitting as well," I say.

Henry and the kids are getting firewood for the fire we're having tonight. So far there's no one at the campground, and the Washingtons have marshmallows. The kids crash through the woods and drop their loads at the fire pit. Henry follows and smiles at Dottie.

"What a racket, children of mine," she says. "We need to get in the habit of moving quietly." Her voice is serious, but she softens it with a smile. They nod.

Corrine plugs her iPod into her ears and then groans. "It's dead! Dad said I couldn't use the car to charge it. Now what am I going to do?"

"Read a book?" offers Hank. Corrine looks at him like he's told her to eat a bug. "Oh, that's right," he smirks, "you're too stupid to read a book."

She rolls her eyes. "You're the dumb one, Hank. You think dead people are walking around."

"They are! I *was* right. Dad told me. They don't want you to know because you act like a baby and will be all like, 'Oh my God, I'm so scared, wah wah wah.'" He grins as she whips her head around to her father in fright.

Henry gives Hank a look that could kill and kneels at her feet. "Corrie, baby, we think it may be true. We don't understand why. It's a virus, like a parasite." Her eyes well up with tears, and she shakes her head.

Henry's voice is steady as he holds her arms and looks into her eyes. "It's no different than it was before. I know it seems scarier, but it's still the same situation. And we'll be okay. I'm going to make sure of it."

She grabs her dad in a hug and sobs. Then she realizes that she's not acting like the teenager she wants to be and lets go. She tries to look calm, but her hands are shaking.

"I think we can spare a little battery time for charging up your iPod," Dottie says. She leads Corrine to the car with an arm around her shoulders and a gentle murmur.

CHAPTER 33

Penny cuts open one of the brown MRE pouches and dumps an assortment of smaller pouches and cardboard containers onto the table.

She lifts them up one by one and reads aloud. "Sloppy joe, wheat snack bread." She turns the little square plastic pouch over. "How do they get bread in here? Fudge brownie. Oh, look!"

She opens a little bag that contains utensils, a napkin, matches and gum, and pulls out a tiny bottle of Tabasco. "How cute is this?" It's a dollhouse-sized bottle and we all admire it. It really is cute.

"Ooh, can I eat one of those, Mom?" Corrine asks.

Dot shakes her head. "We have to eat the stuff that will spoil first. I'm sure you'll be sick of those in no time."

Corrine pouts, but Penny hands her the Tabasco with a wink. Corrine thanks her and sits smiling at its tininess in her palm.

"They're not very good. I had a couple a long time ago," I say to Corrine. My dad had gotten some once and finally let me and Eric try them after we bothered him about it for days. "Promise."

My cheese tortellini tastes like Chef Boyardee, but it smells better than the meat. That reminds me of dog food, although James says it doesn't taste like it. I don't want to know how he knows that for sure. But it's nice to have food that doesn't waste stove fuel. You just add water and drop the bag into a pouch, and the chemical reaction heats it up.

"This is disgusting." Ana makes a noise and pushes hers away. "I'm not eating it."

"Some of the stuff in there isn't bad," Penny says. She roots around Ana's MRE pouch and pulls out a chocolate energy bar and applesauce.

Ana hits them out of her hand and they thud on the table. "I said I'm not eating it!"

She stalks off to the vault toilets with Penny muttering at her back. We all watch her go, except Peter, who eats a few more bites and then pushes his away, too. "Can't say I blame her," he says. Then he rises and leaves his food sitting there so that someone else has to clean it up.

***

I've taken the kids to find perfect marshmallow roasting sticks in the woods bordering our sites.

"It's got to be green, so it doesn't burn. And thin. I'll make a point on it with my knife when we get back," I say, as we scour the ground and trees.

They seem to have made up. I remember how brutal Eric and I could be to each other, and then a half an hour later we'd be playing together like nothing happened. Thinking of Eric makes me quiet.

"Are you okay, Cassie?" asks Corrine.

"I'm fine." Those pretty eyes of hers are as observant as her brother's. "I was thinking of my little brother. I hope he's okay. He's going to meet me where we're going."

She points into the distance. "Is he out there?"

"Yeah." She looks worried. "I'm sure he's fine. Eric's pretty amazing at everything. He'll find me."

She nods like she's not concerned, but as we're walking back to camp she takes Hank's hand for a minute, and he lets her. The fire burns merrily as I whittle their sticks, and they impale their marshmallows to get the perfect toast. We enjoy the warmth while the sun sets, licking sticky marshmallow off our fingers. I wish we could keep the fire going all night.

Nelly and I take first watch. "Maybe *they* should share a tent," I say, about Peter and Ana. "Peter's got to start acting human. I don't know what to do."

"Seriously," Nelly says. "I'm about to take him aside for a little man-to-man talk."

"You mean a man-to-brat talk."

My sympathy for Peter is receding at an alarming rate. I know I could have found a better way of ending things, but I'm trying. Every smile I give him gets a cold stare, every word I say he either ignores or rolls his eyes. I'm getting angry now. He's thirty years old, not three.

"That I do," Nelly agrees. "If for no other reason than the safety of his own hide, he should be pulling his weight."

I feel a little better by the time we wake James and Penny and crawl into our sleeping bag. We got an extra one today, but I left it outside for whoever's on watch. I kind of like sleeping with Nelly, anyway. I don't want to be cold and alone in my own sleeping bag. I have a sneaking suspicion that Nelly feels the same, not that he'd ever admit it.

CHAPTER 34

"What's so funny?" Nelly asks.

"Hm?" I say, warm and cozy in our bag. The tent walls glow blue from the morning light. I finally feel rested, despite the rock that's been jabbing me in the ribs all night. I'd been having that same dream about Adrian.

"You were laughing in your sleep."

I smile, still half asleep. "A dream about Adrian. The same one I had last week. We were at the house."

Something pokes me in my ribs, and I move away from the rock. "I miss him. If I just knew he was okay, I'd—ow!"

This time Nelly pinches me out of my stupor in time to hear Peter unzip the tent door and storm out.

"Crap," I say. "Crap. Crap. Crap." I burrow into Nelly's armpit in the sleeping bag. "Did he hear me?" I know he must have, but I'm hoping that by some miracle he didn't.

"Every word."

Leave it to Nelly to give you the unadulterated truth. Sometimes I wish he would just lie. I burrow deeper, but the smell drives me back out.

"Nelly, your armpit stinks."

"You don't exactly smell like a rose yourself."

I take a sniff and grunt. It's true. I prop my head on my hand and sigh. He shakes his head, like I've done it again.

"What should I do? Should I say something?" I ask. Nelly's good at this stuff.

He shrugs. "I don't know, Cass. This is one of those times where it may be better to say nothing. What are you going to say? Sorry for having a dream about my ex-fiancé? It might just make it worse."

"You are no help, Nels."

I stick my head back into the bag, smell or no smell. The ball of tension in my stomach gets heavier. I wish I had kept my mouth shut. I know it would have hurt my feelings if I were Peter. And on top of it all, I feel stupid that Peter heard me. All the feelings I've kept to myself for two years were just handed to him on a platter. I cringe at the thought. I'd like to hide in here all day, but I really have to pee, so I may as well bite the bullet.

Nelly gives me a sympathetic grimace as I leave the tent. When I get back I join Peter, who's brushing his teeth at the water containers. I bring my toothbrush over and rack my brain for something to say. Finally, I decide to keep it simple but heartfelt.

"I'm really sorry, Peter," I say. "I..."

I know he hears because he looks right at me. He spits out his toothpaste venomously and wipes his mouth before he stalks away. I feel like all I've done is say sorry to him. I feel like shit. And I wonder if I'm a horrible person, since I always, always seem to fuck things up.

CHAPTER 35

"You are not a horrible person and you don't always fuck things up," Penny says, as we fill the water containers at the stream.

"You have to say that, by law, as my friend."

"Not true." She makes gentle splashes in the water with her bare feet. "As your friend I'm duty-bound to tell you when you're being a jerk, and you're not. You can't help how you feel. I mean, yeah, he didn't really need to hear your dream. He was acting like an ass before that, though. You were going to break up with him anyway. You can't be expected to stay with him when you don't want to because of all of this."

I peel off my socks and stick my feet in the water. After getting a good whiff of myself, I feel extra grubby. "I guess. I just hate tension, especially when I've caused it. I wish I could make things better. Or not care. God, this water is freezing! I brought soap to wash up, but I don't think I can do it."

"Maybe you just have to let him work it out, Cass. Just be extra nice for a while. I mean, it is possible that Peter can turn normal suddenly, right?"

"Ha, unlikely. But I will be nice." I fold my hands in prayer. "I'll be like Mother Teresa."

Penny laughs and grabs the soap. "I'm doing it. I'm going to wash this stinky body. Come with me. I need moral support."

She's lost her mind. The air is fairly warm, but the water is snowmelt, and I'm a huge baby about cold water.

"You can have the towel first. It'll be all nice and warm. Please?" she wheedles. "I'll be your best friend. Until the end of the world."

She makes sure the coast is clear and peels off her shirt.

"You have someone to smell good for. That's why you don't care that it's twelve degrees!"

"Duh." She shrugs and grins. "Please?"

She can usually get me to do things by begging, and she knows it. I give in because it's only cold water and I'm thankful she's made me feel better.

"Fine, I'll do it. But only because I love you."

I take off my clothes. My legs go numb as I step gingerly over the rocks in the little pool.

Penny plunges under and comes up howling. "Come on in, the water's fine!"

I shake my head. "I don't love you that much."

I splash with tiny amounts of water to rinse the soap and race to the towel. It might be warm, but since I can no longer feel my skin I can't really tell. I dry off haphazardly. Penny soaps herself up and even washes her hair. She must be in love. I lay the towel on a sunny rock and wrestle my damp skin back into my dirty clothes.

Penny comes up behind me wrapped in the towel and breathing hard. "Whew! That felt good."

"You're insane."

But I have to admit, now that I'm warming up it feels good to be sort of clean. I load up the water while Penny gets dressed and hums to herself. God, I love her. She's like the antithesis of Ana, the anti-Ana.

CHAPTER 36

I change my shirt and stick my clean armpit in Nelly's face. He responds with some sort of comment about how mature I am, but since I'm rubber and he's glue it doesn't stick. I offer Peter a tentative smile, which he ignores. That's okay. I'm going to smile at him until my cheeks crack.

"...nothing now," mutters Henry.

"What's that?" asks James, who's propped up against a tree with the iPad, his head wreathed in cigarette smoke. We charged it up in the car while heading to Sam's Surplus, but of course there's no service here, or possibly anywhere, at this point. Penny sits at the table next to Ana and brushes her wet hair.

Henry holds the little radio up and repeats himself as we watch him spin the dial. "There are no news broadcasts today. Just those recordings, only now they're listing something called Safe Zones instead of treatment areas."

"Hey, Sergeant Grafton in Jersey said something about it being changed from a treatment area into a Safe Zone," I say.

James lifts his eyebrows. "Yeah, that worked out well."

"There's nothing on AM or FM," Henry says. "Maybe I could find something if we had a shortwave radio, but I've had it on since early this morning and I haven't heard a single update."

Henry hands over the radio and watches as James spins the dial and shakes his head. They try the police radio in the truck, but it's dead silent.

"Maybe the power's off. You can't broadcast without power," Penny says.

Henry rubs his chin. "If there's no power at all, then things are worse than I thought."

"Well, I wouldn't be that surprised," Penny says. "Either everyone is panicking and leaving or panicking and staying home. How many people do you think are going to go to work?"

"I once read that the average power station would only supply energy for twelve to twenty-four hours, unmanned. After that it would begin to shut down on its own," James says, ever the font of information.

"No power means no water and food going bad," Henry says. "Which means hungry people. How long until the stores are cleared out? Man, people will do anything when they're hungry. They'll kill for food in a second, they'll take—"

"Little pitchers have big ears," Dottie says, cutting Henry off.

We turn to where the kids sit on the ground. They had been looking through my wilderness survival book, but now they're watching us, the book forgotten in Hank's lap. Corrine fights back tears.

"Daddy?" she says, like a little girl. "I like it here. Can't we stay here where it's safe?"

Henry sits down on the bench and beckons them over. The lines on his face look deeper; he no doubt wishes he could take his last words back. Corinne and Hank could be toddlers by the expressions on their faces, complete with tear tracks through the dust on Corinne's cheeks.

"I feel safe here too, baby. But we have to leave soon. I think more people will come, looking for somewhere safe. And sometimes people will want what we have."

"But we met Penny and Cassie and everyone. They're all nice," Corrine says.

Henry smiles. "Weren't we lucky? And I'll bet lots of other people are nice, too. But we can't take chances. Not when I have to protect you and your mother and Hank. We have to make it somewhere safer than this."

"I'm scared, Daddy."

Henry hugs her to him with one arm and closes his eyes. "We all are, baby. Being brave doesn't mean you're not scared. It just means you do what you have to do."

Hank leans into his father and nods. "I'm scared too, Corr. But I can teach you all about zombies and how to fight them. You've got to get the head, because the brain—"

I don't think a detailed description of the undead is going to help, so I jump in. "Hey, guys, I saw you looking at my book. Did you see the section on walking quietly in the woods and tracking animals?" They nod. "Why don't you practice that? That's a good skill to have. And I just remembered something I have in my pack that I want to show you. A real survival tool."

At Henry's nod they retrieve the book and read it to each other as they move carefully in the brush, rolling their feet with each step. When I come out of the tent, Henry stands there.

"Thanks," he says. "I didn't want to yell at Hank, since he's trying to help. But the last thing Corrie needs is a blow-by-blow account of how to kill them. We do need to talk about leaving, though. Maybe after you're done with the kids?" He gestures at the long pouch I'm holding. "What is that, anyway?"

"Come see. It's pretty cool."

I had forgotten I threw this in the bottom of my bag. I knew it was silly to do it, as it was taking up precious space, but I couldn't leave it behind. I kneel down at the edge of the campsite and clear a patch of dirt with my hand. Then I take a pointy-edged dowel, a square piece of wood, a rock and what looks like a tiny bow out of the pouch. Corrine and Hank kneel across from me.

"It looks like a little bow," she says. "What do you do with it?"

"You're right, it is a little bow. It's called a bow drill. You use it to start fires when you don't have matches. Only really, really hardcore survivalists can start fires without lighters," I inform them, and do my best to look very serious.

Hank's eyes widen behind his glasses. "Can you?"

"Of course I can!" I say, in mock horror. "This is my bow drill, given to me by my dad, who was the most hardcore survivalist I ever knew. We even lived in a lean-to he built in the woods for a month one summer. Just for fun."

They both gasp and look to see if I'm joking, and when they see I'm not, they look impressed. We really did live in the lean-to, but I'm definitely not a hardcore survivalist like I'm pretending. Neither was Dad, but he did know a few tricks.

I show them the pieces. "The stick is the drill. You wrap the bow string around the drill once. Then you put the pointy end into the square piece of wood."

I hold the bow in my right hand. The drill rests in the square of wood on the ground. I turn the rock over to show them the round depression underneath.

"So you hold the bow like this, and with the other hand you fit the rock on top of the drill stick. You don't press down too hard or the stick won't twirl when you move the bow."

I begin to move the bow from side to side. The string that's wrapped around the drill tightens and spins it, first one way and then the other. I do this for a couple of minutes until wisps of smoke appear where the drill and wood meet.

"It's friction!" Hank says.

"Thanks, Captain Obvious," says Corrine, in better spirits now. He elbows her, but they both laugh, excited by the new toy.

"Okay," I say. "To really start a fire, though, we need tinder. That's fine bits of shredded bark or leaves or anything that's very dry. I have some here."

I show them a little ball of fluff and place it at the base of the drill stick. I get into a rhythm again. When the wisps of smoke appear the kids point, and I nod and continue until I'm fairly certain I have a coal. I lift the drill and, sure enough, there's a little glowing piece of wood.

"That's the coal," I say. I guide it into the tinder. "You have to be gentle or you'll put it out and have to start all over again." I pick up the tinder and blow softly until it smokes.

"You need to have progressively larger tinder and kindling ready, if you're really building a fire. But that's how it's done." I hear clapping and see I've gained an audience. I do a little curtsy on my knees.

"What else is in that bag of yours?" Nelly asks. "Books, bow drills, anything else weird?"

"I put all the heavy stuff in your bag so I'd have room." He grins.

"Well, I'm impressed," James says. "I want to learn, too."

"Yeah, because there aren't any lighters or matches in the world," Ana scoffs. Peter snickers.

I give her a big smile, like Mother Teresa would have. "Survival isn't for everyone," I say, in a super-sticky-sweet voice, unlike Mother Teresa would have. I turn to the kids. "You guys are dying to use it, aren't you?"

They nod eagerly and reach for the tools. I coach them until they've gotten the hang of holding all the components in place. Getting a coal is harder; I used to practice for hours when I was a kid.

I sit in a patch of sunlight at the picnic table. Nelly perches on the table while Henry paces at the other end. Ana deposits herself next to Penny and rests her chins in her hands.

I stroke Ana's arm across the table. I know she's scared. I am, too, but I guess I'm better at hiding it, or ignoring it. I should probably be more understanding of how she feels. It's hard, because her general way of being doesn't garner much compassion. She glares at me like she's angry, but I can't figure out why.

"Banana," I whisper, "can I do anything for you?"

She narrows her eyes. "You can stop being a bitch."

I recoil like I've been slapped. I sit open-mouthed and try to think of what I did to her. Sure, I've been irritated by her comments, but that's par for the course. Everyone gets irritated with Ana, and it doesn't seem to faze her at all.

I'm about to respond when Henry speaks. "Dot and I are thinking we should leave tomorrow. I'm afraid of getting stuck here the longer we wait.

It might be best to get on the road before there are too many infected or desperate people looking for food."

I'm still reeling from Ana's comment, and it takes me a minute to process what he's said. It's only been a couple of nights, but the thought of going our separate ways makes me sad.

"I've been thinking, and I haven't discussed this with anyone else," I glance around the table, "that maybe we should stick together. There's room at the house, and lots of food. You guys are heading into unknown territory. Getting enough food for a few months or even the winter, if it comes to that, might be impossible. You're welcome to come with us."

Everyone nods, except for Ana, who's still glaring at me. Peter lets out an audible sigh. I don't really care what he thinks, so he can stuff it.

"We can't," Dorothy replies with a wistful look. "It's so kind of you to offer, and I wish we could, I really do. It sounds terrible to say that." She looks to Henry, who explains.

"When we were at the storage place, Dottie sent out a couple of texts once we figured out where we were going. It looked like they went through, which means that we might have family meeting us there. The chance is slim, but..."

Nelly looks disappointed. "But you have to be there to meet them. Of course."

I want to remind Dot and Henry that it's unlikely their families got the texts, much less that they'll make it there. But I won't be telling them anything they don't already know. If it were Eric I would be there waiting, too.

James breaks the silence by unfolding the map. "Okay, so are we all leaving tomorrow?" he asks, and speaks again when he sees our half-assed nods. "I agree with Henry. We should get going. We're in a news blackout. If the virus spreads as fast as it seems it does, we should be traveling to safety before there are more infected than we can handle."

He runs his fingers through his hair and makes an annoyed noise when it flops forward again. "I've mapped out the route I think we should take. The truck has a third of a tank of gas, so we're going to need more soon. We can get more from abandoned cars with the siphons from the surplus place. I—"

He stops speaking when we hear the unmistakable sound of car wheels on a dirt road.

CHAPTER 37

I grab my pistol out of my pack. Nelly casually rests the shotgun on his shoulder, but I know he can fire it in a split second. A maroon car flashes between the trees. It slows when we come into view and coasts forward. We stand in a cluster, ready to fight. Even Peter clutches a machete in his hand.

A sporty, young guy in a baseball cap leans out the window. His eyes flicker around to assess our friendliness. The passenger, a girl with short hair and a white, fur-trimmed down vest, offers us a tentative smile.

"Hey," he says, to Nelly and his shotgun. "We're not looking to invade your space or anything. We just need somewhere to stay a day or two. Just drove up from north of Paramus, heading to—well, we don't actually know where we're heading to."

Nelly nods. "Not our campground." His voice is friendly enough, but he keeps his tough face on. "You're welcome to whatever site you want. We'd like to hear what's happening out there, if you can tell us. We've been here a few days and haven't heard anything on the radio since yesterday. Name's Nel."

"Brian and Jordan. Listen, I gotta get out of this car. I'm going to go park, and if it's okay we'll come over and talk?"

He pulls into a site a couple down and they walk over. Nelly does the introductions. Brian and Jordan stand and look uncomfortable.

"Sorry," Penny says. She motions at the tables. "Do you want to sit? I know we didn't seem very welcoming, but we haven't seen anyone and didn't know what to expect."

Jordan sits on the bench. Brian stands and surveys the campground. "No one's been here?" he asks.

Penny shakes her head. "We were thinking there'd be more people, but so far no."

"Yeah. The highways are clogged with abandoned cars. We had a motorcycle at first. We passed people walking, but they won't make it this far for a while. When we got out to the country, there weren't many infected, but everyone is holed up anyway. Won't even answer their doors. Or they went to Safe Zones."

"They keep listing Safe Zones on the emergency broadcasts now," James says.

Brian nods. "Yesterday the word went out that treatment centers were Safe Zones. Under protection, that's what it said on TV. We went to the high school by us." He laughs bitterly and looks at Jordan, who has yet to utter a word. She stares worriedly at him, her highlighted hair stringy under her hat, her eyes surrounded by mascara. Besides her vest she's wearing spangled skinny jeans tucked into sheepskin boots. She's dressed in what you would wear camping on a modeling shoot. Under normal circumstances it might be amusing, but it just makes me feel bad for her. None of us wants to be here. She wraps her arms around her waist like she's protecting her vital organs.

"We thought it'd be a good idea. We didn't have much food in the house, like they were saying you should. Our families said they'd meet us there."

We wait for him to continue, and after a minute he does.

"When we finally got there, we found that most of the people who'd been there, soldiers or whatever, were sent somewhere else. My brother and his wife and kids were there. They'd gotten there before the roads were clogged. Because, you know, everyone had figured out that this was worse than they were telling us. I mean, how can you tell people there's no problem when they can look out their window and see the fucking problem wandering around outside? They blew up the bridges to New York. You guys know that?"

His eyes are wide and rimmed with red. He digs his thumb and fingers into them.

"We were in Brooklyn. We got out the night before they blew," Nelly says.

Brian drops his hand. "Yeah? Well, you're the lucky ones. If you had seen the footage they were showing of the city—"

"What's happening there?" interrupts Penny, her face pinched.

"You're from Brooklyn?"

Penny nods, and motions to Ana. "Our mom..."

Brian nods like he knows what she's trying to say. Since only the two of them made it here, I have a suspicion he understands completely.

"Manhattan's burning up. People were running out of buildings right into fucking groups of Eaters. I mean, what can you do? In a fire, you die. Maybe outside you live. If you can climb or run fast, you know? You've got to run fast."

He looks to Jordan for confirmation, but she stares at her feet, arms gripping her sides. "Brooklyn wasn't as bad. Parts were burning, but nothing like Manhattan. The infection is just as bad, but people, at least the people who don't have a death wish, are hiding out for now."

I picture the rows of brownstones in our neighborhood on fire, people spilling out of the apartment buildings straight into the arms of infected. Running across rooftops to avoid the flames and looking to the streets below for a safe spot to escape to.

"Okay," Penny says, the worry in her eyes unabated.

Ana sits heavily on the bench next to Jordan. I glance at Peter, but he's looking down at the ground, tracing an O with the toe of his shoe in the soft dirt. He does it over and over, like he's solving a complex math problem.

"What happened at the high school?" I ask Brian.

His face closes, and I'm positive he's going to tell me to mind my own fucking business. Then all the fight leaves him, and he sighs, shrinking an inch or two in all directions.

"Well, we were there," he says, his voice flat. "My brother Chris, his wife, Jess, and my nephews. We got a corner by the bleachers. One lady told me there were power outages in the cities, no phone service, and I'm thinking that three days ago, three fucking days ago, everything was fine. You know?"

His eyes dart around the group for reassurance.

When his eyes meet mine, I nod. "It was fine." As I say it, I realize it's not true, it couldn't have been. "It seemed fine here, on the East Coast, everyone thought so."

The panic that he might be going insane, on top of everything else, leaves his eyes. "After a while we realized our parents weren't going to make it out from the suburbs. We decided to wait the night and head to them in the morning. It was getting packed in there, and we could hear tons of noise outside. People caught up in all the traffic, honking. Then the little guy, my nephew, Ty—"

He stifles a sob and removes his baseball cap, then puts it back on and moves it side to side until it's settled. Then he takes it off again and folds the brim in half, the way you do to make that perfect crease down the middle.

"Tyler. He had to pee, you know? So Jess took the boys to the bathroom. The honking turned into screams and gunshots, and people were running to the doors to see what was happening.

"So Chris tells us to stay there, that he wants to make sure Jess and the boys are okay. The screaming gets louder, and they're trying to close the doors. But it's too late, and tons of *them*, Eaters, are in. We couldn't see, so we get on the bleachers right as Chris and Jess and the kids come into the gym."

Brian stares into the trees, but he's not seeing them. I can see what he sees. The way the lights in every high school gym cast a garish yellow glow, the bleachers that line the tiled walls, the windows covered with grates to protect them from an errant ball. The way everyone must have been running in circles, their screams amplified and echoing.

"I yelled at them to go back. They could've hid in the lockers, you know? They were surrounded, so they made a run for us. I wanted to help them, but Jordan held my shirt." He looks at her accusingly. "She said I was going to get bitten. They—they got Jess first, just took her and Thomas down. Jess got right on top of Thomas and tried to fight them off. But she couldn't hold them off long."

I know where this is going and wish I hadn't asked, but I don't want to make him stop. He's been watching his own personal horror movie on an endless loop, and now he's vomiting it back up, trying to get it out of him for good.

"Chris was holding Tyler. He's bigger than me, and he was throwing the Eaters to the side. Tyler's arms were around his neck. I thought he was going to make it. So I go to hang off the bleachers and get ready to grab Ty.

"Then he trips. Without even trying, one of those fuckers trips my brother and he goes down. But he gets Ty up on his feet. Yells at him to run to me. Tyler, he tries, he's pumping his legs. He's yelling, 'Uncoo Bri, Uncoo Bri!' I was about to leap down, I just wanted to get to him, but *they* were under me. They must have been pouring through the door the whole time. And his fucking eyes. They're huge and he's running, and then Tyler, h-he runs right into one's arms and…"

The baseball cap brim is folded beyond repair. Brian's eyes are puffy and a worm of snot runs out of his nose. He looks so lost, so like a Little Guy himself, that I put my hand on his shoulder.

"You couldn't help him," I say. It was a hopeless situation. "You wouldn't have made it back in time. You did try."

He nods, but his eyes say he doesn't believe it. All he sees is his Little Guy running for help he didn't give. He raises his arms and I think he's going to shove me, but he grabs me in a hug that takes my breath away. I hold up all two hundred pounds of him, even though my legs tremble with the effort. His sobs are hoarse and shuddering; they remind me of how I sounded after my parents died, when I would cry alone.

Jordan gets up, her eyes shiny behind the smeared makeup. She rubs his back with a hand that wears a diamond engagement ring.

"Bri," she says in a gentle voice. She cranes her head around my shoulder. "Brian? She's right. You couldn't save him, baby. I know how you... I didn't mean..."

He catches his breath and his body tenses. He lets go abruptly, and I stumble until James catches me and sets me upright.

"If I'd gone earlier, if you hadn't argued, I might have. But you held me back. It's *your* fault he's dead. *Your* fault they got Tyler." He grimaces like he's just eaten something disgusting.

Jordan's eyes overflow and she shakes her head. She's gone pale under the spray tan. "Brian, no, it just would have been you, too. Don't you think I wanted Ty safe? I loved him so much. You know—"

He clenches his teeth. "Shut up, Jordan. Just shut the fuck up."

She runs to their car with a sob and slams the door. We all turn to Brian, who looks after her with a face devoid of emotion. I'm thinking that Brian is cracking up a little, just as he seems to fear.

"Sorry," he says. "I've got to go talk to her."

He walks away with downcast eyes.

CHAPTER 38

We've got the beginnings of a plan. We leave at first light. We'll have to part ways immediately, since we're heading in different directions. I think the Washingtons have a good chance, since they can wend their way along small, isolated roads. We're going to cross the Hudson at the base of the park and drive along a network of back roads, also.

Nelly, Henry and James have, after fifteen minutes of manly deliberation, decided on the best placement for kindling and our campfire is ablaze. Dottie insists on sharing what's left of their now un-frozen burgers with us. When we protest, she reminds us in a don't-even-argue mom voice that the meat will spoil. I snicker when Nelly murmurs, "Yes, ma'am," even though she's not that much older than us.

Hank and Corrine watch the flurry of packing with bleak faces from their spot by the fire. They look like they've just seen the world for the first time, and it's turning out to be a much shittier place than they thought. And they're right. The world just went from semi-shitty to never before seen levels of shittiness. I get the last of my stuff in my pack and zip it up. Then I pull a couple of things back out before going to sit next to them.

"You guys packed and ready?" I ask.

Corrine shrugs and looks at the fire, biting her lip to stop its trembling. Hank looks up from whittling his new marshmallow stick and gives me a serious smile.

"I'm ready. You?"

I smile. "As ready as I'll ever be. But I thought that you guys might need something to help you out in the woods, so I want give you these."

I hold out the wilderness survival book and the bow drill set.

Hank's eyes gleam and he takes the pouch with reverence. "Really? We can have this?"

"No, Hank," Corrine says. She takes it from him and holds it out to me. "We can't take it. Her dad gave it to her, it's special."

"That's why I'm giving it to you. It's special, yeah, but so are you guys. I want you to have it. There's another set at the house, along with lots of lighters and matches. You may need it, so it belongs with you. And the book, too. I'll be totally offended if you don't take them."

Corrine laughs at my pout and takes the book before she leans forward and hugs me. "I wish we were going with you," she whispers.

I hug her tight. "Me too, honey."

CHAPTER 39

The hamburgers hold absolutely no resemblance to Alpo, much to my delight. Peter, now answering me with grunts and monosyllables instead of icy stares, rouses himself enough to thank Dorothy. Jordan and Brian appear at the edge of the firelight. They've spent the last few hours in the car, and we've spent the last few hours trying not to be nosy.

Brian looks repentant. "Hey, you guys. I'm really sorry about earlier. And I was way out of line and apologized to Jordan, just so you know. I don't want you guys to think I'm a dick or anything, I'm not. Well, most of the time, anyway."

He smiles tentatively and gives Jordan's hand a squeeze.

Jordan squeezes back. "He's not. It's been hard. Just…horrible."

Penny gestures at an empty spot on the blankets. We offer them burgers, and they eat a little. Dottie tells us a few stories about growing up in the Caribbean, and Penny talks about living in Puerto Rico. I wonder if the islands have fared any better than the mainland. I'm thinking dreamily of warm sun and fresh mangoes and no infected when James clears his throat.

"I know we're trying to keep it light, but I was doing some calculations today and it looks pretty bad. Okay, today is Monday. This all started, as far as we know, on Friday. On Saturday they took out the bridges, and by then there was something like fifteen percent infected. That means that it took a day for the virus to spread that rapidly. The Midwestern states were already somewhere around sixty percent then, and I'll bet they're somewhere up around eighty or so now.

"Worst case scenario, in cities and big towns we're going to see sixty percent starting tomorrow. The smaller towns and rural places have a bit more time. From what Brian said, most people are stuck in traffic jams. That doesn't mean they're going to give up, but they'll have to walk to reach those places. And at least some infected-but-still-alive will make it there, too. And then they'll turn.

"The infection will be everywhere eventually. I think it'll hover at eighty percent for a while, as those people who've found safe places or have provisions hold out. But, depending on how long the infected live, the majority of people will have to leave their homes at some point for food or water. And that's when they'll get infected. Our best chance is what we're doing: going somewhere remote and hunkering down until this blows over."

Ana and Peter's faces are closed, and when he finishes they murmur something to each other. I don't think they believe him.

"When will it blow over, do you think?" Jordan asks, her face eager.

James's face, which has been animated as he speaks, falls. "That's the thing. No one knows. Maybe they won't die until they decompose. Maybe they won't rot as fast as, well, any meat would. It sounds impossible, but so does everything else. So I'm counting on it and planning to be pleasantly surprised if I'm wrong."

Something passes between Brian and Jordan. She gives him a small nod and rests her head on his shoulder as he strokes her hair.

"What are your plans?" I ask them.

"We're heading out tomorrow, too," Brian says into the fire. "Maybe find our parents. We plan on being gone before you guys, while it's still dark."

Jordan twists her engagement ring around and around on her finger, and he puts a gentle hand over hers to stop it. "It'll be okay. We'll be together, right?"

She smiles tearfully and nods. I wonder how he can be so calm, so sure. If he, who saw half his family eaten in front of him, thinks it will be okay, then maybe it will be.

The fire dies down. I'm in no rush to start tomorrow, but when Henry yawns and says they'd better get to bed, we all stand.

"Thanks, everyone," Jordan says in a quiet voice. "Thank you for sharing with us. It gives me hope that maybe everything good isn't completely gone, if people like you guys are here." It's the most she's said all night.

"And you too," Penny says. "Don't forget, you made it up here."

Jordan smiles, but the sadness in her eyes is back. "Yeah. We'll be okay."

CHAPTER 40

It's mostly dark when I feel someone shake my shoulder. Penny leaves the lantern behind after she's sure I'm awake. I roll up the sleeping bag and listen to the rustle of nylon and zipping of zippers outside the tent. I pick up any loose items and try to ignore the hollow feeling in the pit of my stomach. When I emerge from the tent it's a few shades lighter. Wisps of mist hang in the air, and I can just make out Brian and Jordan's car parked in their campsite. I guess they're still sleeping.

The remaining food sits on the table to be divvied up. After brushing my teeth I head over to where Nelly and Henry stand and stare at the five remaining cases of MREs.

"No one wants them, huh?" I joke, and they laugh.

Nelly turns to Henry. "Are you sure you won't reconsider coming along with us?"

Henry sighs. "You don't know how badly I want to. But we've decided to give the family a month, and then we'll make our way to you. If that's still okay?"

"Of course it is," I say. "If for some reason we're not there, look for a path to the left of the house. There's an old maple tree with what's left of a tree house, not too far in. It's the Message Tree. In a hole in the trunk there's a coffee can. I'll leave where we've gone in there."

Henry nods. "Got it. Now..."

He looks at the table. Nelly, who's always on the same page as me, takes one case of MREs and pushes the others toward Henry. The sky is bright enough now to see his eyes open in surprise.

"No, man," he protests. "I can't take all this. What will you guys do?"

"Henry, we're heading to where we know we'll have plenty of food," I say. "We don't have two kids to drag around. This won't even keep you going for that long, so please don't argue." I hold out a revolver. "And don't argue with this, either. I'll give you boxes of ammo for it, too."

"I don't know what to say," he says, his relief warring with his reluctance. "Guns aren't something to just give away right about now. I...but I can't say no to that. Thank you."

"I'm not giving it to you," I say. I raise an eyebrow and look into his kind face with a small smile. "It's a loan. You have to return it, that's the catch. I'll be expecting it in a couple of months."

Henry's cheeks crack into a smile for a second, then his face reverts to its usual serious expression as he hugs me. "I'll get it back to you. I know it's only been a couple days, but—" He stops and thumps Nelly on the back.

"Hey," James says, as he pulls down the second tent, "their car is still here. I thought Brian said they were leaving early."

Suddenly, I think I know why Brian and Jordan seemed so peaceful last night. I can feel something coming from the car. More like the absence of something.

"Henry, keep the kids away," I say.

I walk toward the car, heart pounding with trepidation. At first I think I'm wrong, that they're just sleeping in the backseat. Brian's got his back against the door and his legs run the length of the seat. Jordan's snuggled on his lap, and his head rests on hers, like he was taking a last, deep sniff of her shampoo. His arms, which were probably wrapped around her, now rest limply on either side.

I steel myself and open the door, just to make sure they aren't still alive. I hear footsteps behind me. The others stand there, frozen, until Dottie leans in and feels their wrists.

She shakes her head. "Maybe pills. I don't know."

"Should...should we bury them?" Penny asks.

I'm glad to see I'm not the only one who shakes her head, even though I feel callous when I do it.

"We need to go," Henry says.

"Maybe a prayer," Dottie says. "Jordan wore a small gold cross. I saw it last night."

"Of course," he says. He begins to recite the Lord's Prayer.

CHAPTER 41

Henry closes the trunk and makes sure the twine holding the boxes to the roof is tight. He takes a deep breath.

"So," he says. "I guess this is goodbye."

Hank and Corrine look out the car windows with what they must think are brave faces. But they look scared, with hollows under their huge eyes.

"No," I say. "It's see you soon."

His eyes are warm as he gives a brisk nod and gets in the car. We're following them out to the base of the campground. I ride shotgun while Nelly drives. Right now the ability to shoot a gun accurately trumps the fact that you get a little squished in the back, so Peter and James sit with Ana and Penny. No one sits behind the cage; no one wants to be trapped back there. At the fork in the road we pull alongside their car.

Dottie rolls down her window and gives us a bright smile. "Take care of yourselves."

"You too," Nelly says. "See you soon."

We drive in silence. The ranger booth at the bridge is unmanned. The parking lot outside the welcome center has a few cars in it, but otherwise it's empty.

"We need gas, right?" Peter speaks up. "Why don't we siphon some out of these cars? It doesn't seem like we're going to get gas at a station."

Nelly pulls into the lot. I wish we'd thought to have Henry fill up here. I hope they don't have to stop anywhere too dangerous. James and Peter get to work prying open the gas tank covers while Nelly makes sure nothing lurks around the building. Penny and I walk to the road and watch the muddy Hudson River race under the bridge.

"What's that ahead?" Penny asks, after a while.

A figure limps across the roadway at the far end of the bridge. I rest a hand on my holster. At the rate it's going it'll be ten minutes before it reaches us, but panic wells up just the same.

Penny's voice is strangled. "Um, guys? One's coming our way."

Two more Lexers come into view and follow the first.

"Make that three," I say. I pull my pistol out. They're too far to risk a shot, but I want to be ready.

"We're good," James says. "Let's get out of here."

Nelly turns onto the bridge and drives on the left side of the road, as far away as he can get from the infected. They watch us go past and reverse direction to follow.

At the other end James points at a few Lexers stumbling their way to the bridge. "They must be coming from Peekskill, about five miles south. Good thing we're going north."

CHAPTER 42

We have about one hundred-sixty miles of backtracking on winding roads to traverse before we near the house. We'll be lucky if we get there in five hours. As we start down the first of our dirt roads, I sigh. Nelly glances at me.

"Brian and Jordan," I explain. "Why did they do it? Wouldn't you want to be sure all was lost before you offed yourself?"

"Of course *I* would want to go down fighting. But not everyone's as strong us, Cass," he says.

I think Nelly's made a mistake by lumping us together. He doesn't take shit from anyone. I can't even break up with someone without taking three months to build up the nerve. But I can't bring that up with Peter here, even if the endless stream of Safe Zone locations on the radio might drown it out.

"How about after my parents died?" I argue. "I went crackers after that. I wasn't exactly a pillar of strength."

"Okay, but how could you not go a little crackers, darlin'? Besides, everyone's entitled to one crack-up in their life."

"Yeah? Are you going to have yours anytime soon?"

"Already did, the summer before senior year, when I came out. It was either tell my family who I really was or die. And I mean really die, I wanted to die. I was ready to be ostracized, as long as I could stop pretending.

"One night I was in bed and I couldn't stop thinking about my dad's guns downstairs. How easy it would be to curl up with one and pull the trigger."

He watches the road calmly, but his hands tighten on the steering wheel. He's never told me about the gun.

"I didn't know you were that bad." I want to cry for the kid who contemplated dying. I get a glimpse of how empty my life would be if I didn't have Nelly and touch his hand.

"I was. But I also knew I could survive anything, as long as I didn't pretend to be something I wasn't. So I didn't get the gun, and I told everyone. Anyway, previous crack-up notwithstanding, you are strong. You would never take the easy way out like that, because it wouldn't be the easy way."

It took me two years to admit I made a mistake with Adrian. I'm terrified of confrontation. For instance, I haven't asked Ana why she's pissed at me because I'm afraid it will open up a can of worms, and I like my cans shut tight.

I know that's not exactly what he means. I used to be strong, before my world went up in smoke. It was one of the things I liked best about myself, and I hate how weak I've become. I've spent the past years just surviving, and I hardly deserve a merit badge for that.

I cross my arms and look out the window at the budding trees. "Well, I don't see anyone else in this car downing a bottle of pills, so why does that make me so special?"

Nelly sighs. "You could argue a cat out of its fur, you know that?"

I smile. "What's that, another one of your Texan expressions?"

"Nah, I just made it up. You like?" he says and laughs when I roll my eyes.

He must believe what he's saying. Well, he's right about one thing: I'm not going down easily.

CHAPTER 43

Three hours later the radio still broadcasts the same-old, the New York State road atlas looks dog-eared and we're only about halfway there.

"All right," James, now in the passenger seat, says in a weary voice, "County Road seven thousand three hundred forty-two is the next left."

Every road has a name like County Road 42 or Albany-Jingletown Post Road. They're ridged and potholed, and our top speed is forty miles per hour. I'm thankful we haven't hit any problems thus far, but it's cramped with four people in the back seat, especially since no one, including me, smells very good. But we're alive. I know it's ridiculous to focus on the fact that my right butt cheek is numb when the world is ending.

I vacillate between a combination of worry-terror that makes my chest tighten and feeling bitchy about little things, like how stuffy the car is and how guys think sitting with three feet of empty space between their knees is a basic human right, even when three girls have their knees glued shut in the same row.

It's a while before I realize that I'm not just grouchy. I don't feel well. Every time we hit a curve I close my eyes to take away the sloshing in my stomach, but it makes it worse. I lean my head on the cool window glass.

Penny turns to me. "What's wrong?"

"I don't know," I say between bouts of nausea. "I feel like I'm going to throw up."

"Nels, you'd better stop the car. Cass's going to puke," she says.

He pulls over on a wide shoulder. The cool air hits and my nausea recedes a little. I lean against the truck and close my eyes, glad the world has stopped its jolting. That's when the stomach cramps hit.

"Pack." I gasp, doubled over from the knife twisting in my intestines. They look at me blankly. "Toilet paper."

Penny rushes to the back and grabs the roll. I stumble into the woods. When I return ten minutes later everyone stands outside the truck.

James suddenly stubs out his cigarette. "I kind of feel nauseous too."

"Need the TP?" I ask weakly. "It was tons of fun out there. I wouldn't want you to miss out."

He gives me a wan smile and perches on the front seat, head hanging in his hands. My legs are shaky, and I plop down on the ground, breathing hard. The nausea creeps back.

"I haven't felt right all day," Peter says with a frown. "Did we eat something weird?"

"Everything was packaged," Penny replies. "I guess it could have been something, though. We filtered all the water, so it's not that."

Ana and Peter exchange a quick look.

"What?" Penny demands. "What's the matter?"

It dawns on her at the same time as I remember Penny giving them water duty a day ago. We even showed them how to use the filter properly. Ana looks at Penny meekly.

"You didn't filter the water? Don't even tell me you didn't use the filter, Ana," Penny says, her voice rising.

"We didn't think it would be a big deal. The water looked clean. And it was taking so long," Ana replies. She crosses her arms like she's explained it to everyone's satisfaction.

"That's why they're called microbes, Ana. They're *microscopic*. And what else did you have to do that day? Shopping? I can't believe you guys."

She shakes her head in disgust at them, arms akimbo. I look up at their faces and it makes me dizzy.

"I'm sorry," Peter says, but he looks more annoyed than sorry. "If I had known, I wouldn't have done it."

Their arguing voices get distant. The sun is so bright. I want to close my eyes and lie down right here. Another wave of nausea hits. I try to scramble away, but I throw up violently on someone's shoes. I curl up on the soft dirt and hard pebbles of the road and groan.

CHAPTER 44

I hear the sounds of tents being erected. They moved me somewhere, but I couldn't open my eyes without vomiting. I squint and see a flash of grass in a clearing before it all starts rotating. This time I throw up all over my hands while I crawl toward the woods. Penny crouches next to me with a drink of water and fans the back of my neck. I hope it's new water.

"Oh, God," I moan. I sink down in my own vomit as my stomach cramps. I know it's disgusting, but I can't even care. "I have to go to the bathroom."

The bathroom. Funny. What I would give for a bathroom right about now. Even the vault toilet at the campground would be better.

"Let me help you," Penny says.

I stumble on her until we find a spot in the trees, then she wraps me in a sleeping bag and puts me in a tent. I want to ask where we are and if it's safe, but instead I drift into a feverish sleep.

I'm sick again and again until I feel I might actually wish I were dead. I hear moaning during the night and have dreams that the infected are after me. I can't run, so I hide and hope they'll go past. In the dream Penny tries to get me to drink, but I knock the water out of her hand, because I know that's how they got infected. Finally, twisted and sweaty in my sleeping bag, I wake to the chirping of birds. Penny sleeps next to me. On her other side is a long lump. James.

Penny sits up with a worried frown. "What do you need? What's wrong?"

"Nothing." My voice is dry and raspy. "Water."

She hands me a bottle. I drink and wait for the stomach lurch, but it seems okay. I'm so thirsty I want it all, but I take careful sips instead.

"Did I sleep all night?" My head is still a little spinny and I lie back down.

"You slept all night, twice." Penny looks me over carefully but must think I look okay, because her face relaxes.

"Really? I lost a day?"

She nods. "Not just you. James and Peter got sick, too. Nelly's hit yesterday, but he's not as bad, and Ana and I are fine. We've been taking care of you all."

The last conversation I heard comes back to me. "It was the water?"

I can't believe Ana and Peter didn't filter it. I told them how important it was. But I think they only filled our containers. If they made the Washingtons sick and they had to stop somewhere to recuperate, they could be dead right now. We could have been dead right now, camping out here. Wherever here is.

"It seems most likely. Ana finally told me that they filtered some of it. I guess that was before it got too boring." She makes a face. "So maybe I was lucky enough to get uncontaminated water. We washed all the containers as best we could and refilled them with filtered water. Ana knows how to use that filter now, you can bet on that."

She looks triumphant, like a mother who has taught her naughty kid a lesson.

I laugh. "Thanks for taking care of me, *chica.*"

She smiles. "Of course. Even though you were a pain in the ass and kept trying to knock any drinks I gave you away. You kept saying it would make us moan, too. I was worried about you."

"I was having crazy dreams. Sorry I was so annoying. Sounds like it must have been fun." Penny shrugs and smiles. I motion to the lump that is James. "How is he?"

"About the same as you. Peter, too. It hit them later, so I figure by tonight they'll be feeling better. If you're feeling better, that is."

I nod. "I might actually be a little hungry. Not much, but a little."

"Let me see what I can find that you can stomach." She unzips the tent, then stops and turns to me with an evil grin. "Oh, you'll like this. Remember when you threw up the first time? Well, you puked on Peter's shoes. He was so pissed. It was great. All he could talk about, until he got sick, was how terrible they smelled even though he scrubbed them."

Peter's shoes cost hundreds of dollars. I'm feeling even better now than I did a minute ago. It's amazing how a little morale boost can improve your health.

I smile and close my eyes. "Good. I hope they smell forever."

CHAPTER 45

Three days of people puking has done nothing to improve the aroma in the truck. A bar of soap and limited cold water don't really cut it when you've lain in your own vomit. We've been camping in a clearing down a dirt track. Penny says she and Ana heard some cars go by on the main road. A couple of times they heard distant gunshots and what she thought were explosions.

We're days behind schedule. I'm driving and as jittery as a cat in a room full of rocking chairs, or whatever crazy thing it is that Nelly says. I haven't had much cause to drive, living in the city with no car the past few years. Plus, my dad always said I drove like an old lady, anyway. I'm about three inches away from the windshield, afraid of what's around every bend. Nelly, who's resting in the back, finally opens his eyes and asks me if I want him to drive.

"I'll drive," James offers.

He's perked up in recent hours and sits in the passenger seat. He looks almost skeletal now. Penny offers him a snack every fifteen seconds, pecking around him like a mother hen. I'm pretty sure he likes it.

"I'm fine," I say, and attempt to unclench one of my hands from the steering wheel.

"Dude, you've got the wheel in a kung fu death grip," James says.

I let out a laugh that's tinged with hysteria. I offered to drive, since Penny and Ana barely ever drive and everyone else still felt worse than me, but I probably shouldn't have. At least not in the state I'm in. Maybe it's being weak from sickness, or because I don't believe the ride can remain as trouble-free as the last hour has been, or maybe I'm trying for two crack-ups in a lifetime instead of one. I feel like a baby for being scared, but I try to convince myself I have nothing to prove by driving this stupid, stinky car. It's not like I've spent the past days whining and refusing to do what needs to be done, not like some people I could mention.

"Okay, I'll pull over in a few. Somewhere we can have a pit stop."

The road wends its way through stands of forests, past farmhouses, fields and run-down houses and trailers. When we started this trip the other day there were signs of life: the occasional person outside or smoke pouring from stovepipes. Today most look empty. I can't figure out why the occupants would have left somewhere relatively safe for a Safe Zone.

I guess I might consider it too, if we hadn't already escaped from one and heard about the fall of another. I'm looking for a place to stop, so I'm not prepared when I round a bend and there's someone standing in the middle of the road.

"Shit!" I slam on the brakes and skid to a stop two feet away. There are grunts as everyone in the back hits the front seats. "Sorry! You guys okay?"

"Fine, we're fine," Penny says, not taking her eyes off the road.

A man stands with his back to us. His hair is greasy cowlicks. He looks normal from the back, but none of us is surprised when he turns and his face is slack. A network of purple capillaries stands out on the gray of his face. They look just like the tiny, twisting lines of the back roads we're following on the map. He shambles up to the hood and leans forward. His eyes are cloudy, like grimy old marbles.

"Run him over!" Ana screeches.

Her voice carries out the windows. He moans and pulls himself halfway onto the hood, teeth clacking together. I haven't seen one this still and close in broad daylight. There's a brown crust in between every tooth, like he hasn't brushed in a year. I'm pretty sure it's blood. I can see the bone in one arm, a flash of white in the tangled mess of tissue.

"Cassie," James says in a calm voice. "You might want to go."

I snap out of it. There's a dead person on the hood of the car. His hands scrabble on the shiny black paint as he tries to get purchase, and I'm afraid he'll fly up and crack the windshield. I lightly press the accelerator, even though I want to gun it.

"Jesus, Cassie, go!" Peter shouts, and the creature on the hood gurgles with frustration, or something like it.

"I don't want to crack the windshield," I say, as I speed up. "Hold on to something, everyone."

I swerve and the Lexer slides off the hood. There's a terrible *thump-bump* as we run over some part of him. My breath comes in gasps. We're going fast now, and I have no intention of stopping, ever. I'm so tightly clenched that my hands and neck hurt. Everyone talks at once, but I'm silent, waiting for the next bump in the road, literally and figuratively.

"Sorry, everyone," I finally say. "I should have moved faster there." I feel dumb, like I can't be trusted to keep everyone safe. My cheeks are hot.

"Are you kidding?" Penny asks. "If it were me we'd still be sitting there trying to get me to step on the gas."

"And I would've floored it, and he probably would've cracked the windshield," Nelly says. Peter gives a little cough. "You wanted to take off fast, too. Right, Pete? That's why you yelled for her to go?" There's a warning in his voice.

"Not fast enough to crack a windshield," Peter replies.

I can see him in the rear view mirror; his jaw clenched. He hates when people call him Pete, which Nelly knows, without a doubt.

"Thanks," I say, to everyone but Peter. "I won't be as slow next time. I thought we were pretty safe here, but if that guy is just wandering around..."

"It doesn't look good," James finishes. "I can drive whenever you want."

CHAPTER 46

The houses that looked empty now look menacing; their dead eyes watch us as we go past. I jump every time I think I see a pale face at a window, a corpse inside waiting to be freed. I would think that after days of this my heart would have ceased going into overdrive, but the body knows when it's threatened, and it isn't going to let me pretend otherwise. Maria said the virus lives in the brain, where our most primitive reactions are based. It occurs to me that if I allow my brain stem to do its reptilian job in response, I just might live.

The holster digs into my side in the backseat. It's not an unpleasant feeling. I've never particularly liked pistols. They've always scared me a bit, even though I've shot them more times than I can remember. My dad liked to carry a gun; it was an extension of his body, a tool. Like a hammer. I feel as if I'm using a table saw with no safety cover, no goggles, and my eyes closed. Like any second it might start going off wildly, despite my attempts to control it.

My dad said I was a natural at shooting targets, and I did enjoy it. But I'm not like Nelly, who holds a gun with ease, who never frowns at the weight of it in his hand like it's a venomous snake. I've never wanted a gun for protection, afraid it was more dangerous to carry than anything I might come up against in daily life. But now I'm glad it's here. The heaviness weighs me down, roots me, and reminds me that at any instant I might have to use it. I just hope I'm still a good shot.

There are just over thirty miles left. It doesn't seem like a lot, but it could be impossible. People drive that far to get a gallon of milk around here. Or they did; both small stores we passed were dark.

It's about ten miles to Bellville, the town my family would visit on summer evenings for a scoop of ice cream or Fourth of July fireworks. This wasn't our usual route, but I've spent enough of my life here to have traveled this road before. The farm with the wagon wheel mailbox means we're only five miles away. I say this aloud. Everyone nods, but the car is silent.

Peter's on the other end of the backseat. His profile is still and his eyes flick back and forth at the passing scenery. This morning he mumbled an apology at me, and I tried to be gracious about it. *It's okay, it was a mistake,* I said, and tried smiling at him. His answering smile was bitter, and he went back to loading the truck. He's so angry at me, maybe at everything. Peter's always wanted for nothing, except the things that really matter. He's always had money and charm to fall back on, but now all the superficial armor that protected him is gone.

Maybe somewhere in there is that guy I glimpsed now and again in his generosity or in the gentle way he would treat me, which was so at odds with the way the rest of the world saw him. I wish I could smooth things over. Maybe it's not possible. But he's here, and though I want to kick him much of the time, I'm kind of glad. He may hate me, but I still care enough about him to want him safe.

CHAPTER 47

A painted wooden sign welcomes us to Bellville. A police car sits sideways across the road, surrounded by a jumble of cars. Three men pop up from behind it. One rests a huge rifle on its roof while the others hold their hands up until we stop.

"Okay," shouts a tall, blond man. "Everyone out of the truck."

"Should we get out?" James asks. "Maybe we should just turn around. Is there another way?"

"It's another forty miles of driving, at least," I say. "And no guarantee we won't run into another roadblock." On the plus side, if they've got the town barricaded, everyone must be well.

We spill out of the truck as two men move forward and leave the one with the rifle trained on us. The second man is bulky, with brown hair that looks like it was cut with a butter knife, and small, mean eyes.

"Where you folks headed?" asks the tall one.

I step forward a couple of inches. "Headed to my folks' place, about twenty miles north."

"Any of you sick?"

We shake our heads. It's a good thing we didn't try to pass through here while we were ill with whatever was in the water. They look like they plan to shoot first and ask questions later. We still don't look that great, and there have been an embarrassing number of pit stops today, but all in all we don't look infected.

"Well, we're not letting anyone into town. You'll have to find another way up there."

"We just need to pass through, up Bell Street," I plead. "It'll save us forty miles and we're really low on gas. You can escort us."

He shakes his head. "We don't have time to escort anyone anywhere. Over half the town's gone to the Safe Zone outside Albany. National Guard came through a few days ago and told people it was their only chance. So they took it."

The bulky one narrows his already small eyes. "Why aren't you headed for a Safe Zone?"

"We were already at one in New Jersey," Nelly says. "We got out by the skin of our teeth after the infected got in. I'm sure you're not there for the same reason. You figure you can protect your families, yourselves."

"Damn straight. But we're still not letting you through. Sheriff's orders."

Hope spreads in my chest. "Sam? Sheriff Price?" I ask.

The tall one raises an eyebrow. "You know the sheriff?"

"I do. He'll know my name. Can you please tell him that Cassie Forrest is here?"

Mean-eyes tightens his mouth, but the other answers first. "All right, I'll give him a radio call. Sit tight."

They walk back to the cruiser and speak into the radio. I try not to stare, afraid they'll suddenly refuse to help if we make one wrong move. Besides, the rifle's still on us.

"This is no joke," Nelly says. He leans on the truck, hands in pockets, looking nonchalant. He barely inclines his head toward town. "Don't look. They've got people on the roofs. I've seen two so far."

"They're not fucking around," James agrees. "We'll siphon more gas if they don't let us in. I just want to get out of here."

I nod. It's not worth all of this. I'm about to say so when the tall guy opens the cruiser door and smiles. He walks toward us with Mean-Eyes dogging his footsteps.

"Well, Cassie Forrest," he says, and extends his hand, "Sam's real glad you're here. Name's Will Bishop, by the way. Sorry about the welcome, but we've had some trying to pass through with infected people."

He hooks his thumb at his partner. "This is Neil Curtis."

Neil gives us a nod, and when he takes in our group his eyes linger too long on me, Penny and Ana. His eyes have no depth, like a dumb, unpredictable dog. Some of those dogs are mean, while some are so enamored with tennis balls that there's no room in their brains for anything else. This dog right here is mean, though; I can see that.

James moves forward to block us from view. I appreciate the sentiment, but the past week has made him look frail enough to blow away on a stiff breeze. Neil notices, though, and quickly hides a look that's much too heated. *Mean dog.*

"We'll move the cruiser so you can get past," Will Bishop says. "Sam's down at the Town Hall. You know where you're going?"

"I do. Thank you."

CHAPTER 48

Sam stands outside Town Hall and raises his eyebrows when he sees what we're driving. I jump out as soon as the truck stops and run to him.

He grabs both my hands and gives me a hug. "Cassie, it's been too long. How are you? Are you okay?"

It's so nice to see a face I know that I can't stop smiling. I give him a brief synopsis of our trip as everyone joins us.

"Come along inside," Sam says. He removes his hat and opens the door. "State police office isn't safe. It's where everyone who got bitten went, followed by everyone who got scared and then got bitten there. Thankfully, not too many have made their way here so far."

Sam directs us into a room with old windows that let in the late morning light. He sits on a wooden bench and motions for us to do the same. He looks just as he did three years ago, when he came to the house to tell me about the accident. The deep, dragging lines in his long face are still there. Or maybe they're recently back. This is a crisis that blows a parental car crash out of the water.

"We've got the main intersection blocked off," he continues. "Pretty much everyone's moved down to the junior-senior high school. It's got a generator. We're moving the equipment here to the school office."

"It must be cramped," I say. "I know half the town's gone, but that's still more than a thousand people."

"A thousand? Where'd you get that idea? Most of the town is gone. There're about two hundred of us left, that's all."

"At the roadblock. They said half the town was gone."

"Oh, they're saying that to discourage people from getting the idea they should try to take us on. I'm glad you thought to ask for me, since we're not letting anyone through. One—what did you call them? Lexer? They've been calling them Biters around here. One gets through and that could be the end. Anyway, they're doing the best they can over by the roadblocks. They're all scared."

He puts his elbows on his knees and steeples his fingers. There's so much to think of, and he looks beat-up and bleary-eyed from trying to anticipate it all.

"There's one guy down there, Neil, I think his name is? I understand the un-welcoming committee, but he's..." James trails off with a shrug.

Sam rubs his chin and sighs. "Yeah, Neil's family's lived around here for generations. They're like pit bulls, constantly inbreeding and making a meaner animal. Neil's been doing good down at the roadblock, but he can be trouble. Run up against the law a few times. I'm keeping him close, don't worry."

He turns back to me. "You're welcome to stay at the school if you want. We could use some extra hands. We've got a lot of families left. A quarter of our numbers are children."

I don't want to let him down, but the thought of staying here makes me nervous. I don't want to tell him what I'm really thinking—that they're sitting ducks.

"The house is still stocked up, Sam. And Eric—you remember my brother?—he's meeting me. I'd feel better if we were there. I'm sorry."

He nods. "I figured you'd say that. Listen, you didn't tell anyone where the house is, did you?" We shake our heads. "Let's keep it that way. Some people might just be tempted to come by. I'll check up on you in a few days. The National Guard unit that came through said they're expecting this to be over in a month. Said the Biters would—disintegrate, is how the man put it. We can all last that long, right?"

"Of course we can," I say. This is very welcome news. A month until this is over.

The radio on Sam's belt crackles. I can't understand a word, but he replies. "I've got to run some folks to the north block and then I'll be there."

He clips it back to his belt as we stand. "You've got enough gas?"

There used to be fuel at the house, for the generator, but I don't want to count on it. I look to James, who answers, "We've got about a quarter tank."

"Should be enough to get you to town a couple times. We're conserving gas for the generator, but next time you come down, we should be able to spare some from what we're siphoning."

The sun is bright when we step outside. I turn to Sam and shield my eyes from the glare with my hand. "Why didn't you go with the Guard?"

Sam's hat is back on his head and his eyes are in shadow, but his mouth tightens. "I was in Albany on Sunday. It was a complete fuckshow, pardon my French. People ignoring the curfew, infected wandering the streets. I've been listening on the police radio for the past week and honestly, Cassie, I think—hell, I *know*—they're in over their heads. When I heard the plan was to move us to a *more* populated place, I thought they had to be out of their minds. I offered to set them up here; we could've used the help. But they had their orders. I tried to get more folks to stay, but they felt more secure with the Army." The decision is weighing on him.

"We were in one of those so-called Safe Zones. It might be the least safe place I can think of. You made the right decision."

Even if it won't be enough, it's still the better choice. But they did say a month, I remind myself. It should be enough.

"Oh, Cassie, I really hope so."

CHAPTER 49

We follow the paved road out of town for about twenty miles before the turnoff. I've moved the star ring to my clean pair of jeans, and I use the word clean very lightly. Mostly puke-free would be a better description. I circle the outline of the ring in my pocket and think of the first time I brought Adrian to the cabin.

Adrian and I pulled up at lunchtime, as the last strains of "Take Me Home, Country Roads" died out. It was a tradition that began with my mom's John Denver cassette tape when I was young. I would make them play it on the last road to the house. I had pulled out the CD at the turn and popped it in. Adrian laughed at the corniness of it, but still sang with me at the top of his lungs. After all those months he was used to my idiosyncrasies.

We sat in the car and listened to the clicking car engine mix with the sounds of the house: the soft clucking of chickens, the wind in the trees, a dish clanking in the kitchen.

"Ready?" I asked.

I knew he was nervous. He'd met my parents a few times, but this was a long weekend in their house. A whole different ball of wax.

"It looks just how I pictured it," he said.

I tried to see it through his eyes: the weathered logs of the cabin, the picture windows my parents installed, the porch that ran the breadth of the front, with table and chairs, the porch swing at the end. The flowers my mother babied surrounded the house with a riot of bright colors. But all I could see was home. I hoped that Adrian would love it there as much as I did.

My parents came out the screen door as we retrieved our bags. My dad grabbed me in a bear hug and tickled my neck with his beard. My mom gave Adrian a hug. Her long hair was in a braid and her laugh lines deepened as she welcomed him with the signature warmth that drew people to her.

"You can always tell when Cassie is coming down the road," she said, humming a few notes. She had a soft spot for the song, since she grew up in West Virginia. You could still hear the mountains in her voice if you listened carefully. "Lunch is ready. I made a few things since I wasn't sure what you liked, Adrian."

I translated for Adrian. "That means there's enough food for fifteen people inside."

"No, no, I practiced restraint. There's only enough for ten." She laughed and then swatted my dad when he shook his head and mouthed, "Fifteen."

The wood walls and floor were a warm honey color in the sunlight that came through the loft. When I was a kid I would spend hours painting up there, feeling very serious as I worked in what I thought of as my art studio. There were supplies up there still.

The big farmhouse table sat next to the kitchen, which was open to the rest of the house. Eric and I would tease my mom and say that was why she always went overboard with food: she was feeding the ten chairs instead of the people. It was loaded with cold cuts and hummus, homemade potato salad, three kinds of bread that she probably baked herself, yogurt, some sort of pasta, two pies and lots of fruit.

"There are chips and some—" mom began, as Adrian started talking.

"This looks great, M—"

She cut Adrian off and held a hand in front of her. "You aren't about to call me Mrs. Forrest, are you? Because I refuse to answer, remember? I get enough of that at school all year. Please, please call me Abby."

She put a plate down in front of him while he smiled and promised to never do it again.

"Well, you can call me Pat, or Patrick or whatever you'd like. Just don't call me late for supper," Dad said. Mom and I groaned; he loved to act hokey.

I could see Adrian relaxing. My parents had a way of doing that to people. Dad heaped a plate like he hadn't eaten in days, which couldn't possibly be the case with my mom around. I wanted some of everything, and tried to figure out where to start.

Mom plunked a fork and a jar of her canned peaches in front of me. Now there was no contest. Nothing in the world compares to a home-canned peach; it's like summer in a jar. I stabbed peaches and plopped them in my mouth, their cool sweetness exploding on my tongue.

"Savage!" she said. But she loved that we all adored her food. "That's almost the end of last summer's peaches. I got a couple of batches done yesterday but thought we'd do some more tomorrow. If you want to, that is. You can take a bunch back to school with you."

"Definitely."

I handed Adrian the fork with a half of a peach on it. He ate it in a single bite as we all watched him, like it was some sort of test.

"Wow. That's really good. No, better than good," he said, passing the test, since you could tell he meant it.

"We're having them over homemade ice cream tonight," Dad said. He scoured his beard with a napkin and rubbed his gut.

"I can't wait," Adrian replied.

He smiled at my mom and she beamed back. My dad brought up some problem he was having with the solar, and once they started talking about inverters and arrays, I zoned out. I knew I should pay more attention, but there was always something else I'd rather be doing, like eating peaches.

"Eric really wanted to come, but he couldn't get away," my mom told me. While I would have liked to see Eric, I thought maybe it was good that Adrian wouldn't be on Forrest family overload right away.

"I spoke to him yesterday," I said. "He keeps mentioning one girl in particular. Sounds like she's a tough broad. Kicked his butt climbing some mountain. I think he might like her for real."

"Is her name Rachel?" I nodded. She clasped her hands together. "We met her at parents' weekend, with a group of his friends. She seems like a nice girl. One of those girls that reminds me of horses, you know?"

She saw that I had no idea what she meant. It's no secret that I inherited my flaky side from my mom.

"She doesn't look like a horse, nothing like that," she continued. "She's actually quite pretty. She's like a thoroughbred: all tan, muscular flanks, strong, white teeth and long, thick mane of glossy, dark blond hair. She looks like she just came in from some sort of adventure, even if it was just a walk to the store."

The funny thing was that I knew exactly what she meant. I'd always felt like those girls were a different species from me, with their rosy cheeks and unbridled enthusiasm. I burn in the sun, and even the millions of freckles on my arms have never joined forces to create a tan. My hair isn't a naturally shiny mane; it gets frizzy and puffy from waves that don't quite make it to curls. My thighs tend to wobble and no one has ever said that I look like an outdoorsy girl, even though I do outdoorsy things. In the wilderness I tend to look like something the cat dragged in, not an L.L. Bean ad. But I liked Rachel already; anyone that could kick Eric's butt was great in my book. He could be insufferable; he was just so competent at everything. But he was also impossible to dislike because of it.

Dad and Adrian glanced furtively at us as my dad attempted to draw some electrical thing on a pad.

I shook my head sadly when they looked my way again. "You're both itching to get out there, aren't you? You can barely stand it!"

"Well," my father said, "it would be easier to show him."

I pretended to be defeated, but really I was glad they had something in common. "Go. Shoo!" I flapped my hands dismissively. "You can have the tour later, Adrian. We'll clean up."

Their chairs screeched as they jumped up and left through the sliding glass doors on the back wall. Mom looked fondly after them and began to stow the insane amount of food in the refrigerator.

She came to stand next to me while I washed dishes. "You love him," she said.

Mom was the one person who could always get me to talk about my feelings. I kept my eyes on the sponge and smiled. "I do."

She squeezed my shoulder. "I'm so glad."

Afterward, I wandered around and stuck my head into all the rooms, saying hello to all the familiar books and pictures. Being there after an absence was like a reunion with old friends. My bedroom smelled of the wildflowers my mom had put on the dresser, and I sat on the bed and played with the single ear of an old, ratty stuffed dog I'd won at a carnival long ago.

I looked out to the backyard. Off to the right of the house was a stand of trees, the hammock underneath practically begging me to come and read. The little barn was right behind it, shaded by fruit trees. There were no animals in it; my parents were waiting for retirement to get some goats and maybe a pig for bacon. The chicken coop was full, however. In the fall they would give the chickens to our neighbors, John and Caroline, who were happy to take them.

Blueberry bushes and a huge bed of strawberries sat before the wood and wire fence that surrounded the vegetable garden.

I strolled outside and raised my face to the sunshine, listening to the bugs that tease you with their calls that cut off when you get close. We could never catch them when we were kids, no matter how stealthily we crept. I let myself into the garden. The zucchini that had escaped attention were over a foot long, and the earliest tomatoes were almost ripe. I fingered the tomato plant leaves and breathed in the green, almost minty smell.

I heard laughter and headed for the shed that housed the batteries for the solar. Adrian and my dad were bent over a metal box, nodding. I knocked on the top of it, like a mechanic does on a car, and pretended I had any sort of inkling of what could be going on.

"So, boys," I said. "Any luck?"

They stood. They were so different. Where my dad was broad and pink, Adrian was lean and dark. My dad couldn't tan on a bet, but Adrian was bronzed by the sun. It struck me that they were very similar as well. Not only their interest in self-reliance and insanely boring electrical systems, but they both had infinite reserves of patience. They were solid. Always ready for a laugh and full of kindness. But under that was a core of steel. If provoked, they were a force to be reckoned with. I suppose I shouldn't have been surprised by that revelation, but I was.

Adrian looked mischievous. "Yeah, I think we figured it out. It was the flux capacitor. You guys need a new one."

I rolled my eyes. "You know, I have seen *Back to the Future*. Nice try, though." They laughed. "Mom and I are going down to town. Getting some peaches and there's a sale on canning jar lids. You need anything?"

"More canning lids? That woman has enough lids for a hundred years!" My dad exclaimed, although he didn't mind, really.

"Hey, those lids are what bring you peaches all winter. Pea-ches," I reminded him.

His eyes twinkled. "You're right, Cassafrass. Tell her to get enough for two hundred years, then."

I kissed them both and left them to their flux capacitors.

That night our neighbors, John and Caroline, came over for dinner. You could walk a straight shot through the woods to get to their house. Over the years we'd worn a trail.

While my parents were liberal hippies, John and Caroline were religious libertarians, which made for interesting dinner conversations. People thought it strange they were such good friends, but they were like family.

John sat at one end of the table, spooning pie past his beard. "If you think that FEMA is going to be there when the stuff hits the fan, well, I can't imagine that's always going to be true. Look at the places they've dropped the ball so far." He turned his attention toward Adrian. "What do you think, Adrian?"

Adrian nodded. "I guess I never really thought about stocking up with food for any particular reason. But it would be a by-product of the kind of farm I'd like to live on. Meat stored on the hoof. Preserving the harvest and keeping food until the next planting season."

"Exactly," John said. He knocked his fist on the table. "People think it's crazy to store food, but it's not a recent phenomenon. It was the way things were done up until fifty years ago. You planned ahead for tough times."

"What's crazy is relying on a complex chain to bring food to you, and to believe that every link in that chain will do its part unfailingly," my dad agreed. "So far, it's worked, because any time there's been a problem it's been localized and other areas pick up the slack. But it would only take several areas in the United States to be hit at the same time. A cascading series of events."

"And then you're standing on the FEMA food line, praying there's enough so you can feed your kids," John finished.

It was pretty heavy dinner conversation. I was used to it by now, of course, but I wasn't sure if Adrian wanted the Preparedness 101 lecture on his first visit, even though he seemed interested.

"You know, I think you're preaching to the choir," I said, smiling. I changed the subject. "How are Tom and Jenny?" We had spent our childhood summers playing with their kids. Caroline filled me in.

"I think we're going to sit out on the porch a bit," I told my parents, after Caroline and John had left.

My mom yawned and hugged us both. "We're heading to bed."

My dad was at the stereo. "You guys want this off? Any requests, or can I put on a couple more tunes for you?"

"You choose," I said, and gave him a kiss goodnight. "I love you, Daddy. Until the end of the world."

He smiled. "And after, Cassie-Lassie. Good night, Adrian. Thanks for the help today; in two hours you solved what's been stumping me for a week."

"No problem," Adrian said. "It was fun."

"Fun? You're both hopeless," Mom said, and winked at me.

We headed out into the summer night. The air was still warm up on the hill, so it must have been a scorcher in town. We rocked on the porch swing as we listened to the music through the window screens. "This Magic Moment," by Jay and the Americans, began.

I squeezed Adrian's hand. "It's official. My dad loves you."

"How can you tell?"

"This is my parents' song. He wouldn't share it with just anybody. It's Dad code, he's saying we can have it."

He laughed. "Dad code?"

"Yeah. I can read him pretty well."

"I like him." He sounded wistful. "Both of them."

Adrian's dad split when he was young. From what I'd heard of him it was probably a good thing, but that didn't stop him from missing what might have been.

"I can share," I offered. "Lots of people use my dad when they need one."

He squeezed my hand. "What was that you said to your dad when you said goodnight? Until the end of the world?"

"Yeah, it started when I was little. You know, like I love you more than the stars in the sky?" Adrian nodded. "Like that. One day I said, 'I love you until the end of the world. And after.' It stuck."

We listened as the music swelled. Adrian looked down at our hands and rubbed his thumb in circles over mine. "So, do you think you'll ever say that to me?"

We'd said I love you, but I wasn't very good at expressing my emotions without feeling flustered. I didn't have a lot of experience being in love. Actually, this was my experience being in love.

"Say what?" I asked, even though I knew what he meant.

"That you'll love me until the end of the world? And after?"

I watched his thumb stroke mine. I couldn't look up. All of this came so easily to him.

I forced the words out. "I already do. I just don't say it out loud."

His mouth moved to my ear. "Cassie Forrest, I love you. Until the end of the world."

I shivered, not sure if it was his breath on my neck or his words. I wondered what we both did to deserve this, to have found each other so easily.

I smiled as I met his eyes, and my next words came easily. "And after, Adrian Miller."

His hands were tangled in my hair as I pulled him closer on the creaky porch swing. The end of the song surrounded us, a gift from my dad, and in that magic moment the song became our own.

***

"I can't remember, is this the turn?" Nelly asks.

I start, feeling like I've just fallen out of that swing. "Oh, um, yeah." He turns up the dirt road, which means we're almost there. I pump an imaginary accelerator with my foot. I want to be there so badly, yet I'm afraid, too. I wonder if my parents' ghosts linger there, if they'll haunt me as I walk the rooms.

Here's the tree with the reflector on it, where I would start playing the song. I sing softly to myself, thinking that in the passenger seat no one will hear. Nelly does, though, and he joins in. It forces me to raise my voice, too.

"Oh, great," Ana says. "A sing-along."

Penny squeals. She's an old hand at this song, having spent much of her summers here, at what she called her "country estate," and I feel selfish for having denied her access these past years.

Penny's voice is sweet and clear and purposely directed right at her sister's ear. James gazes at her with a look I recognize. Adrian used to look at me like that. Then he opens his mouth and sings, and my jaw drops at the voice that comes out. It's smooth and low and we look at him in surprise.

James flushes and shrugs. "Middle school chorus."

I remember the last time I drove down this road, and my voice deserts me. I couldn't play this song. My mom and dad were in the backseat, mixed together in a box. Somehow I had thought their ashes would be like cigarette ashes, but they weren't. A little chunkier, a little more *there*, they didn't disperse into nothing the way cigarette ashes do. They settled on the ground and worked their way into the soil. Once I got over my initial surprise it seemed fitting.

Penny and James sing the end in perfect harmony as we turn into the driveway. I can almost hear the music backing them up. They've left me and Nelly in the dust.

"Show offs!" Nelly throws to the back, before he takes my hand and we pull up to the house.

CHAPTER 50

It looks forlorn. The porch furniture has been put away, and the swing is off-kilter. Eric may not have made it here all winter. He doesn't tell me, because I haven't wanted details, although I do like knowing he comes here.

"Ready?" Penny asks.

"Yeah," I say.

Gravel crunches under my feet. My mother's flowers have fallen victim to neglect. I should have been here, weeding and trimming, keeping it tidy. Small patches of ice linger in the shady parts of the yard. Spring comes a bit later up here, but the crocuses and daffodils are sending up their tiny green fingers anyway.

My hand trembles. *It's just a house.* I open the door and step in. Everything's the same, layered with quiet like it would be when we'd come up after an extended absence. All it needs is people filling its spaces. And it isn't just a house. All this time I thought I would be haunted by memories here. Maybe even by ghosts, if you asked me after a particularly bad nightmare. But the memories aren't haunting. There's the wood stove where we would make popcorn on movie nights, the table where we ate countless home-cooked meals, the quilt on the couch that I'd wrap up in on cold, damp days, the shelves full of books, my mom's knitting basket. It's all just stuff, like this is just a house, but it all means something, too.

I'm irritated suddenly, as I realize I've wasted three years that I could have been here, taking comfort in this place. It seems to have become a habit of mine, to refuse the things that would give me comfort.

"This is really nice," James says.

His breath fogs in the air. We need a fire. I feel like we haven't been truly warm for days and days.

"Thanks."

Everyone mills around, touching things, peering out windows. For now this is their house, too. I want them to like it. I've given some thought to rooms, but I want to check with Penny.

I motion her into the kitchen. "So," I whisper, "bedrooms. Are you and James going to sleep in the same room, or should I put you and Ana together for now?"

She fingers the knives that sit in a block on the counter and doesn't look at me. "Um, I think we'll be in the same room."

"Okay." I kick her foot and try to keep from smiling. "Is there gonna be a home ru—"

"Cassie, I swear I'll kill you if you make a comment that has anything to do with baseball bases," she cuts in, and pretends to grab a knife. "But, if you must know, yes, I'm planning to hit one out of the park as soon as possible." We dissolve into giggles.

"What's so funny?" James asks from behind us.

"Oh, nothing," Penny says. We grin at each other.

I clear my throat. "Okay, guys, I was thinking Penny and James in my parents' room. Peter," he looks up from the bookshelves, "you can have Eric's room. When he gets here, we'll figure something else out. Ana and Nelly, one of you can sleep with me in my room and the other can have the office-slash-guest room. Or, since there are two twin beds in Eric's room, one of you can sleep in there with Peter."

Nelly and Ana look at each other. It's clear Ana wants the room to herself, and Nelly capitulates.

"Looks like we're bunking together again," he says to me. "You've proven you can keep your hands to yourself."

"Ha ha. I'm going to the basement to turn on the breakers."

I flip the switches, but nothing happens. Thankfully, the water is gravity-fed, and the solar water heater is separate from the rest of the power. That means hot showers. I sniff my hand, it still smells like puke. I survey the rest of the basement. It's warmer down here than upstairs, above fifty degrees, and light filters in from the ground level windows.

My dad was the electric guy, but Mom was the carpenter. Wooden shelves full of home-canned jars line the walls. There are tomatoes, peaches, green beans, jams of all colors, applesauce and countless other things that were first grown, then harvested, and then preserved by them both. The summer and fall were times of canning jars and giant boiling pots and hot stovetops. It was hard work but worth it, my mom always said. And it was, come January.

Cans and large buckets of food line two walls. They contain flour, wheat, oats, sugar, rice, popcorn, beans, and dehydrated foods, amongst other things. Mom had it down to a science and rotated things out so nothing ever went rotten. She knew what it meant to be hungry; wasting food was anathema to her. Another shelving unit holds canning lids, candles, wax, batteries, lanterns, flashlights, a tub of medicines, shampoo, soap, conditioner, razors, and all the things we used to just run by the drugstore and pick up. I'm used to this abundance, but when I hear a gasp I remember it's not normal to see this much food in one place.

"It's like a warehouse," James says. He runs his hands over the buckets. "There's got to be thousands of pounds of food down here. I've always wanted a basement like this."

He's as crazy as I am. I'm thankful that he doesn't make me feel like a freak for liking all of this.

"Cass's parents planned for an emergency," Penny says. She and I used to come down here and search for interesting treats, like a treasure hunt.

Peter's voice comes from behind. "I didn't realize your parents were hoarders."

I imagine all the ways I could kill him. Maybe he doesn't realize he's insulting them. Maybe.

"They. Weren't. Hoarders," I say. "They were *preppers*. Hoarders take stuff they don't really need, and they don't share it. My parents grew a lot of this food. They also gave it away. They donated to food banks, and they kept enough in reserve to feed us through a hard winter if something terrible happened."

I think about telling him how my mom was so poor growing up that sometimes she went without. That she would hunt for squirrel after school so there was dinner when her dad got home from work, dirty and exhausted. That the last thing she would ever do would be to let others go hungry when she had food. But he doesn't deserve an explanation, to know these things about my mom. And, anyway, I think even if I told him he wouldn't understand. Peter's never had to go without.

I spin around. He's watching me with a bored expression, like he's letting me talk but doesn't believe a word of it. "And imagine that, something terrible happening? No, I don't believe it ever could. How about you?"

My hands tremble with rage as I glare at him. He breaks eye contact first. So this is how it's going to be. Nothing I do will ever be right. At least I know where I stand.

CHAPTER 51

Our meager belongings are put away and a pile of smelly laundry sits in the corner. The house is warming up nicely. Peter sits at the table and eats crackers and peanut butter with homemade jam. I notice the *hoarded* jam is going down easily.

"Should we go see John?" Penny asks.

"He was visiting his daughter last week," I say. "He was planning to call on his way back and come to see me in the city." It's the world's worst timing, to be away from his supplies right now, but at least he's with Jenny.

I head out to the solar shed. The hole in the bottom of the door is not a good sign. Inside, the batteries are strewn everywhere. One of the windows is broken and wires are chewed. Fluffy mouse nests are tucked in the debris, but something larger must have come in and then chewed its way out the door, maybe a raccoon or porcupine. The little fucker must have gone bananas in here. Power would have been nice, but there are plenty of lanterns and the kitchen stove's two LP tanks are full.

I hear something in the woods as I leave the shed. My holster's back in the house, machete, too. It was stupid to go outside unarmed and alone. I grab a piece of metal tubing and creep over the dead grass to the house.

I pick up speed at the sound of snapping branches until I hear a joyful bark that stops me short. It's John's dog, Laddie. He's gray around the muzzle and limps on cold mornings, but he dances around me with a doggy grin.

"Laddie!" I kneel to hug him and get a slobbery lick on the lips. "What are you doing here? Where's your dad?"

He sits and his tail sweeps away the leaves behind him. I hope John's okay; he never would have left Laddie here by himself.

"Hello the house!" a voice rings out.

John strides out of the path between our houses. He looks much better than he did when I last saw him. Caroline died a year ago of a massive heart attack in her sleep. It hit him hard, and it seemed like he was trying to follow her to the other side. His broad frame is still on the thin side, now that

Caroline isn't here to feed him, but his eyes sparkle and his teeth flash under his salt and pepper beard.

"John!" I run into his bear hug and relax in his wool-shirted arms.

He grasps my shoulders and holds me away from him, his eyes moving up and down. "You're okay? You made it here?" he asks, like I might be an apparition.

"I'm fine. We're all fine. Nelly and Penny and her sister and, well—come in and meet them. Why are you here? Why aren't you at Jenny's?"

"The day I was leaving Jenny called and said the kids had a virus and I should postpone a week or so." I gasp and he shakes his head. "No, no, they had bad colds. Fevers, runny noses, coughing. Thank God." But worry crosses his face anyway. "I last spoke to them on the weekend. I tried to call you, but service in New York was down. You know Jenny, she's like her mom, already battening down the hatches. They're pretty rural. I pray they're okay."

"Oh, John, I hope so." I cover one of his calloused hands. "But I am so glad to see you here, I really am. Come inside."

CHAPTER 52

John's booming laugh fills the house as he hugs Penny and Ana, shakes Nelly's hand and is introduced to everyone else. His questions about where we've been get right to the point.

"An Army buddy of mine who's high up at the Pentagon called me last weekend," he says. "Said there were rumors this was a bioweapon gone wrong. That it's ours, something called BornAgain. He didn't know how it ended up all over the world. He called me on a secure line from somewhere underground, and if that's not an indication of how bad this is, then I don't know what is."

He runs his hands through his white-streaked hair. "Told me to sit tight and wait it out. I asked him, 'Wait out what and for how long?' He said he wasn't sure on either count. The party line was a month, but they'd picked that as an arbitrary number. Far enough away to scramble together some sort of military response and near enough that people wouldn't panic when they heard it."

My heart falls. I'm one of those people who heard it and felt relieved. Sam believes it, too. I'll bet the National Guard did as well.

John notices my expression and I explain. "They told Sam the same thing. If everyone's operating under the assumption that we only have to stick it out for a month, they won't be as careful."

Penny and James nod frantically, both thinking of their mothers, I'm sure. Earlier in the week I saw Penny holding James in the trees while his shoulders heaved. When I asked later, she said he'd tried to get his parents to take Bornavirus seriously, but they said he was being his wacky old self. He's sure they're dead, or infected.

James doesn't give the impression of being the toughest guy at first glance, but I think he's sturdier than most. He held it together the whole way here; I never had to wonder if he was okay. We were all scared, but it didn't stop him. He's different, and he's smart.

A light goes on in his eyes. "I was reading some conspiracy theory websites and site said something about a bioweapon. At the time everyone had a theory, so I just skimmed it. I wish I could remember the details."

He closes his eyes and puts a hand on his forehead like an old-timey mind reader. "It said the mutation of a military virus caused Bornavirus LX. Something having to do with soldiers killed on the battlefields being able to continue to fight. Life after death. BornAgain, I guess. I dismissed it as complete craziness at the time, but..."

"It might be true," John finishes. "And the infected are going to last a lot longer than thirty days, from what my buddy said, or didn't say.

"He always ribs me about my food storage, and when he asked how I was set for food, I thought he was joking. I laughed and told him I had years of food and plenty to grow more. 'I know, John,' he said. 'And thank God you do.' The way he said it, all quiet, made my blood run cold."

"Years?" James asks. He drops his hand from his forehead and widens his eyes. And now, finally, I can say I've seen him look frightened.

CHAPTER 53

Unfortunately, John doesn't have any idea about the solar. He'd planned to have my dad help solarize his house, but the plans died along with him. He does, however, have lots of stored fuel and a generator. He's been running it for a few hours at night to keep his freezers frozen. And the best part is that he has a clothes washer. He even insists on taking our laundry back with him, so we can settle in.

"Eric took your generator for the winter," John says.

Eric and Rachel rent a house that's notorious for winter power failures, so that doesn't surprise me. John told me Eric called after the bridges blew and said they were leaving. They planned on hiking here if they couldn't take the roads. He told John to keep an eye out for me, although he wasn't sure I'd made it out. I do my best to imagine them trekking through the woods safely, but they have hundreds of miles to go. Even though thinking about it makes my stomach twist, I obsessively picture them hiking along a trail, filling their water bottles, enjoying the views and snuggling in a sleeping bag under the stars, while I trace a likely route along the map in my head. Maybe if I will it hard enough it'll be true.

"We have heat, a stove, lamps and water," I say. We're probably some of the luckiest people in the world right about now. "I think we can cope just fine. Plus, we get to send out our laundry. It's just like the city."

John bellows out a laugh.

"But you will have dinner here, right, John?" Penny asks. "We've got to fatten you up a bit."

"A little home cooking wouldn't go amiss. And a little company, too. Both my freezers are chock full of meat. I need some help eating it. I'll take out some beef to thaw for tomorrow." He flings the bag of laundry over his shoulder, like a lumberjack Santa Claus. "I'll get going and start this up. Be back with what's clean for supper."

CHAPTER 54

I yank a brush through the snarls in my hair. Even the short shower we were allotted before the hot water ran out felt wonderful. I watched a week of dirt and grime swirl down the drain and allowed myself to think of Adrian. As of a year ago, he was somewhere in northern Vermont. If he's still there I'd bet close to a hundred percent that he's okay. If I know him he'll be building fortifications and gathering people around him right now.

It heartens me that I'm closer to him, although at this point the distance may as well be a million miles instead of hundreds. I just want to know if he's okay. There are people who say they would know if someone they loved was dead. I'm not so sure, but if it's true, then he's still around. I can feel the pull of him all the way down here.

I dress in jeans and a shirt that have been here for years and head down the hall. Ana, Peter and Nelly are sprawled on the couch and overstuffed chairs, covered by a motley assortment of clothing. We're going to need more clothes soon, in the correct sizes.

There's a pot of water and canned tomatoes simmering on the stove. James hums and stirs the sauce while Penny puts the spaghetti in. It looks so normal and domestic, except that James's high-water jeans are cinched tight and Penny's got on a tie-dyed skirt of my mom's. I stifle a laugh and try to help, but they shoo me out. The sun is going down. I set the table and add two solar hand-cranked lanterns. I put two oil lamps on either end of the couch.

There's a knock and John enters with a bag and sets it down. "Got half of it done. I'll get the rest later."

"Oh, thank God," Ana says. "I can't wait to get out of these."

Personally, I think she looked kind of cute in a cuffed-up pair of my mom's khakis. It hurts my feelings that she isn't grateful for the clothes she has on, even though it's probably ridiculous. She paws around in the bag and heads down the hall. I follow and tap on the door.

"Yeah? Come in."

"Hey, Ana." I close the door most of the way. "Can we talk for a minute?"

Her look is unfriendly. "I guess."

"Are you mad at me?"

Ana throws my mom's shirt in the corner and puts on her shirt. She unbuttons the pants and stops. "Peter told me what you said to him. I mean, I knew you didn't like him that much, but I can't believe you would do something like that."

I think back. I broke up with Peter and berated him for acting selfish, but I'm not sure what she means.

I cross my arms and lean back on the computer desk. "I have no idea what you're talking about."

"Peter told me how you told him not to come with us, just because you guys agreed to break up. That's why he didn't come when we had to run. I can't believe you would be so selfish."

She pulls my mom's pants off and tosses them on top of the shirt. My brain repeats everything she just said, and I listen carefully because either I'm living in an alternate reality or Peter is. And in this alternate reality *Ana* is calling *me* selfish. Heat rushes from my stomach to my face.

"That's not true," I sputter. "*I* broke up with Peter, back in Brooklyn. He said he wasn't going to come with us at the Safe Zone, even though I told him to. I've tried to be nice to him. Now he's lying to you. And, of course, you believe *him.*"

Her lower lip juts out as she shrugs and zips her jeans. She doesn't care, just like she doesn't care about the clothes that lay in a heap. Why take care of clothes that aren't hers, that have only been worn for a couple of hours? She gives no thought to John trudging through the woods with our clothes, being nice enough to clean and fold them, to use his stored gasoline to run his generator, and all the other small—but also huge—things that make laundry possible here.

I pick up and fold my mom's pants and shirt carefully on the daybed. I want to smack Ana. I find it impossible to believe that she's completely unchanged by this past week, but the old Ana stands before me—selfish, entitled Ana.

"Whatever," she says. "We just have to be here for a month, right? I'm sure we can get along until we can all go back to our lives."

She gives me a nasty closed-mouth smile. She hasn't been listening at all. I'm not quite sure what she thinks will be left in New York in a month, even if the infection has died out.

"Fine, you believe what you want to believe, Ana."

I hug my mother's clothes to me. My mom always said pretty is as pretty does, and Ana looks so ugly to me with that tight face and misplaced self-righteousness. I head for the door, but then I stop and turn back. I want to wipe that smile off her face.

"But if you ever throw something of my parents' on the floor again, like it's trash, I swear I will beat the living shit out of you. I really will."

My knees knock as I stalk out. I lean against the hallway wall and take a breath. I can't believe I just threatened Ana with bodily harm, and that I meant every word of it. But I still don't care, because the look on her face as I left was worth it.

CHAPTER 55

"Home-canned green beans are actually pretty good," Nelly says, as we finish up dinner. He looks at Penny and James. "Thanks, guys."

Everybody looks exhausted. It seems like a few days ago that we'd passed through town, even though it was this morning.

"You all need to go to bed," John says. "I'll sleep on the couch tonight. Laddie'll let us know if anyone's coming. Tomorrow we'll start work on an early warning system for your house. I've already done mine."

"What's that?" Penny jokes. "Like cans with rocks in them strung on wire?"

"Pretty much," John says with a laugh. "There are some high tech things you can buy if you want to take your chances in Albany, so for now we're going with barbed wire and fishing line."

A little while later I tell Nelly about Ana as we lie in my bed and watch the moon graze the trees.

"I can't believe Peter's lying about it," he says.

"I know," I say. "I can't even look at him."

Angry tears well up in my eyes, and I go silent so Nelly won't hear them in my voice.

"I wish you would let me talk to him, Cass."

"I don't want to start any more problems. Maybe it'll blow over. Maybe some time will help."

"Peter isn't striking me as the kind of person who rises to the occasion. But I won't say anything yet, I promise. You can't let him treat you like this, you know."

I sigh and roll over on my side. "I know, I know. I told you I'm not strong, didn't I?"

He exhales. I think he's gone to sleep, but then he speaks. "I do like this new leaf you've turned over, though."

"What leaf is that?"

"The one where you threaten to kick people's asses. I would've liked to have been a fly on the wall for that one."

"Quiet, you," I say, but I smile. And although a few minutes ago I felt like I would never be able to relax, I drift off to sleep.

***

It's early morning when I wake. I've seen a lot of sunrises recently. I have a feeling there are many more in my future, since we'll be conserving batteries and lamp oil. I love the underwater blue-gray light before the sun finally makes an appearance. When I watch the day dawn, I feel more in tune with it, like we're old friends, instead of being thrust into it midway. For the first time in years, my fingers itch to hold a paintbrush, to blend the colors until I find that perfect shade of blue.

John's got a fire going in the living room, and there's hot water waiting in the kettle. He remembers I like tea in the mornings, bless his soul. I sit at the table where he's scratching out something on paper.

"What'cha doing?" I ask.

"Planning out your perimeter. We'll string up the early warning system, also known as the tin cans," he smiles at this, "a ways out, but close enough to hear. The barbed wire will go inside that line at chest height. It's supposed to catch anything that gets through the cans and hold it until we can get to it. The hill behind the garden's steep, so we'll save that for last. It's the best we can do with what we have. Depending on how this all plays out, I think we may want to dig trenches, too. We'll see how it goes."

He reminds me of my dad, sitting at the table as steady as a rock, working on some sort of plans. It makes my chest tighten. John is the closest thing I have to a dad now. "John, you're awesome. Thank you so much."

I wrap my hands around my mug. The bedrooms are still cold; it was down in the thirties last night.

"I'm happy to do it. Takes the mind off of things." His blue eyes shine in the lamplight when they meet mine. "I didn't think you'd make it here, honey. Not after what they did in New York. When I saw the smoke from the stovepipe, I thought for sure it was Eric, and I wasn't surprised. It was you I was worried about. I can't tell you how glad I was to see you. Almost like Jenny showing up."

I cover his hand with mine, and we sit in companionable silence as the sun rises.

CHAPTER 56

"If I never see another can in my life, I'll be happy," Penny says. She rubs Neosporin over the cuts she got stringing them along the wires.

"A good day's work was had by all," John says, who spent the day securing barbed wire into trees, but he glances at Peter and Ana. They spent much of the day working, but while the other teams of two were getting hundreds of feet finished, they were getting fifty. I've done my best to ignore them.

The barbecue is lit for the thawed steaks. It's chilly out on the deck, but we're still warm from the work. James passes out the few beers we found. Eric probably enjoyed the last of my dad's home-brewed beers; there's nothing but empty bottles.

James raises his bottle. "This is a momentous day." At our curious looks he pulls his iPad from its case, and we gasp at the crack in the screen.

"Yeah, iPad is dead. Gone. I'm pretty sure it's going to be impossible to submit a claim to AppleCare." We laugh. "At first I was terrified at what I would do without it, then I realized that stringing cans is infinitely more useful than Words with Friends. Maybe more fun, too." He winks at Penny, his partner in stringing, and she blushes.

"And number two." He pulls a pack of cigarettes from his pocket. "This is my last pack. I thought I'd enjoy them with a beer. I don't want to be a pusher or anything, but anyone who wants one better get in on this."

"We don't want to smoke your last cigarettes, man," Nelly says, although we totally do.

"I want you to. The longer I have them the more miserly I'll become. I want them gone tonight and to smoke them with friends. Especially friends who will remember, when I'm acting like an asshole in nicotine withdrawal tomorrow, how generous I can be."

He turns the pack suggestively, like we need any more enticement. Nelly and I each take one and lean back in our chairs. Even Penny, the good girl who hasn't smoked since high school, takes one. We all *ooh* at her and she gives us the finger. Peter shakes his head, and Ana moves her chair to the edge of the deck with a sigh.

"What the heck," John says. He slides one out of the pack. "It's been twenty years, but damned if they don't still smell great."

It looks like it's going to rain. I feel good, like we've done something productive, something besides running. Early this morning John and I drove down to the mailbox on the main road and chopped the post down with an axe. We hid the concrete base under some brush. Removing the last vestige of civilization felt like a capitulation, a goodbye.

I watch the cigarette smoke curl up into the trees and look at Nelly. He's got his eyes closed and his feet splayed out. His shoes are damp and muddy. He and James both have big feet and no extra shoes. I add shoes to the mental list of things we'll have to find in town somehow.

For the time being, though, we've decided to stay put. Sam said he'd be by in a few days, and we'll get a status report then. I follow the end of my beer with the last drag of my smoke and hope it isn't another kind of goodbye, though I'm almost certain it is.

CHAPTER 57

I look up from the table where I'm organizing seeds when I hear the rumble of thunder. We've spent the past four rainy days organizing our supplies, chopping wood, cooking, cleaning and getting less sleep due to a watch schedule we've set up.

Ana and Peter sit on the couch. These past days trapped inside with them have been torture. I've found an excuse to head to John's house every day rather than listen to their sighing.

The other night at dinner, when we discussed starting a garden, they looked like they were about to explode. John tried to explain that even if everything went back to normal today at least half the population would be gone. Food would still be scarce and fresh vegetables non-existent. This was not what they wanted to hear. Since then both of them have been sullen and unhelpful, like if they refuse to help it won't come true.

Penny's tried to talk to Ana, but she's in the grip of some powerful magical thinking. I admit it's a lot to take in. All of us have our moments of disbelief, but right now, disbelief will get you killed. The thunder rumbles again, louder this time.

Nelly looks up from loading logs in the wood stove. "Storm's a-brewing."

John stomps his boots as he enters the front door, looking grave. "Those are explosions. I'm pretty sure it's from Bellville. Don't think we'd hear Albany or Pittsfield so far. There's a huge tank of LP at the school, and last I saw Sam they were moving more fuel there. But I bet they had some explosives rigged up, too."

We crowd around him at the open door, but we can't see anything except trees and gray sky. Gas tanks are hard to blow up by accident. Unless they meant to, which would mean they've been attacked. We listen, but there's nothing more. I move to the table and sit down.

"We could use a good antenna," John says.

Every day we turn on the shortwave radio. Aside from the usual emergency broadcasts, we've heard a few broadcasts from other countries. But they haven't been in English or Spanish, the only two languages we speak, collectively. We don't understand them, but they all have the same urgent, fervent rhythm.

One emergency broadcast said a message from the president was forthcoming, but it never came. The past couple of nights we've picked up what sound like Americans talking, but we tend to get terrible reception up here.

"We're going to have to go down there soon," Nelly says. He doesn't look happy about it. "There's stuff we need, no? And we should know what's going on. I don't want to be surprised."

I grab a pad and pen. "We need some shoes for you and James."

Peter shoots me a look. "I need shoes, too. All I've got are sneakers now."

"Okay, Peter, too," I reply.

Penny tries not to smile. I kick her under the table, and she makes a strangled noise. I pinch my leg to keep from laughing and keep my eyes glued to the pad. I know if I even glance at her, I'll lose it. It used to happen in class all the time.

"How about we wait another couple days, and then we scout it out?" John asks. "Whatever's going on down there might have blown over by then."

CHAPTER 58

It's bright and sunny as we climb into the truck. Nelly, John and I are heading to town. Since the explosions, we've heard nothing more, although black smoke billowed into the sky eventually. I've got my holster on and the machete that I'll wear across my back.

"Please be careful," Penny reminds us. Her face is creased with worry. "Just come right back if it's not safe. We don't need anything that badly."

"Yeah," James adds. "You can't leave us here with those two."

He tilts his head toward Ana and Peter on the porch. Peter's arms are crossed. He's mad because he wanted to come. It's the only thing he's wanted to help with so far, but John insisted he learn to use a gun first.

The houses on the road are empty, since most people chose the safety of town. The roadblock at Bell Street is unmanned. The two- and three-story buildings on Main Street with ground floor businesses are all dark, and the sidewalks sparkle with the shattered glass of broken windows.

We head for the school. The only movement comes from trash blowing across the asphalt. From a distance we see that two walls of the school still stand, but the inside is a blackened ruin. It's either still smoking, or the resulting ash is sifting into the sky; I can't tell. I just hope all those people weren't in there.

John pulls into the parking lot, and we take in a scene of total destruction. Bricks, splintered wood and pink tufts of insulation are everywhere. On top of and under and intertwined with the debris are bodies that must have been flung during the explosion. Big ones, small ones, a tiny one that makes me raise my hand to my mouth. They're covered with flies. My mouth fills with thick saliva at the smell.

John stands with one leg out of the car. "Anyone here?"

We wait a few minutes in silence. The taillights of a police cruiser peek out from behind one wall, and we head for it. Sam lies on the ground, dead, behind the bullet-riddled open doors.

"Careful, John," I say. The flies rise from his body in a swirl and then settle down again. I gag. You don't see flies on Lexers, I realize, maybe because they don't decompose normally.

"Shot," John says. "Look at his chest."

Sam's shirt is encrusted with dried blood. He was so worried that he was making the wrong decision to stand his ground. It looks like that's what he died trying to do.

"Jesus," Nelly says. "It had to have been living people."

"Let's go," John says. "They may still be around."

The parking lot is no longer empty when we turn. About twenty Lexers move across the lot, but they're far enough that we can beat them to the truck, although it means running toward them. Nelly and John must think so, too, because they take off at the same time I do. But we stop when four more come out from behind a van. My gun is in my hand. I'm not sure when that happened, but I'm glad it's there.

I stop and sight, just like Dad taught me. *Breathe in. Relax.* I aim for the head of a woman I think I recognize. She bares her teeth and lunges. That's when I remember—she worked at the café and would bare her teeth like this whenever we came in as teenagers, even though we always tipped well.

Left hand underneath to steady. Use the right to aim. Line 'em up. Exhale. I pull the trigger. The sound is loud and my hands jolt. But she goes down, head half gone in a splatter of brown gore. John hits two, and Nelly gets the other. But stopping has given the other Lexers time to get between us and our truck.

John's voice is calm. "Take the ones on your side first."

It's so reassuring that I can't help but obey. The first takes two shots to go down, the next in line takes only one. I miss the next one's head and, after being thrown back by the impact, he staggers closer. I pull the trigger again and hear a click. Six shots. I lost count.

A steady stream of curses flies from my mouth as I shove the pistol in my holster and slide the machete out from behind me. All I can do is stand and wait until he's covered the few feet between us. I hear my rasping breaths, but I feel still. There's nothing else in the world but me and this balding, middle-aged man. Maybe he was an accountant before someone disemboweled him. His intestines hang down, covered in dirt and flakes of dried leaves. His mouth is open and his eyes are blank, but he comes for me like he has twenty-twenty vision.

I raise the machete in a two-handed grip, the way my dad taught me to swing a bat the one disastrous year I played softball, and the only game my team ever won was a forfeit. I step forward and swing like I'm going for a home run. It slams into his neck with a crunch that reverberates up my arms. I can't pull it out to swing again; it must be lodged in his spine. But it's enough. He drops to the ground. I almost follow him down until I release my hold on the handle. John and Nelly stand, guns still raised, but the rest of the Lexers are in a heap, covered in the remains of their head cavities.

"More coming," John says. He points behind us.

More Lexers stumble over the bodies and bricks, which gives us the chance to make it to the truck. John fires the engine before our doors are closed. They slam shut as he swerves to avoid what remains of the school and the people who sought safety inside it.

"Lord, protect us," he says, watching the scene in the rearview mirror. A few limp after us. Some seem to have already forgotten we were there and wander aimlessly.

"I know," Nelly says, breathless. "It's unbelievable."

John shakes his head. "You told me. But when you haven't seen it with your own eyes...dead people walking."

I load my pistol, the box of ammo next to me. Next time I'll wear the double holster. I have a feeling there will be a next time, and maybe a time after that.

Nelly turns in his seat. "Cass, you okay? That was quite a move with the machete."

I click the cylinder home. "I need some practice with a gun. It's been a while. And we need sharper blades. The machete worked, but it got stuck in bone and I lost it." I know it's not what he's asking, but it's all I can think of right now—how to win the war it seems we've been drafted into.

Nelly looks at me closely. His eyes flick back and forth. "Yeah, okay. But are you sure you're fine?"

"She's okay," John says. He doesn't look worried, and I'm glad, because I feel like maybe I should be hyperventilating. But I'm not. "Cassie's tough as nails."

CHAPTER 59

We make it to the little farm goods store without running across anything alive or dead. We find walkie-talkie radios, boots and clothes in peace. I stand watch, but I only see two Lexers way down the road, under a tree, doing who knows what. Waiting for the bus, I guess.

Next stop is the convenience store. The windows are shattered, and the beer cooler is cleared out. I wonder at the people who, when faced with life or death, grab beer and television sets.

As we wade through the crunchy glass, I see some bananas that are way past their prime in a basket on the counter. I grab them and all the apples, which are still okay. I think about taking some cigarettes for James, but it seems mean to bring him more since he's quit. And, anyway, once I look I see they're gone, too.

We only take a few things. Other people, if there are other people, probably need food a lot more than we do. What we're really after is in the back. John breaks open a locked door and leads us into the office. Inside is a big radio.

"Richard Morgan, owner of this shop, he's a HAM radio operator. He's shown me a few times when I've asked. Always wanted to get into it, get a decent radio, but it was always one of these days." John shrugs and gives a rueful smile. "I guess today's the day. What we want most is the antenna."

He heads outside and points out a cord that travels up a little pole on the roof. Nelly stands on the truck and pulls out the staples that hold it to the building. With a grunt he ratchets off the last bolt and lowers the pole. John carefully ties it to the roof. We follow this with some of the radio equipment.

I see a few figures limping our way. We were going to siphon some gas, but we can refill with John's supply, so we head back toward the safety of home. Penny and James are on the porch as we pull up. They look relieved when we step out of the truck unscathed.

"How'd it go?" James asks. "What's happening in town?"

We shake our heads. He nods like he expected no different.

"Did you run into any of them?" Penny asks.

"Yeah," I say. "About twenty, at the school, which is burned to the ground. We had to shoot them."

"Wow," James says.

Penny's eyes widen and she touches my shoulder. It aches from the impact of the machete into bone. The calm feeling has dissipated, and now, suddenly, I'm terrified. I collapse on the steps and drop my head in my hands. The cool breeze turns my sweat cold, and my teeth chatter. Penny leans over me.

"I'm okay," I say. "I wasn't that scared, then."

I look down at my dirty hands and realize I can't tell what stain is what. There are smears of brown and black and something rust-colored. The Lexer I killed with the machete might have gotten infected blood on me. Maybe it's seeping inside, finding a way through a tiny cut and infecting me. I choke back my terror and say, "I need to wash up."

I will not give in to panic, not after the fact. I hear Penny ask if I'm okay as I rush inside.

"Cassie'll be just fine," John says.

He has a lot more faith in me than I do.

CHAPTER 60

At dinner John asks if he can say grace. He always bows his head before dinner, and we've all taken to following suit. I send out my informal prayer that asks for Eric to reach me safely. I ask my parents to look out for us, wherever they are. I thank whoever or whatever is up there that we've gotten this far, because we are so very lucky. If today has shown us anything, it's that nowhere is safe.

"I know we have a lot of different beliefs here," John says. He inclines his head at me, smiling. "But whether we're agnostic or Christian or—"

"One of the Chosen People," James interjects with a grin. "James Gold was James Goldfarb about a hundred years ago."

John laughs. "Or Jewish, of course, I'd just like to give thanks. I don't want to offend anyone."

"No one could be offended by you, John," I say.

He's a deeply religious person, but he doesn't proselytize. He draws strength from his beliefs, something I envy but have never been able to emulate when it comes to organized religion.

He bows his head. "Lord, we thank you that we have food on our table and good friends to share it with. We pray that our loved ones are safe and also have tables laden with food and surrounded by friends. We ask that you help us to protect ourselves in the coming days. And, finally, we pray that the souls of those bodies that walk the world are safe in your arms, Lord. Amen."

"Amen," we all repeat.

Penny wipes her eyes, and even Peter looks like he means it.

There's banana bread for dessert, made from the bananas we rescued. John gave me today's eggs from his chickens to bake it, now that he's got enough in his homemade incubator. He has eight chickens; he wouldn't get rid of any of Caroline's "girls" after she died, even though come summer he's swimming in eggs.

"Tomorrow we're taking a ride," John says. "Target practice for everyone. We shouldn't do it here. Noise seems to attract them."

"Sam was shot," I say. "That means the infected may not be the only thing we have to worry about."

Everyone's confused by the scene we found in town. There were Lexers, but obviously there's someone else out there, too. Someone who killed Sam. Sam, who wanted nothing more than to protect everyone. I can't imagine who would want him dead.

"I want you all to know how to use a firearm safely and accurately," John says. "So, bright and early tomorrow I'll drive over, and we'll head out in the two trucks. I might have a surprise, too."

CHAPTER 61

We've driven through the surrounding state forest to a clearing. If anyone follows the noise they won't know where we live. Ana complained that we were overreacting, but Penny didn't deign to answer her.

"Okay," John says, his eyes stern. "Rule Number One: Never, ever point a gun at something you don't intend to shoot. Loaded, unloaded, it doesn't matter. Got it?"

He stands in front of Penny, Ana, James and Peter, hands laced behind his back like a drill instructor. The four of them nod and hold their guns gingerly.

"Rule Number Two: Treat every gun like it's loaded.

"Number three: Keep your finger off the trigger until you're firing your weapon.

"Number four: Always clean your gun after use. That way it'll work when you need it. You'll be cleaning your weapons later. Any questions?"

"John, I was looking at my gun, and I didn't see the safety," Penny says.

"Revolvers don't have safeties, at least not the kind you're thinking of." He taps his head. "This, between your ears, is your most important safety. Use it properly, and you can't go wrong."

They face the targets he's strung up. Nelly and I stand behind to help with stances and sighting. On John's word they fire, one by one.

Penny holds the gun out by her side when she's finished. "I just don't like holding it. Or shooting it."

"Okay," John says. He watches her reload. "You don't have to like it. Just be able to aim and hit the target. You need to get comfortable with it. Keep going."

The biggest surprise is Peter. Every bullet hits the target.

"That was great! You hit every one," I say enthusiastically. "You're a natural."

John eyes his target. "You say you've never shot a gun?"

"Nope," Peter says.

John claps him on the shoulder and smiles under his bushy beard. "Well, you did great, son. Keep shooting like that and you'll be a better shot than I am one day."

Peter tries hard to keep his face unmoving, but his eyes light up a little. I'm pleased he might have found something he's good at and grin at him. His mouth turns down.

"I don't see what the big deal is," he says, so only I can hear. "You line up the sights and pull the trigger. Anyone with half a brain could do it."

My smile falls as he moves away to reload. I know he was proud of himself. I saw it. It must be because I said something. I pick up a rifle and imagine pointing it at Peter. But that would break Rule Number One, unless I actually shoot him. It's tempting, but instead I pretend the target is him and hit every time.

John and Nelly take John's truck and head to a nearby farm as the rest of us head home. John will only tell us where they're going, but not what the surprise is, saying he doesn't want us to be disappointed if he comes home empty-handed. Back at the house, James talks excitedly about shooting; he was a decent shot. Even Ana seemed to enjoy it. I think they're feeling they've gained some control over all of this.

And they're not entirely wrong: guns saved our lives yesterday. Quiet weapons would have been better, though. There's no sense in inviting more Lexers to the party if you can avoid it. And even though yesterday showed me that I can hold my own, I don't feel brave or like this situation is any more manageable. I'm pretty sure that whoever said facing your fear makes you braver wasn't facing the prospect of millions of walking dead.

CHAPTER 62

John's surprise arrives in the back of his pickup. It's a little mama goat and her kid, both a rich brown with white markings. She looks at us with liquid eyes, and the baby hides behind her between frantic nursings.

John strokes the doe's head. "I was set to buy her this spring. I missed goat milk, and since the grandkids were coming for most of the summer, I figured they'd like to milk her, too. The kid, a girl, was born a few weeks ago. I thought they'd live in your little barn."

I don't know anything about goats, or even goat milk. But I imagine it's got to be better than the milk that comes powdered in a can, which tastes exactly like dried out milk flavored with metal can. He unties and lifts them out of the truck.

"So, is the farmer you got them from okay?" James asks.

"Yeah, he and his wife and three kids, teenagers, are fine. Last name's Franklin. You might remember him, Cassie. They had a petting zoo years ago. We've got a plan to meet up once a week to check in."

I do remember the petting zoo, how the goats used to crack us up. They would eat anything, including our shoelaces and the ends of my sleeves.

"They're so sweet." I laugh as the kid bravely walks over and nibbles on my sleeve just as I remember. "You'd better show us how to take care of them. I don't know the first thing about goats."

The mama goat is named Flora, and James suggests Fauna for the kid. John also brought back hay, and we put a layer in the little pen in the barn. A couple bags of food are included, but John says that goats will eat anything, and now that spring is here there'll be plenty.

And spring is here. Every day I check the strawberry plants out back, and today I saw a bud, which will turn into a strawberry in June. The fruit trees have exploded with blossoms. My mouth waters at the thought of fresh fruit. The apples from the store and John's root cellar are long gone. It panics me to see how quickly the canned peaches are going; they're the last ones my mom canned. I allow myself one small concession to my insanity and hide a jar in my closet.

Seed trays cover every available window spot. Tiny sprouts poke out of the dark soil. I serenade them daily. I don't know if it helps, but my mom used to sing the plants silly songs to make us laugh. She said it made them grow faster, and her plants were always big and healthy.

John's old farmhouse looks like a greenhouse exploded inside it too, and he fights a constant battle with Laddie's enthusiastic tail toppling them. I keep asking John to move in with us, but he refuses. He says it would be too cramped or that his snoring would drive us all out, but I think he wants to be there in case Jenny arrives. Tom's stationed in Germany, and John hopes he's safe on a base somewhere.

Tonight we're going to run the generator and listen in using our new antenna. We've heard what sounded like a report from New Hampshire, but we keep losing them. James has written down any promising frequencies to try.

We make the trip to John's in the late afternoon. A green mist of new leaves has settled on the trees, and birds call as they swoop across the trail. We settle down in John's big kitchen, where he's set up the radio. There's stew cooking on the cook stove, made with stored carrots and potatoes. It smells delicious.

James turns knobs and dials. The handset doesn't work, but we can still listen in. We lean toward the sound like compass needles pointing north. Ana may be most eager; she's been talking about this all day, thinking it'll prove it's not as bad as we think. She helped me plant seeds under Penny's orders, until I finally told her to find something else to do. Instead of planting them carefully, she jabbed the seeds into the soil like they had done her a personal grievance.

I'm doing my best to be civil to Ana and Peter. I try to talk to them like I do to everyone else, except it's hard when it's obvious they can barely tolerate anything I say. They do the bare minimum and talk incessantly about the first thing they'll do when they get back to New York. They have a game they play, which Nelly and I have named Zombie Zagat. One of them names a restaurant or bar and the other lists the best food, the best drinks and all the annoying people they might know in common who frequented there.

There's some static and a voice, an American voice, leaps out.

"Gotcha!" James yells.

We crowd around him and listen to a man's voice reporting our first live news in weeks. "...157th Air Refueling Wing, which is now located at the Mount Washington Regional Airport in Whitefield, New Hampshire. We ask all citizens to disregard pre-recorded broadcasts that offer Pease Air

National Guard Base at Portsmouth International Airport in Portsmouth, New Hampshire as an official Safe Zone. The base was abandoned due to uncontrollable levels of Bornavirus infection.

"The remaining National Guard has removed itself to the Mount Washington Regional Airport and established a Safe Zone in this area. All uninfected citizens are asked to make their way to this location if they are in need of a Safe Zone. We have been in contact with several other locations that are also listing themselves as Safe Zones in the northeast. These are civilian Safe Zones and are not affiliated with the United States government. We know of no other governmental Safe Zones within a five-hundred-mile radius."

That means every other one has fallen. I grab Nelly's hand when I realize that means almost everyone in the northeast is dead. Maybe some are holed up like us, but how many have enough food that they won't have to leave?

"The following locations have been declared Safe Zones in the northeastern United States: The sister towns of Moose River and Jackman, Maine. These towns are serviced by the Newton Field Airport, if you have access to light aircraft.

"Tolland, Massachusetts has room for three hundred people and can help relocate others to another Safe Zone. Follow signs on Route 57 to barricaded area.

"Kingdom Come Farm in Vermont. Located fifteen miles north of Lowell, Vermont on Kingdom Road. Take 105 north, right at Trunk Road, left onto Kingdom Road."

Nelly's grip tightens like a vise. I look at him, and he shakes his head, but something's going on. The broadcaster lists a couple more Safe Zones and continues.

"There may be other safe areas, but at this time we are in communication with these five Safe Zones. Please make your way to one if you are in need of assistance. Note that all persons will be checked for signs of infection and will be barred from entry if they are infected. All obviously infected will be shot on sight.

"The last contact we had with the United States government was a week ago. They assured us that they expected the situation to last only another few weeks."

Up until now the man's voice has been carefully modulated, but now I hear a crack in it.

"However, we have received reports that infected may remain active for a number of years before finally succumbing. We urge you all to remain vigilant as you make your way to a Safe Zone. This broadcast will be repeated every hour and updated every day at seven p.m. Eastern Standard Time."

There's a pause and then an addition in a soft voice. "Be careful out there. Don't take any chances. Travel armed and light. Move quietly. God bless you all, and God bless America."

The radio goes quiet, and we listen to the hiss that's left behind.

Nelly pulls me by the hand that holds his. "Come with me."

I follow him to the porch. He looks excited; his hair is standing up all over the place, and he runs a hand down his cheeks.

"That farm they named? Kingdom Come." He looks down at me as I nod. "I think, well, I'm pretty sure that it's the name of Adrian's farm. I'm not positive, Cass. I know it was in the Northeast Kingdom of Vermont, but it had a name that had Kingdom in it, too. I could swear it."

There's a rush of air in my ears, and I don't hear what he says next. Of course Adrian is running a Safe Zone. Nelly's work boots shuffle on the wood slats of the porch.

"—don't want you to get too excited. I might be wrong," he finishes.

"Okay," I say, but I'm beaming because I know it's true.

It's just how I pictured. I can see Adrian right now, the way his face looks so stern when he's serious, although his eyes are always warm. He would have seen this all coming; he would have started planning even before we did. And if the farm is anything like how he always dreamed, it's close to self-sufficient.

"You're not listening to a word I say, are you?"

Nelly snaps his fingers by my face, but I'm too far gone. I can feel him out there, just like they say. Adrian is alive.

CHAPTER 63

The mood around the table is much more somber. At first I'm riding on a wave of happiness but soon the excitement fades. Knowing—okay, suspecting—Adrian's safe is enough to make me satisfied for now. But the hope that I can reach him dissipates as we figure out how high the infection rates must be.

Peter and Ana sit, dejected, while they listen to the rest of us crunch numbers and shudder at the thought of what's only miles away. I know Penny is trying not to show it, but Maria weighs heavily on her right now. I just hope she can hold out for as long as it takes.

And it's pretty clear now that that will be longer than any of us thought, which supports what John's buddy said. I don't know how it's possible. People decompose. If they're dead it seems impossible they're not rotting away.

"That's the one thing no one could ever explain in all the zombie stories. And I feel stupid even bringing pop culture up as a frame of reference," James says. "But it was always some theory like the microbes that advance decomposition avoid infected flesh. Every Lexer we've seen looks like they're decomposing, just not fast. So maybe some will last six months. Maybe it also depends on climate. It's possible that in the winter they'll freeze and their muscles won't work in the spring."

"Like meat in the freezer," Nelly says. He holds up a piece of beef he's skewered on his fork. "This beef is muscle, just like us. The cells burst open when it's frozen, right? If that happens, then come spring maybe they wouldn't be able to move. Plus, we could kill them while they're frozen."

Ana lets out a little moan at this and runs into John's living room. Penny goes after her.

"Sorry," James says. "I forget not everyone can take talking about it."

"Well, they're going to have to," I say. I studiously avoid looking at Peter. "You have to know things will never be the same if you listened to what that man said."

John's been silent, leaning back in his chair. Now he gets up to clear the table, but not before I see that his eyes are red. I jump up to help and stand by the sink, where he pretends to be involved in washing dishes.

"I'd bet good money on Jenny," I say.

He squeezes my hand with his soapy one and nods. I would've bet good money on Eric too. But he's not here, and he should have been by now. I try to feel him out there, the way I think I can with Adrian, but all I get is a knot in my stomach.

CHAPTER 64

Everyone loves Flora and Fauna. Their antics as they frolic around never fail to make me smile. I once read that before television people would watch their chickens for entertainment. John's talking about bringing half the chickens to live in our coop, plus some of the ones that will hatch soon. Then we'll have two channels.

We've got no refrigerator, except for what the generator keeps cold at John's, so we store the milk there. The milk is great; it's the getting the milk out that's hard. It takes John five to ten minutes to milk Flora, but it takes us thirty.

It's the third week of May, but the actual date means less than it used to. Our calendar is set to strawberry time, so it's a few weeks until strawberries, and we're counting down the days. We've planted the spinach and other greens. The pea plants have grabbed hold of the trellis with their curly tendrils. I found my mom's garden plans from previous years, complete with her doodles and little asides about each plant. It feels like she stands over my shoulder, directing me in her gentle way.

We've all been assigned chores. The only people who actually need assigning are Peter and Ana, who've been walking around like robots since the first broadcast. We've listened every night since. Kingdom Come Farm is always listed, which means they're still okay. A few more Safe Zones have been added as well. Every night I wait, while my heart pounds, until I hear them say those three words: Kingdom Come Farm. Then I say goodnight to Adrian and congratulate us both on another day survived.

We have no way to communicate out. James says the cord may have a short in it. But we listen. We've picked up other broadcasts. There's a group down in Virginia who say that D.C. is completely destroyed. It was bombed in a final failed attempt to stop the spread.

Every day we hear something new from survivors who have figured out access to radios and antennas. People who want to make sure that they aren't the only ones. There's a man in Kansas who says it's not so bad where he is, now that he's killed most of his neighbors, and that he'd welcome some company. Then he plays the guitar and cries before signing off.

Peter knows that we suspect Adrian is in Vermont, and these last few weeks have convinced me that my happiness conversely affects his. The cheerier I am, the angrier he is. He scowls at me and mutters at everyone except Ana. I know that Peter and Ana never hoped to be living on a farm shoveling goat crap, but it sure as shit beats being dead. And, frankly, I'm so sick of them I could scream.

I'm heading out to the barn to check on the goats and punch a wall after a particularly obnoxious comment from Peter, when Nelly falls into step with me.

"Want to take a walk?" he asks.

"No, I'd really rather pitchfork out goat shit." I turn away mid-step and head for the path.

When we get to the Message Tree, Nelly boosts me onto the wooden platform, the only remaining part of the tree house. We swing our legs and watch chipmunks race around with their tails sticking up like masts.

It's nice to blow off work. During the day we're always busy. John's newest project is digging a trench around the fences we made. It reminds me of how my parents used to catch the slugs in the garden. We would mound up dirt and place a small cup of beer in the center. In a day or two the cup would be full of slimy drowned slugs. But slugs are small. This pest control solution entails digging five feet deep and a few feet wide by hand, which should be finished in about twelve years.

Between the digging and chopping firewood, my arms are much stronger than they were. The next time I need to take out a Lexer, I won't be sore afterward. And I think there will be a next time because we're going to town tomorrow. John's working on a long-handled blade in his shop that might be more useful than a machete.

We move the plants in and out of the sun, water them, and sing to them. Well, Penny and I sing to them. Nelly says we're bananas. We fill the generator and cook food. We clean the chicken coop and milk Flora. But, mainly, we dig. Then, at night, we sit around in the lamplight and talk or read or play Scrabble or Monopoly before heading to bed, where we're so tired we fall asleep mid-speech.

Thinking about games reminds me of Nelly and John's project.

"How's the beer coming?" I ask. "We need a night of debauchery and drinking games."

My dad's brewing ingredients are still around. There are a few dozen bottles in the basement right now, filled, capped, and doing whatever beer does while you're waiting for it. I'm dying for one. Maybe those people who grab the beer first thing in a crisis are on to something.

"We'll know in a few days," Nelly says. "I could really use a night of debauchery. And I'm not looking forward to heading to town."

We need some radio parts, and I want to get some stuff for a project I have in mind. Everyone is going. John has a cockamamie idea that seeing what town is like will get a fire going under Ana and Peter.

"You've been quiet lately," I say. "Why the long face? What'd the world end or something?"

Nelly smiles and lies back on the platform, his face sun-dappled. I sit cross-legged above him and watch him watch the leaves rustle.

"I guess I'm just acclimating," he says. "You know, I think I'm getting used to all of this, and then I'll be doing something mundane like chopping wood, and I think, 'Holy fuck, this is all real.' Like half the time I'm in a dream state or something."

I nod. I do the same thing. Or, sometimes, I'll be digging the ditch or pulling weeds and wonder if Adrian's doing the same thing. Those are the good moments, the ones where I feel a tiny kernel of hope that I'll get to see him again.

Then there are the moments I think of Eric and Rachel, or Maria, and I feel sick and desperately impotent. I can always tell by someone's face when they're thinking of their families. There's hope, then desperation and then finally some mixture of horror and resignation. Peter's the only one whose face remains clear; he has no one to fear for. I can't decide which is worse.

"What about you?" he asks. "How's life as Public Enemy Number One?"

I shrug. "It's great, thanks for asking. I always hoped I would be the one everyone hated."

Nelly turns on his side and props his head on his hand with a wry smile. "*Everyone* doesn't hate you. Peter and Ana have decided to hold you responsible for everything that's befallen the world, that's all." He raises his eyebrows. "I know it bothers you more than you'll say. So, since you're incapable of asking for help, I'll ask you. Do you want me to say something to Peter?"

What I want is for Peter to come around and act sensible because he's a decent human being, not because he's threatened with bodily harm. Making people do something they don't want to do almost always backfires.

"They've been doing their chores," I reply. "So what are you going to do, tell them to be nice, or else? Ana was never very nice to begin with. And Peter, I guess he had his moments, although he was nice to me. How can you force someone not to be selfish?"

I twist one of my braids around my finger. I feel like a terrible person when I do it, but sometimes I daydream that Peter hadn't been in my apartment that night. That he was just another person who was out of reach right now. I don't wish him dead, but wishing he isn't here is so close it makes me feel guilty.

"Well, I guess you can't, Half-pint." Nelly tugs on my other braid and flashes me his big smile. "But I could still beat him up for you. Knock some sense into him."

"You're really dying to punch him, aren't you?" His eyes light up. "Stop being such a guy."

I would love to take him up on his offer, but that would only give Peter more fuel for the fire. He already thinks everyone is against him.

"If only it worked that way, you could've knocked some sense into me two years ago, after I broke up with Adrian. Then I never would've met Peter." I wonder where I would be right now. Probably on a farm in Vermont, just like we'd planned.

"Yeah, but then you'd be off in the country somewhere, painting and living some idyllic farm life, and I'd be a corpse shuffling around New York City."

I ruffle his hair. "You? Never!"

But there's a good chance he's right. He might have gone out in Manhattan that night, without me and James to stop him. He would've ignored the signs until it was too late, like most people did.

He sits up. "Bet you a million bucks you're wrong." He sounds so like a little kid that I wait for his tongue to make an appearance.

He's got on his smile where one corner of his mouth goes up and his eyes go all crinkly. I'm overcome with love for my friend, my would-be protector, the guy who knows when I need a boot in the ass. I'm so glad he's here. I can't regret being the reason he is, even if it means being so far from where I hoped I'd be.

"Well, then, next time you're shaking your head because I'm doing something really stupid, remember my stupidity saved your life once," I say, with a superior look.

His eyes crinkle even more. "Yeah, *once*. Out of how many, a thousand stupid things? Those aren't great odds, darlin'."

Then, always the mature one, I stick my tongue out at him.

CHAPTER 65

"I thought you said you'd never shop at Wal-mart," I tease John, as we near the gigantic cinderblock box.

"I did say 'When Pigs Fly,' " he says. "I figure that's pretty much on par with When Dead People Walk. Plus, I'm not shopping, I'm looting." He smiles at me and resumes scanning the road.

Ana and Peter are in the backseat. Nelly, James and Penny follow in the police truck. The trucks and John's fuel drums are full of gas we siphoned on the way down. Pumping all that took a couple of hours, even with a motorized pump to help. You don't know if a car's gas tank is empty until you try it, so there was a lot of wasted time.

"I do believe it's not looting anymore, since there's no one around to care," I say.

"I suppose you're right."

Cars litter the parking lot, like the occupants got here and made a run for it. The electric eye of the front doors has closed for a long nap, but it'll be easy to enter through the gaping hole in the glass.

"Someone's been here," John says, and we pull up to the doors.

"Obviously," Ana mutters.

She's really itching for some conditioner. Apparently, ours leaves her hair flat. I was so upset to hear the accommodations were lacking.

John hops out of the truck and motions for us. I walk over to the clods of mud he examines. "Shoe treads, still damp but not wet. Sometime in the last twenty-four hours, but not in the last ten or so. We're probably in the clear, but just to be sure we'll be extra cautious. We pair up. One shopper, one watcher. Two of us out here."

He checks our weapons over. We look like a ragtag paramilitary group. James, Penny, and John fit radio earpieces into their ears and test them. A holster, a machete, or both hang off every hip or shoulder. John insists we wear our guns at home so we get used to doing everything while armed. Plus, there's no telling when something may stumble out of the woods.

I've got my trusty revolver on one side of my holster, a nine millimeter on the other and a sharpened machete on my back. Penny slings a rifle over her shoulder and looks nervously through the hole in the glass.

We pound inside the door and call out, our voices echoing through the store. It seems like the best way to find the infected; if you call, they'll come running, or at least lurching. Nothing comes.

John teams up with Peter outside and sends James and me into Health and Beauty. Nelly and Penny will head to Clothing, since digging really does a number on one's wardrobe. Ana stands just inside, so she can help where needed.

We switch on headlamps and flashlights as we duck through the door. The cash register lanes stretch out, dark and vacant. They already look foreign, like some relic of an ancient world. It's quiet and feels empty, in the way that no hairs stand up on the back of my neck. But it smells awful. Something in here is very, very dead. In any other situation that would be reassuring.

We creep farther in. The wide front aisle of the store is in shambles. Boxes of crackers and cereal litter the floor, intermixed with clothes and liquids that have hardened to a brown gel. Penny and Nelly head to the back, crunching on Triscuits and Cheerios. Ana's dark eyes are perfect circles, and her face is pale. She's within eye- and earshot of John, but she's the only one who's alone. She holds her gun in her hand, and her finger tends toward the trigger.

"Ana, watch your finger," I warn. "One yell and we'll be back in ten seconds for you, I promise. It's clear right here. You'll be okay."

She moves her finger, the whites of her eyes shining in the gloom, and nods. "Just hurry up." I'm about to say something reassuring when she continues. "I want my turn to get what I need."

I motion to James and turn away before sighing. "Let's go."

We turn down the main aisle and try to keep our crunching to a minimum. It sounds so loud in the silence. I never realized how much noise there was in the world until it was gone. The metal gates at the pharmacy are bent and twisted. The bottles lay in jumbles and heaps. Entire shelves are bare.

"Bet all the good stuff's gone," James whispers as we walk past.

My jeans stick to my legs with sweat, even though it's not so stuffy in here. My heart beats so loud that I'm almost surprised James hasn't remarked upon it.

I fill the bag slung over my shoulder with latex gloves and assorted supplies while James keeps watch. The decayed smell is worse here, and there are huge dark patches of gunk on the floor. I'm pretty sure they're the color of dried blood, but they look black-brown in the headlamps, whose LED glare makes everything look like a black and white movie.

It looks like Hershey's Syrup; that's what they used to use for blood in old horror films. That must have been one hell of a food fight. I raise my hand to my mouth to stifle the insane laugh that bubbles up.

James looks at me curiously. "What's funny?"

"Absolutely nothing," I say, truthfully. "It's just getting to me."

"It reeks. It's even worse over here." He holds his earpiece. "Let's go see about the automotive section. John says all's still clear but to hurry up."

There's a room that leads to the Garden Center on our left, where they put the seasonal merchandise. The stench here is solid; it fills my mouth and coats my skin with a layer of slime. We gag and breathe through our mouths. But now I can taste it, which is far worse than smelling it. I lean on a shelf and retch, but nothing comes out. When I raise my head, my headlamp illuminates the area.

"Jesus," breathes James.

There must be forty corpses piled there, arms and legs splayed and tangled together, so we can't tell where one ends and another begins. We inch closer, ready to run at any movement. When James clicks on his big flashlight, we see gray skin and open unhealed wounds. Every last body has a head wound; someone has killed all of the Lexers in the store.

"Jesus," James repeats, and then speaks into the radio. "Someone's killed all the infected. We've got a pileup by the Garden Center. We're heading for Automotive. Five minutes, tops."

I'm grateful that someone has done this. I feel tremendous relief that other people are out here fighting, surviving. I wish they were here right now. I notice two bodies set apart and motion for the flashlight.

Two girls, both no more than eighteen, are half-propped against the shelves. One wears only a ripped and stained tank top, the other still has on a jacket. They don't have that gray, coagulated look the other bodies have.

Their thighs and faces are bruised and swollen, but I can tell they haven't been dead very long. I wonder if they were infected, recently bitten, but I dismiss that thought immediately. One sits on a carpet of blood, shot through the chest, not the head. The other girl appears to have been strangled with the rope that's still knotted around her neck. And they're the only ones with flies circling and landing on them like some sort of insect airport. Suddenly, I'm very thankful that whoever killed these infected isn't here, because they must have done this, too.

I want to drag them somewhere, away from the pile of infected. Cover their naked bodies and preserve some of their dignity. But there's no time to do things like that now. A little flame of anger flares in my belly and spreads. They survived this far, only to be raped and murdered by some inhuman son of a bitch. Like we haven't got enough inhumanity running around.

"C'mon." James tugs my sleeve. "Nel and Penny are done. They're waiting for us."

We find driving gloves in the automotive section and head out. Ana, Penny and Nelly wait for us at the hole in the glass, their bags full. I gulp in the fresh air outside and fish around in my pocket for something, anything, to get the taste out of my mouth. I find lint-covered peppermint Life Savers and Adrian's ring. I give the ring a rub and pop a candy in my mouth, offering one to James, who looks like he needs it as badly as I do. He accepts it gratefully and spits out the swig of water he was swishing around.

John's gotten the gist of what we saw, and he wastes no time. "Everyone in the trucks, let's go."

His eyes haven't stopped moving and his mouth is tight. We head back onto the road. At the crest of the hill, I turn back and see a beat-up red van and a sports car pulling into the Wal-Mart parking lot.

"That might be them," I say, shaking at how close we came to being confronted with people who rape and kill young girls.

"I had a feeling," John says.

CHAPTER 66

"A na actually had the nerve to complain that everybody but her 'got something' at the store. Like we all got perfume and boxes of candy and she got nothing," Penny says. She looks up from where she's cutting pieces out of my mom's leather coat on the back deck and makes a face.

"Your sister..." I leave the rest unsaid.

"I know, I know. I've tried to talk to her. She's being so obstinate. My mom always said Ana's picture would be next to obstinate in the dictionary."

I can think of a few other words Ana's picture might be next to.

Penny sees my face and cracks up. "Yes, obstinate doesn't begin to cover it. I don't know what to do. Sometimes I can't blame her. This whole thing is terrifying and surreal. But as an excuse, I think that's stretched pretty thin. We all have to do our part, you know?"

"Yeah." I thread the needle of the sewing machine on the table. "I don't know, Pen. You know, Ana's like my little sister, or *was*, when she would actually say more than two words to me. But she and Peter have formed their own little clique of denial or something."

I put strips of elastic and leather under the machine needle and spin the knob on the side with my hand. It's not as fast as a real foot treadle, but it does the job of sewing neater, stronger and faster than I can without electricity.

"So what exactly are we making, anyway?" Penny asks.

"Kind of like armor. I'm attaching it to the gloves. It'll strap over our arms to protect us from scratches or bites. It should protect us from infected blood. Lexers have regular teeth like us. They can't rip through leather."

I think of the horror I felt after I killed that one with the machete, how afraid I was that the virus had made its way into my bloodstream. I'm not usually obsessed with germs, but I've got a raging case of OCD about this.

"Okay. This is one of those surreal moments I was just talking about. I'm sitting in the sunshine in the woods making zombie armor."

James steps through the sliding glass doors to the deck. "Don't you know you aren't supposed to call them *zombies*?" He wags a finger at her. "Every book or movie or whatever, they always call them something else."

"You know," I say, "preppers used to call the people who weren't prepared zombies, too. The people who would want your supplies after everything went south. But you're right, they never say *zombies*. Weird."

Seeing those girls at Wal-Mart made it clear that there really are two types of zombies to fear.

"We call them something else, too," Penny says. "What have we got? Lexers, Biters, Walkers, Infected, Undead, Creepers, Stumblers, Zeds. I'm sure there's others we haven't heard or thought of yet. Plus, unfortunately, this is not a movie."

"Too true," he says, then sits and stretches out his long legs. He's filled out a little bit from the work around here, and his face has changed from pasty to ivory, but he'll always be a string bean.

He rubs the leather on the table between his fingers. "Armor, huh? It's a good idea. We don't know how contagious it is. If it can be transmitted by just a scratch, then we need to be scratch-proof. Full-length leather gloves, or how about neoprene gloves? They'd be great."

"Tell me about it," I say. "But where does one buy neoprene gloves in upstate New York? If we happen upon a sporting goods store, we have to go in and check." I look up from the sewing machine. "I have to say, I'm pretty disappointed my parents didn't stock up on them. How could they not have planned for this exact contingency?"

"Everyone should be ready for the *zombie* apocalypse." James smiles at Penny as he says the word. "And neoprene gloves are an absolute must. At the very least the oceans could have risen until you had oceanfront property and needed them for surfing."

"Two very, very real possibilities," Penny jokes. "Well, actually, I guess only one is still far-fetched. Like I said, it's surreal. My brain can't even keep up."

I pull the first finished glove on and make sure the elastic is snug. The long strips of leather attach to the glove at my wrist and rise up to my elbow. They'll be hot to wear, but I can move just fine. I practice drawing my revolver out of my holster and point it into the woods.

"Hey," James says. "They're actually pretty bad-ass. You look like a superhero. I totally want to play with my pair."

I put my hands on my hips and gaze into the distance, superhero style. "Farmer by day, zombie-killer by night." I point my gloved finger at him. "I'll make yours next."

"Cool."

Penny hands him the paper pattern and leather. "Here, *papi*, make yourself useful."

"Si, *mami*," he says in the whitest Spanish accent imaginable.

Penny and I laugh, and he picks up a pair of scissors and starts to cut, mouth quirking. James's picture should be next to *useful* in the dictionary.

CHAPTER 67

I've finished making everyone their armor, and we're heading out to practice shooting with it on. A jungle of plants sits on the deck and porch. The tiny seedlings are fast becoming food that will go in the ground in a day or two. Right now they're getting used to the outside air during the day, so they'll be strong enough to live outside full time. Ana sets down the watering can and heads to the truck. I think she doesn't mind the garden work; I'm pretty sure I saw her talking to the plants one day, not that she'd ever cop to it.

The screen door slams as Peter comes out onto the deck. He's got on work boots and one of his two pairs of jeans that came with him from the city. They may have been insanely overpriced, but I have to say they've held up well; my cheaper jeans have aged three years. Maybe that can be a selling point if the world ever goes back to the way it was. They can think up some sort of post-apocalyptic tagline for their four hundred dollar jeans.

There's something I don't miss: being inundated with advertisements designed to make you want more, to never be satisfied. Not that I want it this way, either. But there's a part of me that loves this life; it's what I always wanted. I love being in the woods, growing food, making the things we need instead of buying them. I just wish the things we needed weren't sharpened machetes and zombie armor.

Peter avoids my eyes as he comes down the steps. His hair's gotten longer and he's scruffier, but it suits him. He was always too smooth, too groomed. He checks his holster and hooks his fingers under his rifle strap.

We were never soul mates, but we could have fun together. Sometimes, like that night we met, we really talked. Once, after a few too many drinks, he complained about having to go to some fancy party filled with fake people. The society pages would be full of the pictures. I remember when he told me that there were still society pages; I thought they had died out sometime around the end of prohibition. I wouldn't believe him until he showed me, and then I had laughed my ass off at the names and captions, while he watched me with a half smile and glinting eyes.

"So don't go. Come to my house and watch chick flicks," I joked. "Why do you need to go?"

He knew I wouldn't go anywhere near this social engagement and had quit asking me weeks ago. His eyelids were at half mast, and his head rested on the back of his couch.

"If you don't make an appearance then they forget about you, Cassie," he whispered. "You wouldn't understand. I don't want to be invisible."

When he closed his eyes he looked so vulnerable. I reached out and ran my finger over the spiky shadows his eyelashes made on his cheeks. "Peter, you are not forgettable. They don't make you visible. I see you."

But he kept his eyes closed and his breathing became regular. I wasn't sure if he had even heard. The next morning I sat crossed-legged on his couch with my cup of tea, while he sat in the big chair and looked out the floor-to-ceiling windows of his inherited pre-war apartment. I smiled at him, thinking maybe we had reached somewhere different the night before.

"I can't remember a thing about last night. I must have passed out," he said, and glanced away quickly. But I thought I saw the lie in his eyes, the fear that he had said too much and was afraid I knew.

"Oh, you fell asleep, and I got you into bed." But I tried one more time. "Are you sure you have to go to that party tonight?"

His face was casual, but his eyes were sad, maybe. It was hard to tell in the sunlight. "Yes, I have to go."

This Peter coming down the steps looks different but acts the same. Maybe it's that there's no one here to make him feel visible. Maybe that's why he struggles against all of this. Maybe the reason he dislikes me so much is that I know that about him.

He blows past me and hops in the front of the SUV. He gets shotgun privileges now, too, since he's such a good shot. I get in John's pickup. All dime store psychoanalysis aside, Peter's acting like a jerk. And to paraphrase what someone once said: When someone shows you who they really are, believe them. And those moments, the ones I thought were the real Peter, were too few and far between to count.

CHAPTER 68

We've blown as much ammunition as is wise, even though between my dad and John's stores it seems like we could take over a small country. John asks Ana for one more round before we finish up. He's seen why some of her shots are going wild.

Ana puts her gun back in the hip holster and crosses her arms. "No, I'm tired and I don't want to shoot anymore."

"I know you must be tired, but we don't get to do this often, Ana," John says. "So it's best to get it done now. Then we'll get out of here."

He puts out a hand for her pistol, but she has on the same pout as when she was ten and told it was time for bed. She throws up her hands and sits down on a rock. "No! I'm done."

Penny kneels to talk to her, but Ana turns her head away. "I don't want to hear it," she says. "I don't want to shoot anymore. I don't want to do this anymore. I just want things to go back to the way they were. I'm not doing all of this anymore."

This has got to stop. It's one thing if she wants to be a baby about helping around the house. It's quite another when she won't learn to protect herself. That makes her dangerous to be around when she's the one watching your back. I'm sick of everyone mollycoddling her. It's time for Ana and Peter to grow the hell up.

"Ana, things aren't the way they were. They're not going to be," I say, "at least for a long time."

Peter speaks up. "Leave her alone. Not everyone is living out some Laura Ingalls fantasy."

It stings partly because it's true. And because he knows me and is using that knowledge to hurt me, and I hate that he knows me well enough to do that. But mostly it stings because if he really believes that, then what kind of person must he think I am?

"So I like gardening and sewing and canning, Peter. And that makes me happy to be living like this?"

His eyes are cruel, the eyes of a stranger, as he shrugs. I can see how much he dislikes me at this moment, and it hurts my feelings, more than I want to admit.

"I'm just saying that some of us want things to return to normal. That we're hoping they will soon. That it's not crazy to think they might. You're just a bit too happy to be doing all of this, like you've been waiting for it."

He's such an asshole. And I want to scream that it *is* crazy to think things might return to normal soon. It's batshit crazy. My face is hot and my hands tremble. "Oh, you've got me pegged, Peter. Except never once in my fantasy did I wish for two spoiled brats to be constantly snickering behind my back. Sorry that I don't mope around and act like every little fucking thing I have to do is a terrible burden."

Ana narrows her eyes at this, but I don't care anymore; it's the truth, and it's time someone said it.

"Have you ever stopped to think that I'm worried sick about Eric? That my brother is somewhere out there?" My voice rises. I look at Ana. "And Maria? Do you really think that I would want them in harm's way?"

The traitorous tears well up in my eyes. No one takes a crying mad person seriously, and it's so frustrating that my anger is linked to my tear ducts. I think of something mean to say and, instead of holding back the way I normally would, I say it. That's what Peter does. "Maybe you do think that. Maybe you can't remember what it's like to have people you love. People who love *you*."

I'm glad when he flinches. I want to hurt him. I may as well treat him like the person he's accusing me of being.

He recovers from my dig and his eyes go dark. "Well, at least I'm not pining after someone who doesn't love me anymore."

I'm confused for a second, until I realize he means Adrian. Penny's mouth drops open. I step forward with my hand raised.

Nelly puts an arm around me. "Okay. That's enough. Peter, you need to stop. Now."

Nelly's face is expressionless, except for his eyes, which are icy. Peter looks triumphant until he catches sight of Nelly's other hand, tightened into a fist. He takes a step back.

"You two." I point at them with a shaking finger. "You may not *want* to believe things are different. But they are. They are, and if you act like they're not, we're all going to end up dead."

CHAPTER 69

J ohn has timed our target practice for a day when he's supposed to check in with Farmer Franklin. I'm glad when he insists Nelly and I come. I don't want to go back to the house and live in those cold freezes and awkward silences you have when you're fighting with people, when you've said too much.

I already feel bad about what I said to Peter, about no one loving him. It was an awful thing to say, and I deserved what I got back. I sit in the backseat ruffling Laddie's fur, and I replay what Peter said. He's probably right. After all, it's been two years, enough time for Adrian to have moved on.

"He's not right, you know," Nelly says over the crunch of the tires on the dirt road.

We're heading down to where the valley opens up and farms are tucked away in the thick stands of trees. When I don't answer, he turns back to watch me. I shrug and give a weak smile.

"He knew exactly what to say, what would hurt you the most. So he said it," he says.

"So did I. But that doesn't mean he's wrong."

"Look at me." I tear my eyes away from Laddie and look into his earnest face. "He's wrong."

I want to believe him, but he can't know that for sure. I shrug again. The day, which had seemed so bright, now feels like I'm looking at it through a gray haze. My stomach feels heavy.

Peter's right about me living in a fantasy world, but he had the fantasy wrong. Like a little girl who believes in fairies and unicorns, I'd been thinking that Adrian and I would live happily ever after. That belief had given me a tiny bit of hope that this could end well, if we survive long enough. But now I see how foolish I've been. I have to focus on the here and now, not on someone who's probably thinking of me as someone he once loved. If he's even thinking of me at all.

John turns down a long driveway. "This is the place. Richard, that's Farmer Franklin to you, said he'd have some more hay and feed for the goats. That's funny, the gate's open."

We head through the gate to a yellow farmhouse with a porch out front and a wreath on the door. A terracotta planter has tumbled over and spilled dirt down the steps. The wood frame behind the screen door is splintered. Broken glass sparkles in the grass. There's a barn and yard for the animals to graze, but it's empty and that gate is open, too.

"This doesn't look good," John says. He drives around the house over the bumpy grass, but it's empty except for the Franklins' cars. "I've got to check it out."

"You're not going in by yourself," Nelly says.

"Okay, we go in slow. I'll take the main hallway down the house to the kitchen. Nelly, you'll cover the left, that's the family room. Cassie, you've got the right. Dining room with separate entrance into the kitchen at the back."

We nod and open our doors. Laddie stops at the bottom of the steps and whines deep in his throat. John puts a hand on his head. "Heel, boy. Stay."

Laddie watches us mount the steps with worried eyes. John uses his back to hold open the screen and motions us behind him. The smell of decomposition, all too familiar now, wafts out. I hear the distant cluck of the Franklin's chickens, but the house is completely silent.

"Richard?" John yells. We stand and wait, but nothing greets us.

There's a small foyer with a shoe bench, but most people around here reserve the messy entries for the mudroom, usually off the kitchen. That's where you'll find the rubber boots and jackets with hay still stuck to them. I move into the dining room. The painted wood floors creak under my feet as I pass the dining table and chairs.

There are a few empty liquor bottles on the kitchen counters, along with plates of congealed and moldy food. A sun porch runs along the back of the house, but a peek out the door tells me it's empty.

"Cassie." John comes into the kitchen from the hall entrance. "We've found them. Some of them, at least."

I follow him into the living room. The two rooms on this side are furnished with couches, an area rug, and a computer desk. A television hangs on the wall, alongside photos and paintings. It's just the kind of comfortable place where you can put up your feet and get into a movie.

Or it was, because now the colorful throw pillows are scattered and Mom and Dad Franklin sit in two kitchen chairs, dead for many days. The ropes that held them fast while they were alive have sunk into their bloated tissue, but I can see where they come out of flesh and tie underneath. What appears to have been a teenage boy is face-down and splayed on the oak floor, like he was running when he died. The bodies look as if they're being eaten from the inside out, and in places the skin has sloughed off in sheets.

It strikes me that every time I think I've seen something truly awful, I come upon a new horror, something I never even considered. I hold the bandanna I've taken to carrying to my face and breathe. They're so putrefied that it's impossible to see how they were murdered, but it's obvious they were.

"They have two girls. Let's check upstairs," John says.

The upstairs is empty, except where someone rooted through the drawers and didn't replace the contents. On the way down I notice the staircase is lined with photographs, starting with a pudgy blond baby and ending with a family photo, taken at Disneyworld and foil embossed with last year's date. I stare at it until I'm sure.

"Those girls, the ones in Wal-Mart?" I ask. John and Nelly stand at the base of the steps and nod. "One of them was her."

I point at the daughter with long blond hair and straight white teeth. The whole family stands, arms around each other, having the time of their lives.

"How about the other one?" John asks.

I'm usually good with faces, but she had been strangled and her face was too blotchy to see clearly in the dim light. In the picture she's laughing and looking up at her dad, who has on mouse ears and looks so incredibly goofy you really can't blame her.

"She had curly hair, just like her. But I can't say for sure."

John's face is stormy; I don't know that I've ever seen him look like this. His brows meet over his eyes and a muscle flickers in his jaw.

"Let's go," he says. "Obviously someone around here is very dangerous. They don't know about us, and I want it kept that way."

Outside, John opens the chicken coop. We don't spare the time to figure out a way to bring them home, but maybe they'll survive free-range for a while. We kick up dust as we head back down the long driveway, and when it clears I see them pecking around in the grass, enjoying their freedom.

CHAPTER 70

Nelly leans back on the couch with his beer. "This is nice." He takes a swig and makes a face.

"You must mean the company, not the beer," Penny says.

Ana and Peter are sleeping at John's house tonight. He promised them a movie during his few generator hours. I'm sure they're as happy to be there as I am to have them there. After we listened to the nightly radio update, the four of us left. The radio said the same things, but when they mentioned Kingdom Come Farm, I didn't feel that sense of well-being. It just reminded me of how idiotic I am.

Penny holds out her bottle. James, Nelly and I clink our bottles on hers and sip. I shiver when the bitter brew goes down, but it's better than nothing.

"Is it supposed to taste like this?" I ask.

Nelly shakes his head ruefully. "Definitely not. I think I know what we did wrong for next time, though."

I upend the bottle and gulp. I'll never get shitfaced if I don't get serious about drinking. And I'm serious about it tonight. I want this day to be over, and getting drunk and passing out seems like the only way I'll fall asleep. The last drop of beer swallowed, I unscrunch my eyes to find the three of them staring at me.

"That sure cleanses the palate," I say. I wipe my mouth with the back of my hand and reach for another.

"More like destroys the palate," James says. He takes a few gulps. "You know, though, the more you drink, the better it gets."

I nod but don't reply because I'm guzzling the next beer. Nelly holds his bottle in his lap. I wave my hand at him. "C'mon, Nels. Drink up."

He and Penny exchange a glance before he looks at me from under his furrowed brow. Penny's mouth is twisted to the side.

I look from one to the other. "What?"

"Don't forget watch tonight," Nelly reminds me.

We'd been getting lax about it, but the Franklins were dressed in their pajamas, after all. The radios work between our houses, and they'll be on all night.

"I have last watch. By then I'll be fine." I shrug and change the subject. "You know what we need? Music. It's weird to sit around drinking without music."

Nelly looks like he wants to say more, but he drops it, much to my relief. If I have to talk about Adrian or think about him for one extra second, I'll scream.

"Yeah," he says dreamily. "What I wouldn't give to plug in my iPod and listen to a whole playlist."

"I'm just tired of having the most ridiculous songs on Earth in my head," says Penny, who walks around singing jingles and TV theme songs half the time.

We all do. I have no idea why the theme song to *The Golden Girls* has taken up residence in my head, but it seems to be what happens when you're denied any other music.

"There's a windup record player in the basement," I say. "But it only plays seventy-eights. My dad had plans to rig it so it would play all his forty-five records, too. There are hundreds."

I jump up and slam my empty bottle down, almost knocking over the oil lamp on the coffee table, which Penny steadies. "Let's find it! C'mon, James."

I know I'm manic, but I need to do something. I grab a third beer and head for the basement. James follows with a lantern. I see the big wooden box on a shelf in the far corner of the basement.

"Here it is." I pull it out and point to the numerous boxes of records above it. "I'll grab the 78s."

Back upstairs, we unlatch the box and place a record on it. A grinding noise comes from somewhere inside, but the record won't spin.

James inspects it. "I might be able to get it working if I open it, but I'd need better light."

Our nights are dark, the way they were before electric light was common. Our lamps cast enough light to read, but not enough to do tasks that require we see tiny parts. And we don't waste batteries for things that can wait until daylight. I sigh and finish my beer. My nose is numb, a sure sign I'm getting drunk.

"I just wanted a dance party," I say to Penny. She pushes her glasses up and smiles sympathetically. "A stupid, measly little dance party."

I know I sound whiny, but if I can't have the big things, then I want a small one. I crack open a fourth beer.

"Cass and I used to have dance parties from when we were little up until, well, now," Penny explains to James. She grins at me and holds up her bottle.

"Long live dance parties!" I yell.

I crash my bottle against Penny's and lick the splattered foam off my hand. I drink, and now this beer's half empty. That's how I'll see things from now on, I decide: as half empty instead of half full.

"Viva la dance party!" she yells back.

"Oh, Lordy," Nelly says.

Our giggles turn into guffaws, but then my guffaws turn into a sob.

Nelly looks at me with concern.

"Don't," I say, and wipe away the tear that's escaped. I don't want anyone pitying me, to acknowledge how weak I've been. "Please. I've had my one crack-up, remember? I'm fine. Can't we just drink and have fun?"

He looks like he's going to say more, and I brace myself, but he gives in. "Yeah. I think that can be arranged."

He guzzles his bottle as Penny and I cheer him on.

CHAPTER 71

"You're on," James whispers.

I wipe the crust out of my eyes and sit on the edge of my bed. "I'm up. You can go to sleep."

The fire is still going and the living room is warm. I pour a cup of tea and sit at the table. I feel a little better than I did. I wouldn't recommend drinking as a regular problem-solver, but it helped; my feelings aren't as raw as they were. Although when I think about how I believed I could find Adrian and he would want nothing more than to pick up where we left off, my entire body gets hot with embarrassment. I'm such a fool. It makes me angry that everyone knows. And I'm sure Peter is gloating that he's right, that he's exposed me.

I think I see something at the window and freeze, ready to sound the alarm, until I realize it's my reflection. It feels like the night holds only murderers and rapists and walking dead. I'm afraid to look at the windows for fear that a ghostly white face will suddenly appear, bent on my destruction. It's not necessarily a new fear; I've been scaring myself like this since I was little. The only difference is that now it's not only within the realm of possibility, but there's also pretty much a guarantee it will happen eventually.

I decide to make bread instead of sitting here alternately scaring and berating myself. I love making bread by hand, although when my arms are tired from kneading I think longingly of my mother's beloved electric mixer with the dough hook attachment.

I take out the flour, yeast and salt, and measure the quantities I know by heart. I drop the dough on the wooden counter in a puff of flour. I fold it over and punch it, then fold it again, letting myself think only of how it feels under my hands, how it turns from clumpy and sticky to smooth and elastic. I put it in a bowl by the stove to rise and rinse my hands.

I want to call over to John's on the radio, but there's a one out of three chance I'll get someone I want to talk to, so I dismiss that thought. I feel so alone. We're separated from the rest of our families, from the rest of the planet, really. There are others out there, obviously—we hear them on the radio every night—but we may never see anyone else. We may struggle on here and then end up like the Franklins, and no one will ever know how hard we tried.

I hear a noise outside and jump up, hand on the radio, but I recognize the *tick-tacking* of Laddie's claws on the porch. He wags his tail and gobbles his treat happily when I let him inside. He knows I'm a sucker for the pathetic I-need-a-doggy-treat face he's perfected. He climbs up next to me on the couch and nestles his body along my legs as I stroke his head. Now I'm not as scared, since Laddie will alert me to anything in the woods way before it can get to the window. We sit in silence for a while.

"You're a good old boy," I tell him. His tail flops twice. "It must be nice, being a dog, huh? You don't have all these issues with people. You just like them or you don't." He looks into my eyes like he understands. I scratch behind his ears. "And everyone likes you. How could they not? 'Cause you're so handsome. You're the handsomest dog in the world. Yes you are, you puppy-dog. Yes—"

Nelly interrupts my silly baby voice. "You know, there are humans around here you could talk to."

I don't turn around, but I can hear the smile in his voice. "I prefer dog therapy."

He sinks into the chair across from me and yawns. "Of course you do."

The wind-up clock on the mantel reads five a.m.

"What are you doing up? Go back and get some sleep."

"I couldn't go back to sleep," he says, annoyed and bleary-eyed. "It would appear I've gotten used to having company in my bed. Of course, it's completely the wrong kind of company, but I keep waking up and looking for your blanket-stealing lump."

I've been teasing Nelly that he likes sharing the bed but won't admit it. I clap and laugh. "I knew it!"

He pretends not to hear me. I grab the bread bowl while he puts on coffee. The dough has risen, so I punch it down, turn it out and shape it into three round loaves. I place them on the wooden peel to rise and let the oven warm.

"Mmm, bread," Nelly says. He bends over and inhales the yeasty scent. I lean on the counter and try not to smile. "Yeah, yeah, I'm secretly in love with you. I can't live without you. Won't you please marry me, fair maiden?"

He falls to one knee, hand outstretched.

"Oh, shut up," I say, and smack his hand. "You're worse than me. Why can't you admit you need some comfort? At least I can admit to that."

He gets up. "You're a girl. And you suck at admitting it, too."

We turn as John bursts in the front door, still in his pajamas. "Peter and Ana are gone. They took my truck and left a note saying they were going to town."

CHAPTER 72

When Penny raises her head from her hands, her normally placid expression is tight and drawn. The first few shafts of sunlight fall through the window and illuminate every line of worry in her face. She looks old enough to be her mother at this moment, thanks to Ana.

"I'm so sorry, you guys," she says. "I know Ana's selfish, but I didn't think she could be so dumb. What were they thinking?"

"You're not responsible for her actions," John reminds her. He sits at the dining table and shakes his head. "I had a talk with them last night. I told them we weren't going to town for a while. That it was too dangerous. Ana was upset and complained that she was always the last one to get what she needed. But I thought they understood."

"When did they leave?" James asks. He grabs Penny's hand and squeezes.

John shrugs. "At least an hour ago. They were supposed to wake me at four. I woke up and the house was empty. Laddie must've come over here when they left. They're already past town, if that's the case."

"We'll go after them," James says to Penny. "We'll get them back here."

She shakes her head. "We don't know where they've gone. If we start driving around we might attract attention. I won't have that hanging over my head. Or have any of you hurt because of her." Her voice rises. "I can't believe her! I could kill her right now!"

Nelly stands by the front door and watches the driveway. "Let's give them a few hours. Chances are they'll be fine. If they aren't back soon, we'll go looking."

John heads to his house to change. I put the bread in the oven, but when it comes out, perfectly crackled and brown, none of us has an appetite. The rustling treetops sound like car tires on the road, and we all keep stopping, heads cocked, thinking they've returned. But they don't come.

Finally, we put on our armor and holsters. We're silent as we turn out of the driveway onto the dirt road. I'm angry as hell, but I'm also worried. I really do love Ana, and even Peter, in a way. I want them here, even if I don't want them near me, because there's nowhere else that's safe.

When we hit the final curve before the paved road, we almost run into John's truck. Ana and Peter are turned in their seats, watching the main road. John skids to a stop beside them. With a face carved of granite, he takes one thick finger and points it at them, then back up the road toward home. Ana and Peter look like teenagers who've been caught breaking curfew.

Penny leaps out at the house and waits until Ana emerges, looking guilty and afraid.

"I'm sorry," Ana says.

Penny ignores the apology. "I don't even know what to say to you, Ana! I've put up with your bullshit my whole life, first because Papa died and then because, well," she makes quotes with her fingers in the air, "*that's just Ana*. But I'm telling you right now, this has to stop. Your bullshit has to end right now. Today. Do you understand me?"

Ana's eyes are huge and black. She stares at Penny.

"That was not a rhetorical question!" Penny yells, her cheeks red with rage. "No more! Do. You. Understand. Me?"

"Yes," Ana whispers.

She walks past Penny into the house. But Penny's not done yet. She wheels around to where Peter stands, having the good grace to look ashamed. He watches Penny steadily, like he's waiting for his penance.

"I'm not saying it was your idea. I know my sister well enough to know she always gets what she wants. But don't you ever be the one to help her do anything like that again."

Peter nods once and watches his feet as he walks inside. He's always so unflappable, but now he looks shaken and distressed. If he were anyone else I might feel sorry for him.

***

In the evening I head out to the barn to milk Flora. Milking has its own peaceful rhythm once you get the hang of it. I love the smell of the hay and the sunshine that falls in stripes through the slats in the boards, making the goats look like tiny zebras. I'm almost done when I hear Ana and Peter arguing on the far side of the barn. They don't know I'm here, outside in the sheltered area, where I like to do the milking.

Peter's voice is firm. "We have to tell them, Ana. It's not something we can hide. What if they did see where we went?"

"We watched," Ana says. "No one came past. I'm sure it's fine. We don't know for sure if they're even the ones. Do you know how angry they'll be if they find out? My sister's about to kill me as it is."

I pick up the milk pail and creep to the doorway.

"Ana, the sheriff said he was trouble. We can't take the chance."

She's got on her fighting stance. Ana won't back down until Peter agrees. I clear my throat. Ana spins around in surprise, eyes narrowed.

"Milking," I say, and hold up the pail. The milk sloshes from the rage I try to keep in check. I can't believe they'd try to keep something this important from us. "You two need to tell us what happened."

CHAPTER 73

They'd said that the trip to town was uneventful and the stores were empty. We thought that was the end of it, at least as far as danger goes. But it turns out they ran into people.

"We didn't go to Wal-Mart, but there's that town on the other side." Peter looks like he's forcing the words out. He stands in the living room and stares out the window. "We wanted to see what was there. There was a beauty salon. We waited and when we saw nothing we went inside."

Well, I guess Ana got her conditioner. Is there a more ludicrous reason to be willing to die? But, of course, they hadn't been thinking like that. They'd been thumbing their noses at us, showing us that no one was going to tell them what they could and couldn't do.

"We'd just gotten back in the truck when a van pulled up alongside. There were two guys in it. The guy in the passenger's seat was at the roadblock in Bellville. The shorter one."

Mean Dog. Neil Curtis. I say his name aloud and John nods.

"There was some trouble a few years back with Neil and an assault on a woman. I don't know all the details, except that Sam tried real hard but could never get anything concrete on him. Was it a red van?"

The red van that turned into Wal-Mart as we left.

Peter nods. "They asked us where we were headed, and I tried to be vague, like we were just passing through, but then he spotted Ana. He said he remembered us, that we'd been heading north. We said we had been, but we were moving on. There was nothing here for us."

He glances at me when he says this. I keep my eyes on the bookshelves my mom built and read the book titles over and over, repeating them in my head instead of screaming. They didn't just run into people, they ran into murderers.

"It looked like he believed us. He asked us where our gear was. We said we were picking it up as we went along. He told us to go by the Wal-Mart if we didn't mind backtracking. Said it was safe in there, that the Biters were all dead. He offered to take us, since he knew the layout and it was dark inside. We said thanks, but we needed to go. They watched us the whole way out. We drove the long way around so it didn't look like we were coming back here. Then we sat and waited to see if they followed, but they never passed by on the main road."

He says this like we should congratulate him on his excellent spy technique.

"It doesn't matter," I say, my voice barely controlled. He looks away, tight-lipped. "He knows my name from the roadblock, and now he remembers us. All he has to do is look in a phone book and find Forrest. Or find it in the records at town hall, or any number of places."

"That's if he remembers your name," Ana argues. "How many people do you think tried to come through? Why would he remember yours?"

She waves her hands in a crazy fashion, like it's been such a whirlwind of roadblock activity, who could remember anyone?

Nelly points at me, Ana and Penny. "Because of all of you. A man who rapes and murders teenagers, probably killed the sheriff and maybe blew up the school, is going to remember three pretty girls who might be alive and well."

John sits with one fist extended on the table in front of him, nostrils flared. "There's a certain kind of man who gets pleasure out of killing. Some join the Army to kill legally. Some are just straightforward murderers. And a few end up with an opportunity, whether it's here or the Sudan, to give in to their basest desires.

"Neil Curtis strikes me as that kind of man. He's not going to give up, not when he's found something he wants and there's no one to stop him. He'll take time to work it all out and then they'll come. But we'll be ready for him."

It must be like living in the Midwest and being told a tornado is coming straight for your town. A tornado that's just cut a mile-wide swath through three previous towns. It's too late to run. Besides, there's nowhere to run to. So you prepare the best you can and hope it doesn't rip everything you know and love out from under you.

***

The next day we plant the vegetables. Two of us act as sentries, and the rest lower the tiny plants into the soft black soil in predetermined sections. Tomatoes, beans, melons, everything has a place. Every crack in the woods startles us, and we jump up constantly until John comes over from his post.

"It's under control," he says, his voice firm. "I don't think they'll come in daylight, anyway. They'll wait for dark."

Summer is here, I can feel it in the strength of the sun on my back. The grass in the yard is long and soft under my bare feet. Adrian used to say I had hooves instead of feet, because the minute it's warm enough I cast off my shoes and run barefoot over any terrain. My feet hate to be cooped up.

It takes all day, but the plants are in and watered. After dinner we sit in the lamplight, waiting, watching and talking quietly until it's time for bed.

The next day is another glorious one, followed by another. John has us doing small things around the house that might give us an advantage if— *when*—they come. Nelly and I take turns sleeping out in the barn with John, and I'm exhausted and itchy from sleeping on hay.

Peter and Ana have been working hard. We're all angry, but I sense a lessening in everyone else's ire. Not mine. This is the only safe place we have, and now it feels as dangerous as anywhere else. This house was always my safe haven, and they've taken that away from me.

"Maybe they're not coming," Penny says on the fourth day, the relief evident in her voice. She looks at John hopefully.

"No." He cocks his head like he can hear them. "I think they'll come tonight."

CHAPTER 74

A short bark wakes me from my light sleep. It comes from inside the house and is followed by Nelly's voice on the radio.

"They're here."

There's an incredible amount of tension in those two words. I throw back my blanket, instantly alert, and creep to the barn door next to John. The gunmetal feels slimy in my slick hand. It's still dark, but the moon is low.

"Let them show themselves," he says.

He holds a rifle with a scope in his arms. He wants us to see what our intruders' plan is before he does anything. He hands me the other rifle. Rifles are better for distance shooting. I re-holster my pistol.

"Four men so far," Nelly whispers over the radio, as John fits the earpiece in. "Two just went around back."

The moonlight is bright enough to see the two men make their way around opposite sides of the house. One edges onto the deck, while the other slips into the bushes.

"Lights," John commands into the radio, as he sinks to one knee.

The solar spotlight on the deck flares to life and illuminates a figure lifting a crowbar to the sliding glass doors. The other light should be giving a clear view of whoever is in front. John sights and pulls the trigger. There's a loud report and a scream as the man drops to the ground and writhes before going still. I look through the scope, but the second man hasn't come out from the bushes.

A bullet thuds into the wood above our heads. John jumps up. "Back inside!"

I head for the door to the outdoor pen where Flora and Fauna spend much of their days. Two more bullets hit the barn, but the shooter still aims for our original spot. I slip into the pen, John close behind me, and crawl along the ground. I kneel and raise the scope to my eye.

"He'll come back up," John whispers, his rifle raised. "Wait for it."

The form in my scope looks like part of the foliage until it moves. John and I fire at the same time, and he goes down.

Then all hell breaks loose. The sound of breaking glass is followed by shots from in front of the house. My breathing is ragged, but my legs are strong when I stand.

"I'll go to the front. Head to the back and go inside if it's safe," John says.

We hop the fence and run across the grass. At the deck John splits off and heads to the front, where it's now ominously quiet. I look at the man John shot long enough to be sure he's dead and skirt around him to the sliding doors.

A shout from inside stops me. I can see into the living room, but not the hall, where everyone's attention is drawn. Nelly has his pistol in his hands. In the dim light he looks furious. Peter stands ready to shoot out the front window, with frantic glances at the scene behind him. Penny holds a struggling Laddie by the collar with a desperate look on her face. I don't see Ana. Someone must have Ana. The breaking glass was someone coming in down the hall. A surprise attack.

A voice yells, "Put your fucking guns down, I said! Put them down or I'll kill her. I will."

Ana screams. James grimaces as he watches and holds his useless weapon. Laddie roars, but Penny holds tight. If she lets him go, Ana might get shot.

I'll head for the other side of the cabin. The broken window. Maybe I can get in that way, too, and make my way down the hall behind him. I fall into a running crouch just as the wind from a bullet raises my hair and crashes through the door. The shattering glass stings my face and hands. I'm off the deck and behind the bushes as another shot misses. There's a single shot from inside and Nelly's voice rings out.

I don't have enough clearance for my rifle in the thick foliage. I drop it and aim my pistol at the side of the barn, where I think the shots came from, but it's quiet. It's hard to tell; everything in the woods echoes. I crawl through the bushes, heart racing, waiting for that shot, the one I won't hear until it's too late, until it hits me.

When I hit something soft, I let out a scream of surprise and cut it off, quick. It's the man John and I hit, and if he's not dead he's close to it or unconscious. I scramble over, wincing as my knees sink into his torso. I scurry around the corner of the house just as a man jumps out the broken window and races for the road, followed by Nelly. I can't risk a shot.

Laddie races across the back lawn to the barn with deep, angry barks. We were trying to keep him safe inside, but he's gotten out through the broken glass of the doors.

The gunfire in the front begins again, and I stand there, undecided. I was going to follow Nelly, but now I head to the front of the house with my back against the logs, never forgetting that someone by the barn wants me dead. Two men are in the trees on the other side of the driveway, guns flashing as they fire at the other corner of the house, where John keeps them at bay.

They've situated themselves so that there's no clear shot for John or from the house windows, but I'm able to line one of them up in my sights from my vantage point. I aim for his ample beer gut. I don't think about it, don't ruminate on the fact that I'm killing someone, because I don't care. I want nothing more than to see him fall, to choke on his own blood.

Before the gun goes off I already know I have him. It's like down at the school, with the machete. I've entered that serene place in the midst of the terror. The bullet and I have an understanding: I tell it where to go and it does what I ask. He drops when it slams into him, and I cut off his howls of pain with another shot.

His partner makes the mistake I was hoping he would, racing to the other side of the tree. The porch lights up with gun flashes, and John moves forward. Four, five, six shots hit the man with a deafening sound. He does a little jig and flies backward.

Peter twists from his spot on the porch as I move out of the shadows. He turns his gun on me. I freeze.

"It's me, Cassie!" I yell.

Peter lowers his gun, his eyes huge.

"Ana?" I ask.

"She's okay," he says.

I exhale in relief. "There's at least one more behind the barn. Nelly chased one down the driveway. I'm going after him."

"I'm coming with you," John says, and turns to Peter. "We'll go after Nel and the one behind the barn. Two cover the back, two cover the front. Stay inside. I'll call on the radio."

Peter nods and heads in. I hear sobbing before the door closes. John and I walk within the edge of the woods along the driveway. I wish I were barefoot; my boots are too loud on the forest floor. The woods are silent and still. Any creatures who would normally be stirring are holed up, waiting for this storm to pass.

There's a crash at the end of the driveway and two shots. A voice calls out, but I can't make out the words over the sound of an engine roaring to life. They can't be allowed to leave; this has to end tonight. I put on a burst of speed, sprinting on the diagonal through the woods, leaping over obstacles I can just make out.

I jump the ditch and see Nelly standing in the road with his gun raised as the van moves toward him. The windshield cracks as he takes two shots at the driver's side and stumbles out of the way.

"Nelly!" I whisper, so he knows it's me.

I grab his arm to steady him. The van moves past, and I think maybe he's missed, but then it coasts and bumps against a tree. I move forward.

He grabs my shirt. "Don't go yet."

The van door stays closed. Nelly barely puts any weight on his left leg. He's hurt. John reaches the van and eases the door open. The interior light shows the perfect circle of one of Nelly's shots in the driver's forehead. A high-pitched scream from inside the van makes us all leap. Whatever it is, it sounds frightened.

John moves to the empty passenger's side. I jump up next to the dead driver and point my gun into the cargo area, which is littered with beer cans and empty wrappers. A little girl cowers in the corner. Her hands are over her head, and her screams flow one into another without ceasing.

John wades through the trash to pick her up as Nelly flings open the back. She's no more than seven. Her feet are bare, and she wears a flimsy polyester nightgown that may have been pink once. Her long hair is ratty and tangled. She beats on John's arms with her fists, but he keeps his grip.

"It's okay. It's okay," he repeats. "We won't hurt you."

She quiets and swivels her head between the three of us. When she sees me she looks like she might just believe him. Her blue eyes are gigantic and scared, but dry. Even in the weak light from the van, I can see the freckles that stand out in sharp relief from her pale skin.

I reach for her. She pushes off from John and lunges at me. She's lighter than I thought, all arms and legs and skinny ribcage. They wrap themselves around me so tightly it's difficult to breathe. She smells like piss and sweat and liquor. I wonder what they've done to her.

"The one who had Ana ran that way." Nelly points into the woods that lead to the barn and back of the house. He gasps when his weight shifts. "But I wanted to take out the one in the van so they couldn't get away."

"Your leg," I say. His jeans have a ragged hole at the calf surrounded by a dark stain.

Nelly shrugs. "It's just a graze."

We've got to find the last of them, and Nelly won't be able to move fast with his leg.

"Nels, you take her to the house."

I try to hand him the girl, but she digs her nails in and buries her head in my shoulder. We can't have her screaming again, and I can hardly bring her with me.

"Honey?" I ask. I lean back so I can see her face. "Look at me, sweetie. What's your name?"

She looks into my eyes with her distrustful ones and whispers, "Elizabeth. Beth."

She tries to duck back down, but I lift her, forcing her to talk to me. "Beth, do you have a best friend?"

She nods. "Alana."

I talk quickly. "I have two best friends. One is Penny. She's back at our house. The other is right here. He'll take you to the house to see Penny."

I point my chin toward Nelly. He's disheveled and holding a gun, but otherwise he looks friendly when he smiles at her.

I make a face like I'm telling her a secret. "His name's Nelly. He has a girl's name! Isn't that funny? I named him that!"

Nelly makes a face like he still hasn't forgiven me, and something that resembles a smile crosses her features.

"Beth, I need you to go with him and be as quiet as you can. We have to catch the men you came with so they won't bother us anymore."

Her grip loosens almost imperceptibly. "You'll catch them?"

"Yes. I promise they won't hurt anyone else ever again."

She lets me hand her to Nelly. She looks even more pathetic cradled in his big arms. John radios the house to alert them to Nelly's arrival and our plan.

"Let's go," he says to me.

"Careful," Nelly says.

He shifts Elizabeth to his side and grips his gun. I know he'd rather I were heading to the safety of the house, just like I'm glad he is instead of me.

I give him a small smile. "Always."

He turns to limp toward the driveway, talking softly to the little figure in his arms.

CHAPTER 75

When we were kids my favorite game was Manhunt. It was like hide and seek in the woods, except when the hunter caught the hiders they would join the hunt for whomever was left. The last man standing had to make it to the far-off home base without being caught. Or, I should say, last *girl* standing, because I almost always won. I think part of the reason I loved the game so much was that it was the only time my feet were sure and my breath came easily. In school gymnasiums and fields I always missed the ball, got a stitch in my side or came in last. But in the woods, especially in my woods, I couldn't be caught. I would cover myself in leaves, hide in ditches, slog through mud—nothing was off limits. My body knew where it was going and what to do, even though it was only a game.

This isn't a game, and I haven't played Manhunt in years, but I still know where I'm going. The woods are always changing, but the overall feel remains the same. The big stump, the lightning-struck pine—all my old friends are still here.

It can't be more than five minutes since we left the house, but it's time enough for the remaining men to have gotten a plan together. John and I jump the trench, step over the trip wire and under the barbed wire. We make it to the edge of the yard. The spotlight's been turned facing out, so we can't see anyone in the house behind it.

John catches movement to the left and points; it might be the man who had Ana. There's a *thunk* from the right, near the barn. I motion that I'll head that way. He nods and heads left. My hair sticks to my face and my heart pounds. I stop when I hear the voices. They come from the side of the barn, where there's cover in the trees.

I creep out under the fruit trees, which have dropped all their blossoms and gotten down to the business of making fruit. My footsteps are muffled by the petals that still carpet the ground. Two men crouch by the barn, but my view is obstructed by trees.

"Let's just get out of here," one says.

"You heard the shots from the road as well as I did," says the other. "There ain't no where *to* go. We've got to take this place. I'll take out the light and cover you. You run."

I move fast, but I'm still too slow. A wiry figure jumps up. There's a loud crack and the light goes dark. I can't see the one who stayed behind; my eyes are too accustomed to the light to be of much use until they adjust. Feet thump on the wooden deck, followed by a volley of gunfire. As my pupils widen, I see James and Penny standing in the broken glass of the doors, guns flashing.

The other man runs. I take off after him. He's broad and bursts through the woods like an elephant. I hear shots behind me. John. I realize I can see the man twenty feet in front of me. The sky is no longer dark and the stars have disappeared. But if I shoot now, I'll probably just hit a tree and he'll know I'm here.

He turns for the road, not taking his own advice to stay and fight it out. The way he's blindly smacking through the brush makes me think he doesn't know about the perimeter we've made. They must have come down the driveway, where we moved the cans so they wouldn't know we were expecting them, and then gone into the woods. I know I can cut him off if I move fast. It'll keep me out of his line of fire as well. The cool air burns my lungs. I hate running. I swing under the barbed wire, stop short behind a tree and wait.

There are noises far behind me, also following his progress. In the second that I allow myself to think, I hope it's John. The man's closer now; I can hear him grunting. My breathing seems so loud and I try to stifle it, even though I know he can't hear. I close both hands on the gun I hold up against my heaving chest. I'll get him either way. If he gets past the line, I'll shoot him in the back as he goes past.

But he doesn't get through. There's a scream and the twang of metal as he hits the barbed wire and it catches his clothes and the skin under them. I step out from behind the tree into a firing stance. I'm not surprised to see it's Neil Curtis. He's dropped his gun and uses his hands to rip his clothes off the wires that hold him. He manages to tear himself free, falls back on his rump, and scrambles for his weapon.

"Stop!" I yell.

He freezes and blinks up at me. His eyes are the same as they were at the roadblock, empty except for a bit of mean and a lot of crazy.

He puts his hands up with a small, creepy smile. "Okay. You win. I'm going, and I'll never come back."

He thinks I won't shoot him because I'm a girl. He's so used to having his way with women, even if that way includes ropes and guns, that he thinks he'll win this one, too.

"No, you're not," I say, but my hands tremble.

He sees it and leans toward his weapon a few feet away. My finger tightens on the trigger and he stops.

"None of your folks are hurt," he says. It's almost a whine.

I want to laugh. Does he really think that's all that matters? Plenty of other folks are hurt. I just pulled one of them out of a van, stinking of dirt and men. I think of the Franklin girls and their parents, of Sam, of that tiny body at the school, wrapped in a final baby blanket of pink insulation. I shake my head, and my hands stop trembling. Everything inside me grinds to a halt, like it's covered with a layer of ice.

He must see it, and he whispers, "Please."

Finally, I see something in his eyes besides malice. It's fear. He whispers again, his voice cracking. He licks his lips. I hear the other person drawing nearer. I have to act now.

This time he begs. "Please?"

I aim at his chest, considering. Then I raise my gun a few inches and aim for his head. After all, he's just another kind of zombie.

"No," I reply. I repeat it again, louder this time, and look him in the eye. "No."

Maybe he moves for his gun, just an inch. Or maybe that's what I tell myself so I can pretend I don't feel something dark blossoming inside me. Something that revels in taking the life of someone so terrible. I pull the trigger.

CHAPTER 76

John finds me contemplating the ruin that once was Neil's head and tells me it's over. We won. We walk back through the woods with his arm around my shoulders. We pass the body of the one John went after. He's got a goatee of pink foam on his chin. James and Peter come out from the woods across the driveway as we reach the steps.

"They're all accounted for, with your two in the woods," James says. "The little girl, Beth, said that's all there were."

"Good," John says.

I thought the house would look worse than it does. The glass from the sliding doors glitters as Penny pushes it with a broom, and a front window is broken, too. I know there must be bullet holes in the walls and things that are cracked and broken, but I'll look for those later. Nelly sits on the couch, his leg propped on the coffee table. Beth huddles beside him, wrapped in a quilt, her eyes closed. I don't know if she's sleeping, but I don't want to disturb her. He smiles at me, but the corners of his eyes are turned down with pain.

"Let me see," I say softly, and kneel down. The bullet didn't just graze him; it passed through and came out the other side of his calf. But it's close to the skin, so maybe the muscle isn't too damaged. Someone's cleaned and put ointment on it. "I'll bet that hurts like a fucker."

Nelly laughs. "A little."

"That's why my parents stocked Vicodin. I'll go get some."

"I love your parents," Nelly says. He leans his head back and closes his eyes.

When I get back with the pills, Penny's dumping a dustpan of glass into a paper bag that James holds. I make sure Nelly has water and go to help. I don't have to ask Penny how she is; she tells me she's okay with a look.

"Where's Ana?" I ask. I want to see her with my own eyes, to make sure she's still here.

"Lying down. She has a major headache," Penny replies. "You should see her face. Sit down. We've got this. Tell me what happened while I clean you up."

Once I'm sitting at the table, exhaustion steals over me. My thighs feel like they're strapped to the chair. The whole thing couldn't have taken much more than an hour, but I could swear I've been running around all night. I wonder what Penny meant by cleaning me up, but then I look at my arms. They're covered in scratches and scrapes from my shoulders to the tips of my fingers. I must have taken off my jacket at some point.

Of course, now that I see them, the cuts begin to burn. I might have run through the blackberries; those thorns always irritate me the worst. My face and neck burn too. They must look like my arms, but I don't care enough to haul myself out of this chair to see. I hear Peter and John on the porch, talking and cleaning up. Everyone speaks in low voices so as not to disturb Beth, but the tones almost sound reverent. *We're okay; we made it* runs in a low hum under our words. I close my eyes. *Laddie.* I open them again.

"Where's Laddie?" I ask Penny, who's taken a seat next to me with antibiotic ointment and a clean cloth.

She looks around. "I don't know. He isn't back yet."

I force myself to stand, remembering that he ran toward the barn. Penny holds her hands out for me to wait, but I shake my head and step through the doorframe. I whistle and call, but I'm not surprised when I don't hear an answering jingle. I find his body around the back of the barn, his brown fur matted with blood. He could be sleeping. I crumple beside him and pet his still head, wishing he would make those contented, silly grunts.

"I'm sorry, boy," I say. My tears are hot on my cheeks. "You were just trying to help."

I'm going to miss him so much. I'm furious at the men who killed him, who would have killed us.

John and Peter come up behind me. John sighs and kneels on the ground. He runs a hand along Laddie's side and scratches behind his ear. The wrinkly skin around his eyes has gone soft and pink.

"Good boy," John says. His voice is gruff from holding back the tears.

Peter raises his hand, as if he's going to lay it on John's shoulder, but drops it back down at his side. "John, I'm so sorry."

John runs a finger and thumb over his eyes and stands up, brushing off his knees. "I know, son. Thank God we're all okay. That's what's most important. It's no one's fault."

Peter stares down at Laddie's body, lips compressed. It's only now that something awful has happened that he's sorry. He didn't think beforehand. He didn't take the time to see if his actions would hurt anyone. He didn't care, because he thought he'd scrape through like he always does. Even in the midst of the end of the world he's acted like he's entitled to whatever he wants.

I point at Peter. "No. It's *your* fault. I told you we might end up dead. But, as usual, you did whatever you wanted. All you've ever cared about is yourself."

"That's not true," Peter says quietly.

My laugh is bitter, and I feel mean. I want to get him back for putting me in a situation where I had to blow someone's head off, for being the one to tell me that Adrian no longer loves me, for lying about me, for disliking me so much.

"I wish I really had told you not to come with us in Jersey." His eyes widen, caught in his lie. I nod. "We don't need you here, ruining everything. You don't belong here."

"Cassie, I know you're upset—" Peter begins. Something in his face tells me he might be trying to make amends, but he's sounded sincere before.

I hold my hands up for him to stop. "I am way past upset. *Way* past. Just stay away from me, Peter."

I storm to the house, half-wishing it were him with the bullet in his side instead of sweet, protective Laddie.

***

Ana's face looks awful. Her eye on the right side is swollen shut, and her cheek is twice its usual size and three shades of purple.

"Yikes," I say when she enters the living room, where I sit on the couch next to Nelly and a sleeping Beth.

She smiles, then holds a hand up to her cheek and winces. "You should see the lump on my head. I wanted to sleep, but Penny came in every eighteen seconds to make sure I didn't."

It doesn't have the usual tone an Ana complaint has. She touches Penny's hand on the arm of her chair and turns to me.

Her one good eye wells with tears. "Cass, I totally fucked up. I know you're all angry. You should be angry. But I'm sorry, I really, truly am."

I believe her. I get up and hug her gently, brushing her hair back from her hurt side. I don't know why I can forgive her so easily and not Peter, but I can.

"Hey, Banana, all is forgiven." I smile and feel my own scratched face pull a little too tight. "Just don't ever pull a stunt like that again."

Her face is serious. "Never."

I think maybe little Ana has finally grown up.

CHAPTER 77

When we return from getting rid of the bodies, it's early afternoon. Grunting and sweating, we loaded them into the van, and John drove it down the hill while James, Peter and I followed. We left the van in an old meadow down the main road. I thought John might want to bury them, but he said he wasn't feeling very Christian toward them at the moment. I was glad. Then we came home and buried Laddie in the yard.

When I make it back inside the house, Nelly sits alone in the living room with a book, but it's killing him to sit still.

The corners of his mouth turn down. "Beth woke up. She scampered along the back of the couch and tried to run until she realized where she was."

"Where is she now?" I ask.

"Getting cleaned up. Penny said she'd wash her nightgown, but Beth said she wouldn't wear it again. So I think they're looking for clothes."

"I don't blame her." The thought of that dirty nightgown, even washed out clean, is not a good one. "We'll have to get her some clothes tomorrow."

"And window and door glass," John says from where he stands eating by the kitchen sink. "As long as you're up for it."

"I am," I say. I want to get out of here, even if it means visiting with Lexers.

Beth and Penny come into the living room holding hands. Beth's wet hair is combed straight down her back, and her eyes skitter around in their sockets. One of my old t-shirts hangs on her like a dress. Her mouth moves upward a little in response to my smile.

"Hi, Beth," I say. "Are you feeling a little better?"

She nods.

"Are you hungry?" She nods again. "Come and sit at the table with me. I'm so hungry I could eat a horse."

I pull out peanut butter and jelly fixings, applesauce, a jar of peaches and homemade hummus and bread. She sits in a chair, her skinny legs dangling.

"I'm Cassie, in case you forgot."

She shakes her head to let me know she didn't. Nelly told me she's seven, but she's small for her age and looks younger, especially since her eyes are huge with fear and uncertainty.

I smile. "Good. I'm going to make some of everything, and you can have whatever you want."

She slurps up the peaches and a bowl of applesauce and then gobbles down half a sandwich in four seconds. I open jars and spread stuff so she can eat and eat. I tell her about the house and the garden and the plants while she drinks it all in, her eyes round. But they grow less wary as I talk, so I tell her how we made the jam she's eating and how silly the goats look when they prance in the yard. When she's finally slowed down, I ask if she wants to see the garden.

She nods but hesitates. "I don't have shoes."

I kick off my boots and wiggle my toes. "Lucky you! I hate shoes!"

It's her first real smile of the day, maybe her first real smile in a long time.

Beth walks around on the warm soil, her hair drying into a pretty light brown with curls on the ends. I don't ask her many questions. Instead, I tell her about how we got here. Of course, I leave out the scary parts, but when I mention coming through town she speaks up.

"My mom and I were at the school. Then it got blown up right as the Biters came. I heard them say they did it. That's when they took us, me and my mom."

I know *they* and *them* refer to Neil and the rest. They must have used all the confusion to their benefit. I wonder what happened to her mother, but I don't ask. I kneel down to grab a couple weeds.

I look at her, still on my knees. "That must have been so scary."

She looks away. "Yeah." I want to hug her, but she doesn't look like she wants a hug. "Both of them are dead. Both my parents." She looks like a statue the way she's frozen in place. Unreachable.

I hold out a hand. "I'm so sorry, Beth." I understand what it's like to lose your parents. But not what it must be like when they're gone before you're old enough to be on your own.

She puts her small hand in mine but keeps her face turned to the back of the garden, at the forest that covers the hill. *The lower forty*, my dad called it. Her body trembles down to the warm hand I hold as she sobs angrily. She doesn't want me to see her cry. Maybe after the past few weeks she's afraid of showing weakness, of trusting too much. Of being hurt again. Now *that* I understand.

CHAPTER 78

The next morning, John asks Beth if she wants to go to her house to get some of her things. I pull him aside to say it's too dangerous, but he reminds me she's seen a lot worse than we have. That maybe it will help her to have familiar things around, especially when she wakes up screaming like she did all last night. I didn't mind soothing her because I spent half the night awake anyway. I had the dream about Adrian again, except this time Neil's dead hand had crept out from under the porch steps and grabbed my ankle, followed by a leering grin on what was left of his head.

She sits in the back between James and me. Peter's in the front. For someone who's managed to avoid me recently, he's been very present these past twenty-four hours. Bellville looks the same as it did a few weeks ago, except we don't see a single Lexer. John pulls into the school. The bodies of the infected we killed are slowly desiccating on the asphalt. We circle the building, bouncing over debris, and come upon a pile of Lexer corpses in the back lot.

"There aren't any Lexers here," John says, as he scans the school grounds. "I wonder where they went."

"They killed them all," says a little voice. Beth's face is pinched. "They had a game. They called it—" she chokes on the words, "—Live Bait. They tied someone up, and then the Biters would come. They would shoot the Biters while—they made me watch, once."

I put my arm around her slight shoulders. She lets her tears go in little hitching sobs. Peter looks at Beth and then the pile. His face is dark, all knitted brows and gritted teeth.

"Can we go?" I ask.

John puts the truck into gear.

Beth's house is a cute brick colonial. Coming home from school to this house must have been pleasant. The kitchen faces the backyard swing set, and the refrigerator is covered in pictures and drawings and all the things that mark a busy, happy family.

I have a suitcase, but when we're in her upstairs bedroom she pulls one out of her closet. She opens drawers and silently pulls out clothes.

"Do you want me to leave you to get changed?" I ask.

She nods. She's been wearing my kitten sweatshirt as a dress. When I gave it to her this morning her eyes lit up, just like mine would have when I was seven.

I peer into a home office and her parents' room, where the bed is neatly made. The whole place looks like someone is expected home at any minute, but it feels like a museum exhibit: Pre-Apocalyptic Homo-Sapiens.

Beth's changed into jeans and a t-shirt. She fills her school backpack with books and a stuffed animal. She moves painfully slow, but I'm not going to tell her to speed it up, so I sit on the bright bedspread and wait.

Fairy and flower decals cover the walls. A mosquito net hangs over the head of the bed. It's the perfectly magical room for a seven year-old girl. A photo of Beth and a blond-haired woman who looks like an older Beth sits on the bookshelf.

"Beth," I say quietly, not wanting to upset her, "would you like to bring this, too? Or some other pictures?"

Beth nestles it in her suitcase. She looks more and more distressed as the minutes pass. I watch her pick up and discard her belongings, unsure of what to bring.

"You don't have to take everything now. Just the stuff you want most of all. As long as it's safe you'll be able to come back and get more."

She fingers a pair of socks. "Who will bring me back? Where am I going?" Her voice is a whisper.

Tears spring to my eyes. She thought she was coming to get her things before we got rid of her somehow.

I put a hand on her shoulder. "Oh, honey. We'll bring you back. We want you to stay with us. I'm so sorry I didn't tell you. I thought you knew. I hope that's okay?"

Her body sags with relief. "Yes."

That's why she was moving so slow: she was afraid of what came next. She points to my folded kitten sweatshirt. "Here's your shirt back, Cassie."

I put it on top of her clothes in the suitcase. "Would you like to keep it? It looks better on you, anyway. I don't look good in kittens."

She giggles and zips her bag. It was a beautiful sound, that giggle, and I want to hear more.

I point to her dollhouse and Barbies and games. "Do you want some toys?"

She takes them in like she's never seen them before. "No. I don't think I want to play with toys anymore."

I want to take her in my arms and tell her she's safe. I want to insist that she doesn't have to grow up so fast, but I simply nod because she's so serious and aloof. I pick up her suitcase as she puts the straps of her backpack over her thin shoulders. It's so full that it sticks out like a turtle shell. After she leaves the room I grab a handled vinyl box just like the one I had when I was little, the kind that holds Barbie dolls and their accessories. Maybe she'll want to be a little girl again soon.

CHAPTER 79

John finishes installing the new sliding glass door just after the sun's gone down. He pulls the tape off the glass and we clap.

"Thanks, John," I say, as I hand him a beer. We found some of that today, too.

"It was the damndest thing, down in town," John says. He takes a swig and wipes his beard.

We've waited until Beth's asleep to discuss it. The past few days must have caught up with her, because she was asleep with her head in my lap ten minutes after dinner.

"So there are no infected?" Nelly asks.

He wishes he'd gone and tried limping around when we got back to prove he was fine. When he started wincing with every step, he finally sat and pretended he wanted to read. We pretended not to notice.

"Not a one," John says. "Now, there are probably some trapped inside houses that they missed, but they must have killed hundreds, maybe a thousand. Might've been the only good thing those men ever did."

"Except for how they did it," I say.

John tells them what Beth told us about their methods. There's a horrified silence while everyone contemplates being the bait for their sick game.

Ana hugs her knees to her chest. "Well, if there was ever any doubt they deserved to die, there's none now." Her bruises are still painful to look at, but her eye is less swollen. She turns to John. "John, can we go to the range tomorrow? I want to fix whatever I'm doing wrong."

"Let's wait for that eye to heal, hon. I promise I'll get you out there as soon you can see, okay?"

Ana pouts a little and John laughs. "I promise, Ana. We're going to start regular training. I'm almost finished with that tool I'm making, too. But you need to rest."

Ana looks disappointed but doesn't complain like she would have in the past. Penny looks at her speculatively and glances at me. I shrug, but I'm pretty sure Ana has a new project. She's always been single-minded, but it's always been on clothes and money, not armed combat. This should be interesting.

"Beth didn't know she was going to live with us," I tell them. "I don't know where she thought she was going, but we have to let her know we want her. She's trying so hard to be strong, but she's afraid of something terrible happening again."

"Who could blame her?" James asks from the floor where he sits with Penny between his knees.

She nods. "*I'm* afraid of something terrible happening again. Since it's almost a guarantee. Between the infected and what they were saying on the radio..."

The nightly broadcasts have changed from a rudimentary list of Safe Zones to news and descriptions of how various Safe Zones are operating. The broadcast is always from the White Mountain Airport in Whitefield, but a few nights ago they had someone on from the Safe Zone in Maine. A few of the Safe Zones have light aircraft and are flying over the dangerous areas to trade and refuel.

Tonight, Matt Burns, the broadcaster of Whitefield radio, recommended that groups who number less than forty don't broadcast their locations. He said that they're getting survivors from places that were raided by men who found them through their radio broadcasts.

My hopes of contact with Adrian were dashed, but I'm almost relieved. Contact means I'd know what Adrian thinks of me, for better or worse. Every time I start to feel hopeful, I remember what Peter said and my cheeks flush with humiliation. But I can't stop loving Adrian just because he might not love me. That's basically what he'd said to me the night I broke things off.

I trace the outline of the ring in my pocket. There's a faint mark on my jeans where the ring has worn a circle. I want to put it on, but I can't. I'll only put it on when I know for sure. Or I'll get rid of it for good, depending. I think of the other ring, the one I sent back to him even after he told me to keep it in case I changed my mind.

***

It was a year after my parents died. We'd spent much of the past year separated, partly because Adrian was finishing up grad school in the northeast and partly because I'd retreated into a drab and colorless world. I did the bare minimum. I showed up for work every day. I would go out for drinks on Fridays if I had to. Adrian would come down in his old car on the weekends he wasn't interning and try to entice me into doing something, anything, with him. But I never wanted to. The trips we took to look at land

and farms had stopped. I never wanted to leave the city. Really, I never wanted to leave the house. All the joy had gone out of imagining the future. I know now that I had sunk into a depression, but at the time it seemed like everyone had been put on the Earth just to prod me into doing things I didn't want to do. I didn't understand why I just couldn't be left alone. When I was alone I was fine, I thought. Eric would always call and ask how my week had been.

"Fine," I'd say. "How was yours?"

"Cassie," he sighed one day, "I know you're not fine. What happened to that art show? You've never mentioned it again."

I'd been contacted by a gallery owner in the northeast who was interested in my paintings. It was a well-known gallery, and in another lifetime it would have been a dream come true. But I hadn't picked up a brush in a year; I had no urge to. The calls finally petered out.

"I've been busy," I lied.

"No, you haven't. Adrian says you hardly talk to him anymore and that you don't call him unless he calls you. You don't even care whether you see him or not. Believe me, I understand what you're going through, and I know it's hard, but you're closing everyone out. I think maybe you need to talk to someone."

I was annoyed that he and Adrian were discussing me like I was some kind of problem child.

"I don't need to talk to someone, Eric. Maybe what I need is for people to stop talking about me. I'm doing fine. Maybe I'm just different now. Did you ever think of that?"

Another sigh came down the line. "Fine, Cass. You are different. All the life has gone out of you, and I hate to see it. Please think about it. You know I love you, right?"

"Yeah, I know. Love you too. Adrian's here, I have to go."

Adrian walked in and dropped his bag on the living room floor with a smile. He opened his arms and I went to him, but I felt like I was suffocating. I'd always felt safe and loved in his embrace, but now I just wanted to escape. I broke free after a second.

"Are you hungry?" I asked, not looking at him. "Do you want to order in?"

His arms were still raised. He let them fall as I tried to ignore the hurt look on his face. "I thought we could go out. Maybe call Nel?"

I didn't want to go anywhere or talk to anyone. "Um, I think Nelly's busy."

His eyes were bright green, challenging. "He's not. I called him on the way down."

"Let's just stay in."

"Maybe I want to go out and see him."

"Go ahead," I offered. "I don't mind."

"I'm sure you don't," he muttered, so low I almost couldn't hear.

If he wanted a fight he was going to get one. I was still fuming that he and Eric had been trading calls about me.

I stood on the area rug, hands on my hips. "What's that supposed to mean?"

"Just that you never seem to want to see me, to talk to me. You won't even discuss getting married. I know that this year has been awful. I'm not saying you don't have a right to be sad or depressed—"

"I'm not depressed!" I yelled. "Eric told me that you and he are busy discussing my depression. I'm fine!"

"That's right, we've talked. Because we both love you and want you to be the old Cassie again."

His voice was gentle, even as mine rose. His face was full of pity. I couldn't stand it.

"Well," I spread my arms, "maybe this is the new Cassie. Maybe if you don't like it, then..." I trailed off.

He squared his shoulders and his eyes got glassy. "Then what? What do you want me to do? It feels like you don't want me around anymore."

It was true. I didn't want him around, and for months I'd tried to figure out why. I could remember how much I'd loved him, how much I'd liked being with him, but they had become faint memories. I could almost feel it sometimes. It was like after a toothache is gone and you prod the area with your tongue, not quite sure if you can still feel a twinge. I stared at him, unwilling to say the words I'd been thinking.

"What do you want me to do?" he asked again. He sank onto the couch and looked at me helplessly. "I need to know. I need to know if you still want me around. If you still love me."

That's where I should have said, *Of course I do. Just please bear with me a little while longer*. Because somewhere deep down I thought maybe it wasn't really gone. But saying that meant I had to try to find it, which meant unlocking all the other feelings that were locked away with it.

"I—" His face was expectant. "I don't think I love you anymore."

He looked like I had just sucker-punched him. I *had* just sucker-punched him. Out of all the things I could have said, he never thought I would say that. His jaw clenched and he looked away with a nod.

"I'm sorry," I said. I wanted to comfort him, but I didn't imagine I would be much comfort.

He splayed his hands and turned to me. Tears welled up in his eyes. "Why? Can you just tell me that?"

"I don't..." I didn't know what to say. "It's gone. There's just...nothing."

His voice was bleak. "Nothing."

I looked at the little diamond on my hand. It was perfect. He'd combed antique stores all over until he'd found a ring he thought would suit me. I hadn't wanted him to spend any hard-earned money on a ring, but he swore up and down it was a bargain. "And it fits," he'd said. "It was meant to be, just like us."

I twisted it until I finally pulled it off. I felt sorry for causing Adrian so much pain, but, mainly, I felt relief. At the time I thought it meant I was making the right decision. Eventually, I realized that I'd been relieved I could continue hiding and not have to join the ranks of the living. Relieved that I wouldn't have to admit that somewhere in the past year I had forgotten how to be me. I held out the ring.

Adrian looked stunned. "Can't we talk? I can't believe..."

"We can talk," I said reluctantly, not wanting the relief to fade. "But I've felt this way for a long time now. I don't know what there is to talk about."

I don't know how I could have been that cruel. I ended all those years with a few sentences, unwilling to even discuss it. By the end of those ten minutes he looked battered and beaten down. I hated myself for doing it, but I told myself it had to be done. I just didn't love him anymore. I continued holding out the ring.

"Keep it," he said. He looked at me like I was a stranger. "It was for you. Maybe you'll want it again someday."

I gripped the ring in my palm, and we stared at each other for a few seconds. His open, honest face was closed. He shook his head as if in a dream and rose from the couch.

"I guess I'll go."

I wanted this over. "Okay."

He picked up his bag and stood there as though waiting for me to say it had all been a joke.

"I'm sorry," I said again. "I really am."

He shrugged like he didn't believe me and threw his bag over his shoulder. He started down the hallway, but then he turned back. I'd never seen such sadness on his face, and I wanted to take it all back. But I didn't.

"I still love you," he said. "Until the end of the world."

Then he walked out.

CHAPTER 80

Neil's hand comes out from under the porch steps and grips my ankle, followed by what's left of his grinning face. I scream, but it comes out as a wispy little breath. Adrian looks into the trees, deaf to my pleas for help. I wake with Beth sitting above me in the dark.

"Cassie!" she yells.

I've scared her. In my dream it was a whisper, but I could hear the tail end of a real scream right as I woke.

"I'm okay." I try to shake it off. "Sorry, I just had a bad dream, honey. I didn't mean to scare you."

I hold her warm hand and pat the pillow so she'll lie back down. In a few minutes she's out again, her arms flung up with abandon. I head to the living room and tell James to get some rest. It appears I'm done sleeping for the night, so I might as well do watch.

My heart continues to pound. Now I wish I'd kept James up for some inane conversation to calm my nerves. Because even though I know Neil is really, truly dead, I can still feel his cold hand on my ankle. If Laddie were here he'd know just what to say.

The strawberries are in full swing, and I mash a bowl for another batch of jam. We've been gorging ourselves on them. Between John's patch and ours, we've canned pint after pint. Beth cheers every time a jar lid pings when we take them out of the canner. She and Peter place silly wagers on which jar will pop next.

Peter asks what he can do and helps John with everything and anything. Everyone's warmed to him. I guess they can forgive him because it wasn't personal. But I know what he thinks of me, and I can't forgive him for that or for what he's said and done.

Ana begs for target practice, and when she's not getting it or doing chores, she practices with John's new weapon. We've named it The Cleaver. It has a two-foot shaft and ends in a cleaver blade meant to instantly decapitate. It slices through almost anything you put it to, including, we hope, the neck of a Lexer. The other end has a spike, perfect for plunging into the base of the neck or an eye socket. When John explained this, Penny blanched but tried to take it in stride.

I mix the strawberries with pectin and set it on the burner. I measure out sugar and start the oatmeal. At least my nightmares give me ample time to get things done. Once everyone's awake we sit at the breakfast table and spoon up oatmeal. With strawberry jam, of course.

Beth looks at me. "Cassie, would it be okay if I slept in one of the beds in Peter's room? Because, well…"

My face is hot. "Sure, honey. If it's okay with him. I'm sorry I keep waking you up."

"S'ok. I have bad dreams every night, too," she says with a solemn look. "Can I, Peter?"

Peter grins. "Of course, Bits."

We've been calling her Bits. Peter pretended that he thought she was saying "Little Bits" instead of "Elizabeth," and it's become her nickname. She's taken a shine to him, and while I still can't stand him, I can see why. He dotes on her and teases her and insists on naming all her freckles.

He holds his hand up for a high five. "A slumber party every night! But you'll have to ask Nel, it's his bed."

Bits laughs and slaps his hand. He's possibly the last human being I could ever imagine instigating a high five. I don't know what to make of him.

Nelly smiles and moves his stuff down the hall. "I'm ba-ack," he sings.

I know I can't expect Bits to put up with me every night, but I feel like a freak. Nelly might want to start sleeping on the couch.

"Prepare to be tortured. Obviously, no sane person would choose to be in a room with me at night."

"Well, they've never said I'm sane," he says, and tweaks my nose.

CHAPTER 81

"**W**alk the fence line with me?" John asks.

I stand from my mother's flowers and brush my hands on my jeans. "Sure."

First stop is the Message Tree. John steps on a gnarled root and reaches into the hollow. He opens the old coffee can and removes a folded paper.

"I wrote a letter to the kids and Eric, telling them Neil was coming. I told them where we might go, if we had to leave. But we have to agree on where we'd go, so they know where to find us."

I marvel at his foresight. Whenever I think I might be getting the hang of things, he's already three steps ahead.

"I want to put a letter in there for Eric, too."

It's been over two months now. I can't help but think he ran into something he couldn't escape. Eric climbs mountains, he's thru-hiked the Appalachian Trail; he's not easily stopped. He's got to be okay.

I know there was an ulterior motive for John's walk, and I wait for him to formulate the words. "So, Cassie, if we have to bug out should we go to Kingdom Come or Whitefield? We're equidistant from them, so it doesn't matter to me, but I'm thinking it might to you."

He does me a favor by busying himself with the can. When I speak my voice is strangled. "I'd like to go to Vermont."

He nods once. "Well, that's settled, then. Let's walk the line."

We move through the woods, making sure the line is still strung and nothing's caught in it or the trench. John points out deer droppings and a new nest, but I'm thinking of the last time I ran through these woods. As we near the spot my mouth goes dry, and I'm certain I'll see the Neil from my dreams stuck in the wire. But it's the same old woods. Only patches of dirt showing through the leaves give any indication something happened here.

John rests a hand on the barbed wire and looks me in the eye. "You did what you had to do."

He's thinking I'm plagued by uncertainty, but that's not exactly right. I try to explain. "I know, and I don't regret it. I'd do it a hundred more times.

But that doesn't stop him from showing up in my dreams, from thinking about it over and over."

"Cassie, I've killed men before. Bad men, who deserved what they got. And, in Vietnam, men who probably didn't. You carry them with you forever. They haunt you. You wish you hadn't had to do it in the first place, but you did, so you find a way to live with it."

"But I wanted to do it. Not like I knew it had to be done, I really wanted to kill him. I took pleasure in it, John. Just a little."

I've been looking at the spot, and now I look up, expecting to see shock, but his eyes are sympathetic.

"You weren't taking pleasure in killing, honey. You were glad to see someone so threatening cease to be a threat. Not everyone could do that. You know what your dad used to say about you?"

My heart leaps as I shake my head. Sometimes the hardest part is that all I have are memories.

"Your dad said that if he needed someone to have his back in a fight in a dark alley he'd choose Eric. But he said that if he ever needed someone to pull the trigger, it'd be you. He knew you'd do whatever needed to be done. He was the same way. Why do you think I wanted you in the barn with me?"

I'm silent. I never had a doubt my dad would do anything to protect us, but I never realized that I'd inherited that trait. Suddenly, I don't feel like a mass murderer, just someone who protected what was hers. It's not a bad feeling.

CHAPTER 82

John, Peter and Ana return with a new vehicle after a day in town siphoning gas and getting more supplies. John jumps out of the black van and knocks on its hood.

"Our new wheels," he says. "We all fit in it. Plus supplies. That way, we'll be ready to leave at a moment's notice."

"Nice," Nelly says. He makes his way to the van with barely a limp. "It's like the van we left the city in."

"Peter spotted the used car dealership and had the idea to get something bigger. This fit the bill and it's got a full tank," John says.

He claps Peter on the shoulder. Ana grins at Peter, and he smiles back at her. The way they look at each other makes me think there's something more there than friendship. And they are friends: they always volunteer to help each other and walk the line together. They're always laughing. They don't even play Zombie Zagat anymore.

Something like jealousy rises up in me, even though I try to convince myself it's not. They look happy. I try to swallow down the feeling and plaster a fake smile on my face. I stay as long as I can stand it and then head into the house.

I try to sort out my feelings, but there's too many zooming around inside. Jealousy, anger, hopelessness, fear: if you can name it, I've got it. I'm no closer to figuring it out when everyone troops in, laughing. I hear them tell everyone that town's still empty. I can't think with the chattering and want to scream at them all to shut up.

"John?" I walk over to where he's measuring the window glass. "Can I go to your house for a while?"

He turns to me, concerned. "Of course, just turn on the radio so we can contact you if need be. Are you okay?"

I don't look him in the eye. "I'm fine. I just need to be alone for a while."

I sit at his kitchen table and stare out the window. Since that day when Peter and I fought, I feel like everything's gotten worse. There's no imminent threat from either live people or infected, but I don't feel relieved. All I feel is that gray, floundering feeling that overtook me after my parents died. It's underneath everything, trying to get a toehold again.

I refuse to let it. When Peter said Adrian didn't love me, I believed him, but I'm not sure why. It's not like he knows. I grow angrier and angrier at Peter. He does whatever he wants and still comes out with accolades. I clean up his mess, and all I get is feeling left out and sad.

I sit there until everyone comes in for the radio broadcast. Peter, Ana and Bits have stayed behind to play a board game. I wonder if my having left the house has anything to do with it. At least Peter's been staying away from me like I asked him to.

Matt Burns starts in with his usual reports. He names all the Safe Zones, including new ones in Pennsylvania and northwestern New York. Then he talks about the food they're growing in Whitefield, how much work it is to lug water to the plants and the endless weeding.

"So we've become soldier-farmers," he laughs. "Thankfully, we've got Kingdom Come Farm to help us with all the logistics. And we've got one of the leaders or—I don't know, what would you call yourself?"

There's a familiar laugh and my heart stops. The universe must have it in for me today. I want to hear his voice so badly that I must have imagined it. But there it is, calm and measured, an octave deeper than you'd think it would be.

"I call myself Adrian," he says.

I grip the edge of the table as everyone turns to me. I stare straight at the radio. He's alive. Now I know for sure.

"Okay, Adrian. Adrian Miller is here from Kingdom Come Farm in the Northeast Kingdom of Vermont. It's your farm, right?"

"Well, my partner, Ben Sullivan, and I started the farm a year and a half ago. We met in grad school and landed a grant to start an experimental farm. We found an old farm and bought it. We started work on it the winter before this past one and had our first harvest last summer."

I remember Ben. I met him once, before my parents died.

"Tell us about it."

Adrian clears his throat. He hates being the center of attention, and he's nervous.

"Well, we wanted to make it as much like an ecosystem as possible. Where the food grown fed us and the animals, and the animals' waste fed the earth, which in turn fed the plants. Our goal was to even produce the vegetable oil-based fuel that our modified farming equipment would run on."

"You're talking in the past tense."

"Well, we're still doing it, but right now we're more interested in defending and feeding ourselves. We've had about two hundred people show up so far, but we think we can handle many more. The nice thing about the area is that it's pretty isolated and surrounded by mountains. We have neighbors, and we're all working together to make an even larger Safe Zone."

"How?"

"We send out patrols to eliminate any threats, whether they're alive or dead. We're very, very serious about that."

I know the look on his face right now. His jaw is tight and his eyes glow. I knew he was like my dad, but I guess I never realized that he and I were alike in that way, too.

"Bandits, take heed," Matt jokes. "What can people expect if they make it there?"

"Food, a relatively safe place to live, a really great group of people and a whole lot of work. I'm not kidding about the work."

Adrian laughs and his voice softens. "We welcome anyone who wants to join us. When we fly over the more populated areas and see what's become of them, I'm not surprised we haven't had as many refugees as we expected. But I hope people hear these broadcasts and make it there."

"I know you're needed somewhere, Adrian," Matt says. "One last question: Did your family make it okay?"

"My mom was visiting my sister out west. They made it to a Safe Zone in Idaho. I was lucky."

I'm relieved. I hoped they were with him, but this is the next best thing.

"You are lucky. So there was no one else?"

I wait for some hesitation, some sign. But he answers too quickly to even invent a pause where he may have thought to mention me.

"No, there's no one else. They got out just in time."

"Thanks for coming on, Adrian. I practically had to drag him here. But Kingdom Come Farm is hoping that some of you make it there if you can."

Adrian murmurs thanks, and then it's just Matt running through the lists again. I ignore everyone, push back my chair and walk outside into the woods.

The house is mostly dark by the time I go back. I've broken our rule by staying out past sunset by myself, but I don't care. John's on watch, but he only nods at me and goes back to his book. I change into pajamas and get into bed with Nelly. I don't have enough energy to brush my teeth. I lie there and listen to Nelly breathe.

"It doesn't mean anything," he says.

"Maybe nothing means something," I say.

He's silent, but he grabs my hand in his rough paw as we fall asleep. At least this time I don't have to see Adrian in my nightmare, since Neil and I are alone on the steps.

CHAPTER 83

In the morning I start to transfer the star ring to my clean jeans. When I realize what I'm doing, I stop and put the ring in my top drawer. I've made my bed and should stop feeling sorry for myself while I toss and turn and have nightmares in it. I head to the kitchen and start pancakes. Penny comes in with Flora's milk as I'm flipping the first batch.

She stands next to me and puts her head on my shoulder. "Hey, lady." I know she wants to bring up Adrian, but she doesn't. "Love you."

"Love you," I say. "How's *your* love life?"

"It's good." Her face is guarded.

"*Please*. You're all aglow with love and you won't even tell me about it. I've been a shitty best friend, and I'm sorry. I didn't mean to make you think I didn't want to hear it."

She smiles and raises an eyebrow. "Aglow?"

I nod. "Aglow. Now sit down and have a pancake and spill it."

In the garden I'm still smiling at Penny's furious blushing when she told me she loves James. And as I yank weed after weed, I realize I really am happy for her. It makes me feel a little better, like I haven't turned into a completely awful person. Bits kneels next to me and pulls up the tiny plants she's sure are weeds.

"Hey, Bits," I say. Her freckles have multiplied, and there's color behind them instead of that fish belly white. "How'd you sleep?"

"I had the same dream, but Peter held my hand until I fell asleep."

I laugh inside because Nelly did the same thing for me. I've regressed to being a seven year-old.

"Do you want to talk about the dream? Sometimes if you tell someone it might stop, or at least not be as scary."

Fear fills her eyes. Then she nods and speaks so low I have to lower my ear to her mouth.

"Remember the game I told you... where they would tie up...?" I nod and grab her hand in mine. "Well, the time they made me watch, it was after my mom tried to leave with me. That was—my mom was the bait. That's what I keep dreaming about."

I'm frozen to the spot. *Those motherfuckers.* For a moment I wish Neil were in front of me so I could shoot him again. And this time I'd drag it out, nightmares or not. She shakes with sobs and I pull her into my arms. After a long while, she quiets. I cradle her face in my hands and look in her eyes.

"We'll do everything we can to protect you," I say. "Do you believe that?" Her head nods slowly, half scared by my intensity. "Do you know that we love you?" It may have only been a couple of weeks, but we do. She shrugs and looks away.

"We love you." I turn her chin back gently. "And I'm so happy we found you."

"That night gave you nightmares," she argues.

"Honey, this world could give anyone nightmares. I'd have worse nightmares if you were still with them."

The corners of her mouth turn up, and she puts her small hand in mine. "I want to show you something," I say. "Have you ever read the Little House books?"

She shakes her head. "I have—I mean, had—them, but I never read them. My mom was going to read them with me."

I look closely, but her face is eager, not sad. "I still have my set here. Let's go find them."

It's doubtful that talking about something so horrific is going to stop her nightmares, but she already seems a little lighter. So do I.

CHAPTER 84

"We need moving targets," Ana says.

I glance at where Peter chops wood but feel it's probably prudent to keep my mouth shut, so I just nod. All the work outdoors has turned her light brown skin the color of cinnamon. She's covered in a sheen of sweat that makes her glow, unlike the rivers of unsightly sweat my body creates. She's intent on mastering every weapon there is, and it's all I can do to keep up.

"No, thank you," says Penny, who's taking a break on the grass. She tries hard, but she's too gentle. Plus, her glasses slip when she gets sweaty. Sweet, quiet Penny is not made for this world, and it scares me.

"At least I can shoot a gun," she says.

I remember her firing out the back door that night, and my worry lifts a little. I pick up the cleaver again and thrust it forward. My thigh burns from what must be lunge number one hundred today.

"Yeah," I say to Ana, "let's not wish too hard for that one. I'm fine practicing on air and wood."

"You guys know what I mean," Ana says, like she wasn't really wishing for it.

"Yeah, we do," Penny and I say at the same time and then laugh.

Peter walks over. His t-shirt is stuck to him, and even Penny raises her eyebrows at what's under it and then grins when I roll my eyes.

"Hey," he says to Ana. "Can I show you something John showed me?"

"Of course," Ana says.

He stands behind her and places his hands over hers on the shaft. "Like this." He moves her arms upward. "You'll probably need to swing up a little to connect with the neck."

She leans into him, and his arms stay around her a moment longer than necessary. Peter glances at me and pats her on the shoulder as he backs away.

"There you go." He turns to me. "Do you want me to show you?"

"I have eyes, I saw," I say. "No thanks."

Our gazes lock. I keep mine cold and hard until finally he raises his shoulders and walks back to the woodshed.

Ana shakes her head. "Can't you guys just get along?"

I shrug. "Let's practice."

***

We have a barbecue on the Fourth of July. John says there'll be hunting in the fall, so we might as well enjoy the last of the steaks. Penny finds some old sparklers in the junk drawer, and Bits races around with them.

"When's your birthday again, Bits?" John asks, while we sit on the deck and eat.

"November twenty-eighth," she and Peter say at the same time.

She giggles. I have to admit that Peter's good with her. The other night she had a nightmare, but by the time I got down the hall he was talking her back to sleep. When I checked later I saw he'd fallen asleep with his head on her bed, her hand still in his.

I felt something soften that night. Until the next day, when he suggested my mother's marinara sauce needed more basil, in his insufferable way. I handed him the spoon and told him to suit himself. He finished dinner and, of course, everyone said it was great.

"Hey," Nelly says. "Let's go to town tomorrow. My leg is healed and I want to run free. Actually, I need more unmentionables."

"I need to get some stuff too. Feminine hygiene and such." I wink at Penny, who makes a face telling me to shut up, so I wink again.

"Fine with me," John says. "Or I can stay here if I'm not needed."

Ana chews her steak and nods enthusiastically. "I'm going! Maybe we'll run into a Lexer."

We all groan, and Nelly gives her a half-smile. "One can only hope."

"I'd like to go," Peter says.

I can't spend all day in the car with him. I change my mind. "I'll give you a list, Nelly."

Peter looks my way and his hands tighten on the chair. I wait for him to say something obnoxious, but they release and he lets out a breath. "You know what? I have some stuff to do here. Either James or John can go with you three."

I smile and get up to make a list.

CHAPTER 85

Town is still eerily quiet. We head to Wal-Mart for the same reason people did before the world ended: it has most everything we need.

It looks the same as it did, although it might smell worse. Nelly and I head to the back to see about ammo, while John and Ana head to the other end. We grab what's left and snag Bits a backpack for a BOB. The stench in Health and Beauty is unbearable, but this time I'm ready with a perfumed bandana. Nelly gags until he finally takes the other bandana I offer him.

"Just a couple more things," I say.

I throw some shampoo and soap in Nelly's bag. We go through it like crazy, even with not showering as much as we used to. I grab every box of condoms I can find. Nelly raises an eyebrow.

"I thought we'd start being friends with benefits," I say. His bandana puffs out when he laughs. "They're for Penny, dummy."

"At least someone's getting lucky."

"Seriously."

Ana looks disappointed when we leave without a single undead altercation. We're loading the stuff when we hear the drone of a motorcycle coming up fast. John turns the key in the ignition and we ready our weapons. There's no time to leave.

The motorcycle turns into the lot, followed by an RV. The motorcyclist waves his hand in the air for the RV to stop and pulls up within shouting distance. He's a big guy in black leather, with long gray hair, but he looks friendly enough.

"Hi there," he yells. "Name's Zeke. You mind if I come closer?" He opens his jacket to show us a holster. "I've got one weapon holstered. Sorry, I won't take it off, though."

John nods his assent and holsters his gun but indicates we should keep ours out. Zeke heaves himself off the bike and lumbers over. Up close he looks to be in his fifties.

"You're the first live people we've seen in days," he says with a smile. "Mighty glad to see you, too."

We introduce ourselves. Zeke tells us that he's come all the way from Kentucky. "We're headed to Whitefield, New Hampshire. You've heard of the Safe Zone there? We figured we'd throw in our lot with them."

"You're a long way from Kentucky," John says.

"Tell me about it. Had to give a wide berth to all the major cities. New Jersey was a complete and total nightmare."

"So nothing's really changed," I say with a grin, before I can stop myself.

Zeke stares at me, and for a moment I'm afraid I've insulted him with my joke. But he throws his head back, showing a set of perfect white teeth, and laughs until his cheeks are red and drenched with tears.

"Oh, man, I needed a good laugh," Zeke says, as he blots his face with a bandana.

John insists Zeke's companions get out and stretch their legs. At Zeke's word they spill out of the RV like clowns out of a tiny car. There's a family with two kids, three sisters, two sets of married couples and assorted single people. We exchange brief stories.

"We barely made it out," says the mother of the family. "We almost lost my husband, but Zeke came by and helped us."

Every story involves Zeke, and I watch him with growing fascination. The man has picked up these assorted people and is leading them to safety. He's like the anti-Neil. We tell them about Neil and what to expect inside the store but that there's plenty.

"Thanks. We've run up against some murderous folks, too. So, do you have plans to head to a Safe Zone?" Zeke asks.

"We're pretty well set up here," John says. "But we have plans to go if necessary."

Zeke strokes his chin and nods. "Right now y'all are pretty lucky. No Eaters here. But we've noticed they're forming into huge groups. We've been calling them pods. Like a group of whales? They don't seem to pay each other any mind, but they stick together. Also, they seem to be on the move. Maybe looking for more of us, now that the cities are mainly empty."

Ana's face is desperate. "Do you know anything about New York City? Brooklyn in particular?"

Zeke shakes his head. "Sorry, I don't, except there's one group broadcasting out of the city. But keep your eye out for those pods forming up. Figured we'd be safest among a lot of people up north, especially once it gets cold."

"Zeke, what did you do before all of this?" I ask. "Were you military or something?"

"Nah. Name's not even Zeke. They started calling me Zeke for Zombie Killer, as a joke. Z.K., get it? Martin George, D.D.S., at your service."

"You're a dentist?"

He laughs his big laugh again. "Yup, so if you get a toothache, you'll know who to look for."

We wish them luck and watch them head into Wal-Mart before we leave. I wonder if we should have asked them to stay with us, but where would we put them all? John must be thinking the same thing.

"I do wish we had more people," he says. "Maybe we should talk seriously about moving to a Safe Zone before winter. But traveling to it's going to be dangerous, and I hate to chance that, unless we're forced to."

"I like where we are," Ana says. "I might want to try out these weapons, but I haven't lost my mind."

CHAPTER 86

"**C**an I talk to you?" Peter asks.

My head shoots up so fast it hits Flora in the side and she gives a *baa* of protest. I stop milking and spin around. Peter leans against the wall, hands in his pockets.

My own hands tremble and I clasp them together. "Okay."

"Can we try to be friends?"

I remember asking him the same thing not too long ago. "I thought you didn't want to be friends."

His face is expressionless, but his eyes are full of some emotion I can't read. "Well, I would like to be now. We have to live together. I'm trying really hard, Cassie."

He sounds irritated that I don't appreciate his effort.

"Only you would have to *try* to be nice, Peter. So you've spent the past month being an active participant here, but that doesn't erase how you've treated me or what you've said."

"Can I apologize? You know, I think Adrian—"

I can't believe he's bringing up Adrian. I stand so fast I knock over the milking stool. "Don't even say another word, Peter. I already know what you think. You made it very clear and, actually, it's none of your fucking business." I know my face is bright red, and it's all I can do not to scream. I blink back tears. I will not cry in front of him. He shifts uncomfortably against the wall. "And you don't *offer* to apologize. Or *ask* to apologize. If you're really sorry, you just apologize."

His face is red now, too. Whether it's because he's angry or embarrassed, I don't know and don't care.

"Can I start over?" he asks.

"You can do whatever you want, Peter. With absolutely no repercussions. I'm pretty sure that's been established." It may be unfair, but I say it anyway. His face falls for a second and then tightens back into its normal expression. I grab the milk bucket and stomp to the house.

***

Nelly brings me another tray of dried peas. I pour them into a jar and use the pump to remove any excess air. James cuts green beans and Penny loads them into jars for the canner. No sooner have we caught up than Bits comes in with another bowl.

"Peter says there's tons more up high where he can reach," she says.

"Goody," Penny mutters.

Her hair is stuck to her temples with sweat. It's a hot day and every window is open, but the breeze is non-existent. Add all the running burners, and the kitchen is an oven.

"Thanks, Bits," I say, and take the bowl.

Bits grabs a few beans and munches on them like she's been doing all day.

"Hey, Bits, you'd better not eat too many."

She looks worried and her chewing slows. "Why?"

I try not to smile. "Too many fresh green beans can turn you green. I guess you didn't know that."

She considers what I've said and watches me carefully. "Cassie, I know you're kidding!"

We grin at each other. "My mom almost got me with that one when I was little. I think you figured it out faster than me, though."

She bites the tops off another handful, like she's daring them to try to turn her green, and skips out the door with a wave of her hand. We've been reading the Little House books, and she's thrilled to be doing the same things as Laura. She's been bugging us to get a pig so we can butcher it in the fall and build a smokehouse. John told her he'd see what he could do.

"I'm freakin' dying," Penny says. She lifts her hair and fans her neck. "How did your parents do this all summer?"

"You just picture all the jars lined up on a shelf in the winter and it cools you down," I say. She looks dubious. "Okay. You sweat your ass off, but it's worth it anyway."

"Plus, we really have to do it," James says. "We're going to need food." He chops the latest installment of beans and whistles.

"Have you *ever* been angry, James?" I ask. I wish I could take a pinch of him and sprinkle it on myself.

He looks confused. "Sure."

He catches Penny's head shake out of the corner of his eye and puts his hands on her waist. "I don't get angry at you because you're perfect."

Penny blushes. I make a face, even though I think it's cute. "Yeah, yeah, young love," I say. "Seriously, even when you're angry you only seem half angry."

He shrugs. "I just don't get all worked up about stuff. I never have. Life's too short, especially now."

I know he's right. I tell myself that over and over again, hoping it will sink in.

CHAPTER 87

John actually found a skinny, neglected pig for Bits. She's named him Bert, and she tries to clear the table before we've eaten the food on our plates so he can have it. I'm not quite sure how the whole butchering in the fall thing is going to go. I have a feeling we've acquired a pet pig.

Bits is so good-natured she seems impossible to spoil. When I see the photograph of Bits and her mother, I try not to imagine her tied up, screaming. Or forcing herself not to scream, desperate for extra seconds before the infected reach her. I wonder if it was that much worse because she knew she was leaving Bits unprotected. I hope she can see us and her heart is at peace. I hope she can hear me when I promise her we'll do the best we can.

Bits still believes in fairies. At first I thought it strange, but we live in a world with zombies, so maybe fairies aren't so farfetched. We planted a fairy garden and we lie in wait for them in the grass. We haven't caught one yet, although once I watched Peter surreptitiously sprinkle glitter over the plants so she would find it in the morning.

Peter tries to be civil to me, even though, at best, I pretend he doesn't exist. At worst, I'm bitchy and short-tempered with him. It seems like no sooner do I think something mean than it comes out of my mouth. I'm not proud of it at all, but I can't seem to stop.

I'm on a ladder in the barn, nailing the loose boards. It's looking like a real barn these days, with hay and bags of feed stacked up for winter. Bert snores in his pen, Flora and Fauna hop around and the chickens cluck softly. It even smells like a barn, in a good way.

I turn to say something to Nelly, who's mucking out the goat stall, and the ladder wobbles. "Shit!" I yell.

I grab the wall to steady myself as Peter appears. He grips the base of the ladder and looks up at me. "The ground's uneven here. I'll hold it while you finish up."

I don't want his help. I don't want to owe him anything, not even a *thank you*. I whack a nail and shake my head. "I'm fine."

"I don't want you to fall," he says.

I don't know why he can't just leave me alone. "Peter! I. Don't. Want. Your. Help. Leave me alone."

Peter's shoulders stiffen. He lets go and leaves the barn quietly, although he gives the door a good slam. I give the nail another whack and try not to feel guilty. The ladder steadies again, and I look down at Nelly's stern face. I know that look.

"What?" I ask.

"Remember how you used to tell me that Peter was a nice guy underneath all that bullshit?" I nod and look away. "Well, you were right. Hey, can you believe I'm admitting you were right?"

He's joking to soften the fact that he's reprimanding me, but I still feel heat creep up my neck.

"He's doing everything he can to show he's sorry, Cass. He took me aside to apologize for having been a jerk, even before all this went down. You have to see how much he loves Bits, how good he is with her? He has risen to the occasion. It just took him a little longer and one big mistake."

I nod again, but I'm so ashamed I can't look at him.

"You've never held grudges. So why now? You need to forgive him for what he's said and done. You've said your share at this point, too. And stop holding him responsible for the things he's not responsible for.

"You don't know what Adrian's thinking. Neither do I. Neither does Peter, for that matter. And there's no way to know right now. So stop acting like you know, first of all, and stop taking it out on other people. We all have our own shit we're going through. Adrian's alive, be thankful for that."

I think of Eric and what I would give to know his fate. Of everybody else's families and how desperate we are for news of them. I once said that knowing Adrian was alive was enough, and it was true then. I've gotten so mixed up.

"You're being mean, Cassie, and you aren't a mean person. Give Peter a chance to prove he's changed, okay?"

He reaches his hand up. I grab it but keep my eyes on the dust motes swirling in a patch of sunlight. He squeezes once. "Love you, Cass. I'll leave you alone."

I watch him leave and rest my head on the ladder rungs. Nelly's right. I've denied Peter the one thing I want most for myself: forgiveness. Instead of understanding it might have been impossible for him to be the person I expected him to be, I've been punishing him, nursing hurts and grudges and holding it against him. Which is exactly what I fear Adrian has done. That he can't forgive me for having been weak and lost. I haven't been able to forgive myself, so I didn't think Peter deserved it either.

It's time to let it go. To accept that whatever is, is. To embrace and enjoy what I do have. Because I know that right now, in comparison to the rest of the world, it's an awful lot.

CHAPTER 88

I wait until Peter's alone on the front steps carving away at a small stick and force myself over to where he sits.

"Taking up whittling?" I ask, and try to smile.

He drops the stick and raises his hand in the air. "I don't know, maybe. Does that meet with your approval?"

His voice is exasperated, on the defensive. I fight the urge to storm off. I haven't said a nice word to him in a month, so why should he know that I plan to now?

"I didn't mean... Peter, I'm sorry for the way I've been treating you."

It comes out in a huge rush and my voice cracks at the end. He looks up from his folding knife with a lined brow that smoothes out when he sees my face. I motion at the steps, and he scoots over so I can sit. It's shady and cool out here in the afternoon. I've brought my mother's flowers back from their sorry state, and I take a deep breath of the scented air before I continue.

"I haven't been fair to you. I know you've been trying and I've made it harder. I've been feeling sorry for myself instead of being thankful for all of this."

I wave my hand at the woods and the house and even him. He picks up his stick and turns it over in his hands, then looks sideways at me with the corner of his mouth turned up.

"Taking a page from my book," he says. "I'm sorry too, you know. I thought I could get away without saying it to you for some reason. I don't know why it was so hard for me to do." He shakes his head.

I shrug. "You were mad at me. I haven't handled things very well, have I?"

"Better 'n I did," he says, like we're two kids having a fight.

I smile. "I mean, the break up could have gone smoother. I'm sorry about that."

It's his turn to shrug. "It was coming for a while."

"You knew?"

"I'm not that oblivious, you know. I knew you would break up with me sooner or later. I just held on as long as I could. I thought maybe at some point... But after that night, the one before that party?"

I nod. So he was awake.

"After that, it was just a matter of time. I'm surprised it took as long as it did."

"Well," I say. "I'm not very good at breaking up with people."

Except once. I know he knows what I'm thinking. I'm sure Ana's told him the whole story.

He looks cautious. "Can I say something? It has the A word in it."

I let out a shaky breath. "Sure. Let's get it all out."

"I know what he said on the radio, but I think you're taking it wrong. You automatically thought he wasn't talking about you. But what if he's talking *to* you?"

"What?" Peter's out of his mind. There was no cryptic message in there.

"Maybe he didn't want to go on the radio and pour out his heart to someone he thinks doesn't miss him. But maybe he said there was no one else so that you would know, just in case you were out here listening. Cassie, think about it. 'There's no one else.' "

I look at Peter like I've never seen him before. Maybe he's right. Not that it was a message, but that I've been thinking about it all wrong. *There's no one else.* Maybe I still have a shot. And a tiny voice reminds me that I know Adrian, that he never would have gone on the radio willingly; he would have sent Ben or anyone else. Maybe he wanted me to hear his voice. Just in case. It's a tiny coal of hope and I'll protect it, but I won't let it consume me. Maybe one day I'll know.

"When did you get so smart?" I ask.

He grins and gets that arrogant look on his face, but it's only for show. "Only recently," he admits, and looks down at his stick again. "Only after Bits and that night."

"I'm sorry for what I said, Peter. About no one loving you. It's not true, you know. And, Bits, she loves you, well, to bits."

"And I'm sorry about putting us all in that situation, but I can never be truly sorry it happened. We saved Bits."

I nod. I've thought that myself.

"She reminds me of my little sister. She was nine when she and my parents died." He twists the stick with shaky hands and glances at me. "I've never told anyone this before."

He exhales. "The night they died my sister was going to a birthday party at one of those arcade places. You know, the kind that have Skee Ball and other stuff?

"We lived in Westchester. We weren't loaded or anything. My grandmother was the kind of person who held money over your head, and my dad had washed his hands of her. We saw her on holidays. He was a lawyer and made decent enough money. We were happy."

He smiles and stares into the trees across the driveway.

"So that night Jane, my sister, wanted me to come with her. She practically begged me, but I didn't want to be seen with a bunch of nine year-olds by anyone at school and I was old enough to stay home alone. So I told her no way and they left. The next time I saw them was at their funeral.

"At the wake I heard people talking about the accident. My mother and father had been killed instantly, but what everyone had kept from me was that my sister hadn't. She must've been stuck in her seat, because she died of smoke inhalation from the fire. Her nails were bloody, like she'd been trying to release herself, but the car was so twisted she couldn't undo the buckle. Maybe if I'd been there I could have gotten her out. But I was selfish."

The stick twists faster and faster. I put my hand over his. All these years he's been carrying this around, angry at himself.

"No, Peter. You were *twelve*."

He drops the stick and holds my hand. A tear rolls down his face. "After that it was easy to be like my grandmother. To be selfish, since I knew that's what I really was. I didn't have anyone else. After a while I forgot there was any other way. Poor little rich boy, right?"

I shake my head at his disparaging laugh. My mother always said that everyone carries so much inside them that we never know about. That's why she was so kind to everyone. As usual, she was right.

"Bits is like my second chance at a family. A chance to protect Jane. It's ridiculous, I know."

"No, it's not. Not at all."

He places my hand back on my knee with a gentle pat and wipes his eyes. We sit so close our shoulders touch. I hear plates hit the table for dinner and footsteps at the front door. Whoever it is must see us sitting here because the footsteps recede again.

"We're all your family," I say, and I mean it. He smiles and looks down. It's just like my dream, except I'm sitting with Peter.

"You and Bits have the dirtiest feet I've ever seen." He laughs and wipes his eyes one last time. He glances at me again. "Can I say one more thing?"

"Of course."

"Do you love Adrian?"

I stare up at the treetops, watching crows circle. "I always have. I just told him I didn't."

He elbows me in the side. "Well, why would you go and do something dumb like that?"

"Thanks a lot," I say, and elbow him back.

He stops smiling and his eyes grow serious. "Cassie, if you really loved him and he knew it, really knew it?" I nod, because he did and because I know he loved me back. "Then he still loves you. Believe me, no one would let you go that easily."

My cheeks are pink, but it's more of a happy warmth than a blush. I see he means it, and it's one of the nicest things anyone's ever said to me. "Thanks."

He picks up his stick and taps me on the knee. I take it and tap him back.

"So, are we friends?" I ask.

"Yeah, finally, I think we are."

I look at his work boots. They're so different than the kind of shoes he always wore. They look good on him.

"Hey, Petey." I bite my lip to keep from smiling. "Sorry about your fancy shoes. You know, the whole puking thing."

He laughs and leans back on the top step. "I deserved it. But I really did love those shoes."

We lean against each other for a little while longer, listening to the sounds of our family in the house, and then we get up and join them.

CHAPTER 89

I've volunteered to do the thankless task of placing new jars of food behind the old in the basement. All the flour and other staples we've scavenged we use first because my parents packed theirs to last for ten or twenty years. I wonder if we'll still be taking refuge here in ten years. It's a sobering thought, and I try to banish it by humming anything but the *Golden Girls'* theme song, so I don't hear Nelly behind me until he speaks.

"Whatever would you do without me?" He stands with his hands on his hips and looks gallant.

I put on a southern belle accent. "Ah don't rightly know, suh."

"You've been humming for days, and I can't help but think my Come to Jesus talk had something to do with it."

"Nelson Everett, modest as usual." He huffs on his fist and rubs it on his chest. "But right as usual, too. Come and help."

"I knew I'd get roped into doing work if I came down here."

"There's always work in the summer. Just think of the long winter days we'll while away by the fire, growing increasingly bored and insane."

He groans and sits on a five-gallon bucket. "Don't get me wrong, being alive is cool, but the thought of all of us, all winter, is a tad bit depressing. Think we could find me a boyfriend before the snow flies?"

"Maybe next year we'll head to a Safe Zone and find you one."

I try to keep how much I would like to be at a certain Safe Zone out of my voice. It's not that I want to leave here; I just wish for five minutes alone with Adrian. Five minutes to see how he feels about me. I smile brightly.

Nelly smiles and shakes his head. "There's no maybe about it, darlin'. If I have to watch you walk around all lovelorn for two more years, I'll strap you to my back and walk you there myself, fighting off zombies the whole way."

I laugh at the image but squint at him. "I'm not so bad, am I? I've been trying."

"You haven't been whimpery at all, but I still know."

"Of course you do." I sigh. "So it's celibacy for us. Unless you want to switch teams for the winter." I wink lasciviously at him.

"No, thanks," he says dryly. "Although you'd be my first choice. Maybe ask me again in February."

"Think of all the little Nelson Charles Everetts we could have running around." I pat the imaginary head of one of them.

"Okay, that just made up my mind. No way." He runs a hand through his hair until he looks like he's been electrocuted.

"Well, we need a project. Is it just me or have you noticed that Ana and Peter—"

He grins. "Um, yeah. Even Bits has noticed. She asked Ana if Peter was her prince the other day. Ana got all flustered, it was great." He shifts on the bucket as he laughs, and I hear an ominous creak.

"Well, Ana's not the problem. I think Peter likes her, too, but he's treating her like a little sister-best friend. I'm going to find out why." I push the old cans of beans to the side and stack the new ones behind them.

"You're okay with it?"

Nelly jumps to catch a can before it crashes. He holds it and searches my face.

I shrug. "Yeah. Why wouldn't I be?"

"Oh, I don't know," he says, like I'm dumb. "Some people feel it's weird to have their ex-boyfriend dating their little sister."

"Come on. She's not my little sister. Plus, Peter and I should have broken up forever ago. I have no feelings except friend feelings for him."

"Well, maybe you should save him for February for yourself, just in case I'm unavailable."

I cuff him on the back of the head. "Shut up. You'll come around, I just know it."

I lean sexily against the shelf with a hand on my hip, but my hand slips and he bursts into laughter.

"I am now forced to rescind my offer, since you laughed at my sexy pose. You'll be sorry." I cross my arms and he grins. "Anyway, I'm going to find out what Peter thinks of Ana. It'll give us something to do besides moving those cans of beans and putting the new ones in the back." I point to where what looks like a thousand cans of beans sit waiting.

"Seriously?" He lets out a dramatic sigh before he moves to the shelves and starts to shuffle cans around.

CHAPTER 90

Halfway through the third lap between the cabin and John's, I stop with my hands on my knees. I was not made to run. There's a knife in my side and my lungs burn. I might be dying. Ana's ponytail swings jauntily as she jogs in place in front of me. She's actually smiling. I hate her.

"That's only a mile," she says.

"That's about a mile more than I can usually run." I sink to the ground. "Dying. Go on without me. Remember me always."

She frowns and nudges me with a sneakered foot. "You are not dying. Stop being such a baby."

Ana's new interest has turned into an obsession. And while these past weeks have put me in the best shape of my life, I am not as driven as she. I want to be able to kill things, not be a superhero. Or be a superhero without having to run ten miles.

"I just need a minute."

It's soft and cool down here on the forest floor. Ana bounces on the balls of her feet. I know she wants to continue, and I've no intention of getting up anytime soon.

"Go ahead, Ana. I'll see you on the way back." She nods and starts toward John's. "Or never."

"I heard that!" she yells, as she hops off a tree root with a burst of speed.

I watch until she's out of sight. Ana's still headstrong and bossy, but now she has a vulnerability she always kept hidden. I'm trying to encourage it. It's the main reason I'm running through the woods like an idiot, killing myself.

I kick off my sweaty sneakers and wait until the burning in my lungs subsides. I have to stay ahead of her if I'm going to escape her clutches, so I yank myself up using a low branch. I pass the shed and see Peter and James inside. They've been trying to figure out the solar power for days.

"How's it going?" I ask.

They look up and smile. I like having Peter's reaction to me be a smile instead of a scowl. It's nice to smile back at him, too.

James pushes his hair back and sets down a manual. "Well, I think I might have an idea. Unfortunately, I know computers, which is about as helpful right now as being fluent in ancient Greek. We're going to need a bunch of stuff, most importantly, new batteries."

He's being modest, though. He fixed the radio and helped John with the generator wiring. I bet we'll have power eventually.

"We can go tomorrow," I say. I lean against the wall to massage my legs and look at Peter to see if he's in.

"Sure," Peter says, his mouth quirking. "Boot camp making you sore?"

"I am not built for speed."

It comes out before I remember its double meaning. He looks like he's about to comment, but he must think again, because he closes his mouth and raises an amused eyebrow. Peter's so different that I don't think of him as the Peter I dated. I just pretend I've slept with his evil twin brother.

I blush and change the subject. "She's relentless."

Just then Ana runs past and waves. Her footsteps head around the shed, and then she's past the window, waving again.

"She's definitely single-minded," he says. We watch her run into the woods.

"She can sure fill out a pair of Wal-Mart yoga pants though, eh?" He looks at me strangely but stays silent. Nelly says I have no finesse in these situations. "She's really pretty, don't you think?"

"Of course," he says.

"And she's smart and has a great sense of humor. You probably know all that, since you guys are such good friends."

"Why do I feel like you're trying to sell me something?"

His face is impassive, but I think I see a twinkle in his eye. James stands behind Peter, his shoulders shaking with silent laughter. I glare at him.

"I'll get started on that list for tomorrow," James says, barely containing his mirth as he leaves.

Peter looks at me suspiciously. Nelly was right, I have no finesse. I'm going to have to get right to the point. "Well, I was thinking that you and Ana would be good together. She likes you, you know." I grin at him.

He looks everywhere but at me. "This is weird, Cassie. My ex-girlfriend trying to set me up with her little sister. Who is also too young, by the way."

"She's not my sister! So we dated, now it's done." I put my hands on my hips. "I think you like her, Peter."

He looks a little pinker under his tan, but it's hard to tell. I've always liked teasing Peter. I can't help it. He's so self-assured that I have to make sure he's a fallible human like the rest of us.

"She's young. And what am I going to do, ask her out to dinner?"

He hasn't denied he likes her. Now we're getting somewhere. I make a face dismissing his argument.

"She's twenty-five, not fourteen. I know you're an old, old man of thirty, but I think somehow the chasm between your ages can be bridged. Plus, what might have been a big age difference three months ago doesn't mean anything now. And a lack of restaurants hasn't stopped people from getting together over the last gazillion years."

He shrugs, but his eyes are thoughtful.

"And that's the last thing I'll say about it," I say, and turn to go.

"Cassandra," I hear, as I get through the door. "If that's true, I'll sign over every dime I have to you, if and when this is all over."

He sounds serious, but I know when he's amused, so I wave a hand and skip away. This is a bad idea, as my hamstrings are half their usual length. I yelp and stagger as Peter chuckles. I give him the one finger salute and limp to the house to the sound of his full-blown laughter.

CHAPTER 91

The parking lot of the Radio Shack's strip mall is strewn with vehicles. It looks like someone attempted to build a barricade using metal drums in front of the nail salon; they're lined up three deep in a semicircle under the overhang. The lot is empty, though, and anyone who used it is long gone. We haven't traveled this far from the house yet, but Radio Shack's our best bet for the electrical stuff we need.

James points out the window. "Hey, there's an automotive parts store. We can get the marine batteries there, I bet. Then we won't have to stop again."

The store is a big square island that sits catty-corner to the strip mall in the same parking lot. Nelly wedges a crowbar between the doors until they bend open. Everything is in place; I guess no one desired auto parts before the world ended. Rows of car and boat batteries line the shelves in the back.

"Dude, this is perfect," James says.

We relax. There's nothing in here, and we only saw one Lexer on the way. It would lull me into thinking they've died or rotted away, except that Matt in Whitefield has reported sightings of large groups of infected, walking and walking. Zeke must have made it there, because Matt's been calling them pods, too.

"Do some of you want to bring the list to Radio Shack? You can take the truck and come back to pick me up. I'll drag all this to the front. Peter, you know what we're looking for as well as I do," James says.

"Someone should stay with you," Ana says. She turns to me. "Cass, you want to?"

I shrug. "Sure."

I walk to the front to grab a cart and watch them drive to Radio Shack. James wanders the aisles like a kid in a candy store, throwing things on top of the batteries. He's muttering something about some kind of controller when I see a flash of movement in the parking lot.

"James, I just saw something."

We scuttle to the front windows. Ana throws boxes and bags into the back of the pickup while Nelly watches the lot.

"Sorry," I say. "I saw one of the bags and didn't know what it was."

He pats my arm. "Better safe than sorry."

The second cart is soon overflowing, and James is dreamy-eyed as he looks it over. "I used to build radios when I was a kid. Maybe we should go to Radio Shack, see if there's anything else I could use."

I wouldn't mind going over there. I'm getting uncomfortable with having split up. My hands are sweaty in my leather gloves, and I want to load the truck and leave.

I hear the shout at the same time I see the mass of ragged forms. Nelly, Peter and Ana stand with their backs against the nail salon's broken window, inside the ring of metal drums. The gunfire starts and the infected fall, but dozens more press forward.

Those metal drums are the only thing keeping the three of them from being overwhelmed. There's an opening on both sides of the semicircle where the barrels don't meet the wall, and the infected feed through them like cars in a bottleneck. Nelly attempts to move one, but they must be full; it doesn't even budge.

James and I run into the lot and take shots from behind a car. We take out the stragglers, but not the ones closest to our friends for fear of shooting one of them. They've dropped their empty guns, and now they slash into the oncoming bodies one by one.

Ana screams. Her body slams against the cracked glass of the nail salon window, and she fights to right herself. I get a glimpse of hands just inside the salon, tangled and twisted in her ponytail. Nelly jabs his machete at them but has to turn and fight off the next Lexer that's been funneled to him. Peter's got his hands full, too. He slashes a neck and shoves the body to the side, but there's only seconds before the next.

The cords in Ana's neck stand out as she twists and fights. Her face is desperate, and, even worse, it's tired. Someone has to take out the Lexers in the nail salon.

I turn to James. "I'll get the one who has Ana."

He nods. I reload my pistol and hand him my nine millimeter. I don't take the time to hide; I sprint as fast as I can around the side of the building. The glass back door of the nail salon is locked. I crash my cleaver into it and bust out the jagged edges.

I step over scattered bottles of polish in the storeroom and into the front. Pedicure chairs run along the left wall, and manicure tables fill the right. There are two Lexers at the window. They're getting in each other's way, which may be the only reason Ana is still on the other side. There's a spike of glass under her back, and every time she hits it she yanks up, but she won't be able to do that forever.

I move the cleaver to my left hand and take out my revolver. I don't see the Lexer coming at me until a second before he knocks me to the linoleum and follows me down. The air whooshes out of my lungs, and the pistol skitters across the floor.

I can't get up. He must weigh two hundred pounds, but I manage to get the cleaver shaft under his chin. He bites the air inches above me. Clotted black strings drop off his bottom lip and pool on my chest. My biceps shake with the effort of pushing against every lunge. I can do two, maybe three, more lunges. And then that rotten, disgusting mouth will find its mark on my face or neck. It won't matter where; I'll be as good as dead. Pure panicky terror gives me another burst of strength. I scream with the effort as I buck under him and roll free.

I scramble back and my head slams into a footbath. For a moment it all goes black, until I feel hands grab my boot and I begin to slide. I grasp the edge of the footbath and kick as hard as I can. There's a crack as my foot breaks his cheekbone. It knocks him down, but he immediately rises to his knees. It's not fair, the way they feel no pain. The way they don't stop. The way they don't get tired, or scared, or out of breath. He hisses and reaches for me.

"No you don't, fucker. Not today," I hiss back.

I grip the cleaver like a battering ram and send the flat end under his chin. It slices cleanly through the vertebrae, and he crashes to the floor. My feet slip in the viscous fluid from his decapitated head, and I slide to the window where Ana blindly punches behind her. The two Lexers bite her leather-clad arms, but her armor does its job. The broken glass protects her head, and with each attempted attack they cut deep, bloodless gashes in their faces.

They haven't noticed me. I turn my cleaver to the spike side, level it with the brain stem of the first and slam it home. I yank it out. The other lets go of Ana and starts for me. I hardly need the force I use to get it through his eye socket. Ana spins around, her face terrified and relieved, and leaps onto the barrels. A litany of curses fly from her mouth.

She stabs the spike into the top of a Lexer skull. "Mother!" She grunts and stabs into the next. "Fucker!" She flips around her blade and decapitates one.

She dances down the barrels, slamming her cleaver spike into their heads or eye sockets and ripping it out again. She reaches the end of the line on Peter's side and then turns to Nelly's. He holds his machete by the hilt, with the last of the infected skewered on the end. Its hair is torn out fuzz and its face is half gone, teeth exposed. Its hands struggle and flail. It's mindless, or it's mindful only of us, which is just as terrifying.

James, who's been slowly advancing and killing Lexers from behind, comes up and sinks his knife into its neck with a crunch. It slides off Nelly's machete to the ground. When I step out of the salon, Ana races into my arms. We don't hug so much as hold each other up.

"Thank you," she whispers.

All the fear I've kept at bay hits, and I swallow hard. "No, thank *you*. All that horrible running paid off."

Ana barks out a laugh. We assess the damage. Lexers lie in the parking lot, but most are piled around us. We hop onto the barrels, not wanting to step on, or worse, in, the infected, and practically fly home.

***

We've hosed ourselves off and taken showers. Our clothes and armor soak in a cocktail of cleaners no virus could possibly survive. Ana's waited until last to shower, and when she finally enters the living room, running a hand through her damp hair, we stop dead. Where there used to be the long chestnut colored hair that Ana painstakingly hot-ironed, there's now chin-length hair that gets even higher in the back. Nothing's going to get a handful of this hair. She tries to look nonchalant, but she's nervous.

"I love it," I say. "I really do."

It accentuates her cheekbones and her graceful neck. She looks older, more sophisticated. She smiles, but pulls at the ends like she's trying to lengthen them as everyone murmurs agreement. Peter stares at her, and I catch his eye and tilt my chin up, telling him to say something.

He swallows. "You look gorgeous."

Ana beams, and I realize it was his reaction she was most worried about. If his face is any indication, she's got nothing to fear.

Penny's mouth hangs open. "I can't believe you cut your hair off. Don't get me wrong, you look amazing, but I just can't believe *you...*" she trails off with a shake of her head.

"I'd rather be alive than have nice hair," Ana replies.

"Who are you and what did you do with my sister?" Penny asks. She smiles and moves forward to touch her sister's hair in wonder.

CHAPTER 92

Bits picks basil leaves off the stems under Peter's tutelage. He's making some sort of pesto. Tomatoes, sprinkled with goat cheese, sit on a platter. His dinners are always fancy, and before he's done we're milling around the kitchen like begging dogs. I set the table and get out a bottle of wine we found. There isn't much wine, but this dinner should have something special to go with it. And John's got strawberry wine brewing in his basement.

"Smells good in there," Nelly says, as he sniffs through the back door screen. He's been digging, and every inch of him is covered in dirt. "Pete, maybe you'll teach me how to cook one day."

Peter leans toward the door and laughs. He doesn't mind when Nelly calls him Pete now. "You'll just slather it in barbeque sauce."

"Damn straight," Nelly says. "I'm a Texan."

He leaves his mud-caked boots outside and heads for the bathroom. The table looks nice with the wine glasses, which starts me thinking.

When everyone's seated I jump up and clap a hand over my mouth. "John, we forgot to check the tomatoes in your garden today! They were ready to burst as of yesterday."

John looks at me calmly, obviously thinking I'm blowing this out of proportion. "Well, we'll just leave it to tomorrow."

"What if tomorrow they're too far gone? All that wasted food? What if it's the difference between life and death?"

I think I may have taken the melodrama too far, but no one looks suspicious. I move behind Nelly's chair and surreptitiously hit him in the back.

He chokes on his tomato. "I'll help," he says, and looks longingly at the pesto.

"Pesto is great at room temperature," I say. He mutters something and I grin. "Penny, James, John? There are lots of tomatoes."

"I don't remember that many tomatoes," John says, his brow creased.

"I saw a lot," says Bits, who thinks five tomatoes is a lot. But I'm not going to argue.

"Okay." John heaves himself up. "Food'll still be here after dark, but we should get the tomatoes if you say so."

I wave at Ana and Peter to sit back down. Ana's back was pretty badly wrenched, and we've been trying to make her rest.

"No, you guys stay," I say. "We have enough people. Ana, you shouldn't bend over! Peter, you cooked it, so you should enjoy it."

I see the light dawn in his eyes. I smile serenely and pour wine into their glasses. He glowers at me. I hum a little tune and consider lighting a candle, but it's not dark, so that might be overkill. I wink at him before I slip out the door. He shakes his head and sighs, but there's a smile playing on his face when he turns back to her. I'm counting it as their first date. We walk the path to John's, and the memory of my and Adrian's first kiss makes my insides bump.

***

It happened on our third real date. We'd been out in a group, too, but Adrian hadn't tried to kiss me, on a real date or otherwise. I'd begun to think I'd misread the signals. Nelly cornered me at the bar after our second date.

"So?" he demanded, eyebrows raised.

I sighed. "So, nothing. He hasn't even tried to kiss me. He asked me to go hiking on Saturday, so I think we have a really good time together. Well, I do, anyway. But maybe we're just friends."

Nelly looked skeptical. "No way he's just friends, not with the way he looks at you."

"What do you mean?" I nudged Nelly's arm.

Nelly took a long swig while he thought. "It's like he goes all soft. He smiles like you're a little kitten or something."

"Most people don't want to make out with kittens. Maybe I'm like one of those mangy old kittens you can't help but feel sorry for. Who's cute in a ratty sort of way, so you give them extra attention?"

Nelly laughed. "You are blind, girl. Blind, I tell you. But okay, I'll just go ask Adrian why—" He lifted his beer at Adrian, who sat at the bar and smiled at us while he talked to someone.

I grabbed the back of his shirt and spun him around. "Don't you dare!"

He grinned. "I won't. If he kisses you on Saturday. If not, we have to get to the bottom of this."

On Saturday, Adrian picked me up in his beat-up car. He opened the door for me and walked around. I reached over and unlocked the driver's side door, just like my dad had taught me, since my dad thought he still lived in 1970, when no one had those little clicker thingies that unlock all the doors. But Adrian's car had the knobs you pull up, and I smiled as I followed my dad's date etiquette. Adrian apologized for the car's general appearance, but since I had no car, I said his was still nicer than mine.

"Plus," I said, "I have one criterion for cars: they have to not break down, leaving you stranded on lonely dirt roads or desert highways. That's it. A radio's nice, too." I rubbed the door like I was trying to make friends with it.

"Well, this must be your dream car, then." He smiled and shook his head.

"What?" I asked.

"You're just different. In a good way."

I wondered if being different in a good way made me more desirable or more like that ratty kitten.

We walked a few miles alongside a creek before we stopped to eat. There was frost on the ground every morning that late in the fall, but the sun had come out to warm up the day. My fingers and toes were cold, though, and I wanted some of the hot chocolate I'd packed. A flat boulder that jutted out over the creek made a good picnic spot. The water eddied and pooled around it, and the long-legged bugs that skate across the water were everywhere. There was a splash every time a fish came to the surface to gobble one up.

Adrian reached into his pack. "I have salami and a turkey, too."

"I love salami," I said.

He held the neatly-wrapped sandwich in the air and smiled. "I know. You mentioned it once."

I tried to recall a conversation that would have demanded I list my favorite lunch meats, but I knew there probably wasn't one. Who knows why I had decided to share that little gem with Adrian. But it gave me hope. You wouldn't remember someone's favorite sandwich meat if you didn't care. I think I saw it on a greeting card once.

I vowed to keep my favorite dog breed and tampon brand to myself, at least for today, and smiled back. "Oh, thanks."

I watched the crimson and gold leaves drift into the creek for a farewell ride down the gentle rapids. It reminded me of something.

"You know, I once read that there's really no reason for trees to change their leaf color in the fall," I said, as I set out the thermos and cups. "They use the sugars and nutrients in their leaves to put out all these colors, instead of bringing it into their trunks and using it. When I read that I wanted to go hug a tree. Or say thank you or something. I'm sure they don't do it for us, but maybe they do it just because it's beautiful."

There was silence. I looked up, already regretting having said something so weird. He was watching me, and now I did see what Nelly meant about that look. It was gentle, but it was also curious, and I squirmed a little under its intensity.

"Hey," he said softly, "I really like you, Cassie."

"I like you, too," I whispered.

Everything inside crashed and whizzed when I said it. Until Adrian I had a strict policy of keeping feelings to myself in a relationship, especially since mine always fell short of what the other person had for me.

"I was hoping you did." He cupped the side of my face and his dimple creased. "Tree hugger."

My laugh rang out. Before I could say anything he was close, then closer, and then his mouth was softer than I thought it would be. My stomach dropped the way it does on that first big roller coaster dip. His hand rested on my collarbone and I put my palm on his chest. When I felt his heart beating as fast as mine, I grabbed a fistful of shirt and pulled him closer. I didn't recognize myself. This girl who grabbed shirts and nipped softly and would have done absolutely anything on that rock right then was new to me.

When we parted I could feel two spots of pink burning on my cheeks. My breathing was shallow. I was embarrassed that my desire was so apparent until I saw it on his face and in his unfocused eyes.

"Your hair is such a pretty color," he said breathlessly. He rubbed a lock between his thumb and forefinger.

I shrugged. "It's brown."

He tilted his head to the trees. "No, it's the color of oak leaves once they've fallen. They're brown, but that red still lurks underneath. Russet."

"Oh." I liked having russet hair instead of brown.

Adrian poured cocoa. I leaned back and watched him. I wanted to kiss him again.

He looked up. "What are you thinking?"

"I wasn't sure you'd ever kiss me," I said, surprised I'd said it out loud.

"I wanted to, but I meant what I said before. I like you, and I don't want to mess it up."

He looked shy suddenly, but when his eyes met mine they were direct. I wondered how he could say what he felt without being terrified. Or, maybe he was but didn't let it stop him. Maybe I could learn to do that, too. He handed me a cup, and I blew on it to have something to do while I thought of something to say back. I remembered that he'd asked me what I was thinking.

"You won't mess it up," I said, with what felt like all the air in my lungs. "Not if you kiss me again."

So he did.

***

Bits points at the two small buckets of tomatoes. "See? Lots of tomatoes!"

I laugh at the confused look on John's face and come clean. "Peter was yapping about not being able to take Ana out to dinner, so I thought I could make it a romantic dinner without it being weird. The opportunity presented itself and was too good to pass up."

"I had a feeling you guys were up to something," Penny says, and looks at Nelly.

Bits's smile gets wider as we talk. I've got at least one ally.

Nelly raises his hands. "Don't look at me. I would've been much smoother."

I may have no finesse, but it's nice to think about somebody else's love life besides my own.

"How about I make you all some P.B. and J at John's?" I ask. "Just to tide you over until we go back." Everyone groans at the thought of the meal at the cabin, which is as gourmet as it gets out here. "Oh, come on, it's for love! You'll still get your yummy dinner."

Bits spins and sings the song from Sleeping Beauty. Nelly picks her up and waltzes her around. They follow me into the house grumbling, but love is in the air and the peanut butter sandwiches go down a lot easier than they expected.

CHAPTER 93

It's a good thing I love the garden, because it feels like I should pitch a tent out here sometimes. If we're not weeding, we're watering or picking or mulching or drying or processing what we've picked. The tomato plants are pushing five feet tall and are laden with red and green globes. The melon patch smells sweet, and we've already had a few watermelons ripen. Nelly taught Bits how to spit the seeds, and she takes great pride in holding the world record. Cracking into the thick skin of the first watermelon was like a religious rite. Fresh fruit used to be something you grabbed at the store. Now it's something you eat when it ripens and savor as best you can until next year.

All of us girls are in the garden picking beans. Bees crawl over every flower, enjoying the sunshine and getting ready for winter, just like us. The boys, as I think of them, have gone to find propane for the stove. I wanted to go, but then I wondered why I wanted to assist in picking up a two-hundred pound tank. I worry about them as I search among the tangled vines. I haven't forgotten our last trip. That's the real reason I wanted to go. I feel like if I'm there I can control things and make them come out all right, even though I know it's an absolute fallacy.

I try to let my worry go. I've gotten better at letting things go in the past few weeks. I can't make Adrian still love me, I can't change the course of this virus, I can't protect everyone I love, I can't walk around with my nails digging into my palms from the stress of it all. But I can annoy Ana and Peter until they finally get together.

"So, Ana," I say. "What's going on with you and Peter?"

She goes very still. "Nothing." She pulls back and looks at me, wide eyed. "I swear, Cassie."

She thinks I'll be mad. I've been going about this all wrong.

I put out a hand to stop her stammering. "Ana. Ana, it's fine. I know you've had a crush on him for forever. And he likes you back, you know."

He face relaxes and she bites her lip. "Oh. Do you think so?"

"I know so. I asked him."

She dips her head, and her hair hides her face while she smiles. "You did? I thought maybe, a couple of times, that he might. Although, look at me."

She points to her stained tank top and self-consciously runs a hand through her short hair. Her arms are covered in dirt and scratches, and she doesn't have on a lick of makeup. She's gorgeous.

"Ana, you know you're beautiful. Your skin is a burnished gold and your hair is shiny." She looks more upbeat as I continue. "Your hands are graceful and your bottom plump. You smell always of roses and—" She throws a bean at me, laughing. "No, but seriously, you don't need any of that. He likes you and you like him."

"And you're okay with it?"

When it's come to boys, Ana's never cared who or what she goes through to get them.

"I insist. You two are driving me crazy. All those long looks and lingering touches. Ugh." I pretend to puke and get hit by ten beans.

Bits comes tearing around the house. "They're back and they have a surprise for everyone!" she yells, then turns and races back again.

The back of the pickup is full. There are two propane tanks strapped in the bed and a tangle of metal that I realize are bicycles and a rack. Bits squeals when she sees the purple one that's hers. She hops on and rides around in circles.

"We got one for everyone," John says. "There was a guy who fixed up bikes and sold them down in town. We'll attach the rack to the van roof and keep a couple up there. This one here is yours, Cassie."

He holds out a red bike. Penny looks from John to my face and bursts out laughing.

When everyone looks to see what's so funny, she says, "Cassie can't ride a bike."

Six faces turn to me in disbelief. My face must be crimson. "I fall off bikes. I can get going, but then suddenly it all gets crazy and I go out of control."

"Crazy?" Nelly smirks. I'm so glad my inadequacies are amusing to him. "Why am I not surprised?"

Bits makes another circuit. "It's easy, Cassie," she says. "Maybe you need training wheels until you get the hang of it, like I did."

This comment elicits so much laughter that I find myself laughing too. I've always longed to hop on a bike and go breezing off somewhere, but I end up crashing. I don't know what happens. One minute I'm fine; then the next I'm headed for the curb or a tree and I freak out.

"I can help you," she continues. "I remember how."

"Thanks, Bits," I say, and struggle to keep a straight face. "I'm going to need all the help I can get."

***

My first bike lesson on the dirt road ends in the usual tragedy. I put my feet on the pedals and balance, but the front wheel strikes a rock, which makes the fork wobble, and I close my eyes and run into a ditch.

"Why are you afraid of the bike?" Peter calls out from the driveway as I lumber up.

I wonder how long he's been watching. Bits stands next to him, my own personal cheerleader.

"Because it wants me dead," I reply.

He laughs. I feel self-conscious with an audience that isn't just Bits, so I walk the bike back.

"I taught Jane to ride," he says. This is the third time he's mentioned his little sister in the past month. In the entire year we were together he'd never even told me her name. "If a six year-old can do it, you can. Just remember this: the bike is your friend. The bike doesn't want you dead." He smiles at my look of doubt.

Of course the bike wants me dead, they all do.

"Now say it."

I laugh. "No way."

"Yes way. Say it, Cassandra."

This will never work. I roll my eyes and say in my most sarcastic voice, "The bike is my friend. The bike doesn't want me dead."

"Good." Peter pretends I'm not acting like a two year-old. "Now get on it. And don't close your eyes. That's what you're doing, right?"

"How did you know?"

He winks at Bits. "My sister did the same thing. Now, go!"

I don't want an audience. I'll never be able to balance.

"You can't look," I say. "Close your eyes."

Bits giggles, and Peter bends down so she can cover his eyes. "Okay. I can't see."

I get back on. The bike picks up speed, and right away I feel like I'm out of control, but I fight the urge to close my eyes and land in a relatively safe heap. I grip the handlebars and keep going. The wind kicks up my hair and cools my neck. This must be why people ride bikes. It beats the shit out of running. When I've gone a ways, I stop and turn the bike by walking it. I'm not about to attempt what seems like some sort of daredevil maneuver, even though Bits and probably every other seven year-old in the world can do it, and I head back.

My eyes are trained on the road, and only when I hear whistles and cheers do I look up. Bits is too busy clapping to cover Peter's eyes any longer, and they both watch my approach. I brake in front of them, feeling both extremely proud of myself and like the world's biggest dork at the same time.

"I can ride a bike!" I say. "Sort of."

"You did great!" Bits says. "We'll practice together!"

Her eyes are so sincere that I bend down and give her a kiss. "Thanks for the advice," I say to Peter. "It worked. Now, if only you'd take mine."

"I will, Cassandra. If you'll stop bugging me about it."

"Done and done," I say.

But we both know I have no intention of doing anything of the sort. He stares at me sternly, but his mouth twitches, and I stare back until he cracks a smile. I salute them both and head to the house on my bike. I don't fall once.

CHAPTER 94

The sun hides behind dark clouds, but I wake at dawn, as usual. Rain means there's less to do, so we can sleep in. I once thought eight in the morning was early and eleven was reasonable on weekends. I decide to try for eight this morning. I bury myself under the covers, but after a few minutes I sigh and give up.

"I used to get home at this time after a night out, not wake up," Nelly complains.

He has one arm under his head as he looks out the window. I stretch my arms and point my toes. It doesn't hurt as much as it did. My body's gotten used to all this exercise.

He snaps out of his reverie. "That's two nights with no nightmares, right?" he asks.

I nod. "How did you know?"

"I tend to notice being pummeled and woken up by screaming most of the time. So, I also tend to notice when I'm not."

I kick him under the blankets. He yelps and moves his legs. My feet are freezing, even in the summer. Adrian always let me tuck my icy feet under his thighs. He would clench his teeth and smile while I sighed with contentment.

"I think the nightmares are gone. At least for the time being." I can't say why that's the case, but I'm pretty sure it is. I'm starting to feel like me again.

I throw back the covers and grab clothes. When I open my top drawer, I see the glint of silver and pick up the ring. It's warm in my palm. I place it on the bathroom sink, and when I'm dressed I slip it in my pocket. That's where it belongs since it makes me happy. No matter what happens. I pat it gently and head out to make breakfast.

***

The cutthroat game of Monopoly has ended, and we all sit around, listening to the rain pelt down on the metal roof when there's a crash in the kitchen.

Penny stands among the remnants of a bowl. "Shoot. Sorry, Cass."

I keep telling her that this is her house, too, but I know she feels bad about breaking something of my parents'.

"Please, Pen, it's fine. Hey, remember when I broke your mom's vase?"

We were twelve and I'd been showing Penny some goofy dance move I'd made up. Penny grins, remembering how when Maria came home she wasn't angry. She put on music, asked me to show her the move, then proceeded to do it around the house while we laughed our asses off.

If only she were here or we knew she were safe. My fear is reflected in Penny's eyes before she turns her gaze back toward the smashed crockery. When she looks up, her smile is back.

"This is such a movie day," she sighs. "Most of the time I don't miss TV, but on a day like today..."

"A movie," Bits says. She looks like someone's just offered her a trip to the moon. "I wish we could watch a movie."

John laughs. "Well, ladies, had I known how desperate the situation had gotten, I would've said something sooner. Why don't we watch a movie at my place while we run the genny?"

We allow ourselves almost no excess electricity. The generator stays at John's and runs the freezers for a few hours a day to keep things frozen. It powers the radio and washing machine, charges batteries and tools. Gasoline is a very finite resource, and we want enough to last us through the winter.

"Yes!" Bits shouts, and throws her arms around John's neck.

She's become so demonstrative in recent weeks. I've been the recipient of at least a thousand butterfly kisses. And while her nightmares haven't disappeared, they don't come as often. She trusts us so completely it terrifies me we'll fail her somehow.

"Well, we definitely shouldn't make any popcorn," I tease.

She grins. "Caa-ssie! Yes, we should! And my Barbies and your dog have to come, too." She races down the hall to retrieve the toys she's started playing with again.

"Wow," Nelly says. "That kid really needs a movie, huh?"

When *The Princess Bride* ends, we all sigh. Spending time in another world really was like taking a trip to the moon. I could watch movies for a week straight.

"Well, it's about time for the seven o'clock broadcast," John says.

We eat the remaining popcorn while we wait. I steel myself for Adrian's voice, even though I know it's unlikely, but it's just Matt, running down the list of Safe Zones, and one's missing.

"The Safe Zone outside of Allentown, Pennsylvania has been compromised," he reports. "The survivors described a pod of Lexers several hundred strong. Their exact losses are unknown but very high. Some survivors are reported to be in the Safe Zone in Starlight, Pennsylvania."

He reminds us that pods of this size could mean a change in the habits of the infected. The report ends a minute later. I guess even Matt, who seems to have taken a real shine to being a radio personality, doesn't have the energy to be cheerful.

"Okay," John says. His mouth turns down. "We need to start working on fortifications tomorrow."

I try to imagine the group of Lexers we ran into at the Radio Shack times nine.

"We could never fight off that many, either," I say.

"Nope," John replies. "That's why we have the van."

Any magic the movie left behind has evaporated by the time we head back. Bits holds my hand and waxes on about Princess Buttercup. At least she's still happy, and I want her to stay that way. The thought of her, alone, defenseless, makes me grip her hand tight.

"Ouch!" she says.

I loosen my hand. "Sorry, honey." But it's all I can do not to tighten it again, I'm so worried.

CHAPTER 95

John distributes ammo to each of our backpacks in the van. He has some MREs, and with the remaining ones from Sam's Surplus, we have food for a few days.

"Yuck," Penny says, when I stick some in each bag.

John smiles. "Ah, they're not so bad. You should see what they used to feed us in Vietnam. It tasted a lot worse and weighed a ton, too."

"But they had cigarettes in them back then, didn't they?" James asks longingly, wheeling a bike over for the rack. He hasn't had any since his last pack.

"They did, and that was the best thing about them."

"Well, they should give extra combat pay based on the food alone," Penny says. She adds another sleeping bag to the back. "I think that's it."

John laughs. "James, I need help with the shutters. We'll cut 'em at my place and drive over."

Locking the bike down, James says, "Sure thing, boss."

While they work on the shutters, I work on letters for the Message Tree. I write a new one to Henry Washington, telling him we'll be in Vermont if we're not here. I remember how I thought I was lucky that I had no children to keep safe. And now that I do, I see I was right. There's the fear I'll have to watch her die, and, possibly even worse, that I'll die and she'll suffer some horrible fate scared and alone. I think of small, serious Hank and work hard to imagine him full of life instead of shambling and rotting in the woods somewhere.

I write to Eric. I tell him about the ring and thank him for saving it for me. I tell him he was right—about the ring, about Adrian, and about the infection being so much worse than we thought. I tell him he saved me by making me promise I'd leave New York. I tell him I love him and am picturing him and Rachel hiking through the woods, having the time of their lives, because that's how I always think of him. I tell him to meet us in Vermont when he can.

***

It's only three o'clock, but the house is dark. The inside of every window and door in the living area is covered. John's made frames that fit around them so the plywood shutters can be easily hung. They have small hinged doors for viewing and firing a gun.

"I have one for the hallway," John says. "I didn't have enough wood for the bedrooms, but those windows are higher. We can make this a panic room of sorts until we get more. We'll put them up every night."

"I feel like we're on an episode of the A-Team," I say. When everyone looks at me curiously, I explain: "I used to watch the reruns with Eric. Remember at the end they would always build a crazy vehicle or fortress or something?"

James's face had been sober as we sat in the dark and imagined being surrounded, but now his usual smile is back. "That was my favorite part."

"So, do I get to be Face?" Nelly asks.

"You and Peter can fight for it," I say. "But I'm Murdock, he was my favorite."

"You know," Peter says. "That doesn't surprise me one iota."

He and Nelly high five each other. What is with the high fives?

"Well," James says. "I know there's no question that I'm B.A. Baracus. I've been told the resemblance between me and Mr. T is striking."

"That's what attracted me to you at first," Penny says to James, who crosses his arms in a Mr. T pose.

"I pity the fool who messes with my plywood shutters," James says in a deep voice, which makes us laugh.

Even Bits laughs, although she has no idea what we're talking about. And when she mimics James and says it, with her scrawny arms crossed and her tiny voice as deep as she can make it, we lose it completely.

John pretends to be disturbed. "Okay. We'd better take them down. I think the dark might be getting to you all."

CHAPTER 96

It's seven in the morning, but the day is already hot, humid and still. Nelly washes the breakfast dishes while we sprawl out in the living room. There's so much to do, but none of us feels like moving.

"It's hot," Bits whines from where she lies flat on the floor.

"It is," Peter agrees. "I think you're starting to melt. Look at you, you're oozing into the wood."

She giggles. I fan her with an old magazine, and she closes her eyes and pants as the air rushes past.

"It's too hot to do anything," Penny says. She looks at me with one eye squinted, just like she used to in high school. "Should we cut school?"

It's the best idea I've heard all morning. "We totally should. We should go to the pond."

Bits sits up. "Pond? Like swimming?"

I nod. "Yep. We have to walk about a mile, and it's kind of muddy and gross, but we can catch frogs and salamanders. And swim, if it's not too icky for you."

"It's not! Can we really go?" Bits leaps to her feet, the heat forgotten.

I look to John, who nods. "We'll have to check it out first, Bits, make sure it's safe, but I don't see why not. I still have the kids' frog-catching nets at the house."

"Can we have a picnic?" Bits asks. "And, Cassie, can we paint? Outside, like you were telling me about?"

"Sure." I love to see her so excited and wish for the hundredth time that she could have a normal childhood. I point to Nelly. "We'll just load up our pack mule to carry it all."

"Hee-haw," he says.

"That's a donkey, silly!" Bits laughs, before running off to find something to wear.

John and Peter radio us to come down. The pond is a tiny tributary of the creek that runs through my parents' land and ends in a beaver dam. This time of year it's buzzing with dragonflies and frogs and surrounded by cattails.

By the time we reach the pond we're dripping with sweat. John and Peter stand in the clearing around the water and survey the surroundings. I strip to my bathing suit and spray Bits and myself with sunblock.

"Hey, *blanquito*," Penny says to James. "Come and get some of this."

She sprays James, and I eye her tan enviously. "I hate you," I say. She responds with a grin.

Nelly drops his bags in the grass and pulls off his shirt. "I'm going in. You with me, Bits?"

"Yeah!" she yells. She runs into the muck at the water's edge and turns back. "Ew, it's gross, but not too gross. The water's warm, though. Come on!"

I make my way to the water. I love it here, although being so far from the house with no early warning system makes me nervous.

Bits squeals as frogs plop into the water while we wade in, the mud squishing between our toes. "There's one, Cassie! And another! There's, like, a million!"

Nelly runs past and dives in. He comes up spouting water and goes under again. Bits doggy paddles around me and talks incessantly. The water is cool and feels wonderful. I'm about to dunk myself when my ankle is yanked out from under me.

Suddenly I'm in the water up to my neck. I gasp for air to scream. In an instant I can see how it will all play out: The bite on my ankle, the slow death, the way they'll have to finish me off when I'm finally dead so that I stay that way. I kick until its grip releases and grab Bits just as Nelly pops up, rubbing a red mark on his chest.

"Sorry," he says with a sheepish grin. "I guess I kind of forgot things like that aren't funny anymore. This is definitely gonna bruise. Nice karate moves, by the way."

"Oh my God, Nelly!" I hold my hand over my heart. "You scared the shit out of me!"

I splash him as hard as I can. Bits joins in and laughs as he takes his punishment with a smile. Peter, who'd raced over when he realized something was amiss, picks up Bits and cradles her in his arms. She nods, and he tosses her into the water with a splash.

She comes back up squealing. "Again, Peter!"

John keeps an eye on the woods. We haven't seen a single Lexer up by us, since we're on a steep, remote hill, but there's no guarantee it'll stay that way. When I've had my fill, I head to the blankets to set up the paints. I show Bits how to mix the colors, and we sit in the sun with our brushes, our bodies cool from the water.

A shadow looms behind me. "Hey, that's really good," Peter says.

I fight the urge to cover my painting. "Oh, no, it's not. It's terrible."

He crouches next to me. "Well, in thirty minutes you've made something better than I could do in a year, so I think it's good. I've never seen any of your stuff."

"Yeah, you have. That painting in the living room?"

It's a painting of the vegetable garden in bloom, with a woman, my mother, in the shadows, tending to it.

"You did that? Wow. Whenever I pass by I think how I'd like to step into that world. The colors are like in a dream: all bright and liquid, but creamy."

I smile and nod. My mother always said it's what she'd dreamed heaven must be like. "Thanks. I do like that one, but I'm rusty. We've got to practice if we want to get better. Right, Bits?"

She nods and points to her canvas, where she's painted three thousand frogs sitting at the water line. "Look at mine, Peter."

He moves to hers and stands with his hand under his chin, like a serious art buyer. "I love it. I really like your use of the frogs. We'll hang it up when it's done, for sure."

"We're going to have a gallery, Cassie said! And I'm going to put on an art show." She cleans her brush and wipes the sweat off her brow. "Can I swim again? I'm hot."

Nelly and Ana are in the pond, so I nod. "Sure, then we'll have lunch."

We watch her lope to the water and smile as Nelly tosses her in the air.

"I love that kid," I say. "I was worried she'd be too scarred from all of this, but she takes it all in stride." I shake my head. "I don't think I could be so strong."

"I know." Peter watches her giggle as Ana pulls her through the water. "She amazes me."

"Doesn't it scare you?" I need to know if I'm the only one. "That we won't be able to protect her?"

He nods, his face fierce. "I'll do whatever I need to do to keep her safe. I love her so much. I didn't know it was possible—" He breaks off and looks away, blinking fast.

I rest my paint-covered hand on his shoulder. "I know. She knows it, too. Maybe that's why she's so happy, because we all love her."

Peter puts his hand over mine and smiles. He looks happy, at least as much as is possible while thinking of things like this.

"We'll do the best we can," I say, no longer feeling so alone in my fear. I yank on his hand and stand up. "Now, how about a game of chicken? I know Nelly and Ana are in."

His teeth flash. "C'mon, we'll whoop their asses."

CHAPTER 97

I've slept late, for once. Nelly must have snuck out as a little birthday present. I've always liked having a birthday in August because it meant I could spend it here.

Bits stands at the end of the hall and slips away when she sees me, cackling madly. She's been acting suspicious and innocent for days, in the way only little kids can. There are pancakes on the table, and the shutters lean against the wall at the far end of the living room, taken down for the day.

Penny's in the kitchen cleaning up. "Happy birthday!" she says with a hug. "How does it feel to be old?"

"You'll find out in four months. Until then you're too young to understand."

"Happy birthday! When I'm as old as you I'm going to wear makeup!" Bits yells, apropos of nothing. You'd think it was her birthday, the way she's dancing around. "Twenty-nine, that's old!"

I stoop and pretend to walk with a cane to the table. Bits sets something on my head. I reach up and feel soft fabric.

"It's your birthday crown," Bits says. "I always get a birthday crown."

I take off the purple felt crown with a star sewn on the front.

"It's absolutely beautiful," I say. "Did you make it?" Her smile is wide. She nods and I squeeze her tight. "Thank you so much. I'll wear it all day."

I load up my plate and get more birthday wishes from the others. Nelly comes in with a pail of milk, and I thank him for letting me sleep.

"Thank you for letting me sleep, birthday girl," he says, as he rubs my shoulders. It's been weeks with no nightmares.

I find Ana in the garden. I know she'll know what's ripening, since she's always in here.

"There's so much," she says. "We have to get canning again tomorrow."

"I'll do some tomatoes today," I say.

"Let's just say the stove will be in use today and you will be out of the kitchen. If I say any more Bits will kill me."

I laugh. "Got it." I smell the tomatoes we're picking and sigh.

"I know," Ana agrees. "And they actually taste like they smell."

I compare the Ana of four months ago, flipping her hair and scowling, to the one that stands here. She must know what I'm thinking because she shakes her head.

"I know. Gardening. Who would've thought?"

"I could've sworn I saw you talking to the seedlings."

"I totally did, when no one was looking. I wanted to sing to them with you and Penny, but I just couldn't. Like if I did I would be admitting to all of this. I didn't want it all to change." She raises her shoulders and places tomatoes in the crate by her feet. "I still don't."

"Me, neither." I think of the years I wasted after my parents died. "I'd like to go back to the way things were but do a few things differently."

"Me too. But Mama always says dwelling on the past gets us nowhere, so for once I'm going to listen to her."

"She's right." I have recent experience with that. "And speaking of the future, what's with you and Peter? And I'm totally prying, so tell me."

She holds her hands out and a crease appears between her eyebrows. "Nothing. Sometimes I think he wants to kiss me and then, nothing. I have no idea. It's driving me crazy. I like him so much, Cass." Her voice has softened. "He's the first guy I've ever liked that I actually *like*, you know?"

I know all about that. "I'm on it."

***

Nelly and I run the generator in the afternoon after Bits orders me out the door until dinner. John's house is quiet and cool. We lounge around in his living room while the freezers run.

"So, I have something for you," Nelly says from the couch.

"A present?" I ask.

"Yeah." He looks uncertain. "But I don't know if you'll like it."

"How could I not like anything you gave me? Hand it over!"

He pulls a little jewelry box out of his pocket. Inside is a silver chain of tiny, hand-twisted links. It's old-fashioned looking and I love it instantly.

I kneel and give him a kiss on the cheek. "It's so pretty. Thank you."

"I know you don't wear much jewelry, but it's for the ring. Maybe you don't want to wear it on your finger, but it might get lost in your pocket."

I stare at him for a few seconds, wondering how he knew.

He raises an eyebrow. "We live in the same room. Plus, I know you, darlin'. But you don't have to use it for that if you don't want to."

"I do." I thread the ring on the chain and hug him after he clasps it. "How do you always know what I need?"

"I just think to myself: If I were a klutzy, flaky, artist-type, what would I want?"

"Very funny." I touch his knee. "No, really. Thank you, Nels, for always being there for me."

"You're there for me, too." He shrugs, embarrassed by the sentiment, and reverts back to his normal self. "Just so you know, I'm expecting a kick-ass birthday present now."

I wink. "I'll see what I can do."

CHAPTER 98

Bits insists I be blindfolded and pulls it off while everyone yells, "Surprise!" There's a beautiful, lopsided and heavily-iced cake, obviously her work, surrounded by homemade pizza and beer. But the best part is my dad's wind-up record player. When I open my eyes, James drops the needle and "Happy Birthday Sweet Sixteen" blares out of the speaker. He's fixed it to work with 45s.

"It's a dance party!" Bits says. "Penny said you wanted one."

My eyes prickle as Penny smiles at me. I'm so lucky to have friends who know what you want and try their best to get it for you. I hug them, one by one.

"Don't worry," James says in answer to my unasked question. "John checked the volume. You can't hear it down the driveway."

I relax. I grew up on this music, because my parents did, and hearing it makes me feel like I've really come home. We teach Bits the twist, the swim and the mashed potato. Even John dances, because the mood is contagious, although he swore he wouldn't. There's a lull while Bits looks through records and we eat.

"How about this one?" she asks. " 'This Magic Moment?' "

Penny gently takes it from Bits and glances my way to see if I've noticed.

There's a twinge in my heart, but I nod. "That's one of the best songs in the world. It was my parents' song. You should play it."

The opening chords begin, and my chest constricts more. This song is my mom and dad; it's Adrian. But then Nelly comes with his hand out, and I rise to my feet. It hurts, but suddenly I understand that it's better to feel something than nothing at all. And I find that once I give into it, it lessens, and all that's left is love.

***

Peter's in the kitchen cutting carrots and cucumbers into sticks. I jump up on the counter and swing my feet.

He flicks my crown and smiles. "Hey there, birthday princess."

"Hey," I say. "So, are you ever going to kiss that poor girl?"

His hands go still. "Cassie, I have a lot of money. A lot. It can all be yours."

I wave a hand. "I don't care about your money."

"Yes, I know." His eyes glint. "I always thought it was refreshing, but right now it's just bothersome."

I scream with laughter. He starts to chop again, but I touch his arm. "No, really, what are you waiting for?"

He looks out the window into the night, then turns to me, his eyes anxious. "I don't want to ruin things."

I remember being told the same thing. If he feels that way about her then it's only a matter of time.

"But you guys are perfect for each other," I argue. "You won't mess anything up. Are you worried about the kissing? You have nothing to worry about, Pete. I know from experience."

He blushes to the roots of his hair. I hear what I'm saying and think I should have skipped that last beer, but I don't feel drunk. I feel good and silly.

"Just think, you guys could open the world's first post-apocalyptic boutique together."

I put my hands in a frame like I can see it.

He laughs despite himself. "Cass, what has gotten into you tonight?"

"I'm just happy."

I can't wipe the smile off my face, and he grins at me. Peter always seems to be holding back a little, like he's afraid to laugh too hard, but this smile is genuine.

"I'm really glad to hear that. Even if it does result in your being even weirder than normal."

I'm not dropping this. "You won't mess it up."

"We're such good friends. What if we're here for ten years? I had to be sure it's the kind of thing that could last for ten years."

He's talking in the past tense, though, so he must already have decided.

"That's the way it's supposed to be. You should be friends, or it'll never work. So, is Ana a ten-year kind of girl?"

"Yes." He actually looks shy, and my smile widens. "Yeah, I think she is."

"Then stop waiting. We may not have much time, so don't waste it. It'll be my birthday present!" I clap at my idea.

"You want your ex-boyfriend to hook up with another girl as your birthday present." Peter shakes his head in wonder as he picks up the plate and turns to leave.

"I just want you guys to be happy." My voice is wistful and he turns back with questioning eyes. "Haven't the two of us wasted enough years of our lives being unhappy?"

His smile is sad. "You're right, we have."

"But not anymore."

"No, not anymore."

A current of that new happiness passes between us. We grin at each other, and I realize that Peter's become one of my very best friends. I'm so glad he's here. He nods and turns again.

I jump off the counter and smack him on the behind. "Go get 'er, tiger!"

He leaps a foot into the air. "You know, maybe I liked it better when you weren't speaking to me."

"No, you didn't."

"No, I didn't," he says with a smile.

A few more dances and I sit the next one out. Bits decides on "Breaking Up is Hard to Do."

Peter pulls a record from the pile. "After that's a slow one," he says to Ana, who's eating a hummus-covered carrot. "Save it for me?"

She stops chewing and smiles, her face shining. Then she swallows hard and gulps some water.

I wink at her. "Peter knows how to waltz and fox trot and everything. He had to learn it for the cotillion."

He rolls his eyes. "There was not a cotillion, Cassandra."

I knew that, I just like to bother him about being rich.

Ana laughs and bites her lip. "I won't be able to keep up."

Peter smiles. "I barely remember the steps, anyway. You'll do just fine."

I turn away to hide my huge grin. It's finally going to happen between them, and I didn't even have to use my gun. I was starting to consider it as an option. Nelly spins a giggling Bits as her song begins. I eat my cake and decide that, in a strange way, this might be the best birthday ever. There's so much to celebrate, even if there's so much to mourn.

"Nelly!" Bits screams.

The fear in her voice makes me drop my fork and spin around. Nelly holds her in his arms. She points to the windows, her mouth open in a silent scream. It looks exactly how I'd thought it would, all these years of avoiding windows at night, afraid I'd see a ghostly face looking in. The screen of the window above the couch bulges in from the pressure of the infected. They press their mouths against it, snarling and moaning.

"Jesus Christ!" John yells. He never swears, and I'm not sure if it's an oath or a plea for help. "Get the shutters!"

We spring into action. The wood usually seems so heavy, but I lift it like it's nothing. James races to help and tightens the screws. Peter and Ana get the other porch window and hold it there, their muscles straining as they force it back against the onslaught. The screen must have ripped through.

Nelly has set Bits down, and he hauls the sliding door shutters across the room. She stands on the rug, pale and whimpering. I run to Nelly, and we get the boards there right as the glass breaks. They must be everywhere. A pod.

Neil Sedaka finishes singing about being true, and in the silence I hear Flora and Bert and the chickens screaming and clucking. And, of course, those horrible, ghastly moans.

The shutters buck under us. I turn my back to my board and push against it, but my feet slip millimeter by millimeter along the floor. Just when I think I can't hold it any longer, Ana's next to me, and we connect with the frame. John's steady hands fasten the bolts.

Hands at the other higher windows leave slimy tracks in their wake. Faces appear and bite at the glass before they fall back; maybe they're standing on other infected. Penny's lugged the shutters to their respective windows, and we attach them. It makes me feel a little better that we can no longer see them and they can't see us. My mouth is dry, and the sweat that runs down my back turns to ice when I realize we're completely surrounded. We're trapped.

"Fuck," Nelly says. "We're fucked."

"We don't know how many are out there," John says. "I'm going to the loft to check it out. Shoes and armor on, everyone."

We do as he says. The house echoes with the banging. A window breaks in one of bedrooms, but they can't climb up, and Penny has closed the doors. I shrug on my holster and tend to Bits, who stands like she's in a trance. I put on her shoes and zip up her jacket.

I hug her stiff body. "It'll be okay."

John leans down from the loft. "There are too many of them, with more coming out of the woods. We can't make it to the van."

I climb the ladder. They're everywhere. They crawl up each other onto the porch and pace in the driveway. They surround the van at the corner of the house.

"If we can get them over here somehow, I can go out the hall window for the van," John says.

"We can break the loft window and climb out, shoot our guns, maybe throw a lamp," I say. "Fire might attract them."

John nods in the dim light. We head back down, and John explains the plan.

"I'll stay up in the loft," I say. "As soon as I hear the van, I'll throw the lamp and come running."

"*We'll* come running," Nelly says. "I'm coming with you."

Penny clutches Bits on her hip and nods with wide eyes. I hold the oil lamp I plan on using. It casts a flickering glow on our faces, like we're telling spooky stories at summer camp. There's no time to say anything else; the pounding has gotten louder and the shutters are holding, but they shift with each thump. They've bought us time, but maybe not that much, not with the number of infected out there.

Nelly and I climb to the loft. I use my cleaver to crack the windows, and Nelly pushes out the glass with a chair. We step out onto the porch roof.

"Up here!" I yell.

We kneel at the edge of the roof and aim for their heads, even though we're only trying to get their attention. There's no way to kill them all, but there's no sense in wasting bullets. Their hands reach up and wave like they're at a rock concert. The air is foul, filled with the stench of death. They're trampling my mother's flowers, which should be the least of my worries, but I hate them even more because of it. Nelly strips the armor off his arm, and I see the glint of metal in his hand.

"What are you doing?" I ask.

He draws the knife across his forearm and blood wells up. "Giving the people what they want."

He holds his arm out. The blood runs down and drips onto the infected. The instant it hits, they go insane. The moaning and hissing is so loud it attracts the stragglers to the front, and when they smell the blood they join the crush.

The motor of the van revs to life, and he gives his arm one last shake. I pick up the lamp and aim for an empty spot. I think again of that year of softball. It certainly would have served me well to practice more. I never would've guessed those skills might save my life; I'd always thought playing softball might be the thing that killed me.

I heave the lamp and it shatters and the oil ignites next to one of the infected. We slide down the ladder and run for the hallway.

The van is backed up to the window. Peter and Ana stand on either side to shoot at anything that gets too close. More Lexers move our way, the distraction short-lived. James helps Penny and Bits into the van. There's a crash of wood followed by the terrorized squeals of Bert and the goats. Bits covers her ears and stares at me with wide eyes as the rest of us make it in.

The van rocks as bodies slam against it like caged animals. John guns the engine. I hold onto my seat as we bump over the grass and plow down anything in our way. I wonder if I'll ever see my beloved house again, and I turn to take one last look. And as the lamp oil ignites the tattered clothes of the infected and the flames race up their backs onto the porch, I wonder if there will even be anything left here to see.

CHAPTER 99

We spend the night in the van. The only one who gets rest is Bits. The rest of us sleep in fits and starts, waiting until there's enough light to safely move on. Penny bandages the deep gash on Nelly's arm.

"That was what drove them over the edge," I say. I grimace as I remember the noises they made when the blood hit. "Does it hurt?"

"Nah," Nelly says. "It's fine."

We leave when the sky is streaked with yellow. There's a faint orange glow in the direction of the house. I tell myself we're too far to see a fire and it's the sunrise, but I don't believe it.

James has planned a route that skirts around Bennington, but it's jammed with abandoned cars, so we stay on the main road. It's wide enough that we can weave our way around obstacles. We pass farmland choked with weeds and dandelions. In some places there are signs of a struggle, strewn bodies on the ground and cars tipped off the road. In others it's the same woods of the northeast I've run in my whole life. On one lawn a Lexer sits in the sunshine like it's enjoying the beautiful summer day. It stumbles to its feet, but by the time it's on them we're gone.

"There's no one," Penny says quietly. James takes her hand.

The houses become more frequent as we head into Bennington. We pass the Friendly's restaurant where Eric and I would give ourselves ice cream headaches eating Reese's Pieces sundaes. We'd slam the ice cream and then gulp our water, which would taste warm by comparison. I smile at the memory and watch John weave through an old roadblock where the ground is littered with black garbage bags.

"What's funny?" Nelly asks.

I'm about to answer when we hit a bump. There's a popping sound and the van shudders. John drives a few more yards and stops.

"Everyone stay inside," he says.

He walks back and rips up the plastic to reveal boards of wood studded with nails. His face is tight when he returns and leans in the window. "Every tire's flat. They must have abandoned the roadblock when things got bad. We need four tires or a new vehicle."

Penny buries her head in her hands and moans. We spill out of the van and blink in the sunlight. It's early in the morning, but the sun already feels hot enough to burn the back of my neck. My shirt sticks to me. I'm not sure if it's from the sun or the fact that we're standing in the middle of a deserted street, exhausted and with nowhere to go. There are cars past the roadblock and we try them all. The few that have keys won't even turn over.

Peter pounds a fist on the roof of a hatchback. "Damn it!"

James points at the buildings down the block. "That looks like Main Street. How about we head there and see if there's anything. We need to go west on Main anyway."

"We may as well drive the gear down," John says.

The wheels grind on their rims as he rolls along beside us. Main Street is a line of brick buildings with wooden storefronts. There are no cars, only a wide expanse of asphalt.

"James has an idea," Nelly says. "He saw some houses with trucks and RVs as we drove in. Maybe we can find keys in the houses. We'll take the bikes and go while y'all wait here."

Penny looks at James in desperation. "I don't think we should separate."

"Pen, we can't all go," James says softly. "We don't have enough bikes, even if all of us could make it. We'll be gone an hour at most."

I don't like it either, but I don't have a better plan. Not only do we need a car, but we also need one big enough to hold us all.

A sign on the corner building says Bennington Brew Company & Pub. It's a three-story brick building with ornate white moldings around the windows. I think I see something move as a curtain in an open second-story window twitches. I watch as it flutters again, but there's nothing else. It must have been the breeze.

"We can wait in the van or in here," Peter says. "Maybe we should check it out."

Inside, sunlight enters through the huge windows, making the polished oak and brass of the bar shine. The front room and back kitchen are empty. We unload the van and pile the bags by the bar.

"Peter and I will clear out the nails at the roadblock so they can get through. We'll be gone fifteen minutes. You girls stay here with Bits. Put on the radio," John says, and he and Nelly each put an earpiece in. I place the radio on the bar.

"Be back soon. Promise," James says to Penny, who nods mutely.

I feel a sense of foreboding as the lock clicks on the door and am suddenly sure they're never coming back. I watch as they pass the side windows, willing them to be safe. When they move out of sight, I notice Bits. She watches me carefully, her face devoid of hope, and I realize it's a mirror of my expression. I force myself to smile.

"Be right back," I say, and head to the kitchen where I spotted some bottles of fancy ginger ale. Back in the main room, I pull out four glasses and stand behind the bar.

"What are you doing?" Bits asks.

I try to look mysterious while I pour the ginger ale and follow it with grenadine syrup. I find an unopened bottle of maraschino cherries on a dusty shelf. I drop a few in each glass and slide Penny, Ana and Bits their drinks.

I lift mine in the air. "Shirley Temples. To the girls!"

Bits grins. The four of us clink glasses and sip through our tiny red straws.

"Yum. It's been forever since I've had one of these," Penny says. "I bet it would be good with vodka." I reach down and pull out a bottle of the cheap stuff, since all the top shelf liquor is gone. She shakes her head and laughs. "What's it, eight in the morning?"

"It's a brave new world," I say. "Cocktails at eight in the morning are practically necessary."

There's a burst of static from the radio. "Cassie." John's voice is forceful but not panicked. "There's a pod coming our way. Be ready to let us in and lock the door."

"Copy that," Ana answers. Penny and I run to the door. They fly past the windows and race into the bar. Penny slams and locks it behind them.

"I think they saw us," Peter gasps.

We wait in silence, hearts pounding. A cacophony of groaning tells us he's right. Lexers appear in the side windows. There's a crash as one throws itself against the doors. I don't know if they can see well, but milky eyes peer in like they can. No one breathes. Bits sits on the stool with her drink clutched in her hands, halfway to her mouth.

The doors give a little. The lock holds, but it won't for long. The gold of the deadbolt shines dully as the doors crack wider. The room is dim now, the streams of sunlight blocked by the crush of bodies outside the windows.

"In the back," John says.

Peter grabs Bits in one arm and two backpacks in the other and backs through the kitchen door. We follow with as much as we can carry. The last thing I see are our Shirley Temples, my vain attempt at normalcy, waiting on the bar.

CHAPTER 100

The banging is muffled in here. I peer out the door window into the alley. There's a parking lot directly behind us, but it's on the other side of a chain-link fence. The only way out might be to the left, where the alley narrows and leads to the next block, but several dumpsters block my view of the other end.

"I'll see where it goes," John says. He opens the door. "It's clear. We'll go down the alley to the street. Let me see where Nel and James are."

He explains the situation into the radio and then listens. "There's a pickup they can take. They're getting it and coming our way. They'll be at the end of the alley. Only take your daypacks, in case we have to run."

I throw Bits's little pack on her back and grab my daypack out of my backpack. It has food and ammo and first aid supplies, the stuff you don't want to leave behind. There's an explosion of glass in the front. They'll be in soon.

"Let's go," Ana says. She closes the door with a gentle click once we're out.

"We'll—" John begins, but before any of us can move he's yanked us to the ground behind the dumpsters. Infected are coming down the alley. Thanks to John they haven't seen us.

"Where are you?" John whispers into the radio. "Change of plans. You're going to have to come to the parking lot behind the bar. We're behind the chain-link fence." He pauses. "We're going to have to try."

He turns to us. "A few more minutes. They'll call when they're close."

A garbage can in the alley crashes and rolls away with a clang. I peer through the crack between the dumpsters and see at least a dozen in my narrow field of vision. They're forty feet away now.

"How are we going to get over the fence?" Penny's voice is so quiet I have to read her lips.

She, Ana and Bits hunker against the building's wall. Peter's crouched next to me, against the dumpsters, his jaw clenched. He gestures for me to look in the crack again. The alley is packed. There won't be time to get everyone over the fence. John, on my other side, takes a look and runs a hand down his face.

"We need a distraction," I whisper to them.

It worked at the house. There's silence as we think. I run through any number of scenarios and dismiss them all. There's nothing to do but run and hope for the best.

Peter's breath is warm on my ear. "Remember what you said before we left the city?"

His eyes search mine. I have no idea what he's talking about or why he's bringing it up now. He sees my confusion and leans forward again. "That sometimes we do things that jeopardize our own safety because we love someone?"

Of course I remember.

"I'll be the distraction," he whispers, loud enough for John to hear. "I'll jump up on the dumpster while you all go over the fence."

It won't work. He'll be surrounded in seconds. I shake my head. "You'll never make it out."

His gaze holds steady, and I see by the set of his face he already knows this. I gasp and shake my head again.

"Three minutes," John whispers. "We'll only have a minute before the ones on the side of the pub come around. He's going to back up to the fence."

I turn back to Peter and whisper-shout in his ear. "No!"

Peter watches Bits, who's raised her head and looks at us in terror. He smiles at her, and I can just make out the words he mouths: *It'll be okay.* He turns back to me, and although his face is resolute, there's fear in his eyes. It reminds me of Neil, right before I shot him, but it's different. They shine with a light that reminds me of the paintings of saints in churches. The martyrs.

"It's the only way," John agrees. "But I'll do it. You go over."

I can't believe we're having this argument.

Peter shakes his head. "No, I'll just jump up there with you. More distraction. You can get them to the farm, I know you can." His eyes are desperate and his next words are choked. "Promise me you'll get them there."

"I swear," John says. He clasps Peter's arm and looks him in the eye. "I swear I will."

Peter nods once and exhales through his clenched jaw.

John raises two fingers and motions to the fence. Two minutes to find an alternate plan. I look around wildly. We can't just let him die. There has to be another way.

Peter's poised to jump up. His hair and face are soaked, his pupils dilated, the blackest I've ever seen. I can hardly see through my tears. I want to fight, to shout, but there's nothing I can do to change this.

I hold out my hand and whisper in a cracked voice, "Love you."

I need him to know that we love him like he loves us. Our fingers are icy as we grasp each other's hands.

"Love you," he mouths, his eyes red.

Then, reluctantly, I let go. Ana's across from us, unable to hear our whispers. Her eyes move in confusion from Peter to me and back again. They widen in horror. Peter points his chin toward the fence and gives her a soft smile. Her face pales and her jaw drops. He parts his lips, about to speak, but John gathers Bits in his arms and whispers, "Now!"

Tires peel into the lot and a pickup swings wide and backs up to the fence. Peter leaps onto the dumpsters and bangs his machete on the brick of the building.

"Hey!" he yells. "Over here!"

The Lexers turn to him as one. It's our cue to run, but Ana doesn't move. Her mouth is still open, and she's frozen in a crouch.

I grab her arm. "Ana!"

She rises to her feet. We hit the fence with a metallic bang. Ana, the most nimble, is up and over in a flash. We lift Bits into her arms, and they drop into the truck bed. The fence wobbles and screams as the three of us climb. My jeans catch on the top, and I free fall into the truck, onto Nelly's bicycle. I ignore the pain and scramble up to kneel against the tailgate. I shoot through the fence at the Lexers at Peter's feet.

Peter fights. He hacks them with his machete and then dances back and fires point-blank into their heads. They can't reach him and it's driving them crazy. There's a brief moment when I think we can get to him; we can back into the fence, knock it down. But then more Lexers pour into the lot. James hangs out the window and fires at the encroaching wave.

John pounds on the roof of the truck. "Go! Go!"

The tires squeal. Ana and I fire at the infected that surround Peter, but it's a drop in the bucket. Peter looks up as we move away, and before he turns back I swear I see something like happiness pass across his face.

Nelly jumps the curb to the street. I hang on to the tailgate, but I don't look away. I don't care about the infected around us. I keep my eyes on Peter and watch him fight with every ounce of strength he has until we round the corner and he disappears from view.

CHAPTER 101

Nelly pulls into a clearing and leaps from the driver's side. His hair looks bleached in the harsh sunlight, as white as his face. "Peter," is all he says.

"It was his idea," John says. He raises his big body out of the truck and jumps to the dirt. He holds his hands up, like he's explaining his innocence to a jury. "He wouldn't let me..."

James holds Penny tight. Bits is in her arms, eyes closed. There's no way she could have fallen asleep in the fifteen minutes of bumpy riding. Not after what just happened.

Nelly looks diminished standing there, like he's slowly shrinking. My knees hurt from the metal truck bed. I'm still kneeling, still clutching the tailgate, still looking toward Peter. Ana is, too. Her breath hitches.

Nelly opens his mouth. I want him to say something, anything, that will make this horrible, empty feeling subside. But, instead of words of comfort, he gulps in air like a fish out of water. Then Nelly, who I've never seen more than teary-eyed, leans on the truck, buries his face in his hands and sobs. Blood runs down his arm, soaking his shirt, and it snaps me out of my stupor. I crawl to him. It's the cut on his arm. The bandage is gone, and the cut's opened back up.

I cradle his head to my chest like a mother would. "Your arm."

He nods, and when his crying subsides he speaks. "We had a scuffle getting the truck." His cheeks are soaked with tears, and he uses his good arm to wipe his face. "The bandage got ripped off. I dropped my glove at the house when I cut my arm."

"Let's fix it," I say, glad to have something to attend to.

We sit under a tree. I pour water over the deep wound. The edges are red and irritated. I squeeze antibiotic ointment onto my finger.

Nelly grabs my hand. "Put on a glove." His voice is sharp. "Or let me do it."

"Nels." I smile at him. "Please, I think I know you well enough—"

He looks at his arm and smiles to offset his brusqueness, but the crinkles near his eyes are missing. "Cass, he grabbed my arm before I killed him. I just realized he could have gotten something on me. In me."

For a moment I'm frozen to the core. Then I shake my head. The chance is too slim. "You're fine, Nelly. But I'll put on gloves anyway, okay?"

He nods like he's satisfied and leans back against the tree. John's coaxed Ana to where we sit. She hugs her knees to her chest and stares into the woods, one hand on her cleaver. Bits's head rests in Penny's lap. When I'm done, Nelly takes the gloves and shoves them in his pocket.

"We need to move farther away from Bennington," John says.

"We need to go back and find Peter," I say. Ana looks my way quickly and then turns back to the woods.

"Cassie," John says. "There's no way Peter's—"

"Alive?" Everyone winces. I picture Peter as we left, back against the wall, surrounded on three sides by infected. "I know that. But we can't just leave him."

I envision Peter's handsome face turned rotting and gray, and it's almost more than I can bear. I want to punch something. I'm so angry that, for once in my life, my eyes are dry.

"We have to," I say, yanking grass out of the ground. "He would want us to—" I don't want to say kill him, because he's already dead, and because it sounds so awful, "—take care of him." Ana jumps up with a sob and walks into the trees.

"Peter didn't sacrifice himself so we could go back and put ourselves in the same situation," John says gently.

Of course he's right. There's nothing to do but keep going, keep running, forever wondering what's happened to another person I love.

I catch a glimpse of Ana in the trees and stand. The fern-covered ground muffles my steps, but Ana knows I'm behind her and waits for me to catch up. I hold out my arms, and she falls into me with heartbroken sobs, just like when she was small and had to let go of that little rabbit. I run my hand over her short, silky hair and murmur words that don't help at all—I know this from experience—but I say them anyway.

CHAPTER 102

J ohn insists we eat before we move on. No one's eaten anything of substance since last night. There's trail mix and MREs and energy bars. I stare at the food blankly until he hands me a bar. I unwrap it and eat methodically. Chew and swallow, drink. Repeat. We've been waiting for Bits to wake, but she's still out. John says that as long as her pulse is okay, she is.

Ana, Nelly and Penny sit in the cab of the truck. Nelly has a clean shirt in his pack, and before we leave I watch him bury the old, bloody one under a carpet of leaves. We lay Bits in the truck bed with her head in my lap, and I stroke her hair as we rumble up the road.

"It's going to be at least two hundred miles from here," James says. As he closes the map, I notice the hollows under his cheekbones and eyes. "The truck doesn't have enough gas. And at this speed it'll take us until night, if we don't have to stop."

"Truck's diesel," John says. "As long as we can find another diesel and a container of some sort, I can puncture the fuel tank from underneath. Easy enough. The hard part's finding one, and with fuel still in the tank. Otherwise, we'll need a new vehicle."

The sun is blazing, so I hold my jacket over Bits's face to keep it from getting burned. Her face twitches until, at last, her eyes flutter open. She closes them, struggling to forget, to sleep, but the tears slide out. I wipe away the tracks they make.

She sits up and inches into my lap. I wrap my arms around her, just barely able to hear her whisper, "Peter."

"Oh, honey." I brush her hair away from her ear. "He loved you so much. He loved all of us and wanted us to be safe." I don't know how to explain, but she nods like she gets it, like the old soul she is or has become.

We pass through a few small towns. Pretty towns with ugly groups of infected, so we don't stop to look for a new vehicle. The isolated houses we pass have no cars in their driveways, or they're useless. The truck kicks up dust that covers our skin and crunches in my mouth. I'm drinking the last of my water when we slow. A jumble of cars litters the road. There's no way around. One side of the road is trees, the other a drop-off to a stream.

Nelly hangs out the window. "Should we go back?"

James consults the map and shakes his head. "Did you see all the Lexers in that last town? There was a huge group after we passed. No way should we go back through there."

"Then we'll move them," John says. "I can pop them into neutral from underneath, and we'll push them to the side."

It takes longer than expected. Two hours later we're shoving the second to last car into a ditch, when I notice Nelly wince.

"You should relax," I tell him. "I think you need stitches, but at the very least you shouldn't be pushing thousands of pounds around. How does it feel?"

"It hurts a little."

I can tell he's trying to play it down. "Let me see."

I try to lift the bandage, but he moves his arm away and does it himself. The wound is bright red and puffy around the edges.

"It's getting infected," I say. He pulls his arm back nervously, and I look him in the eye. "With a regular, run-of-the-mill infection, Nels. There's some amoxicillin in the first aid stuff. I'll go get it."

By the time I find the bottle and hand him two pills, the last car has been moved. We fill our water bottles at the stream and rinse off the dust. The cold water soothes my sunburn. Ana's face is blank as she rinses herself off; she hasn't said a word since the woods. Penny shoots her worried glances but says nothing. None of us is okay right now, so asking seems ridiculous.

Bits and I sit in the cab with Nelly. We stop twice more to move cars, and since traveling at night is too dangerous, it's obvious we won't get to Kingdom Come Farm today. The thought of Kingdom Come used to fill me with equal parts excitement and dread, but now I'm just numb. It doesn't seem possible we'll even make it. I obsess over all the obstacles we could hit, but I can't think this way. We have to get there, if only because of Peter. I won't let him die in vain.

Hot tears escape and race down my cheeks. I close my eyes to stop them and slide my ring along the chain. I concentrate on the bump of the ring over the links until I'm in control again. Bits is curled up next to me, and the pressure of her body is like a blanket. I feel sleep steal over me, and I'm so tired I give in.

The truck swerves and I'm thrown against the door. My eyes fly open, ready to fight whatever's in the road, but there's nothing.

"Sorry!" Nelly yells out the sliding back window to where the others grip the truck bed in surprise. Sweat runs down his flushed face, and his chest rises and falls way too fast.

I lean over Bits and put my lips to his forehead. I can feel the heat before I even touch him. "Nelly, you're burning up! Pull over."

He wipes the sweat with a bandana. "It's hot outside. I thought it was just that."

He pulls onto the shoulder. After he puts the truck in park, he leans back and closes his eyes.

James speaks through the back window. "What's going on?"

I walk around to the driver's side. "Nelly isn't feeling well. He has a fever."

John stands next to me. "How's your arm?"

Nelly opens his eyes and blinks to focus. He fumbles with the edge of his bandage and lifts it. It's worse. The wound itself is puffy and purple. A pink streak moves out of it and up his arm. It resembles sunburn, but I know it's not. That streak means it's infected, and now the infection's moving.

"Okay," John says. "You need more antibiotics. Cassie, get him some?"

I find the bottle of amoxicillin and spill four into Nelly's hand. "Take them all." I hand him the water. "You need to really knock the infection out."

Nelly does what I say and turns to John. "It may be the virus."

John nods and rests a hand on his shoulder.

"Stop," I say, angry. "It's just an infection."

Nelly turns to me matter-of-factly. "Cass, remember the man on the Thruway? Remember the bite on his arm?"

I nod. His wound had these streaks too, traveling out from it like roads on a map. Penny comes up behind me and gasps when she sees Nelly's arm.

"It looked like this," he says to John. "All my joints hurt. Just like they said they would on the news."

"Let's not jump the gun," John says. The only thing that gives away his doubt is the way his hand runs over his eyebrows. "That can describe any major infection. Let's see how these antibiotics help. You rest while I drive."

Nelly insists on riding in the back so he can stretch out. Penny builds a makeshift tent by draping John's shirt over two packs to keep the sun off his face.

We circumvent several larger towns that are probably too dangerous. Nelly's asleep in minutes. I want to peek under the shirt to make sure he's okay, but I don't want to disturb him. His chest rises and falls. Whether or not there'll be a next breath is all I can focus on. It's supplanted the empty feeling, but it's definitely not an improvement. John spies an old cabin on a hill in the late afternoon and turns up the overgrown drive.

"I thought we'd stop for the night," he says. "It's about as safe as we'll get. I don't want to keep driving only to stop somewhere that's full of infection."

Nelly sits up and I rush over to him. "How do you feel?" I touch his head. It's still way too hot.

He gives a weak smile. "Not much better, darlin'. But I might be hungry."

I help him into the cabin. There's a main room with a rotting table and two chairs by the glassless front window. The wood stove is orange with rust. The smaller room has glass in its window and a cot mattress on the floor. A couple of moth-eaten wool army blankets rest on rough-hewn shelves. They don't smell great, but they'll do. I drag the mattress to the main room. Nelly sits on it and leans against a water-stained wall.

Bits kneels next to him and holds out her little water bottle. "Nelly, do you want a sip of my water?"

Nelly recoils slightly, but she doesn't notice. "No thanks, Bits. Make sure you don't drink out of my bottle." He looks around in alarm. "Where is it?"

"In your bag," I say, and place the small pack next to him. "No one drank out of it."

He puts his arm over it protectively. James carries what little we have inside and sets it on the table.

"What do you want to eat?" I turn to Nelly, but his eyes have closed. "Bits?"

She looks over the food listlessly as I open an MRE pouch. Her eyes light up when I pull out Reese's Pieces and a pouch marked Fudge Brownie.

"You can have them." She sits by Nelly, candy in her lap, but doesn't eat it. "Is something wrong?"

"I thought Nelly might want some. Whenever I'm sick I like sweet things. I'll wait for him to wake up."

The hopeful look on her face makes me want to cry. The only store-bought candy she's had in a month, and she wants to share it. "You're so sweet. But you go ahead and eat that, honey. There's more for Nelly if he wants, okay?"

She lifts the brownie and takes a bite. I spoon something into my mouth that tastes like apple pie filling, but I don't care enough to check. The sun is going down, and we're drooping like flowers from heat and exhaustion and mourning. Penny bustles around in an attempt to clean and organize our stuff. She tries to be cheerful, but it's a relief when she finally gives up.

James blinks from the strain of looking at the map in dim light. "There's over a hundred miles to go and only an eighth of a tank of gas. We'll work on that tomorrow, I guess? Depending on how Nel feels."

Nelly sighs. His eyes are red-rimmed. A drop of sweat falls off his nose when he shivers. I grab a blanket and tuck it around him.

Nelly speaks through his chattering teeth in little bursts. "I'm just going to say it. I think I'm infected. I don't know how long it takes from one little scratch, but you can't sit here for days while it runs its course. You need to get going tomorrow."

"Jesus, Nelly!" I say furiously. Like I'd just go on my merry way. "If you think for one second I'm going to leave you here, you are out of your fucking mind!"

Everyone looks aghast. Even Ana, who sits in the corner staring into space, has looked up.

"Nel, you must be delirious," Penny says in her soft voice. "We don't know what it is. And even if we did, we're not going anywhere."

He nods as his teeth clack together. I give him six more tablets of amoxicillin in the hope that it makes a dent. There's a pouch of electrolyte juice mix in one MRE, and I use the enclosed heater to warm it. Nelly's hands are so shaky I need to steady the cup for him. It's like now that he's admitted to thinking it's LX, he'll let us see how bad off he really is. Either that or he's going downhill fast.

CHAPTER 103

Once Nelly began shivering so badly that it scared even him, he let me crawl onto his mattress. He's hot as a furnace, and even though I know his chill is inside, I try to warm him. My arms feel miniscule around his broad trunk, but it seems to help. He finally drifts into sleep with only an occasional tremble.

Bits and Ana sleep under the other blanket. James has Penny wrapped in his arms like a teddy bear. John takes first watch. He sits with a flashlight and checks our weapons. Maybe Peter was right: John knows what to do. We never would have gotten those cars off the road today without John's expertise. I shut my eyes and see Peter on the dumpster, so I open them and stare into the darkness until they close in exhaustion.

Nelly's worse when I wake for watch just before dawn. His face is red and his breathing's labored. When it's light I force him to wake and take the last of the amoxicillin. He can barely swallow, and he turns his eyes to watch me without moving his neck. A few more pink streaks have joined with the first. They're at his biceps now.

"Can you eat?" I ask.

He shakes his head. He won't drink either, no matter how much I coax.

"Cass." He blinks to hold back tears.

I know he's working on some sort of goodbye speech, but I can't hear it; I'll die if I have to. I tuck the blanket under him. "Nelson Charles Everett, if you're about to declare your undying love for me, then you can just save it until you're better."

I grab his good hand and give a choked laugh.

"Can't you even be serious now?" he asks, but he manages a small smile. "I'm on my deathbed here."

"No, I can't." I point at him. "I learned from the master. And it's not a deathbed. It's a disgusting stained mattress. You can't die on it, it wouldn't be fitting."

He gives my hand a weak squeeze and drifts off but opens his eyes a moment later. His bright blue eyes have gone icy, and he turns to me with a wince. They remind me of the hazy eyes of the infected. A knife of fear stabs my gut, but when he smiles he's the same Nelly.

"Love you, darlin'."

I smile and try to keep the despair out of my voice. "Love you back."

***

When Ana wakes she sits outside on the grass and ignores Penny's attempts to talk. She's not in shock, at least not the medical kind. If she were a store she'd have a Closed for Business sign in the window. Penny and James offer to search for a replacement for the truck. I don't like the idea of her out there. Penny feels Nelly's head, and when she stands her eyes are puffy and resigned.

"Pen, maybe you should stay here and I should go." I touch her sleeve. "You aren't..." I don't want her to go, but I don't want to leave Nelly, either.

"I can shoot okay." She shrugs, but her hand strokes the earpiece of her glasses. "I don't want to sit here while James goes."

"You'll look for more antibiotics? Stronger ones?" I've already clarified this a dozen times, but I figure once more can't hurt. "And be careful?"

She nods as she ties her hair back in a bun. Since Ana's hair incident, I've taken to winding my hair into two buns when we're somewhere dangerous. Nelly calls me Princess Leia, and James makes all kinds of nerdy Star Wars jokes that I don't get.

She smiles. "Hey, I thought Mother Hen was my job. You just take care of Nelly."

I try to smile back. "Okay."

We hug tight and then they're gone.

CHAPTER 104

It's been several hours, but there's still no sign of Penny and James. Bits picks wildflowers; I sit in the doorway where I can see her. It seems like everyone is disappearing.

Nelly hasn't spoken since dawn. He's lapsed into unconsciousness, and the streaks are moving fiercely to his shoulder. A sheen of sweat covers his face. His features look sharper, the skin moving away from the bones, like an old man. I pat his good shoulder.

"Don't worry, Nels. You'll be okay." I feel like I'm lying.

He breathes heavily. Peter might have gone through this, except he was all alone, desperate for a drink, for a gentle hand. I can only hope that he was eaten so thoroughly there wasn't enough of him left to turn. I would never say it out loud to the others—it's such a sick prayer—but I have a feeling they think it too.

I rifle through every backpack again hoping that something that will cure Nelly has magically appeared. Of course, there's nothing, so I stomp around. Bits comes back in with a handful of flowers for Ana, who gives her a distracted smile.

"Cassie," John says in a gentle voice. "Are you okay?"

"No, I'm not okay. It's not fair!"

We survived all these months and now look at us. We'll never be in the clear. John nods his head in agreement, in acceptance, which makes me angrier.

"Why are we even trying?" I demand. "What's the point? Peter's dead. Nelly—" My throat closes.

John sits on one of the rickety chairs watching me while Bits huddles next to him. The tears come, and I wipe them away angrily.

"I don't get it!" I yell.

"Everything happens for a reason—"

I cut him off. "How do you know that? That everything happens for a reason? How are you so sure? Because I'm pretty sure there's no good reason for all of this." I wave my arm to encompass the whole world. I pick up the empty, useless amoxicillin bottle and throw it as hard as I can. It hits the wall with a sad little *thwack*. I look for something better to throw, but everything is too precious to destroy. Instead, I slam the water bottles into a line. I stack the food and arrange the weapons by the door as loudly as I can. Everyone jumps at the louder noises, but I don't care. Nelly doesn't budge, and that's the only thing I care about. Here I am, allowing another person to die right in front of me. I won't do it.

"There's a hiking trail on the map that cuts through to another town. I'll find a pharmacy or something. I can take one of the bikes. I'll get something stronger for the infection."

John's eyes are full of pity. "Cassie, it's too dangerous to go on a fool's errand when James and Penny will be back."

"It's not a fool's errand, John! They've been gone for hours. What if they don't come back?" I feel awful as I say it, but it's true. Ana closes her eyes as I continue.

"Amoxicillin is the weakest antibiotic in the world. There are others: Erythromycin, Cipro..." I can't think of any more, so I stomp my foot in frustration. "I'll find something. I can't just sit here waiting for help that might not come. I'm not going to let Nelly die. I won't!"

"We don't know—"

"That's right, we don't know! It could be a regular infection. We need something stronger."

"You're right, Cassie. It could be a treatable infection. But I don't want you risking yourself to find out it's not. Wait a while longer. Please." He raises and lowers his palms in an effort to calm me. "I know you're angry. We're all angry. It doesn't seem fair, honey. But we don't know what God has in store for us, what His plan is."

I can't believe that this might be someone's—or some*thing's*— plan. That all of this is some sort of test. Some fucked up experiment designed to watch us fail.

I shake my head. I don't want to live in this kind of world, not if it means losing everyone I love, one by one. I'd rather die quickly and get it over with. A fury I've never felt before rises in me—a blind rage that vibrates through my body. I don't care about being quiet, or how unfair I'm being, or whether or not I'm heading into danger. I need to do something to release it, so I pick up the empty chair and throw it against the wall. Bits whimpers when it crashes to the floor, but I'm too far gone to stop.

"What, did He think to himself, 'Oh, I know, I'll kill all the kind people and babies and kids? And not only will I do that, but I'll make them fucking zombies, too, to finish off the rest?'" I scream this at him, even though none of it is his fault.

I throw on my pack and snatch my cleaver. John watches me calmly. I know how badly he wants me to stay, but I won't be able to live with myself if I don't do something.

"I'll come with you," he says.

"No, you need to stay with Nelly, in case he wakes up. You—you take care of him. I don't know if there is a God, or what His plans may or may not be. But my fucking plan is simple: Nelly lives. That's it. I don't think it's too much to ask."

I look up at the ceiling. "So, God, I'm going to town now to get some medicine. Do me a favor and work with me here. Thanks."

I fly out of the cabin and stand at the top of the hill. My chest heaves. I feel like I'm drowning. I know that if I give into this sadness, I'll never make it back, so I focus on my anger. I blow on that coal of rage and fan it into flames. I hear footsteps behind me and pray it's not John. I've no space for apologies right now. But it's Ana, with her pack and weapons. Her face is set and serious.

"No one else is dying," she says. Her eyes are hard and her lips thin into a grim line. "Not if we can help it. Let's go."

We start down the dirt road to the trail. Nelly's bike is way too tall, but I manage the bumpy, rough miles to town. I don't even think about falling and don't close my eyes once.

CHAPTER 105

W e find a phone book at a gas station on the outskirts of town that lists an urgent care. A tourist map says it's only a half mile away. Ana and I sit on the counter and eat Snickers bars that have melted and hardened and re-melted in the heat, but they're still tasty.

Ana wears black pants, black leather hiking boots and a black tank top. With her cleaver and her gloves she looks like some sort of hiking ninja. I tell her this and she smiles.

"Thanks for coming with me," I say.

"And miss this?" She laughs, but her smile fades quickly. "We have to try something. If we could have helped—"

She stares out the window at the gas pumps, blinking rapidly. I don't know how many times I've replayed those moments in my head, trying to think of something else we could have done.

I jump off the counter and face her. "I'm so sorry, Ana. It's—"

"It's stupid. I think maybe I loved him. I think he liked me a lot."

"No," I say. "He loved you." I'm not sure if it'll make it worse, but she should know. "I saw him look at you. He loved you, Ana. Believe that, okay?"

I put my hand on her knee so she'll look at me and see that I'm telling the truth. She nods and wipes her tears away.

"Okay. Thanks, Cass." She jumps off the counter and changes the subject, so she doesn't cry again. "Ready?"

"Ready, ninja-girl."

The road into town is full of abandoned cars and littered with empty bottles, plastic bags and cans, the detritus of fleeing humans. The streets are lined with beautiful old houses under an even older canopy of trees. It seems like any minute a Fourth of July parade might come marching past. It's a storybook street, except for the battered screen doors ripped from their hinges and the windows with jagged black holes. Rotted bodies lie on overgrown lawns, so fully consumed by Lexers that they didn't turn. The lucky ones.

We're careful when we park our bikes at Green Mountain Urgent Care, since a lot of sick people went to the hospital at the end. And some might still be there, buzzing against the windows and doors like trapped houseflies.

We step into the stale air and gag at the smell. Beyond the intake desk is a hallway lined with doors. Two are closed and something bumps around in them.

"Thank God they're too stupid to open a door," Ana whispers. "Can you imagine if they were smart, too?"

I shudder. We'd have been dead long ago. We creep past and pause when we hear a whispery slithering sound, but nothing rounds the corner at the nurses' station ahead. Another closed door reads Pharmacy. Ana raises her cleaver as I pull out a pistol and fling it open. The room is empty, except for shelves of medicine bottles, and my legs grow weak with relief. I feared the room would be stripped bare.

We check the bottles by flashlight. I find the names of several antibiotics I've never heard of in a medication book on the counter and locate them on the shelves.

"Get some liquid ones," Ana suggests. She shines her light on some tiny bottles and pockets them. "They might work faster."

She stuffs a handful of needles in her bag before we step into the hall. Clipboards fall to the floor by the nurses' station as three Lexers stumble toward us. They're desiccated like mummies from the heat of being trapped inside for so long. The swishing sound of their stick legs rubbing together follows us as we rush out the door. We mount our bikes and watch them press against the glass with gnarled hands and gaping mouths.

"Fuck you, assholes," Ana mutters. I know exactly how she feels.

We're almost out of town when we run into a small pack gathered in the only open part of the street, between the abandoned cars. We can't get past.

"We can take them," Ana calls.

Our only other option is to find another way out, but we're likely to run into an even larger group. Our bikes clatter to the ground, and we draw our cleavers from behind our backs, afraid guns will attract more.

We stand shoulder to shoulder and let them come to us. The first to reach me is a gray-haired woman wearing a skirt and silk blouse. Her glasses still hang around her neck on a gold chain, and her jaw bone is exposed. The tendons that connect it to her skull contract as she snaps her teeth together.

I am not getting killed by a fucking librarian.

I ram the flat blade into her neck. Her head severs from her shoulders easily, a testament to John's weapon-making skills. The next one, a young guy still in his tight biking outfit, separates from his head too. There's no blood, just a sick splatter of gore. A growl escapes my lips. I hate them. It might not be their fault—they were just people once who wanted to live as badly as I do—but they're making my life a living hell.

I flip my blade and back up to wait for the next two: teenage girls with dirty, sparkly t-shirts. Out of the corner of my eye I see Ana kick a short man to the ground and take the heads off two more before spinning her blade one-handed and stabbing the one on the ground through the eye.

The girls are close enough to each other that they could be whispering secrets in the school hallway. I puncture one of their eye sockets, then the other—two wet crunches in quick succession. Ana grunts as she shoves her blade home on the final Lexer and he drops to the pavement.

We stand with our cleavers at the ready, but nothing else surfaces. I walk to my bike and grab my water bottle. I'm out of breath from fear and exertion. Ana looks past me and raises her cleaver again. Her hair glimmers as she spins and sticks it under the chin of a teenage boy wearing a Nascar T-shirt, who has come out from behind a crashed minivan.

I huff my thanks and take a swig of warm water. "You really are a ninja," I say. She's hardly broken a sweat.

Ana laughs. "We make a good team."

I'm amazed at how easily we dispatched them. Our practice has paid off.

"Let's get the hell out of here," I say, and we mount our bikes and move on.

CHAPTER 106

My thighs burn with the uphill effort of the way back, but I ignore the pain. Every turn of the pedals brings me closer to Nelly, who may not have much time. A little voice whispers that he may already be out of time, but I ignore that too. The shadows are lengthening when we get back to the cabin, where a VW bus sits out front. Inside, James and Penny sit near Nelly, while Bits and John open a can of pilfered soup.

"We ran out of gas," Penny explains after she hugs us. "We had to walk, but we finally found some old hippie's house. That's where we got the car and stuff." She points to a pile of sleeping bags, lanterns and food. It's a good haul, but she doesn't look happy. "There was no medicine. We stopped at every house we could. The town was too infected. I'm so sorry, guys."

"We got it," Ana says. She slings off her bag. "We found some."

"Any problems?" John asks.

"Nothing we couldn't handle. Even the infected knew not to mess with Cassie today."

I smile grimly and take up my post near Nelly. He looks worse. His wound is a deep purple, and it smells. That voice whispers that it smells just like the Lexers do, but I tell it to go to hell. His skin is dry; he's sweated out every ounce of liquid. Ana empties out her bag, and I begin to crush some pills when she stops me.

She holds up a needle. "We should inject them."

"I'm afraid it won't help if we do it wrong."

"I'll do it," she replies, her face determined. "I know how."

She picks up a bottle and uncaps the needle. "Mama took me to the classes she taught when I was little. I watched the nurses learn to inject and draw blood." She sticks the needle in and sucks up a syringe full of the clear medicine.

"Some of them fainted, but I was fascinated, even though I knew there was no way I'd ever be a nurse." She squeezes the plunger to remove the air. "But I remember the steps: Find the vein."

John clamps his hands around Nelly's good arm until the veins are more prominent.

Ana nods. "Okay, just about at this angle, push it in." Her hand is steady as she slips the needle in. A curl of Nelly's blood swirls in the neck of the syringe. "Got it. Now inject."

She pushes the plunger slowly. When she withdraws the needle, I press a wad of napkins onto the bead of blood. I hold Nelly's hand and jump whenever a tremor passes through him. I keep my holster on because I know I'm grasping at straws. I have to be realistic.

John suggests we move Nelly into the other room so we don't disturb him, but I know the real reason: if Nelly turns we'll be able to stop him before he does much damage. I wonder how long it takes. Do you die first and then turn hours later, or is it instantaneous?

Everyone takes turns sitting with me and Nelly. We wipe his head with a cool cloth. Penny hands me a cup of soup, which I ignore after one bite. I stare at Nelly and will his chest to rise. Ana gives Nelly another dose of antibiotics and takes Bits to bed. Penny gives Nelly's forehead a kiss and whispers something only he can hear. Then she kisses my head and leaves.

John lowers himself next to me. "I'll take first watch of Nelly."

"Wake me if—" I stop when he nods. "I just—I know it won't really be him, but he deserves someone... there, you know?"

"I will, I promise."

John lays a hand on my shoulder. He's so kind that I remember to feel guilty. "I'm sorry about earlier, John. I wish I could have unshakable faith in something like you do."

He shakes his head. "Oh, hon, this has tested my faith. But when I believe, when I trust in something bigger than me, I can handle whatever comes my way. That's how I made it through when Caroline passed. Someone told me a long time ago that there are many paths to Heaven. I believe that."

"I can't believe in any one thing that way." Right now, though, I really wish I could.

"You don't have to hold to any one belief. I don't think God minds. What you did today? Risking your life for a friend? You can't get much more Christian than that.

" 'Greater love hath no man than this, that a man lay down his life for his friends.' John 15:13." He means me and Ana, but I know we're both thinking of Peter. "Lie down, hon. I've got it."

I kiss him on the cheek and get in my sleeping bag. And before I close my eyes, I hedge my bets by apologizing to God, too. Just in case.

CHAPTER 107

I wake with a start in murky light and see Nelly lying on his pallet. John sleeps upright against the wall at Nelly's head. He's fallen asleep on watch; he's never done that. Nelly is pale, his face slack. I watch for the rise of his chest, but there's nothing.

I stifle a sob and inch closer. I draw my pistol with a trembling hand. I can't be sure how long he's been dead, how long it will take him to turn, if he does. We're going to have to take care of him.

It's not really Nelly. It's not really him.

I stick out my foot and gently prod him. An eye flutters. He's turning. I hold out my gun, trigger finger ready.

It's not him, not him, not him.

"Cassie." John's voice is soft as he tries not to startle me. "Put down the gun. He's okay. Nel's okay."

I hear what he's saying, but it doesn't compute. My fingers are tight on the pistol grip. "What?"

Then I see Nelly's chest rise. It does it again. It's barely moving, but he's breathing. He opens his eyes and turns his absolutely alive, beautiful, pale face to me.

"God: zero. Cassie: one," he croaks, and his cracked lips turn up.

I sit dumbfounded for a moment and then throw myself on him. I knock his arm when I kiss him on his hot, but no longer fiery, forehead, and he winces.

"Sorry, sorry!" I say. My grinning face is inches from his. I kiss his forehead again, just to be sure.

"Thirsty."

I hold the bottle and he drinks greedily. Penny, Ana and Bits rush into the room. The sight of Nelly stops them like it did me, and then they move forward. James stands in the main doorway and grins.

"I saw a few hours after the second dose of antibiotics that he was getting better," John says. "I knew he was okay when he said a few words and drank a little. James agreed when I woke him for watch. I didn't want to wake you. You both needed sleep."

Nelly lets me inspect his arm. It still looks terrible, but the red streaks are receding. I feel like I've won the lottery. It really worked.

"Thanks, Half-pint," Nelly whispers. He looks like he might cry, and it's enough to start me off.

"How's that for an early birthday present?" I ask with a sob. "Kick-ass enough?" He gives a weak laugh. "Ana's the one who shot you up. She did a great job."

Nelly blows her a kiss and she blows one back. "But Cassie's the reason we went to find medicine," she says.

"I heard." Nelly looks at me with shining eyes. They're back to their normal shade of blue, and it makes me want to leap on him again, but I content myself with giving his hand a kiss. "I think everyone in a two mile radius heard. She doesn't get pissed that often, but when she does, not even God is going to defy her."

"Sorry about that," I say, embarrassed.

I stretch out my other hand and pull Bits into my lap. She still has half the bag of Reese's Pieces she's been saving for Nelly crumpled in her hand.

I hug her tight. "I didn't mean to scare you, Bits. I don't know what came over me."

She shakes her head like it's okay.

The first rays of sunlight stream through the filthy window, illuminating dirt and cobwebs and stains I don't even want to know about, but every decrepit bit of it looks beautiful. Nelly's alive. He closes his eyes, but I don't worry this time. I know he'll open them again.

"You're like your mom," John says. "Slow to anger. But the slow burns make the huge infernos. It's not always a bad thing."

He's right: my anger wasn't a bad thing. Nelly's back from the dead, and for once in this God-forsaken world, that's a good thing.

CHAPTER 108

"I love this car," I say from behind the steering wheel of the VW. It's all gleaming wood inside, with a tiny fridge, sink and two bench seats. The outside is unblemished white and teal and chrome. Somebody else loved this car.

"It's not a *car*," Nelly says. "It's a *bus*, or *camper*, or even a *van*."

"Whatever. I love it. It has a spice rack! How many people have a spice rack in their car? If we make it all the way there in it, think we can keep it?"

"Sure. We'll go on road trips. Visit the zombie-filled countryside."

He's still pale and his arm is painful, but after three more days of antibiotics, he's truly on the mend. We've been waiting to leave until he's strong enough.

"Smart-ass." I go to give him a light smack but feel his forehead instead. It's blessedly cool.

He ducks away. "How long are you going to insist on feeling my forehead every ten minutes?" He hasn't had a fever in two days.

"Forever. Get used to it. Are you sure you're okay to leave tomorrow?"

He rests his good arm on the window and takes a breath. "Definitely. Tomorrow's as good a day as any to die." He raises his eyebrows at me. I can't tell if he's serious.

A remnant of that overwhelming sadness and rage passes through me. "No! You're not allowed to die. I didn't save your ass so you could just go and die again. Promise me."

He keeps his eyebrows up. I know it's ridiculous to make him promise something he has no control over, but I don't care.

"Okay, Cass. I promise not to die. Ever."

"That's more like it." I ignore the sarcasm in his voice. It makes me feel better, which might be even dumber than exacting the promise in the first place.

Penny comes out of the cabin and throws backpacks in the rear. "We're ready to go first thing in the morning."

Her hair hangs greasy and limp in its ponytail. I wish I could shower. Showing up greasy and stinky is not how I hoped I'd see Adrian for the first time in two years. I know it shouldn't matter in the grand scheme of things, but if he's not happy to see me, it would be nice not to feel physically repulsive to boot.

Penny gets in the back and sighs. "I love this car."

James arrives with canned food right as she speaks. "It's a bus, sweetie. Not a car."

I ignore Nelly's victorious look.

CHAPTER 109

"Forty miles to go," James says, in answer to Bits's tenth, "Are we there yet?"

She's been serving us water a few drops at a time so she has an excuse to run the sink incessantly. We've had to move a few cars, but as the terrain gets less populated there are fewer obstacles.

It's a beautiful drive. Adrian and I dreamt about living up here one day. The mountains are green, like in lower Vermont, but they're craggier and wilder. It seems like you could take a few steps off a trail and be lost forever. But it's also a place of gentle valleys and neat squares of farmland. That farmland is now overgrown and the farmhouses are empty. I count the miles and translate it to minutes. Forty-five minutes left to go. Thirty-five. My mouth is dry and my hands are clasped so tightly my forearms hurt.

"More water?" Bits asks.

I force my lips into a smile and nod. She pirouettes to the sink for a refill. She's almost as grubby as the night we found her, but she's excited instead of terrified. She cries for Peter in her sleep, and since he soothed her most nights, it's another blow when she wakes and realizes the nightmare's real. But she's resilient. I hope resilient enough for this world.

Thirty minutes. The water washes over my parched tongue without touching it. I wish it would drown the butterflies in my stomach. Twenty-five minutes. Twenty.

"Someone's moved the cars off the road," John says, and points to the ditches where abandoned cars lay.

The farm-bordered road gives way to the lawns and houses of the town before Kingdom Come. We brace ourselves for the infected. There's at least one group in every small town, and they always come out when they hear a car. We pass town hall and a village green, but no Lexers lope after us. The general store has a sandwich sign out front. Next to it is a metal drum with a hand pump and hose. The sign reads:

GAS IN DRUM. FOOD INSIDE STORE.
TAKE WHAT YOU NEED.
PLEASE BE CONSIDERATE OF OTHERS AFTER YOU.

"Wow," James says. "They've cleared the town out and even have a pit stop. They must have their shit—" he looks at Bits, who grins, "—um, stuff together, huh?"

We turn onto a dirt road that twists through woods until it opens up at a small farm. The sign reads Cob Creek Farm, but we can't see it because the tree-lined driveway ends abruptly at a tall wooden fence that surrounds the house and outbuildings. The fields outside the fence are planted with corn. We pass more fortified farms. One has a chain-link fence and another a cinderblock wall. Our barbed wire and shutters seem like child's play in comparison.

John squints at the sign ahead. "Kingdom Come Road. Here it is."

He makes the turn. A cabin perched atop a framework of legs stands in a clearing. A ladder leads up to a platform outside the cabin door. A man on the platform raises his hand, and John slows to a stop. A blonde woman climbs down the ladder. She holds a rifle but smiles when she motions us out of the van.

"Hi. Sorry about the guns." She notices Nelly's bandaged arm and her smile fades. "Are any of you infected?"

"No," Nelly says. He peels back the gauze to show his wound, which is obviously healing. "I got sliced with a knife."

Her grip on the rifle relaxes. "Sorry, we've got to be careful. I'm Shelby. Welcome to Kingdom Come. Go up the road about a quarter mile, you'll see the gate. I'll radio ahead."

The corrugated metal gate must be ten feet tall. Two guys in jeans and t-shirts stand next to a door set into the wall beside it. A chain-link fence heads into the trees for as far as I can see. I don't know how they've managed all this, although if you have enough people, I guess you can get anything done.

The one with a handsome, rugged face and blue eyes leans an arm on the van window. "Hiya. I'm Dan. You here to stay or just passing through?"

"Hoping to stay," John says. "We're friends of Adrian Miller. You know him?"

Dan laughs. "Of course. It's his and Ben's farm. We're all just visiting."

He winks at me and Bits then grins when she gives him a lopsided wink back. The gate slides open to reveal more tree-lined road.

"You'll see a small gate up a bit. Maureen'll meet you there," Dan says. "I'll see you all around. Welcome."

Penny leans over and puts her hand on mine to unclench it. "It'll be fine."

I wish I had her faith.

CHAPTER 110

A shed with a stovepipe sits right before a bend in the road. A smiling, pleasantly-rounded older woman walks out and waves.

"John?" she asks. "I'm Maureen. You're going to follow me through the gate on my bike. I'll show you where to park, and then we'll figure out everything else. Sound good?"

John nods. "Lead the way."

We gasp as the farm comes into view. A white farmhouse with a huge front porch stands in a clearing surrounded by maple trees. An apple orchard, the trees twisted with age, runs to the left. A greenhouse and two gigantic barns are set back, with animals sitting in pens in the sunshine. Cabins and tents dot the back of the land, and behind them is the biggest vegetable garden I've ever seen. A far off fence glints, and beyond it are fields of crops.

The farm itself is beautiful, with its red barns, white house and groves of trees, but most breathtaking is the ring of mountains it sits nestled within. We're surrounded by a circle of solid green. It makes me feel tiny, insignificant and safe. I know how Adrian felt when he saw this place and wish I'd been there. It's perfect.

We head behind the house to a post and beam building and park next to an ambulance. I pick my jeans off my thighs as I hit the dirt. The banging of pots echoes out of the building's back doors.

Maureen points toward the noise. "We call that the restaurant, where we make most of the food. Are you hungry? Lunch officially starts in a couple of hours, but there's always something around."

We shake our heads. The only thing I want to know is where Adrian is, but I can't seem to open my mouth and ask.

"Okay." Her eyes are kind as she takes us in. "I'm thinking you won't mind being together in a tent? We've got an empty one. They're actually pretty nice. I bet you guys would like a shower, too."

"Yes to all of the above, ma'am," says John, who's become our spokesperson.

Maureen's cheeks get even rounder when she smiles. "John, don't ever call me ma'am again. And I don't know the rest of your names."

We introduce ourselves as we follow her to the tent. It's cozy and light inside, with cots, bunk beds, a small bookshelf and a wood stove that vents out the roof.

"Hm," Maureen says. "It might be a bit tight. We're building cabins, but they won't be ready for a few weeks. There are spaces in other tents if you want to spread out."

The thought of splitting up makes me uneasy and, judging by the vigorous shaking of heads, I'm not alone. I'm pretty sure we'd cram all seven of us into a two-man tent if we had to.

"This is great," Nelly says. "Really."

"Okay. Think of me as your cruise director." We laugh. "Today you'll just get the lay of the land. Tomorrow we'll talk about your jobs here and all that. Where are you from?"

"New York City," James says.

Her eyes widen. "Have people been getting out?" James explains that we left early on. "Well, I'm glad you made it. You'll meet some of the people who live here later. They're all great. We're like a family."

I open my mouth, but Nelly beats me to it. "Actually, we're good friends with Adrian Miller. Is he here?"

"Adrian's in Whitefield. The plane's expected back before dinner. We trade our expertise and food with the guys there." She clasps her hands and beams at us. "He'll be so happy to hear you've come."

I'm filled with disappointment, but also the tiniest bit of relief, because I've been terrified of this moment. And I hope with all my heart that Maureen's right.

***

Maureen takes Penny and me to find clothes while the others wait at the showers. A room built onto the restaurant holds bins of clothes organized by size. I find jeans, a tank top and hoodie for me and outfits for the others. Maureen and I wait with my stack of clothes while Penny searches for pants for James.

"Thank you for the clothes," I say. "This is so great."

"Isn't it?" she asks. "When I got here this was all in its beginning stages, but we've got a system down now."

"Adrian's very organized."

She leans against a table. "Yes, he is. Everyone loves him. How do you know him?"

"We met in college." I don't want to tell her the details. If he's not glad to see me, at least I won't be known as the ex-fiancé right away.

"You know him well?" I nod and watch the occasional person walk by outside. "Then you know he's quiet, but somehow he gets everyone to do what needs to be done. Maybe they don't want to disappoint him."

I hesitate, but Penny's still busy, so I ask my question. "Is he dating anyone?" I keep my voice light, like I'm looking for gossip. It must work, because Maureen leans in conspiratorially, her eyes wide.

"Not anyone! Granted, there are more men than women here, but I've seen him turn down some very obvious offers."

The butterflies are back. *There's no one else.*

"I heard that last summer he had a fling with one of the summer interns," she continues. "It was hot and heavy for a while, but when summer ended, so did the fling."

Jealousy flares. I know I have absolutely no right to be angry, but that doesn't stop me from picturing Adrian, *hot and heavy*, with someone else. I want to throw up.

Maureen puts her hand over mine in a motherly gesture. "And I'm getting the feeling that was not something you needed to hear. I'm sorry. I do tend to go on. TMI, my daughter calls it."

I squeeze her hand and swallow down the bitter feeling. "No need to be sorry. I asked. Is she here? Your daughter?"

Her eyes fill before she blinks them clear and smiles. "No, she lives in Florida. I don't know if she's okay. I lost my husband on the way here."

"I'm sorry. We lost someone on the way, too. And my brother, he was supposed to meet me but never showed up."

Maureen sighs. "I don't know anyone who hasn't lost someone. We just go on the best we can, don't we?"

Her gentle voice reminds me so much of my mom that I want to hug her. I don't think she'd mind if I did.

Penny walks over. "Okay, found jeans for the string bean. Thanks, Maureen."

CHAPTER 111

The shower is just warm water running from a barrel through a showerhead, but it feels incredible. I lather up my and Bits's hair and feel some of the horror of the past week wash down with the suds and run under the pallet we stand on. Before she left, Maureen asked if I wanted her to find me at the restaurant when the plane was on its way. When I nodded, she squeezed my hand and promised she would.

We unpack in the tent before heading to lunch. The dining room has exposed beams and an assortment of tables, benches and chairs. Kitchen workers continually refresh the food at tables in the back. It's the height of summer, so everything is fresh. I pour a big glass of cow's milk for Bits, who gulps it down and asks for a refill.

"You know, I think you may love that coffee more than me," James says to Penny, who drinks a mug of coffee with cream like it's a religious experience.

She cracks open one eye and smiles before closing it again. "You may be right."

My food looks delicious, but I can't eat it. The main lunch rush has ended, but the room is still full of people. Most of them look to be between twenty and fifty years old, although there are some kids and older folks mixed in.

The way they talk and laugh makes it seem like everyone here really does get along. Whenever someone catches our eyes, they smile or wave. People who pass our table make sure to welcome us, but they don't press us for information. Probably because we sit here wide-eyed and shell-shocked from the sheer amount of people and the unbelievable fact that we're safe. We don't need to spend every moment listening for the rattle of cans or the crunch of something walking in the woods.

Maureen steps through the wide front door, and I tense up. She shakes her head. No plane yet.

She pulls up a chair and smiles. "You all clean up well. Are you settling in all right?"

"Just fine," John says, and runs a hand through his damp hair. "Say, I was wondering how it works here with jobs."

"Well, we try to get people to do whatever interests them. Let's see, there are the gardens and crops, of course. Then there's construction, managing the electrical system, guards and patrols, water, livestock, kitchen and preserving. Lots of people do a little bit of everything. There's a schedule where you sign up."

"I'd like to work in the gardens," Ana says. "Can you be a guard and do that?"

"Sure. Most adults take guard shifts. It's the patrols that are more dangerous." Ana's eyes light up at that.

"So you know about gardening?"

John tells her about the gardens we left behind.

Maureen looks impressed and then enlightened. "No wonder you didn't fall on the fresh produce like you hadn't seen it in months. That's what most people do when they get here, you know. You guys already know this stuff, then. Everyone will want you on their teams, for sure. I knew a bit about flower gardening before I got here, but this has been a learning experience. The only thing I ever did was open a can, not put things in one and cook it up."

She laughs and turns to Bits. "And you're Beth, right?"

"Yes," Bits says through the cookie in her mouth. "But most people call me Bits now. Like Little Bits."

"Well, Bits, I know of at least two kids your age who would love to play with you. How about you and one of your friends come with me after lunch to find them?"

Bits nods and drains the last of her milk. Maureen waves someone over. He's on the small side but packed full of muscle, with curly brown hair and a friendly face I remember. It's Ben, Adrian's partner.

"Ben, these are some friends of Adrian's that arrived today," Maureen says.

"Hey." He smiles. "I heard people came but didn't know you knew Adrian." He shakes hands as Maureen introduces us. She gets to me last.

"I've met Cassie," he says. Something flickers in his eyes when he smiles at me. It might've been uncertainty. *Join the club, Ben.*

"Hi, Ben," I say. "This place is absolutely gorgeous. I can see why you chose it."

He thanks me and talks a minute longer before he's called away. His gaze lingers on Ana as he says goodbye. She gives him a polite smile and looks down at her cloth napkin. If I'm an awful flirt then Ana is a natural-born one, but she doesn't look up again until he's gone.

We help bring the dishes to the kitchen. It's huge, with several wood cook stoves and a pantry. I stop and look out a window on my way to the trough sink. They all have a gorgeous view of the mountains; I've never seen anything like it.

Maureen comes up. "The plane will be here in about thirty minutes. The landing strip isn't far. There's an equipment shed that doubles as a pilot hang out. You can wait in there if you want."

My feet are stuck to the ground. Nelly pries the tray out of my hands, takes it to the sink and returns. "Do you want me to come with you?" he asks.

I shake my head. As much as I love Nelly, I don't want him to witness what's probably going to be something I'll never want to talk about with anyone.

CHAPTER 112

I follow Maureen down a side road to a shed with a small loft and windows. "I have some stuff to do outside," she says. "But if you need me, I'm out here. Should I leave the door open?"

I nod. "Thanks."

I can see the runway, a wide swath of brown cut into a field. I pace the room and look at the maps on the wall without seeing them. I try sitting, but I can't sit for more than a minute before I jump back up and pace again.

I run through all of the possible reactions Adrian could have to my presence. Almost every one of them makes me cringe. The best I can hope for is that he still loves me and eventually he'll forgive and trust me again. I broke his heart, after all.

I take a gulp from my water bottle with trembling hands. My heart thuds, my head is full of white noise and I'm covered in a cold sweat. So much for the shower. "You'd think you're going to the guillotine," I say out loud. Great, now I'm talking to myself.

I've lived without Adrian before, but I wasn't really living. I was just killing time. And now, especially now, I want to eke out every moment of happiness I can. Three years ago I found out how it can all end so quickly, but I didn't learn the lesson it should have taught me: to hold tight to the things I still had. Instead, I forced them away.

I think of Peter and how he never had the chance to tell Ana how he felt. What's most important is not that I like Adrian's answer, but that I pose the question in the first place.

I hear the engine before I see it and step to the doorway to watch. The white plane circles and comes in for a landing. It hits the ground and races along the strip until it stops fifty yards away. The door opens.

I rehearse what I'm going to say for the hundredth time and wipe my palms on my thighs as Adrian steps out. He wears jeans, black work boots and a jacket, which he takes off to reveal an olive green t-shirt. He leans back inside the plane to say something, then waves and turns.

He looks the same as he always has: the cheekbones, the ever-present dark stubble and the nose that turns his looks from pretty to handsome. I know every inch of him, from his ugly toes that I would tease him about, to the scar on his temple from the chicken pox when he was five. But it's been so long that he also looks new, like a stranger.

Maureen moves to him, a rake in her hands, and he touches her shoulder as she speaks. Adrian not only makes you think he wants to hear every word you say, he really does. She gestures toward the shed, and he goes still. I wonder what he's thinking. I know I should go out there, but I can't.

His mouth moves, and at her nod his jacket drops out of his hand onto the dusty ground. He spins and moves toward me. I back into the shed and listen to his boots pound the path. In that awkward moment when he comes in and stops, that's when I'll say what I've practiced. I'll get it all out before he can say anything: how sorry I am, how ashamed I am that I hurt him and how I never stopped loving him.

I take a deep breath as he strides into the shed. His eyes match his shirt, and they're full of disbelief.

"Adrian, I'm—" I begin, but he doesn't stop. His steps never falter as he makes his way over and folds me in his arms. His heart beats as fast and hard as mine.

"You're here." His voice is like a prayer. "I can't believe you're here."

He holds my face up to his. His hands are rough and cracked and smell like gasoline. I don't think I've ever felt anything as wonderful as those hands on my face.

"I'm so sorry. I—" I try to get the words out, but his mouth covers mine in a kiss so raw that I can't do anything but respond. I can't even remember what I wanted to say, because I'm lost in the kiss I've dared not imagine for two years. He feels the same, tastes the same, and it's like coming home.

It's so much more than I deserve. Why did I think he would hate me? I'm the kind of person who might not forgive so easily. He's an open book. There's nothing but joy in this kiss and the way his hands hold me like I can't possibly be real, like I'm something precious. A sob escapes and he pulls back, although he doesn't let go.

"What's wrong? Is this—?" His hands drop. I want them back on me, even if I don't deserve them.

"I'm so sorry," I say. "I'm so sorry for what I said to you. For what I did. I just want you to forgive me."

His brow creases, and his voice is tender. "I already have. A long time ago. I love you."

It makes me cry harder, and he wraps me in his arms. We stay like that, with his chin resting on my head, the way we used to.

"I couldn't stop thinking about you on your birthday." His voice rumbles in his chest when he speaks. "Where you were, if you were safe, so I had them fly to the cabin the next day. We're not supposed to use fuel for that, but I didn't care, I couldn't take it anymore. The house—" his voice breaks, "—it was burned to the ground. Lexers were everywhere. I made them fly back and forth, over and over again, trying to see if one of them was you and—" He stops and his body shakes.

I rub his back. "I'm okay."

"I was so sure you were okay. So sure. I knew you could get out of New York. But when I saw the house, I thought I was too late. I hated myself for not coming sooner."

He blames himself, when I'm really to blame. I shake my head against his chest. "No. I should've contacted you somehow. I was too scared you didn't want to talk to me, so I didn't."

He loosens his grip and raises my chin with his hand. "I would never want—"

"Adrian!" A young, fair-haired guy clomps into the shed. "Oh. Sorry, man." He looks more intrigued than sorry.

"What's up, Marcus?" Adrian asks, but he doesn't move and holds me tighter so I can't move away.

"Um, there's something smoking in the electrical shed. We kind of need you."

"Where's Janine?"

"She's at Cob Creek for the night. We heard the plane, and they sent me for you." Now he really does look apologetic.

Adrian sighs. "Okay. I'll be there in a few."

"Sure," Marcus says, looking at me curiously before he leaves.

I smile at Adrian. I can't believe I'm standing here in his arms.

"You okay?" he asks.

I'm better than okay. I stand on my tiptoes and kiss him softly while I cup the back of his neck. He gives me that gentle look, the one Nelly called soft a million years ago.

"I love you," I say. "I really do."

"Good." We laugh, because that's what we used to say, and it's nice to be back there.

A girl with a buzzed head pokes her head in and winces like she got the job no one wanted. "Hey, A. Sorry, but there's really a lot of smoke."

Adrian nods. "Coming right now. I'll meet you there."

I give him a gentle nudge. "Duty calls. Go put that fire out. We're all in one of the big tents in the back."

He looks at me incredulously and grabs my hand. "No way. Come and put out the fire with me. And who's *we*?"

He pulls me out the door, and we walk up the path as I tell him.

CHAPTER 113

Adrian drags me around the entire afternoon, not that there's any real dragging involved. When he pees I have to stop myself from following, and I pace outside the bathroom until he returns. Our permanently-linked hands get curious glances when he introduces me while attending to a million tasks. I must look like a maniac; I can't stop smiling.

He takes me to the unfinished cabins and pulls me through a doorway. The walls are filled with insulation, and it's fitted with a wood stove made out of a metal barrel. Everything else in the world has fallen apart, but this place is growing.

"How did you do all this?" I ask in wonder. "It's incredible."

"No it's not." He shakes his head and sits on a low shelf built onto a finished wall. "While everyone else was trying to get to safety, I was already safe. It was just a matter of recognizing what was happening and doing something."

"No, it *is* incredible, because instead of closing the farm, you opened it up. You welcomed people. You've inspired them to do all of this." I point out the glassless window.

He shrugs and looks down. He thinks that anyone would do what he's done. He doesn't realize how rare he is. I think of how this works to my benefit because I've never been sure that I deserve someone so intrinsically good. Maybe no one's good enough for him.

"I love you," I say.

He keeps his head lowered, but I see his dimple and know he's smiling. He draws me to him and loops his pinky through the ring on my neck.

He runs it along the chain. "You still have it. Why are you wearing it around your neck?"

I'm embarrassed by my superstition. "I felt weird putting it on. Like I shouldn't wear it until I knew."

He glances at me. "Do you want to wear it now?" I know his question is about more than putting on the ring.

"Yes," I whisper.

He removes the ring and slides it on my left ring finger.

"It still fits," he says, and kisses my hand. "Just like us."

I can't find my voice to reply, so I bring his hand to my mouth and brush my lips over his fingers, one by one. When I look up, his eyes are hooded and so hungry that my breath catches. He stands and lifts me onto the shelf. I pull him to me and taste his lips, his tongue, his neck. He twists a handful of hair behind my head.

"You're so beautiful," he murmurs into my mouth.

Everywhere his body touches mine is warm and liquid, like we're melting into each other. His hand runs under the waistband of my jeans, and I arch into him. The skin under his shirt is so warm, so smooth. There's no way I can stop, I think, right before the cabin wall behind me begins to shake with the pounding of hammers. I jump in surprise and knock Adrian's head with mine.

I rub my forehead and grin. "Ow! Sorry."

Adrian looks so silly with one eye squinted closed that I break into laughter. He holds a hand to his head and smiles.

"Isn't there any privacy in this place?" I shout, still grinning.

He takes my hand. We fall through the door into the late afternoon light, and he waves at the people who hammer siding onto the cabin.

"Not much. But being one of the owners has its perks. I have my own room in the farmhouse. I'd been thinking of giving it to a couple, but..."

I squeeze his hand. I want to be in his room with him, but now that I'm cooling off I feel shy and can't say it. This is not uncharted territory with Adrian, but I feel like a virgin on her wedding night. A bell clangs somewhere.

"It's dinnertime," he says. "Maybe we'll find Nelly and Penny, finally." We went by the tent earlier, but they were off exploring.

Nelly spots us as we walk in and pulls Penny's sleeve. He rushes through the crowd and, upon seeing our intertwined hands, gives me his wholesome grin that manages to convey something naughty. He and Adrian hug and pound each other on the back.

Penny squeezes Adrian's face in her hands and smooches him on the lips. "I never thought I'd see this beautiful face again!"

Adrian laughs and spins her around. We're attracting all kinds of attention, but most people are smiling. Some look wistful. I think of how Maureen said we've all lost someone, and I feel a tiny bit guilty that we've been found.

CHAPTER 114

The dining room is almost empty. A few people play cards or talk, but most have gone to their quarters for the night. We've pushed ourselves back from the table and sit in lantern light. Bits made a friend named Jasmine, and they sat under the table giggling until Jasmine's bedtime. Now she's on my lap, limp with sleep. We were up at dawn today, and she's exhausted.

Nelly's taken on the job of telling Adrian our story: Brooklyn, Jersey, the Washingtons and the campground, Neil's gang and even Zeke, who Adrian knows. Zeke did get to Whitefield like we thought.

When he tells the story of Peter, his voice lowers, and he makes sure Bits is still asleep. Somehow he manages to include Peter without mentioning that we dated. I don't plan on keeping it a secret, but it's something I need to tell Adrian in private.

"He must have been a great guy," Adrian says. He notices Ana's wet cheeks and hands her a napkin with a sad smile. "I wish I could thank him."

He touches my knee, and his eyes go to Bits. It must be a shock to have me arrive with a seven year-old who belongs to me, to all of us, but she's already won him over. I saw him sneak her a precious pack of gum when he thought no one was looking.

When Nelly and Ana tell him about my insistence that we find medicine for Nelly, I stare at the floorboards. They've painted me as some avenging angel, and Nelly mimics my throwing things around.

I roll my eyes. "You were barely conscious. I wasn't that bad," I say to Adrian, although he looks impressed.

"Yes, she was," Nelly says with a wink. He leans back and yawns.

John rubs his eyes. "I'm ready to hit the sack. It's been a long day."

He scoops Bits up and cradles her like a baby, and the rest of us rise.

Adrian takes hold of my hand. "Ready?"

I nod. We walk into the dark and say goodnight. It feels strange to be sleeping apart from the people I've spent every day and night with for months.

"Hold on," I say to Adrian, and run to catch up with them.

"I wanted to say goodnight again," I say. "I'll miss you guys."

I plant a kiss on a sleeping Bits. I hug them, saving Nelly for last. "I'm used to sleeping with you," I whisper in his ear. "I'll miss you."

His laugh cuts through the night, and I can just make out his smirk in the dim solar lights that mark the path. "Darlin', if you miss me? You're doing it wrong."

CHAPTER 115

The interior of the house is lovely, with big windows and old-fashioned moldings. The stairs creak as we make our way up. Adrian points out the bathroom and opens a door at the end of the hall. "This is me," he says.

Huge windows line two of the walls. It must have a beautiful view during the day. He flips a switch, and an electric light comes on. I walk to it in awe.

"Wow, a real, honest-to-goodness light," I say. It seems so bright. I've gotten used to the dim circles of light lanterns throw off.

"Another perk. We'll have them in the restaurant soon, running off the solar."

There's a queen-sized bed and a desk covered with organized piles of papers. A bookcase full of books. A wardrobe holds what I know are neatly-hung clothes behind its wooden doors. Adrian's the neat one, while I'm the slob. A painting between the windows catches my eye, and I move closer.

It's one I made for him, of the spot where we first kissed. I painted it how it looked just after. It all runs together, the way it would if your eyes were a little unfocused. The colors are brighter. The yellows and reds of autumn leaves and the gray of the rock mix with the foamy silver of the water.

"You hung it up," I say, surprised he didn't pack it at the bottom of a box somewhere. I think of the bin that only existed because of Eric, and it makes me feel terrible.

"Of course I did." He comes behind me and puts his arms around my waist. I lean into him and close my eyes.

"I didn't want to give up on you." His arms tighten. "I came down to New York last spring to see you. I wanted to know if you'd changed your mind. I thought if you had you might not want to..."

"Admit it? Apologize?" I say. I want to kick myself.

"Kind of. I thought maybe you'd punish yourself by thinking I wouldn't want you anyway."

I nod. He knows me so well.

"But when I came, it was a Friday, and I saw you getting into someone's car. Some guy's car. He kissed you on the top of your head, and you smiled. I thought you might be happy again, and I didn't want to mess that up."

Nelly said Adrian stopped emailing him about a year ago. It must have been then. "That's not true." He tenses and his voice is tight. "I was angry at you. For moving on when I didn't want to, and I didn't think you would either, not really. So I decided to believe what you told me. I hoped that you and the dark-haired guy with the nice car were happy, when I wasn't fuming."

The dark-haired guy with the nice car. "That was Peter." I'm not aware I've said it aloud until his arms retract and he moves away. But I want him to know. I don't want to lie. I don't even want to omit.

"That was Peter? The Peter who—?" he asks.

His face is completely blank except for his eyes, which are burning. I know what he must think of me at this moment. That since I lost my new boyfriend I came to find my old one, who just happens to be somewhere safe. Adrian may be trusting, but he's only human, and I haven't shown myself to be trustworthy.

I turn to face him. "We dated for a while. But it was over before we left New York."

He won't look at me. His expression is similar to the night I last saw him and, once again, it's my fault. The day feels like it's collapsed in on itself.

"It's true," I plead. "He and Ana were sort of together. We were just really good friends."

I reach for his hand, but his arms are folded tight, and he doesn't release them.

"Adrian, I've never—" I was going to say that I've never lied to him, but that's not true. I used to never lie to him, but then I did, and it was a huge one. "I've only ever lied to you once."

"Oh yeah?" His voice is flat. "And when was that, Cassie?"

I hate the way he says my name, like it's a curse. I want him to look at me. I pull his arm, and he turns reluctantly. I don't know how to make him believe me, so I just tell him the truth.

"It was when I said I didn't love you."

I pray that it shows in my face as I wait for him to tell me to go. But it must because the hardness leaves his eyes, and he crushes me to him. We kiss, and this time there's no one to interrupt.

My stomach swoops down to my feet, just like it did that first time. The colors of my painting swirl behind my eyelids. His body quivers when I pull off his shirt. My clothes dissolve under his rough hands. We make our way to the bed, and my last conscious thought is to wonder how in a million years I could have ever willingly given this up.

And Nelly was right: I don't miss him at all.

***

I wake at dawn and creep to the bathroom. My eyes shine, and my lips are swollen from Adrian's scruff. When I get back to the room, he's still asleep, one arm thrown above his head. I crawl under the covers and rest my head on his chest.

"I love you," I whisper, not wanting to wake him.

His arm strokes my back. "Say that again," he says, his voice sleepy.

"I love you."

"Again."

I hear the smile in his voice and raise my head. He looks at me with luminous eyes, and his mouth is curved.

"I love you," I say.

"One more time."

I sit up. The view out the windows is just what I thought it would be. I trace the curve of his cheek with my finger. "I love you. Until the end of the world."

His smile widens. "And after?"

I turn to the windows and think of what lies beyond the relative safety of that beautiful ring of mountains. Then I turn back and smile at him even as something cold climbs up my spine. "And definitely after."

EPILOGUE

I'm in the kitchen, blanching and peeling tomatoes for canning. It's a huge crop, and if we want to have enough to last the winter, we'll be working for the next week straight. The autumn air has the chill of winter in it, but it's not unwelcome this year. We hope that the cold will freeze the infected and give us the opportunity to finish them off. And we hope the ones we miss will end up like frozen meat, their muscles useless in the spring thaw.

It's repetitive work but comforting. The thought of this food sustaining us in the dark hours of February does make it less arduous, like my mom always joked. I can almost feel her here with me, canning tomatoes like we did every fall. It doesn't escape me that I'm living the life I wanted, with Adrian, and my heart gives a little hiccup. I know my parents would be glad to see it, too, barring the fact that there are hordes of undead roaming the world.

Bits stands next to me and helps to peel. Maybe I'm creating those same comforting memories for her, even in the midst of the end of the world. She has many mothers now, and we all love her fiercely. She's our hope for the future, the reason we want to create a future. I smile at her, and her face lights up. Maybe all the horror she's seen hasn't completely destroyed her childhood. I hope it hasn't.

A radio sits on a window ledge next to one of the cook stoves. We have them everywhere in case there's an emergency and we have to head to the fences. The crackly voices on the radio announce things that need fixing, requests for help and even the occasional wisecrack. I find it amazing that humor has survived and that everyone here works to get along. I have a huge family now.

Almost every day there's a radio call that people are at the gate, people who heard the broadcasts and made it here. But so many fewer than we'd hoped. We get one and two at a time. Last week there was a whole family, kids and all, and we rejoiced that they were alive, one intact family among millions of broken ones. I thought of the Washingtons and desperately hoped they were another exception to the rule.

The reports say it's gotten worse out there, and people won't be able to make it here in the winter. That means many will be dead by winter's end from cold, hunger or infection. My thoughts are so loud that I miss the last radio call over the clanging of pots and jars.

"What did they say?" I ask. "I think I heard my name."

"It sounded like it could have been. I think there's someone at the gate, but I'm not sure," says Mikayla, a bubbly caramel-skinned girl, who was here studying organic farming practices when Bornavirus hit.

Mike, down at the first gate, continues on the radio, "He's headed up to the second gate now. Looks like Rambo, but Shelby says his jeans used to cost four hundred bucks." He laughs good-naturedly. "Nice guy, needs a bath and a nap."

My heart races. I think about stopping to call back on the radio. To clarify. But I don't want to. I don't want to be told I'm wrong. I want to believe for one minute more.

I grab Bits's hand and turn to everyone. "I think it's someone I know."

"Go!" they shout, smiling.

Everyone dreams of the day when the someone at the gate may be for them. I grab our sweaters and look for my shoes in the pile by the door. I can't find them, so I give up. Bits looks at me like I've lost my mind as I drag her out the door and run across the gravel driveway. I know that Ana and the others may not have heard the radio just yet. I don't want to raise their hopes, but I can't stop myself.

I turn to Bits. "Go get Ana. Tell her to come to the gate."

She nods, her eyes wide, and takes off for the garden. I continue down the driveway, where the trees are dropping their leaves; shades of orange, yellow and red litter the road. My feet slap the ground, and I can hear my breath. I haven't run like this since before we got here. I was running for my life then, but now I'm running with hope.

I race past the second gate and wave to Maureen. I come around a bend, and there he is. He walks with Dan, who's probably telling him about the farm. I stop, panting, as he looks up. His shirt is dirty and creased, his hair flops in his eyes and his jeans are more brown than blue. A pistol sits on his hip, a rifle on his shoulder and a machete hangs from the other hip. Rambo, indeed.

"Peter!" I yell, and run to him.

His teeth are white against his smudged face when he smiles. I don't know that I've ever seen him so happy. That's not true, I do: In those pictures of him as a kid. He's a dead ringer for that kid now, minus the freckles.

I almost knock him down when I reach him. His pack thuds to the ground as he hugs me. I can't believe it's him. It's Peter, who was dead; we all knew he was. I remember his face when we pulled away, how for an instant he'd looked happy, and I hug him tighter. I don't realize I'm crying until I try to speak. "How?" I croak, but I can't say any more than that.

"There were people in the building. Upstairs. They dropped down one of those ladders you hook to the window."

That curtain in the window. It wasn't just the breeze. I shake my head at his luck, our luck, and cry harder.

Peter's eyes gleam. "When'd you turn into such a crybaby? Last time I saw you—crying. Here we are again—crying."

I can't stop my tears, but there's no way I can let him get away with that. "Must've been the same time you found a sense of humor."

He laughs. "That's my girl."

Then, finally, the tears stop, and I beam at him. "Not anymore. Your girl is up in the gardens, on her way down. We're all here. We all made it because of you."

I know he was afraid to ask, and the final bit of worry leaves his face. I want to tell him about how we got here, about Nelly, how Ana helped save him. But there's time for that. *Time.* That's something we don't take for granted anymore.

Pure joy bubbles up, and I see it in his face, too. He laughs and spins me around and around like we're ballroom dancing but stops short as Bits and Ana come around the bend. Bits flies into his arms with a scream of joy and wraps her appendages around him like an octopus.

He kisses her on the nose and inspects her face. "Bits, you got so many more freckles! I see one named Morris right there."

Bits's smile is blinding, and her tomato-stained hands hold on tight. "Peter, I missed you so much!"

Peter hugs her close. "I missed you, too, baby girl. So, so much."

The rest of our group, and Adrian, have made it down the road. They hug Peter and ask a million questions at once.

I introduce Adrian, who shakes Peter's hand with a smile. "I've heard a lot about you. I'm glad you made it here."

Peter flashes me that gigantic grin again. I wink back and look for Ana. She stands apart, wearing a wide-brimmed hat that keeps the sun out of her eyes in the garden. She's always out there, when she's not trying to rope me into some sort of exercise or finding Lexers to destroy. She chews her lip and stares at Peter, uncertainty all over her face.

Peter whispers something in Bits's ear. She jumps to the ground with a nod and smile. Peter makes his way to where Ana stands and stops a few steps away. Then, in a gesture that's almost courtly, he holds out his hand.

"You know," he says, with the hint of a smile, "I never did get that dance."

Ana laughs and reaches for his hand. Her hat hits the ground when he pulls her to him and waltzes her around. Peter hasn't forgotten the steps at all, but Ana keeps up, just like he said she would.

"Dance party!" Bits calls out, her voice echoing through the trees.

She takes Adrian in one hand and Nelly in the other and dances like she hears music. My dad used to grab my mom and dance her around the house, me and Eric, too. If we protested, he'd say, *There's always music playing somewhere. You just have to listen.*

I have to believe that still: that there's music playing somewhere out there. That somewhere else people are dancing. And, as Nelly spins me around, I think I can hear the faintest tinkle coming from far off. Penny and I link arms to skip in a circle and then cry with laughter when Nelly and Adrian copy us. Bits has roped Dan into the party, and he swings her through his legs and throws her in the air.

We must look ridiculous out here, dancing on a dirt road. But I don't care because we can hear the music, and it's getting louder. It drowns out the moans of the broken bodies that wander the world, unaware they're destroying everything they once loved. It soothes the pain of the broken families and broken hearts we all have now.

James lands on Penny's feet with every step, but I can tell he hears it, too. Even John nods along. Adrian catches me and holds me close, twirling Bits to Nelly as she squeals with delight. I'm full of happiness and hopelessness at the same time, laughing and crying at once. I don't even know which tear is for what. Adrian smiles and brushes them with his thumb.

The hopelessness begins to recede. I mourn for the way the world was, but I have faith it will go on. When I was a kid and promised to love my parents until the end of the world and after, it was meant to be silly. It was impossible. When the world was over, it was over. But it turns out that's not true. We may lose this after all; humans may become a mere blip on the radar screen of history.

But I'm not so sure about that, because the world has already ended, and we're still here.

ABOUT THE AUTHOR

Sarah Lyons Fleming is a wannabe prepper and a lover of anything pre-apocalyptic, apocalyptic, and post-apocalyptic. Add in some romance and humor, and she's in heaven.

Besides an unhealthy obsession with home-canned food and Bug Out Bag equipment, she loves books, making artsy stuff and laughing her arse off. Born and raised in Brooklyn, NY, she now lives in Oregon with her family and, in her opinion, not nearly enough supplies for the zombie apocalypse. But she's working on it.

Visit the author at www.SarahLyonsFleming.com

Other books by Sarah Lyons Fleming:

The *Until the End of the World* series
Until the End of the World (Book one)
So Long, Lollipops (Peter's Novella, Book 1.5)
And After (Book two)
All the Stars in the Sky (Book three)

The City Series
Mordacious (Book one)
Peripeteia (Book two)
Instauration (Book three)

The Cascadia Series
World Departed (Book one)
World Between (Book two, coming in 2021)
World Undone (Book three, coming in 2022)
World Anew (Book four, coming in 2023)

ACKNOWLEDGEMENTS

Writing a book is exciting, difficult, frustrating and a whole lot of fun. And when you finally have something to show, your brain makes you second guess every word you've put down on the page (or at least mine does).

Thankfully, I had people who encouraged me and told me I did have a good story to tell and a decent way of telling it:

My mom, Linda Isaacs, who cheerfully read, loved and critiqued every draft. Well, except that first draft, which no one but me and my computer will ever see. She bugged me about when the next one would be ready, and said the story never grew boring. Hard to believe, but she sounded sincere, even if she is my mom.

My dad, Bill Lyons, who read and re-read and told me how awesome I am (I think he might be biased, though). I might never be the crazy human that I am had he not camped with us in a lean-to for a month, or handed me *Malevil* the summer going into fifth grade.

Thanks to my early readers:

Rachel Greer, my first non-family reader, who gave me tons of encouragement in a long email I must have read ten times.

Jamie Arest McReynolds, who sat at her computer and read it in three days, ignoring children and everything else, and then told me what she loved and what could be changed. Jamie's husband, Shawn, a guy I hope I get to meet before our post-zombie apocalypse meet up, gave great mechanical advice. A bucket and a screwdriver, duh!

Allie Birchler and Danielle Gustafson, whose advice on a few key parts made the book all the better. Paulette Letson, my mother-in-law, who read and added her voice to the ones who loved it. Larry "Big La" Isaacs, my step-dad and all around good guy.

Will Fleming, the King of Grammar (a.k.a. my husband). His observations, suggestions and grammatical corrections are always thoughtful, honest and astute. Believe me, if you find a grammatical or stylistic error the fault is all mine. And, as someone who knows writing, his encouragement and kind words made me believe that maybe I really did have something here. Thank you, Ruggles! (It deserves more exclamation points, but I know better). I don't think it's possible to express how much I value your opinion and advice.

And to Sadie and Silas, the children who would only nap with their feet in Mama's lap. If I hadn't been trapped under y'all for all those years I might never have decided to see if I could write a book. So, thanks, you goobers. But sleeping through the night would be cool. Just sayin'.

Printed in France by Amazon
Brétigny-sur-Orge, FR

15834994R00228